WITCHERY IN HIS TOUCH

"The man threatened Queen Eleanor," Raimond explained, "and tried to steal her treasure. He had reason to hide. If he died, his shade will surely come to dwell with us if we speak of him again."

"But where would he have gone?" Alyse asked. "If he still lives, where would he be?"

Raimond began to play idly with the hem of Alyse's new shift. "Do you not grow weary of these questions, wife? Would you not prefer to hear what the Saracen ladies wear beneath their silken gowns?" He drew her into the shelter of his arms.

"I wish you had never come to this place," Alyse said.

"And never taken you to wife?"

"Even that. If this matter goes wrong, you will lose your honor, and live in exile."

"That would be no hardship, with you at my side."

Alyse smiled and blinked back tears unshed. "I will be with you, my lord husband."

"Then you will need to learn, my lady wife, what the Saracen ladies wear beneath their silken gowns."

She brought his hand back to rest upon her thigh. "Tell me, Raimond."

His hand closed upon the thin linen of her shift. "I will show you."

There was witchery in his touch, strong enough to turn her thoughts from the future. For that long summer night, all questions ceased . . . .

BOOK YOUR PLACE ON OUR WEBSITE AND MAKE THE READING CONNECTION!

We've created a customized website just for our very special readers, where you can get the inside scoop on everything that's going on with Zebra, Pinnacle and Kensington books.

When you come online, you'll have the exciting opportunity to:

- View covers of upcoming books
- Read sample chapters
- Learn about our future publishing schedule (listed by publication month *and author*)
- Find out when your favorite authors will be visiting a city near you
- Search for and order backlist books from our online catalog
- Check out author bios and background information
- Send e-mail to your favorite authors
- Meet the Kensington staff online
- Join us in weekly chats with authors, readers and other guests
- Get writing guidelines
- AND MUCH MORE!

**Visit our website at
http://www.zebrabooks.com**

NIGHT FIRES

LINDA COOK

Zebra Books
Kensington Publishing Corp.

http://www.zebrabooks.com

For Barbara J. Gislason
and Jeri Smith Youness

ZEBRA BOOKS are published by

Kensington Publishing Corp.
850 Third Avenue
New York, NY 10022

Zebra and the Z logo Reg. U.S. Pat. & TM Off.

First Printing: November, 1998
10 9 8 7 6 5 4 3 2 1

Printed in the United States of America

PROLOGUE

*Parlar degram ab cubertz entresens,
e, pus no ns val arditz, valgues nos gens!
We will speak in secret ways;
candor is no help, so let our wits prevail.*
—Bernart de Ventadorn,
trobar to Aliénor of Aquitaine

Midnight. June 1, 1193 St. Albans, England

It was a trap. From the beginning, he had known it was a trap.

Raimond deBauzan turned from the dying hearth and took up his sword. He would wait no longer; weary of blood and treachery, he had begun to imagine the scent of both in the stale air of the empty house.

The merchant's house was deserted, but not neglected. There was no dust, nor any sign that thieves had discovered the modest treasures of the place. The servants had fled, leaving a nervous young boy who had opened the door to Raimond at nightfall. The lad had tended the fire and brought a jug of harsh wine. And disappeared.

"Damnation." A scarred fist slammed onto the cold surface of the table, sending the earthen jug wobbling against the rim of the wine cup. The echoes sounded twice before the darkness swallowed them. And the deep silence returned.

Raimond poured the last of the wine and pulled his damp, steaming cloak from the bench before the fire. He was a man of the sword, not a creature of intrigue. Had he left the battle-fields of Palestine for nothing more than murky scuffles with cutpurses and spies in the dark streets of St. Albans? Two days after reaching England's shores, he had yet to sleep the night through in a good English bed or take his ease in the smooth, pale body of a good English whore.

A grim messenger and four men at arms had waited at Dover with fast horses and a summons which had revealed little and demanded much. Now, two hellish nights later, Raimond had reached St. Albans alone, only to find an empty house and no sign of the promised envoy from Hubert Walter, bishop of Salisbury.

The heavy blood of anger pulsed in Raimond's temples. He cast the dregs of the wine upon the embers and turned away from the brief, acrid stench. The bishop's messenger was a dawdling fool. Or he lay dead upon the road north from Windsor.

DeBauzan winced as he buckled on the heavy broadsword in its stained leather scabbard. Deep within his shoulder, a shard from a Saracen dagger sent pain, brief but intense. That infidel steel had sowed delirium and fever, sparing him a butcher's task at Acre when—

"Enough." Raimond kicked the last log to crimson-edged embers. In the flickering shadows of this chill, dim house such thoughts would bring madness. He needed warmth. Light. Wine. A woman. "Damn them," he growled again. "Walter can find another fool to wait for his black-hearted ferrets."

"Black-hearted?" A woman's voice drifted among the shadows.

Raimond felt the hairs of his neck bristle. There was only one such voice in the world. He turned slowly, his hand upon the pommel of his sword.

The voice came again. "Ferret? I was a dove—so the poets said."

His eyes narrowed. She had to be there, in the shadows beyond the room.

"And now, the years encaged have turned this dove to hawk."

"Queen Eleanor." His own words rang loud and sharp to Raimond's ears. Had he imagined that low, mocking voice calling him from the past?

The silence deepened; even the faint scrabbling of mice within the walls had ceased. Raimond closed his fist about the cold iron of his sword's hilt.

The voice returned. "I have a task for you, Raimond deBauzan."

The shadows had darkened, shifted. And formed into her image. Eleanor of Aquitaine, dowager queen of England, her face yellowed in the dying amber firelight, stood within the low doorway.

The rustle of her hem and the deep scarlet shimmer beneath her cloak dismissed the last of Raimond's doubts. Mortal or ghost, Queen Eleanor had not abandoned her rich silks, nor had she lost the disciplined grace of her bearing. Only her eyes, dark and terrible, revealed her present grief.

"Your grace, they did not tell me—"

"They sent you here. That was all I required." She turned her face from him and moved to the hearth. "I have much to say and little time to do so."

In the tense, uncertain times two decades ago in Poitou, Queen Eleanor had not been so dismissive, even with the most insignificant of her own servants. The years had indeed turned the dove to hawk, an ancient, black-eyed hawk with no care for civility or courtesy, looking only to her purpose—

Raimond set his jaw and waited for the dowager queen to speak. It was already too late to evade her demands, whatever they might be. Raimond saw his hopes of a fortnight's hot revels vanish - extinguished by the distracted, calculating expression on Queen Eleanor's face.

He smothered an oath as he pulled the heavy settle-bench closer to the fire and spread his cloak upon it. With slow, practiced grace, Eleanor took his outstretched hand and seated herself to face the diminishing flames. The long, bejeweled fingers were as beautiful as he remembered, but very cold.

"A moment. There is wood outside—"

"Stay. Do not build the fire. I have come at this dark hour for a reason." Her voice, which overlaid Languedoc's rich accents with the brisk cadence of privilege, had not changed with age. "My escort waits outside. They do not know whom I meet. Do not let them see you, deBauzan. Swear you will not."

A secret task. Not an honest piece of butchery to be done for the crown in the light of day, but a thing to be done in the shadows. By St. Thomas' holy blood, this was ill fortune. After two years with Richard's army on a pilgrimage of brutal intent, Raimond deBauzan craved a few months of peace, far from the demands and restless ambitions of his Plantagenet lord. Instead, Raimond had reached his father's keep to find forty hard-eyed mercenaries waiting to send him across the sea to England.

Raimond closed his mind to the thought of what those wolves in armor would have done to his father's lands had he not gone with them willingly. The mercenary troop had refused to tell the aged, furious Rannulf deBauzan where they would take Raimond, nor had they allowed the old warrior a moment's private speech with his son.

"Well, Raimond deBauzan? Will you swear?"

"Your grace," he said, "you have my oath I will not speak, but my presence here is no secret. Mercadier and forty of his men rode with me to Calais."

"They put you on a ship to Dover. They know nothing beyond that." Queen Eleanor stared into Raimond's eyes for a long, uncomfortable moment. "I have called a council here," she said at last, "to find ransom for Richard. He must be freed quickly, lest he lose his kingdom as well as the ransom-price."

There had been a hint of aged, frightened desperation in her voice. Raimond drew a long breath and tried to find words to answer her. "Your son is the greatest warrior king in all Christendom, your grace. The emperor, though he holds King Richard, would not dare to harm him."

For an instant, Raimond saw a bitter brightness about the queen's eyes. She turned her face from him. "I did not summon you here to speak of a mother's fears." After a time, the fierce whisper came again. "I speak of freeing your king by harvest time."

"Ten thousand silver marks and two hundred noble hostages cannot be found and moved so quickly."

"So they say in the streets of London." The dowager queen's hands were fisted at her side. "One hundred thousand is the true sum, deBauzan. Ten times the amount first named. The emperor asks the impossible, and Philip of France urges him to remain firm. That young vulture will take whole provinces while Richard is confined. I need the ransom sooner than my deputies will find it."

Blessed St. Thomas, Raimond swore silently, deliver me from this woman's scheming. "Your grace," he began, "I have nothing but my sword to offer you. I have no lands, and I brought nothing—no plunder from the Holy Lands."

The black eyes softened at his last words. "You brought your king away safely from Palestine. If he had listened to you, if he had not changed the plan—"

"No one could have foreseen—"

"You found an honest ship. Richard heeded the counsel of a brigand and suffered for it. For all your sins, deBauzan, you are a clever man and worthy of our trust. Will you turn that wit and honor once again to your king's welfare?"

Raimond tried to focus upon her words. He had not slept since his ruined homecoming at Bauzan, and he needed every shred of wit he possessed to deal with King Richard's determined mother. He drew a deep, desperate breath and rose to stand before her. "Tell me, in plain speech, what you want, your grace."

Eleanor's smile vanished. Raimond deBauzan had never been a sweet-mannered courtier to be led by the nose. And the years in Palestine had done nothing to soften his blunt speech.

The dowager queen's dark gaze narrowed and passed slowly over the tall knight before her. The large, rangy frame he had inherited from his warrior father had filled out with dense muscle earned in combat and hardship. The eastern sun had scorched the color from his thick hair, leaving a shining, silver-gilt frame for that strong Norman face.

Two years in the Holy Lands had claimed the lusty, warm-hearted innocence of Raimond deBauzan and had left in its place a cold, intense austerity.

Eleanor caught her breath. She knew (what woman knew better than she?) what Palestine could do to a man. In this cold-eyed warrior, she saw no trace of youthful appetites and idealism. Would it be folly, an old woman's last folly, to entrust Richard's future, and her own, to this stern stranger?

"Swear that you will keep secret what I ask of you. Should you refuse me, you must never speak of this night."

There was a long moment of silence. When he spoke, there was no trace of emotion in his voice. "On the Holy Sepulcher, I—"

"No. On your sword. Swear on your sword."

His gaze flashed a warning.

Eleanor waited.

At last, a thin smile touched his weather-burned face. "If I learn your secret but refuse your task, your grace would be foolish to let me leave this house alive. Better to ask that my oath be sworn upon my hopes of living past dawn."

"I will have your oath on your sword, Raimond deBauzan. When you hear what you must do, you will see I bear you no ill will in this matter."

His smile vanished. "You have forgiven me, then."

"For Poitiers? I forgave you long ago."

Raimond deBauzan waited, as he had promised, until the moon went down. Before dawn, he unbarred the scullery door and left the silent house.

The servant lad had left a single torch burning in the bracket before the stable door; it cast a long shadow beyond the bay gelding Raimond had bought in London. It illuminated, just beyond the edge of that shadow, the figure of the small servant boy, bound and gagged.

"You were long enough, my lord. I thought the old woman had left you dead." Hugo Gerbrai, captain of the Bauzan garrison, slouched over the cropped mane of his horse. The torch light flickered upon the dried lather and sweat which covered the roan's bowed neck. Gerbrai made an impatient gesture. "What did the queen want?"

Raimond frowned down at the small figure lying trussed against the stable door. He growled an order.

With a scrape and a hiss, Hugo drew his sword and reached down to the white-eyed servant to slice through the rope which bound the birdlike ankles. "There, boy," he grunted. "Be gone."

In silence, Raimond listened to the child's sharp footsteps receding far into the blackness at the end of the passageway. He turned his gaze back to the burly man slowly sheathing his broadsword. "May I hope you treated the queen's guard with more respect?"

"That young alley rat nearly robbed me of the choice, Fortebras. He was halfway out of the stable to warn them when I stopped him." Gerbrai sighed. "Well, Fortebras? Tell me what the old woman wants and I'll send word to your father."

Fortebras. Strong-Arm. He had forgotten that name, won upon the Bauzan training field a lifetime ago—before Palestine.

"My lord?"

Raimond shook his head. "Tell my father I am well. Tell him I will return when I can. Say no more than that."

"That won't be enough to keep him from marching upon Falaise to demand your safe return."

"Stop him."

"He took offense, seeing you ride off with Mercadier's filthy butchers. Your father and Ivo will march to Falaise if you're not back within the month." Gerbrai's mount sidled away from the stable door.

Raimond caught the slack of the reins beneath the muddy bridle. "Stop him. He will anger the queen, and accomplish nothing but—"

Gerbrai leaned forward. "Tell me what she wants from you. Then I will be able to stop him."

"How did you find me?"

"Followed you to Calais and bought rumors from the harbor rats. Paid a merchantman to take us aboard and try to keep your ship in sight. And at Dover, paid more gold to learn your destination. We were too few to do anything but follow you and watch—"

Raimond glanced into the darkness beyond the loom of the torch. "How many did you bring?"

"Twelve. Erec, Alain, and ten men at arms from the garrison. They are not far from here—waiting at the abbey gates."

"Send two of them back to stop my father."

"And the rest?"

"Come with me."

"What does she—"

Raimond put up his hand. "I will tell you what she wants, but the others must know nothing of it. Agreed?"

"Agreed." Gerbrai shifted in the saddle. "Well, Fortebras? Speak. What caused the old crone to send her vultures to drag you here?"

Raimond led his large gelding forth and doused the last torch in the water trough. He climbed into the slick, rain-soaked saddle and turned his mount away from the feeble light of dawn. "Later. I'll speak when this nest of serpents lies a full league behind us."

"By St. Cuthbert's great toe, Fortebras—"

"Not before."

Dusk, 2 June, 1193 Morston, Cornwall

She never left the valley now, never walked far beyond the bailey walls. Never out of sight of that sway-backed, crumbling heap.

As if she knew he was watching.

He had come twice before and waited for her in the shadows of the tor. A twelvemonth ago, he had seen her moving among the flocks brought down from the hills for shearing. And at harvest time, she had spent four days in the oat stubble, in the small field north of the keep. Never out of sight of the walls.

As if she knew he was watching.

He had not waited in idleness. It had been easy to find others. The pig girl the first time, then the old shepherd. They had come to him, rushed to him when he showed his face, picked up the small bundle of cloth at his side, had helped him to this place. It had been so easy. Before the end had come, each of them had told him all they had known of Morston's lady.

He squinted into the low sun as it disappeared into the sea, and turned back to the broken body caught in the gorse at the base of the tor. There was no need to move it, no need to touch it, save to search the twisted neck for warmth or pulse. The tumbled sprawl of the shepherd's corpse would not reveal his deed.

The shepherd had been an old man, awkward and slow. His death would surprise no one. It was not a great sin to have killed him.

The dead pig girl had troubled him for days, even though her death was not his sin alone. Though she knew it not, Alyse of Morston had shared that sin. Because of her, two people had died.

If she would stray, at the right time, a little closer to the tor, it would be ended. But the lady never left the rotting hovel she called home.

She was a coward, clinging close to the walls of the keep.

As if she knew he was watching.

CHAPTER ONE

West Coast of Cornwall, 15 June, 1193

Raimond deBauzan rode north from Chilcheton with eleven of his father's most trusted men, three pack horses, and a shivering, disgruntled priest sent by the vicar at St. James to guide them to Morston.

"That priest is either a fool or in the pay of brigands, Fortebras. He leads us away from the coast." Hugo Gerbrai pulled a mist-sodden cloak across his chest and glared at the hunched figure riding before them.

Raimond frowned into the pale sun. "He keeps us to the high ground. Let him be."

" . . . had three years in Palestine, with Saladin's devils at your throat, and came back to Christendom to follow that cross-eyed churchman in circles across this cold place . . . call it summer, do they?"

"They do."

" . . . and that priest wears a face that could kill a mule at ten paces. He is not eager to reach your new lands, I think. Or to deal with your lady bride."

Raimond turned in his saddle to glance at the short column of men riding a few paces behind him. "There are some among us with faces to match the priest's. When we reach my lands, I'll send them back.''

"You do that and your father will have their hides on the bailey gates." Gerbrai fisted a thick, gloved hand towards the silent riders. "We will stay by your side, every man of us, until you fetch the old woman's trinkets back to her and—"

"Hugo—"

"They cannot hear in this wind. Cold enough to freeze their ears closed, for all it's June. The devil's breath, it is. That priest says it blows for a fortnight at a time. This is no place for you, Raimond."

"It is mine."

"It's the backside of the known world. Take the woman, if you want her, and when you take the jewels to Windsor, keep going. Your father's lands—"

"—will be Ivo's."

Gerbrai sighed. "Ivo will need a strong man at his side. The people look to you—"

"They look to Ivo now, as they should."

"If you don't want to cast your shadow over Ivo, then put away your sword and be his steward. Better that, Fortebras, than following that Plantagenet madman back to die in Palestine, or selling your sword to that other lunatic in Paris. How long, Fortebras, before you hire yourself out to the likes of Mercadier for a season, and then another, then—"

"How long, Gerbrai, will you bait me? My sword is not for hire, and I will be no man's steward. Not Ivo's, not any man's. I have these lands now; they will be enough."

"You will stay here, freezing your balls every time you ride your boundaries, with only the stinking sheep to muster? God knows, the least of Ivo's vassals will have more than this wind-blasted place will give you."

"It is mine, and I will keep it."

"They owe you more than this. God's truth, our king's mother holds his life cheap if she rewards your deeds at Acre with this poor place. Is there nothing more for you?"

Raimond tightened his grip on the reins. "This is what I have, and I would be a fool to leave it untended while I whine at Eleanor Plantagenet's feet for more lands. If these lands are not rich, so be it. I'll have a few years of peace, with no one lusting after what's mine.''

"Well, you will have your peace, Fortebras. This place is so far from comfort that no thief would care to find it.''

"There will be no brigands at my gates. The priest has said that Kernstowe has a stone keep, in good repair.''

"And the priest has said that the smaller holding, your lady's manor, is so poor that her people are near starving each spring.''

Raimond snorted. "And you believed him? When a churchman begins to speak of poverty, he wants a bigger chalice for his chapel. They're all the same. They think we came back from Palestine with our saddlebags full of gold.''

Gerbrai shook his head. "Would he expect a rich man to come to this place, to claim these lands? No, Fortebras. I believe the priest was speaking the truth.''

"If you let that lad run to the kitchen when he pleases, my lady, he'll have nothing to cover those skinny shanks next winter.''

"Don't call him back. He's young and hungry." Alyse Mirbeau watched her smallest worker scamper over the shearing fence and run toward the kitchens. Wat was a good lad, but too frail to be of much help with the milling ewes still penned outside Morston's crooked stockade.

"Nor will there be food to spare for that child if the wool isn't ready for market when the Kernstowe wagon comes.''

Alyse sighed and turned back to lift the rolled fleece at her feet. "We're nearly done, Hawise. Let him go.''

Hawise shrugged. "He's a puny lad. Hardly fit to work.''

"He will grow.''

"Aye, that he may.''

Alyse turned away from Hawise's flat gaze. Six summers ago, when Wat had been a fat, untidy babe in his young mother's arms, there had been many sacks of wool and bags of grain to sell at Dunhevet. The hungry times had begun when William of Morston had sold half the harvest grain and a pair of oxen to pay the old King Henry's crusade tax. When the young King Richard had raised his army, Harald deRançon, lord of

Kernstowe, had taken away Morston's young men to train as foot soldiers. Sixty villagers had watched them go. Only forty women, children, and greybeards awaited their return.

Alyse took an armful of her shearing and started towards the wool shed. Before the men had left, the daughter of the warden would not have worked with the shepherds, covered in dust, pricked by burrs and straw from the unwashed wool, smelling of oily fleeces. Now, Morston desperately needed labor, and Alyse was as strong as any of the folk who remained in the village.

"Is that the last of them, my lady?" Hawise waded through a dense mass of shearings to prod the wool sack hanging between the rafters.

"There are three more to come."

"Well, the bag is not near full. When this lot goes in, it will still be lacking. Mayhap those lazy lads missed some ewes this morning."

"Egbert went to look for them."

"He'll find no more, my lady. We lost more to the wolves than ever, those lads being so young and foolish . . ."

"They did the best they could, Hawise. Do not let them hear you speak so."

The two women began to pile the new wool against the timber walls. The faint body warmth remaining in the fleeces cast a delicate mist into the cool shadows of the shed. Rising from the floor, the vapor shifted in the drafts and gathered beneath the uneven belly of the canvas sack. A rising gust penetrated the rough walls to force the clouded warmth into a pale, lazy spiral.

Alyse moved back to the door, her fists clenched into painful knots.

Hawise glanced at the curling mist and pushed the last of the fleeces into the corner. "It be our good fortune King Richard has ended his quest. Father Gregory told Egbert that the first of Chilcheton's men came home a fortnight ago. Did he not tell you?" She looked up, puzzled by her lady's silence. "Did he not tell you, my lady?"

"Yes, he told me." Alyse stepped past Hawise into the thin sunlight and wiped the sudden cold sweat from her forehead.

Hawise wedged the door shut. "I prayed that our men would be home by harvest time."

Alyse turned her face to the cold sea wind and drew a long breath. She too had prayed for Morston's men, but she had little hope that they would return. DeRançon had chosen so many—all of the young ones, and most of the full-grown men. None of them had trained with weapons before they had taken the cross, but all of them had gone willingly to learn, lured by the bishop's promise of salvation and the lord Harald's tales of Jerusalem's golden cobblestones. So they had gone, and the lord Harald deRançon had remained at Kernstowe, his own small army of seasoned men-at-arms still with him to defend the keep and force tolls from travelers.

"They should be home long before the harvest," Alyse said. So they should, if they had survived. There had been no word, no message sent with the three Chilcheton men who had returned that first winter from the army's training camp at Messina.

Alyse had traveled with her mother's husband to Chilcheton to ask those early survivors how the Morston men had fared. They had found three thin figures huddled around the kitchen fire, their skin darkened by sun and the yellow tinge of wasting sickness. Of the Morston men, they had learned nothing. The camp had been large and crowded, and the Chilcheton men ill from the day they had reached Messina.

A year later, there had still been no word. The crusading army had seemed as far away as the thin moon that shone upon Morston's newly ploughed fields.

Hawise cleared her throat. "My lady, will you go to Chilcheton for news?"

Alyse shook her head. "We will hear soon enough." After her mother and William died of the fever, Alyse had not dared to travel even as far as Kernstowe for news. The sooner she called attention to herself, the sooner the crown would remember Morston, and give it to a new lord. Alyse, only a stepdaughter to William of Morston, had no claim to the lands. She would be sent to a nunnery, if there was an abbess willing to accept an educated but dowerless young noblewoman.

She would go, right willingly, when she had done her last task. When she was free of her promise, she would find peace.

The sea wind gusted again; across the narrow bailey yard, the granary door swung open and crashed against its timber frame. Hawise turned to the storage shed. "Those stupid lads! They've left the last fleeces in the granary. I'll bring them out, my lady, if you take—"

"No."

"You said you didn't want—"

"No. Leave them. Leave them there."

Hawise's eyes widened at her mistress's sharp tone. "I'll get those lazy numskulls to do it."

"Tomorrow. Close the door."

With a small shrug, Hawise turned back to the door. "It's men's work, it is. Time they came back." She pushed the rough timber panel into place and looked back over her shoulder. "Mayhap King Richard will find a husband for you when he returns, Lady Alyse."

"Mayhap." If he did, the marriage would not last beyond the first night. No, it was the nunnery for Alyse when her time at Morston came to an end.

"Emma says the old queen may send for you and take you back to France. Find you a husband, remembering your good mother's service to her."

"She will not remember."

"Not remember?" The woman drew closer and raised her face to stare at Alyse. "You are angry, my lady?"

With effort, Alyse attempted a smile. "No, Hawise." Such mistakes—small slips of the tongue, failure to hide her fear, to mask her anger—were dangerous. Already, Hawise's surprise had become curiosity. "No," Alyse said again. "Why should I be angry with Queen Eleanor? She is old, now—so old that she may not remember I exist."

Hawise's sharp features relaxed into concern. "She would not forget your lady mother. And remembering her, Queen Eleanor will think of you."

Alyse nodded and twisted her sea-damp hair back from her face. "Call the lads in, Hawise, before young Wat eats their pottage as well as his own."

Her smile faded as soon as Hawise disappeared behind the wind-ravaged corner of the keep. Hawise was wrong. Queen Eleanor had shown no sign, over the years, that she wished to remember Philip of Mirbeau's widow and her daughter. Even after the old king died and the queen gained her freedom, Eleanor of Aquitaine did not send word to Alyse's family. Had she forgotten the coffret she had charged Isabelle Mirbeau to keep hidden beneath Morston's rough hearthstones? Alyse had spent the last of her dead parents' store of silver pieces to send word of their deaths to the dowager queen; there had been no answer, no release from the vows Isabelle Mirbeau had sworn to her royal mistress.

Alyse forced the latch bar across the wool shed door and gave thanks to St. Morwenna that most of the ewes had survived the winter. In such things she would find her salvation—in the hard struggle to keep her people from starving—not in futile hopes that Queen Eleanor would release her from her dead parents' promises and reward Morston by forgiving the villagers the new ransom tax. For the past four years, Queen Eleanor had been free to go where she pleased, to do as she wished, and she had sent no help to Morston. No word.

If, one day, it pleased the dowager queen to turn her attention to Alyse's plight and offer to arrange a marriage, Alyse would choose a nunnery instead.

Isabelle Mirbeau's only child was already beyond the queen's help.

"Morston's two fields are not large, but they are good fertile land, nonetheless." Father Gregory halted his mule and pointed down to the narrow valley tilting towards the sea. Above the water, almost at the edge of the high black cliff, was a crooked timber tower squatting among an untidy cluster of huts. Around the hovels, a crude embankment of stones and turf offered the suggestion of a curtain wall. "In the past, with more men to work the fields, the settlement fed sixty souls. Now"—his voice descended into an embarrassed hush—"the lady Alyse has said she cannot pay King Richard's ransom tax."

Gerbrai rolled his eyes. "The tax from that poor place would not buy a morning's kindling for the hearth in King Richard's prison. The lady Alyse showed good sense to refuse.''

The priest bristled in sudden indignation. ''We are all liable for the ransom tax, my lords. Even the poorest of us. At Chilcheton, we gave our finest silver chalice to the king's deputies, leaving us with only a wooden gilt cup for the altar and—'' He broke off and glanced back at the packhorses. ''Kernstowe's late lord Harald deRançon had vowed to bring gold from Jerusalem to Chilcheton should his life be spared. We would have used it to replace the chalice. Alas, he has perished and cannot keep his vow.''

A strange rumbling cough emerged from Gerbrai's deep chest. ''You would have had no gold from him. The Saracens kept their city and their riches. The packhorses carry iron, priest. Weapons for my lord Raimond's men to skewer enemies''— Gerbrai glared down at the cleric—''and thieves—''

''Your lord will find no thieves—''

''—and those who lead him in circles across this godforsaken land—''

''Peace, Hugo.'' Raimond deBauzan turned to the red-faced priest. He looked north, down to the rocky coast, to the drunken confusion of timber and turf perched above the sea. He drew a long breath. ''A strange place to build a keep.''

For once, Gerbrai was speechless. Raimond filled the silence. ''The place is too close to the cliffs. A little damage to the western foundations would send the bailey wall into the sea.''

Father Gregory shook his head. ''It is written in the Dunhevet abbey chronicles that in the time of our King Stephen, near forty winters ago, the face of the cliffs below Morston collapsed in a single night. The keep remained, as it was a little east of the slide. The rocks fell down and filled the cove. The ships can't go there now.''

''Then the keep is not needed. That ragged shore protects the land from even the smallest ships. Or is there a landing place up the coast?''

''No, my lord. This was the only safe harbor. The seas are so great here that not even a fishing boat may be brought close to Morston. The young lads go down the cliffs for birds' eggs, but none dare to put a boat in the sea.''

Raimond frowned. Queen Eleanor had chosen a clever hiding place for her treasure. It was easy to see how Morston, a strategically useless settlement with small cultivated fields, wild moors, and no harbor, had escaped the attention of King Henry, King Richard, and now Count John. The place should have been abandoned long since.

Hugo Gerbrai nudged his horse forward between Fortebras and the priest. He squinted into the northerly breeze. "That's it? Why, an army of a hundred men could not defend that mess of rotting timber. A party of ten men could burn that crooked keep and knock down what is left of the embankments in a short midwinter morning. This is no great gift the Plantagenets have given you, Raimond."

"Hmm."

"Not so." Father Gregory pointed inland. "Your lord also holds Kernstowe, to the north and east of this place. There are rich lands and a fortress strong enough to withstand months of siege."

Gerbrai grunted. "Then let us not stop here. This puny place will hold no welcome for weary men. Look at it, my lord. A drunken keep ready to slip over the cliff, and the barns and huts more crooked still. And for the rest—is that a chapel? At Bauzan, your father has bake ovens built better than that hovel. My lord, your father's cattle are sheltered better than these folk."

Raimond shook his head. "We will stop here first."

Gerbrai frowned at the sky. "Look at the sky, Fortebras. Black clouds. They are an omen, I think."

"Storm clouds, not omens. They bring us nothing worse than rain. We will stop here first, to speak with Alyse Mirbeau. Father Gregory will tell her of Queen Eleanor's wishes."

The priest turned back in alarm. "My lord, it would be better if you told her."

Gerbrai laughed. "It will be no hardship to tell the woman she is to be plucked out of that magpie's nest to live in a good stone keep. She should be happy to wed the new lord of Kernstowe and leave this place to the crabs and the gulls. If, indeed, she hasn't already taken refuge elsewhere." Gerbrai urged his mount back to the small company of men at arms waiting restlessly below the vantage point.

The priest spoke again. "The lady Alyse is surely at Morston, my lord. She never leaves."

"You know the lady, Father Gregory?"

"Well enough, in days past. She came as far as Chilcheton once a year with her stepfather. After her parents died, she never traveled. But I come to Morston from time to time. She is—she is an energetic lady, sensible of her duties. Hard-working."

Raimond smiled. If the lady Alyse had not stirred from this place since her parents died, it might be because she honored her duty towards Queen Eleanor, and watched over the treasure in her family's safekeeping. She would no doubt be relieved and grateful to pass the burden to him. He would reward her with a trip to Windsor when the time came to return the dowager queen's treasure. The lady would be pleased, perhaps a little overwhelmed with her good fortune after her years of vigilance. It would be a fine thing to have a wife in whom such loyalty ran strong. A fine thing—

Beneath him, Raimond heard Gerbrai order the Bauzan men up the grassy slope.

He gathered his reins. "Why are you reluctant to tell Alyse Mirbeau she will be wed? I was told she is a quiet, biddable lady."

Father Gregory coughed. "She . . . has a quiet way about her at times. There are—some would call her biddable. Yes indeed. A good Christian maid, she is. Honest. Very honest. She is most forthright and . . . honest."

Honest. Forthright. And the priest had still not agreed to tell her she would be wed. Raimond's smile narrowed. Would he find his bride a termagant? Was that what the old priest, in his roundabout way, was telling him? Queen Eleanor had given him a harpy to wife. Was this revenge for Poitiers, after all?

Father Gregory coughed again. "And comely. The lady Alyse is comely. As for her character . . . she is a good lady. It is no great privation to have a wife of strong character, provided she be honorable, as the lady Alyse most certainly is . . ."

Hugo Gerbrai returned to hear Father Gregory's last words. "She is nineteen years old, is she not? Protest no more, priest. If she were all that fine to look upon and had good sense as well, a shrewish nature would not have kept her unwed. She should have taken a husband four years ago. If she were all you say she is, there would have been some minor knight willing to have her before now."

"Enough, Hugo."

Gerbrai ignored Raimond and glared at the priest. "My lord will go carefully into this marriage."

The priest bristled afresh at Hugo's words. "I will not have my meaning misconstrued. The lady Alyse is a fit wife for a good man and I will hear no evil of her."

"Leave off, Hugo. Enough talk of the lady. I will wed with her and expect she will be . . . a fit wife." Raimond gathered his reins. "We will rest at Morston this night and go on to Kernstowe tomorrow."

Gerbrai rolled his eyes. "Priest, tell us of Kernstowe's late lord. Had deRançon no kin to dispute the queen's gift of the lands to Lord Raimond?"

Father Gregory relaxed, obviously happy to speak of something other than the message he must give to Alyse Mirbeau. "He has kin in Normandy, none near enough to question the queen's wishes. DeRançon was the only son. For this reason, he did not join King Richard at the outset of the crusade. He paid the Saladin Tithe and sent many men, from Kernstowe and from Morston, to Palestine. Later, when his father died and he inherited the fief, he took the cross and traveled to join the king's army in the Holy Land."

"Why then?" Raimond asked. "He still had no heir."

"His wife had died, after five years of barren marriage. It was over two years ago, my lord, near the time Lord William of Morston and his lady were stricken with the fever. The young lord Harald deRançon set out for Palestine alone—his men at arms were already abroad in King Richard's service. They say he never reached them."

"He died during his passage to Palestine?"

"So it seemed. He left Kernstowe and was never heard from again. Our abbot believes he saw deRançon in London later that year, but it is not clear that he ever reached the coast. The Templars say that he did not embark with the supply ships last spring. He may have met misfortune on the road. The crown declared his lands vacant and charged his warden to pay his taxes to Count John. Rolf Nevers, the Kernstowe steward, has done this.''

Gerbrai halted on the last broad hill above Morston and spat contemptuously. "Surely this is the nether end of Richard's realm. Fortebras, you have been given a crooked wooden tower, ready to fall into the sea, and other lands held by a lord who may or may not have died traveling from this godforsaken, wind-blasted land on his way to court. And you will have a wife from this abandoned corner of nowhere who is either too shrewish or too plain to have tempted any man to claim her.'' He spat again.

"Enough, Hugo. I'm to wed the lady.''

"No—do not say that. Raimond, I would have you see the lady Alyse before you swear before this priest to take her to wife.''

There was no reasoning with Hugo Gerbrai when he was determined to protect a son of Rannulf deBauzan. Raimond drew a long breath and pointed ahead. "Look there—in the field near the sea. Those lads must be Morston folk. They have seen us, Hugo. We will go down.''

The clouds continued to gather about Morston, as if drawn there by its precarious bulk. The wind rose, and with it came the rain. Raimond deBauzan, new lord of Morston and Kernstowe, arrived at his domains in a heavy downpour, cursing the poor, narrow, muddy track he followed. Hugo was right. This place seemed beyond the end of the civilized world.

Alyse Mirbeau peeked between the broad timbers of the chapel door and uttered a word her gentle mother would not have recognized.

It had been foolish to hope that the travelers would not stop to seek shelter. Alyse had seen them appear, indistinct figures riding through the rain, on the edge of the moors above the keep. They had turned to descend the narrow track down to the walls of Morston. Thirteen mounted men leading five pack horses crowded into the small bailey yard among the storage huts, and tethered their large, well-fed beasts to the bars across the wool shed doors.

Three newly shorn ewes bolted into the bailey and skidded to a bleating halt just short of the largest of the horses, a great black monster with a close-cropped mane. The shepherd lads were nowhere to be seen.

Alyse watched in dismay as a rotund man with a short, grizzled beard approached the door of the keep and set his fist to the warped timber. Behind him, the broad-shouldered figure upon the black destrier called a low order and dismounted. The bearded one lowered his fist and shrugged.

The leathern hinges of the door were sagging wet as Alyse wedged the chapel door open and stepped outside. She raised her face to the driving rain and shook her head. Her hair was dirty from the shearing pen and the cold force of the water was a blessing. The fine spray of mud from the puddles beside the chapel steps was not.

Father Gregory from Chilcheton was there, looking oddly small and frail as he made his way through the crowd of intruders to join the heavy-handed men beating at the door of the keep. They were large and heavily armed, and easily outnumbered the Morston folk gawking from the kitchen shed. Why would a small, well-equipped army stop here? Were they the crown's tax men? Had they come to demand a tithe?

Last month, when Father Gregory had come to Morston to hear Father Anselm's confession, Alyse had ignored his talk of a crown tax to ransom King Richard from imprisonment. Had King Richard's royal deputies sent these men to force her to pay? These were hard men, clothed in well-fitting small armor, their horses strong enough to carry a fully armed man into battle. These were not the kind of men a clerk of the exchequer might send to ransack a remote manor, looking for hidden coins.

No, these were warriors.

The rain lightened into a hard-blowing mist. Father Gregory smiled and gestured towards the keep.

There was no help for it. The travelers must be greeted,

offered food and drink, and encouraged to cross the moor to Kernstowe's hearth before they demolished Morston's small stores of bread and ale.

To delay was to risk that they would stay here this night, to eat and drink their way through all that they found in the kitchen.

Lady Alyse Mirbeau squared her shoulders and walked towards the small army gathered before the keep. If they proved angry when she sent them on their way, it was better to risk a struggle, or even death by those heavy broadswords, than to face slow starvation in the wake of their greed.

"You there, boy. Where are the stables? Stables. For the horses." Raimond glowered at the half-grown, weedy child who stared, eyes bulging, at Shaitan. Like the few other folk gathered to cast hungry looks at the pannier packs, he seemed deaf and mute. Hugo had persuaded the old woman in the doorway of the keep to allow his men to carry their saddlebags into the tower, but the horses were still without shelter.

Father Gregory had gone aside to speak with a bedraggled shepherd girl standing ankle-deep in the muddy area which served as a courtyard between the small stone chapel and the keep. The girl's thin woolen gown was soaking wet, clinging closely to her young form. She raised a slender, smudged arm to push her rain-darkened hair from her face as she turned, obviously dismayed, in his direction.

Raimond revised her age upwards. Those pert, full breasts so inadequately covered by the soaked cloth belonged to a woman full grown. God's blood, it had been a long time since he had had a woman. Even muddied and drenched, this woman was uncommonly fair. If she proved willing, he would bed with her to take the edge off his lust before his wedding, thus sparing the lady Alyse Mirbeau a wedding night with a bridegroom too long deprived. Yes, the shepherd girl would do very well.

Raimond smiled in anticipation.

The woman did not smile back.

Raimond saw Father Gregory's frown as he drew near with

the bedraggled girl. Could the priest read his mind? Raimond turned back to his horse and the urchin boy.

Shaitan shook his massive head and bared his teeth.

The spindly boy bolted into the keep.

The woman muttered something brief and angry. She turned to face Raimond. "There is room in the byre up the hill for some of the horses, my lord." The muddy girl indicated a dilapidated barn outside the bailey wall.

Raimond glanced at the barn, then at the woman. To be honest, she did not look willing. It was a pity. Mud or no, there was nothing he would like better than to take her with him and have her in the hay. Later she might warm to him and—

Father Gregory cleared his throat. "Lord Raimond, this is the lady Alyse Mirbeau. I have told her of Queen Eleanor's letter, and of the"—he stepped back from the woman and made a feeble gesture—"and of why you are here."

There was a smudge on the woman's smooth forehead and sodden, lank bits of straw in her hair. "I must bid you welcome to Morston, Raimond of Bauzan," she said. Her voice, cold as the driving mist, held no real welcome. Nor was there any warmth in her eyes.

No, she did not seem pleased with him. Disheveled as she was, her manner and tone were haughtier than those of the proudest damosels at Windsor. No matter. Raimond knew very well how to thaw the ice from such ladies. He smiled and pitched his voice low. "Lady Alyse, I am well pleased by your welcome. We must speak—"

"So says this priest. Wat won't come out again, he's afraid of your horse. Would you stable the beast yourself? I will await you in the guardroom." The woman stalked away towards the oaken door, leaving Raimond, Father Gregory and Shaitan staring after her.

The priest coughed nervously. "The lady Alyse was taken aback. She had no thought to wed, she said."

"No matter. She will get used to the idea."

"It might be best to leave her to think about it for a time, my lord."

"Tell her I'll see her in the guardroom, as she suggested, within the hour."

"I would advise you to wait until—"

"Within the hour, priest." Raimond watched his future wife wring a small stream of muddy water from the hem of her gown in the warped and listing entrance of the keep.

So that was his bride. Raimond shrugged and turned to lead Shaitan towards shelter. There had been no surfeit of sweetness when the Lord Almighty created that young woman. If she knew the proper way to address a knight who had showed her courtesy, she was not willing to use those gentle words. Still, she was fair of face and form, and would be even comelier when bathed and fitly dressed.

She would come to like him well enough. Women always did.

The guardroom occupied the ground level of the keep, near the kitchens. There, warmed by two wall hearths, the bachelor knights and men at arms of Morston two generations ago had taken their meals at the long trestle tables and stored their weapons. At night, they had slept upon pallets across the rush-covered floor.

When William of Morston had brought home his new wife and her small daughter seventeen years ago, the guardroom had been in disuse for many years. Morston had not supported enough men-at-arms to put even a portion of the soldiers' quarters to good use. The village people, and even the kitchen maids, did not care to leave their small huts to sleep in the groaning, settling timber tower which overlooked the sea from precarious foundations. Today, Raimond deBauzan's small company of men filled the dusty guardroom, warming themselves before the fires and steadily depleting Morston's last barrel of ale.

Alyse climbed the narrow stair to the small chambers above the noisy men. She needed to clean the mud from her face and put on dry clothing before facing that man again. And somehow, she had to find the words and the courage to brazen her way through the dilemma the tall Norman knight had presented. Alyse pushed open her chamber door.

"There you are. There's hot water on the fire. Your mother's blue mantle would be best, would it not? You cannot face him looking like a peasant lass. Father Gregory says he will stay long enough to wed him to you. The betrothal tonight, he says, and the wedding soon after. And so we are lost. Lost. What will we do?'' Alyse's aged nurse stifled her desperate question beneath a flood of muttered complaints concerning the clothing chest's heavy lid.

Alyse held the oaken panel open. ''Do? There are many things we could do, Emma. Run away. Ask the Abbess at St. Ursula's to take us as scribes. Appeal to Queen Eleanor, if she's still in England. For now, I will ask for time. I will tell him to return a few weeks from now. We will have time to think.''

Emma located the blue wool and slammed the lid down. ''The man brought an army with him. We'll never get past them.''

Alyse dipped a scrap from an old linen shift into the steaming pot, and began to scrub her face ''Then we'll wait for them to leave.''

''What if they won't go? What if the new lord stays here?''

''I will insist that he go. He must be eager to see Kernstowe after seeing how poor we are at Morston. He will lose interest, Emma. Where is the comb? I can't find the comb.''

''Under the washrag . . . he's not a man to be easily put from a task. Father Gregory says he is a knight of hard reputation who has won much honor in Palestine.''

''Humpf. He won little else but honor, I think, if his present reward is lordship of Morston and Kernstowe. He must have been landless. He will see to his larger holding and forget this poor place.''

''Give me the comb. Are you trying to pull out your hair by the tangles? This knight was landless, perhaps, but not without influence. He is the second son of Rannulf of Bauzan, a lord of Normandy.''

''His men called him Fortebras . . .'' Alyse stepped out of her muddy gown and grimaced as she saw the state of her scratched, grimy arms. ''. . . some guardroom name, fit for a mercenary. He is probably a bastard son.'' Alyse's frown deepened. Her ankles were even more deeply scratched and bruised.

No matter. Having seen her so, that Lord Raimond or Fortebras or whatever he called himself would be less likely to pursue the marriage. Even now, he should be ordering his men to remount and continue to Kernstowe.

"Oh no, he's no bastard. He is the younger brother of a childless heir. Those men down there are from his father's garrison at Bauzan."

Alyse looked up. "You have not been idle, Emma. The man has barely arrived and yet it seems you know all about him."

The older woman hung the discarded gown upon a peg beside the hearth. "The family is known to me," she said.

"How—"

"—and you didn't find me hiding in the chapel when they arrived, my lady. Father Gregory was most happy to give me news. If you didn't spend your days in the fields, dressed as a serf and covered in straw, you would be able to greet a traveler at the door. Properly. And hear the talk." Emma began to plait her lady's hair into a long, thick braid.

"And who would help with the shearing if I sat here all day? God's teeth, Emma, I will act my role when our king releases Morston's men from his service. Then we will all act our proper roles, not before."

"Calm yourself. Those men will hear you and begin to speak of treason in this house. Do not anger them by speaking ill of King Richard."

Emma helped Alyse don a soft gown from the oaken press and placed a faded blue mantle upon her shoulders. "There, now. You begin to appear as befits the lady Alyse Mirbeau. You have such a look of your mother . . ." Emma's voice cracked in a sudden sob. "Promise him anything, my lady, but make sure he leaves Morston today. We need time to recover—"

"Hush, Emma."

"Whether you wed him or not, he will be the new lord here, and you will not be free to dig—"

"Emma! Do not speak of it. Do you want them to hear?"

"You should have seen to it before now. I told you so. Now it may be impossible. Merciful Mother of God, what is to become of us?"

"Hush, Emma. Be still."

"What do you intend? Will you leave it? Forget it? You cannot—"

"Forget it? Never. After all that we did—" Alyse crossed to the eastern wall and looked through the single narrow window. Beneath her, the sodden thatch of the granary roof moved in the wind. "I see it every night. It haunts my dreams, Emma."

"What if this knight has the old queen's trust, if he knows what we have done for her sake? If he demands it now, all is lost. He will find—"

"He may not know," Alyse cut in sharply. "He was given the land. There must be many such grants for King Richard's men. The queen may have given him the charter, but she may not have told him what we have. Do not look for trouble, Emma. I will make sure that Raimond deBauzan leaves us in peace long enough to put all to right."

"But if he knows—if he wants it now, he will—"

"Be silent!" Alyse's reddening gaze turned back to the window. "I will manage to do it. Somehow."

Emma gathered her lady into her arms. "Forgive me, Alyse. All must be well, my lamb. God will help us."

Beyond the narrow window, a pair of larks rose and darted through the heavy mist, out to sea. Alyse watched them as they vanished into the grey sky. With care, and with luck, she too would disappear. When she had done what was necessary, when the time was right, she would go. The Norman lord—and his justice—must never find her.

CHAPTER TWO

Raimond had not known the late Isabelle of Mirbeau, but he pitied her now. Looking out through Morston's narrow, lightless arrow slits, he imagined how that Poitevin lady must have missed her sun-warmed homeland.

During the journey to Morston, the Chilcheton priest had told Raimond the little he knew of the lady Alyse's family. The late lady Isabelle Mirbeau, widowed by King Henry's soldiers and bearing her infant daughter in her arms, had followed her queen into imprisonment at Salisbury and had never seen her own country again. William of Morston, summoned to Salisbury to receive a small inheritance from a mercer uncle, had returned to his lands with a wife and a stepdaughter, an odd, grey-eyed child who had passed her first winter at Morston ill with fever, close to death. The child had recovered, and had grown strong, but her mother had not flourished. The lady Isabelle had given her new husband no heirs of his own.

And her daughter had known nothing of the world beyond this harsh land above a cold sea.

Through the shutters set into the east wall of the guardroom, Raimond saw a confusion of huts, sheds and a small church huddled close by the shadow of the listing timber keep. The bailey wall, an arc of rough stonework following the natural rise of the black coastal rock, had not been completed; it stopped abruptly a short distance from the chapel, leaving the crooked church vulnerable to any marauders who might find Morston worth their notice. A timber gate, too low to stop a siege machine and so ill-fashioned that the newly-shorn sheep moved easily between its planks and the chapel wall, sagged upon iron hinges to complete the crumbling defenses of the keep.

Morston's ancient landslide had swept the edge of the cliff down into the water, taking the western bailey wall with it; the edge of the abyss was now close beside the seaward wall of the fortress, leaving barely enough room for a man to edge past the rough timber tower above the dizzying chasm. The western arrow slits were useless; only sea birds moved across their range.

Raimond paced from one embrasure to the next, frowning at the stonework defenses which remained on three sides of the keep. He saw that Morston's wardens had tried, in times past, to maintain the crude embankment which barricaded the keep from the small fields beside it. Those ancient repairs had begun to crumble under the ravages of wind and salt.

He returned to the western wall and stood in the sharp cold slicing into the room through the embrasures. Here was no comfort for a widow from the lush lands of Aquitaine, where solid strongholds overlooked broad rivers and fertile fields. Yet, Isabelle of Mirbeau had kept faith with her second husband, settling in this damp wooden tower with no escape from the sound of the grey sea.

Isabelle must have grieved to see her daughter's childhood pass here, far from the warmth and enlightenment of Aquitaine's society. For all her cool disdain, the girl Alyse looked and smelled like a shepherd's daughter. Her speech lacked any trace of the subtle charm of her Poitevin forebears; her blunt, abrupt words would be more at home in this guardroom than in the solar of her mother's ladies. Raimond looked speculatively at the precarious stair leading to the sleeping chambers. He had not yet intruded that far, to see what lay above this room. Was there a solar for the ladies in this abandoned place? No mother, however diligent, would have been able to train her daughter in these surroundings to understand a noble lady's ways. The lady Alyse was the proof of that.

Raimond moved back to the hearth to warm his hands. He had not expected to find an exquisite lady of delicate demeanor in this place. To be honest, the lady Alyse was fairer than he had dared hope she would be. Plain spoken as the woman was, she would be a meet wife for him. She would not expect, or even welcome, the elaborate mazes of words that pale courtiers used to tempt noble ladies at Poitiers, Rouen and Windsor. Those women of the court who had taken Raimond into their beds had done so without cunning verses to praise them; they had seemed content to find his lovemaking far more flattering than his speech. The lady Alyse would be as well pleased, God willing.

The room darkened and the hearth began to steam as the rain returned to blow against the keep. A pale grey haze spread through the air, driven by the sharp sea breeze still whistling through the western arrow loops. Raimond scuffed his boot across the rough-hewn stones fronting the wall hearth. Was it here that William of Morston had helped his lady wife hide Eleanor's jewels? Or had he placed them beneath a bedchamber hearth, where only his wife and the serving maids would enter? Or had Isabelle brought the jewels to this keep without telling her new husband, and hidden them alone? Had she ever told William of Morston that this poor settlement held a queen's parure?

A gnarled piece of root rested atop the heap of firewood beside Raimond's boot. He took the twisted wood and prodded the joining between the two smallest stones. If Isabelle had acted alone, how skillfully could she have hidden the coffer? Had she told her daughter what she had done?

Raimond cursed under his breath. Queen Eleanor should have sent for her damned baubles when she had first gained her freedom, while Isabelle of Mirbeau had still lived. She would have saved Isabelle's family from the past four years of misery. Indeed, William of Morston and the lady Isabelle might have escaped the fever which had killed them, had they been free to leave this unwholesome place.

He broke the wood across his knee and flung the pieces into the flames.

Gerbrai and the others had made themselves comfortable, drying their wet cloaks before the spitting flames and removing the rust from their weapons in a clutter of axes, spears, rags, and ale cups on the narrow tables. Their voices, warmed by shelter and drink, echoed from the bare wooden walls of the room. Hugo Gerbrai's deep bass began to chant a crusader's marching song, with words which had proved bawdy enough to send many a Sicilian maiden's family scrambling to close the shutters as King Richard's army had passed.

Raimond saw a flash of pale blue cloth appear at the top of the stairs, hesitate and then draw back. He stood and looked about him; it was useless to try to quiet the men. They were far enough gone in their cups of Morston ale to be forgetful of decorum in this grim place. If the lady Alyse did not care to join the crowd of men in her guardroom, then Raimond would have to go up to her chamber.

Raimond mounted the stairs in a rush and found his lady in a small, bare hall which opened upon two bedchambers. She stood, grim and straight as a foot soldier facing his first enemy action, before the nearest chamber door. Only when Raimond came near enough to touch her did Alyse take one small step backward. A brief flash of annoyance crossed her features, as if she had not wished to show her nervousness.

She looked better now. With the straw out of her hair and the mud washed from her face, Alyse Mirbeau was more than passing fair. Her hair was a rich, glossy black, dark as any Saracen lady's tresses; the small, straight nose and determined chin were comely enough, but the eyes—cold, somber and grey—did not welcome Raimond's gaze.

Gerbrai's voice rose again, followed by a shout of laughter from many voices. Raimond saw a flush of vexation upon Alyse Mirbeau's pale cheeks. "My lady, the men are weary of their travels and—they mean no harm. Is there some quiet place where we may speak?"

Her features stiffened in alarm. "I said we would speak in the guardroom," she said.

"And I ask that we find a quiet place." By St. Cuthbert's

great toe, the lady was not yet his wife and already she showed a willful, angry nature. Or was it fear?

He reached to stroke her arm, with the same slow caution as he would use to steady a restive horse.

She looked down at his hand upon her sleeve, then at the bedchamber door. Raimond could feel her arm become tense as she turned her cold gaze back upon him. "Not here," she said at last.

Raimond smiled. This country-bred lady would not trust him in her chamber. Did she not know that a man's passion would rise as hot, if not hotter, if the opportunity came to play love games in less common places? His smile broadened. If the lady Alyse expected that her husband's lust would be limited to the darkness of the bedchamber, this summer would hold a goodly, pleasant revelation for her.

"Not here," he agreed. "Where, then? Above, on the sentry walk?"

"No. It is not safe." She frowned. "Why do you laugh, my lord?"

With effort, he contained his mirth. "Not safe, you say? Lady Alyse, there is no place in this keep which is safer than any other. Have you not climbed that big hill to the south of Morston to see the lines of the walls from there? This place is rotten, my lady. I have a mind to pull it down before it falls."

There was a brief flash of triumph upon her face, then the solemn stare with which she had first addressed him. "You can see, my lord, that your men—you and your men—must not stay here. So many—such large people will cause the floor to shift. If you start within the hour, you could reach—"

"We will risk it for this night."

"As you wish."

There was a slight movement within the chamber, and the slow whisper of silk upon silk. An older woman emerged from the shadows, dressed in folds of ragged carmine splendor. Above the vivid mantle, her face was so pale that Fortebras could see the blue pulse in fragile temples. Alyse made a small gesture. "My lord, here is Emma des Roches."

"My lord Raimond," the old woman murmured.

Her voice was pure Angevin, and held none of the slight

halting that Raimond had heard in Alyse's speech. The woman had not done the work of a peasant maid in this desperate place; her hands, though fragile with age, were slender and white.

Raimond nodded in the older woman's direction. " Are you my lady's kinswoman?" he asked.

"Emma was my nurse," Alyse said, "and my mother's nurse before."

"You were with the Lady Isabelle and Queen Eleanor at Salisbury?"

The older woman glanced at Alyse, then back to him. "Yes, my lord."

Raimond saw a second wary look pass between the women. "The dowager queen has given me William of Morston's land," he said, "and Harald deRançon's estates at Kernstowe."

"You saw her? You saw Queen Eleanor?"

"Yes."

"She must seem very old," said Emma.

Was there a rising note of hope in her question? Raimond nodded. "The queen is, of course, very old. But she is in good health and much concerned with the governing of King Richard's lands in his absence."

Emma closed her eyes.

In thankfulness, or in resignation? Raimond extended his hand. "Come, Lady Alyse. We will talk in the chapel."

She ignored his outstretched arm and moved past him to the stair.

They descended unnoticed by the guardroom crowd, now gathered around Hugo to listen to his bellowed rendition of "Fair Rosamond."

Alyse scowled at Gerbrai's song. "The ballad is treason. Queen Eleanor did not poison Rosamond Clifford," she said. "In my mother's lifetime, she never allowed that liars' song sung within these walls."

"Hugo means no harm, madam. But if the song offends you, I will ask him not to sing it in your hearing."

"Yes." She looked away from him. "Tell your man when we return. We will speak in the chapel now, before the sun sets." She continued down the stairs.

Raimond shrugged and followed her. "Hugo means no disre-

spect to the dowager queen. He sings the song because it amuses
him. Believe me, my lady, none of these men actually believes
the lady capable of murder.''

Alyse stopped abruptly on the stair and turned to face Fortebras, her eyes wide and staring. ''My lord?''

Raimond repeated his words slowly. ''Queen Eleanor is no
murderess. None of my men listening to the song believe the
dowager queen would take the life of her rival.'' Alyse's grey
eyes closed briefly, as if banishing a terrible vision. She turned
to continue down the stair.

Raimond followed, shaking his head in puzzlement. It
seemed his future wife was skittish as well as bad-tempered.
Maybe deaf as well. With each passing moment, she revealed
another cause for him to proceed carefully. He sighed. He had
had years of freedom to find a wife to bring him lands, and
neither he nor his father had given more than a passing thought
to the matter. Now, it was too late. The choice of his own bride
was a luxury Raimond would never know.

Still, the slender woman descending the stair before him was
fair enough, and the soft blue folds of her mantle did not
completely conceal the subtle sway of her hips. A man could
forgive her grim temper and sullen words if she gave even half
of the lusty bedsport her body promised.

The kitchen was as crowded as the guardroom; giggling,
wide-eyed women were bringing out Morston's reserves of
smoked meat and firing the bread ovens. Alyse Mirbeau uttered
a soft oath at the sight.

Raimond cleared his throat. ''Hugo told them to feed my
men. They have not eaten since morning.''

The lady did not seem embarrassed by the blunt reminder
that she had neglected her duties toward hungry travelers.

''They will have to sleep on the guard room floor.''

''They will.'' Raimond saw Alyse's gaze turn towards a thin
child carrying firewood to the ovens. ''There will be supplies
at Kernstowe,'' he added. ''I will replace what we use.''

''If it please you, send the food. This winter was hard.''

Alyse took a dark cloak from the wall and led Raimond
outside, along the line of flat stones which cut through the
muddy ground between the keep and the small chapel.

She pushed open the door. "Father Anselm?" she called.

Raimond looked within. "Your priest isn't here. Father Gregory was looking for him earlier."

"They must be in Father Anselm's hut." She stepped back. "We will find them—"

"No. Stay, Lady Alyse." He took her arm and drew her with him into the small stone chapel. "Stay here and speak with me—if it please you." Raimond nodded briefly in the direction of the plain, bare altar, and turned to pace across the small room.

Alyse clutched her cloak around her and watched Raimond de Bauzan move restlessly past the damp walls of the church. He was a large man, much larger than any of Morston's folk, taller by a full hand than her stepfather had been. His hair was unearthly bright. Even in the dim light of the chapel, the silver and gold streaks in his hair shone of the sun.

She recognized the color, though there was no one at Morston, no living soul she could remember with hair which mingled the colors of precious metals. But in her mother's book, a small volume of prayers made for Isabelle by the monks of St. Radegunde's Abbey on the occasion of her marriage, there was a warrior saint with such hair. Azure-garbed and holding his sword before a crimson dragon, the holy knight stood guard upon the first glowing page of Isabelle's book, and the pale richness of his hair was as bright as the holy light which surrounded his noble profile.

Raimond stopped and considered her briefly. "Are you ill?"

Alyse looked away. "No."

"You look ill." His voice, low and hoarse, should not belong to a man with the face of a warrior angel. The sun of Palestine was strong, they said, and hot enough to burn away the rain and roughen the throats of those who passed over the deserts.

He began once again to pace across the width of the chapel. Alyse had seen a wounded wolf move like that, shortly before he had attacked the staves of his wooden cage and broken free. Kernstowe's steward, having displayed the animal for his lord's amusement at the Dunhevet midsummer fair, had watched helplessly as the savage beast had mauled a serf and escaped the screaming crowd.

Raimond paused and stared at the drape of the blue mantle across the swell of Alyse's breasts. Her body flushed warm under that azure regard. He was more dangerous than the wolf, she realized. The wolf had not tempted her to step closer, to touch the white gold of his hair. Alyse clenched her hand beneath the folds of her mother's mantle. These thoughts of angels and wolves and saints would keep her from her purpose.

He turned away and rubbed his shoulder.

"Are you in pain?" Alyse asked.

"No. I have an old wound. It stiffens in the cold."

Alyse thought again of the injured wolf and took a small step backward. "Shall we return to the keep?"

"No. We will stay here. Alyse, Father Gregory has spoken to you. You know that Queen Eleanor has given me the lands of Morston and Kernstowe to hold for King Richard."

She nodded silently.

"She has also given me your hand in marriage."

"I have no thought to marry."

"Even so, the crown has given you to me. As we speak, Father Gregory and your priest are arranging the wedding." He began to pace once again.

Alyse willed herself not to shrink back when he moved towards her. "It will not happen," she said. The pacing continued. Had he heard her? "We will not marry."

He stopped before her. There was no anger in his eyes. Mild surprise, nothing more, was in his voice. "Why not? You cannot continue here; you are not William of Morston's heiress. The land reverted to the crown when he died, and now it is mine."

"I understand. Morston is yours now. The lands. Everything. But I do not care to marry, and will ask for a place at the Convent of St. Ursula in Exeter."

He shook his head. "What is this talk of a convent? If you had wished a religious life, you would have been settled in a convent before this day. You had no lands of your own to concern you. Why, in all your nineteen years, did you not ask your parents to place you in a convent?"

"I do not have to make excuses to you."

"You are making them now, Lady Alyse. Queen Eleanor has found you a husband and now you decide you are destined for a convent. That is an excuse to avoid wedding me."

His voice was low and flat, as if her answer would make no difference to his plans.

Alyse had a sudden, terrible wish to strike him. "Why do you question me as if I were a criminal? The queen has given you two fiefs, Lord Raimond, and, as you so courteously reminded me, I have nothing. Take your lands and be damned, then. Leave me in peace. I will be a nun."

Raimond was half tempted to let her do just that. He did not want a shrewish wife, no matter how beautiful she was. But Queen Eleanor had included this woman's hand in the charter setting forth the grant of Morston and Kernstowe. He would be foolish to reject any part of the letter—he must take both the lands and the lady or lose them both when Count John realized his mother had been generous to yet another of Richard's followers. The king's brother would use any ploy to challenge the gift.

Alyse raised a trembling hand to push a wisp of hair from her face.

Raimond drew a deep breath and softened his voice. "Lady Alyse, you are overwrought. An hour ago, you learned that you will be a wife, My wife. Time will prove this is no disaster, my lady. Deal with me honestly and you will not regret wedding me."

"I regret this matter already, Fortebras. Tell Queen Eleanor it is not possible."

"Lady, the queen has written, signed and sealed her royal wish, on behalf of King Richard, that I take charge of these lands and wed you. This I shall do."

The grey eyes closed briefly. And opened to look beyond him, to the shadows behind the simple altar. "All right, deBauzan. I agree. As you say, you have a royal decree and it is your right." Alyse drew a ragged breath and continued. "Go, then, to Kernstowe to claim it. I will wed you within the month.

Here or at Kernstowe, as you wish,'' she concluded in a breathless rush.

Raimond searched that cool grey gaze. The lady had capitulated too easily after that brusque beginning. An ugly doubt formed and flowered within his mind. Alyse asked that he go on to Kernstowe, leaving her here until the wedding. What would she do within that time? Bolt into some drafty convent, as she had wished, or—

Or did she desire to be left alone at Morston for a different reason? Did she know of the jewels? Would she collect Eleanor's treasure and leave?

Or—was she showing a maiden's fears, shy of sharing his bed?

"You wish me to leave you here alone until we wed?"

"Yes. I would finish the shearing." The lady was unskilled at deception; anxiety was plain upon her face.

Raimond began once again to pace. The old queen should have sent a courtier, a patient man to make his way through this lady's smokescreen of half-truths and excuses.

Alyse turned back to him. "You have seen Queen Eleanor?"

Raimond nodded. "At Windsor."

"Will you take me to Windsor?"

"After we are wed."

"How soon after?"

"A few weeks from now—by summer's end. She told me to bring you to her, Lady Alyse. You have something she wants."

She shrank back as if he had struck her. "What do you mean?"

Raimond smiled. She knew. In that brief, unguarded moment, the lady Alyse's alarm had told him that she knew of the treasure. "The queen remembers your mother, Lady Alyse. She would have an account of your mother's life here. And she would have you bring her the jewels she gave your mother for safekeeping."

"My mother had no jewels," Alyse said.

Raimond placed his hands upon his lady's shoulders and felt rough cloth beneath his fingers. She wore a peasant's cloak. To live in poverty while guarding a queen's treasure must have been a cold, bleak task. "Come, Alyse," he said. "Your task is finished. Tell me where to find the queen's property."

Her breath caught as she stifled a soft gasp. She raised her chin and stared up into his face. "There is nothing here for the queen," she lied calmly.

Raimond dropped his hands. By St. Peter's bones, she was a cool one. Raimond willed his lips not to show his amusement at her audacity.

"As for the marriage," she continued quietly, "I will follow you to Kernstowe in a fortnight, if it please you."

Raimond was growing weary of the lady's resistance. "No, that would not please me. It is my wish to wed you here and take you with me to Kernstowe, Lady Alyse. You will ready yourself to marry as soon as the priests can manage. Tomorrow or the next day. That is my wish and that is what you will do."

There was sudden, cold fury in her eyes. "Very well," she said. "You have cast aside your fine court manner and spoken plainly. So shall I. You have a letter from the queen, ordering this marriage. You have Father Gregory to support your claim. You imagine that there is treasure hidden here and you wish me to find it. You have ten brutish soldiers now occupying Morston, ready to back up your demands. But you will not wed me, Raimond deBauzan."

With effort, he managed not to touch her. "You speak as if I wished to ravish you. I did not bring those men here to frighten you. I came here with the honest intention to wed you, with the crown's blessing. Lady, these are unseemly accusations."

"Unseemly? Is it unseemly to turn away a stranger who demands my promise of marriage a mere hour after he first claps eyes on this place? I think not."

"Peace, Lady Alyse—"

"I do not even need to turn you away. No, you are the one who will soon be running back to Windsor to refuse this marriage."

She paused, breathing in short bursts. Raimond frowned. The woman was speaking nonsense. Was she mad? Was this the reason she had remained unwed to the ripe age of nineteen years?

He placed his hands upon her shoulders once again and felt

her shrink from him. "Calm yourself, Lady Alyse. I mean you no harm." Raimond slid his hands from her shoulders to her upper arms. "No one will go running to Windsor. We will speak again tomorrow when you are less distraught."

"No. Hear me now. Listen to me, my lord. I am not . . . fit. You must not take me as a wife."

So that was it. His bride knew she lacked a noblewoman's manner. "Your untutored ways concern you? You need not worry, my lady. It is not important to me. When we go to Windsor, you will find many women at court who will help you learn the proper dress and such things."

"Will you let me speak? I am not talking of manners. I am speaking of—chastity." She made a small, swift movement to straighten the rough woolen cloak upon her shoulders. "I am not chaste."

Her words hung in the silence between them for a long moment. Raimond's eyes wandered from her still face down to her red, chapped hands, and back to where her small teeth had bitten her lower lip.

"And who might your lover be, Lady Alyse? Old Father Gregory? That skinny lad, Wat? And where do you meet him? Out there in the wool shed? Here in the chapel? Lady Alyse, your excuses grow weaker and weaker. First you say you are destined for the nunnery, then you claim you have a lover. I have traveled across most of the known world, Lady Alyse, and never have I seen a place less likely than this crowded, poor place for a lady to lose her chastity. And never have I met a lady less likely to offer her virginity to a secret lover. Is there nothing you will not say to stop our marriage?"

He saw her flinch at his angry bellow. Raimond muttered a curse under his breath and tried to soften his words. "Enough of this nonsense, my lady. Let us find Father Gregory."

"No, my lord. Listen to me. You are not listening to me! I am unchaste." Alyse Mirbeau pulled free of Raimond's grasp and stormed towards the altar.

"I swear before the Holy Cross, Raimond deBauzan. I am no maid. I—am—no—maid!"

Like the blows of a mallet, her words assaulted his disbelief.

His forehead throbbed painfully. "It is true," he whispered. "You are unchaste?"

"Yes. Unchaste. Unclean. Do you understand? There will be no marriage between us."

God's bones, he was weary. He ran a hand through his hair. Was she lying? Shrewish as she was, she did not seem unchaste. He looked her hands. They were shaking.

Alyse edged closer to the altar. The hem of her mantle trembled above leather shoes worn thin with use. This woman was not the mistress of a knight. Had she been forced?

"Who did this?" Raimond growled.

In an angry, swift moment she turned from retreat to aggression. "You are not my confessor."

She shielded a lover, then. A lover who had left her in this desolate place alone. "Who is he?" Raimond repeated.

He saw the lady glance towards the candle stand. Did she think to attack him in God's own house? He would not take a madwoman to wife, royal decree or no. If she had been debauched, he would send word to Windsor to refuse the marriage and suggest that the lady's lover be compelled to wed her.

"I ask you once more, Lady Alyse. Who is he?"

"You have no right to ask."

"I have every right, my lady. Who is the man?"

"I will not tell you." Her fingers whitened as she gripped the candlestick.

"You would protect your despoiler? Why do you shield a man who took your maidenhead and left you unmarried? You are—you are foolish."

"It is not your concern, Lord Raimond. You have your new lands and I go to a convent. Your men may sleep in the guard-room tonight, as they are too drunk, by now, to ride towards Kernstowe. Father Gregory is free to go back to Chilcheton. And I—I will be gone within the week."

"Put it down, Alyse."

His hand descended upon her wrist before she could raise the heavy iron staff; she closed her eyes against the blow she knew would follow. There was nothing, though. Nothing but the pressure of his hard palm, heavy but not hurtful. Against her breast, the heat of his arm raised a strange, flowering shiver within her body.

Alyse released the candle stand and snatched her hand away. "This is God's house. Do you mean to do violence here?"

"No, madam," he said in his hoarse, rich whisper. "I mean to wed you."

CHAPTER THREE

The faded scars on deBauzan's jaw cut white slashes across a darkened, angry visage, below hard eyes which had gone black in the shadows of the sanctuary. If only he would move aside and let her leave—Dear God, she was cold. She wished herself safely back in her bedchamber. Emma would be worried, waiting by the fire—

If only he would not stare at her so. If only that impassive face would give some hint of what he would do next. If only he would move aside. If only he were not so big—

"When?" he asked in a rasping whisper. "When did you lie with this nameless man?"

To ignore his question would demand more courage than Alyse possessed. "Years ago," she said.

"Then you do not—you did not carry his child?"

"No." Alyse's heart began to hammer at her ribs. Why was he asking her these questions? Did he suspect it was Kernstowe's last lord who had taken her? Did he fear she would try to claim the fief on behalf of a bastard heir to deRançon?

"Whoever he is, be he knight, or serf, or priest—"

Alyse flinched at his brutal words. "I will not listen—"

"—does he live within my lands?"

Does he live? The words deBauzan had chosen were closer to the truth than he could know. Alyse swallowed. "No."

"Have you done with him? Or will I find him crossing my lands to find you?"

By night, my lord. He waits by night, ghost fires flickering in his eyes. Watching.

Alyse crossed her arms beneath her cloak. Even here, beside God's altar, deRançon's angry ghost had followed her. Blessed Virgin, she prayed, take the shadows from my mind—

"Answer me," deBauzan said. "I want the truth."

Alyse swallowed her fear. "I have . . . I will not see him again."

"Swear it."

Deep within her, anger boiled into fury at his demand, but her fear was greater still. "I swear upon the Holy Cross," she said, "that I will never lie with the man again." Not until death, when she too would be trapped in the grey mist, where deRançon waited.

Alyse raised her eyes to Raimond deBauzan's face. There was anger, but no scorn in his eyes.

She felt a wild, careless urge to speak again, to tell this man how she had come to be shamed, and why deRançon would never again touch her in this life. She wanted to tell this hard-eyed knight what she had done, to rid herself of the secret which encumbered her thoughts, and shadowed every word she had spoken to him.

She would be mad to do so. Raimond deBauzan's opinion of her, good or bad, true or unfair, would make no difference in the few days that remained to them. Before the fortnight passed, Alyse would leave Morston to seek the cloistered peace of Saint Ursula's convent. A false name would shield her from deBauzan's pursuit.

If he had come before—before her trouble, she would have given him anything he asked. For all his blunt speech, there was warmth in his gaze, and a harsh beauty in his features. Raimond deBauzan might have stepped straight out of Isabelle Mirbeau's tales of the old life in Poitou, of warrior courtiers whose honor was as hard and bright as their swords. Like a tall, stern vision of another world forever lost to her, he had come into Alyse's barren life a year too late.

She would have been safe with this man. His protection would have kept her out of harm's way—out of range of deRançon's scheming. And with luck and good will, she might have found love with him as well.

But he had come too late. By midsummer morning, she would leave Morston forever, and Raimond deBauzan would never know why.

"Lady Alyse," he said softly, "you will tell me who he is."

"What will you do if I refuse? Beat me?"

A look of disgust met her words. "Is that what you expect?" He made a small, impatient gesture. "Keep your secrets until we are wed, if you wish. But you will tell me when you are my wife."

"I will not."

"Madam, I do not ask his name in order to torment you."

If she answered this question, others would follow. If Count John heard of her deed, he would hang her for killing his vassal. And because poor Hund the blacksmith had helped her bury deRançon, he would be accused as well, and suffer many tortures before they finally put him to death. This new lord would find poor Hund, wherever he had gone, and give him to Count John's justiciars. Even Emma, old as she was, might not escape John Plantagenet's vengeance.

Alyse pressed her fist to her mouth and looked aside. She must not tell.

Raimond watched Alyse Mirbeau's face during the long silence following her stammered answers to his demands. It had seemed, for a brief moment, that she would speak again, to offer some explanation of how she had come to be debauched.

Debauched—it was not a word to use to describe this lady. Her proud, erect carriage and fierce eyes in no way resembled the soft, knowing slyness and the languid grace of the women of the Angevin and English courts. Those ladies were wise enough to keep their virginity for marriage to a noble lord and begin their erotic exploits once they were safely wed. No, Alyse

Mirbeau had little in common with those worldly noblewomen who had offered him the freedom of their beds and their bodies.

Alyse Mirbeau would not give herself easily to a man who did not honor her. A mere hour in her presence had been enough to convince Raimond of that. The lady must have been taken by force. Why, then, would she refuse to name the knave?

Raimond sighed. He was not a man to dwell long on such questions. In his youth, he had learned the intricacies of erotic intrigues; he thought no ill of the women who had tutored him in unsanctified arts of love. He had known courtesans and Saracen maids as well as the married ladies of Henry Plantagenet's court. Virgins held no special allure for him, although he had expected eventually to marry one.

Raimond believed Alyse Mirbeau when she said she had put aside her lover. If the lady were deceitful by nature, she would have remained silent about her first man and would have cozened Raimond, with the usual contortions and chickens' blood, to claim a virgin state on her wedding night.

She had sworn before the altar that she was no maid. Would she honor a marriage vow before that same altar? Would she be a true wife to him, and give him sons—true sons of his own get?

He must come to some sort of truce with the lady before she left the chapel. It was obvious that there was more to her tale than she had revealed, but he could learn no more of it this day. He had already pressed the lady Alyse as far as he had dared. She seemed ready to hurl herself into the sea in anger. Or despair.

Alyse Mirbeau had put her fist to her lips, hiding her lower face from his eyes. Her fierce grey gaze had not left him. Those were not the eyes of a liar. Raimond saw anger and desolation there, but not deceit.

His own face must be no great reassurance to a skittish lady. To find peace in this marriage, he would have to give his bride more than questions and show her more than frowns. No woman, however unchaste, would welcome an angry bridegroom to her bed. With deliberate care, he stroked the heavy braid which rested upon her mantle. "Your hair—it shines like the wing of a bird. Will you unbraid it for me, Alyse?"

She pulled her hair back over her shoulder and made a small sound of surprise when he kept his hand in place, immediately above her breast. He could feel the beating of her heart beneath his palm. "Lord Raimond, I want—"

"You shall have what you desire. I swear it." He sensed that her pulse was faster, wilder now; the lady Alyse was not indifferent to his touch.

She twisted away from his hand. "Take me to see Queen Eleanor before we wed. I will explain to her why she is wrong to bring us together."

And I will show you, my lady, how right we would be, together in my bed—He lowered his hand. "It is not possible, Alyse. The queen's charter links my lands to marriage with you. If we go to Windsor and leave these lands unprotected, Count John will give them to another."

"You are willing to take an unclean woman to wife in order to keep these lands, Lord Raimond? You will not risk your precious charter to question the terms?"

Raimond ignored the sneering belligerence in her tone. "Yes," he said. "I will do what I must to be sure of these lands. And you, my lady, have much to lose if you refuse me."

She looked aside. "You will regret this, Raimond deBauzan."

"And what of you, my lady? What future would you have if I renounce you? Is it likely that the abbess of St. Ursula's would welcome a lady both penniless and unchaste?"

Her jaw was trembling. "I would risk rejection by the abbess before wedding a man who would take a dishonored wife in order to keep his lands," she said.

"My lady, you have the tongue of a viper and the temper to match. Do not give insult where none has been offered you."

"No, you have offered no insult yet. But if we were wed and your lands were secure, you would have no further reason to refrain from scorning your dishonored wife."

So that was it. She feared he would punish her for her folly.

Raimond reached for the hand covering her mouth. "When we are wed, I will offer no insult where none is provoked." He held her tight fist within his hands and began slowly to coax her fingers to uncurl. "I do not believe that an unwed girl sprouts warts and two heads if she carelessly loses her maidenhood. I do not wish to spend months in Windsor in search of another wife. I will stay here, take you to wife, and tend these lands. I want children from your body and an honest trust between us. Let us wed, Alyse, and put the past behind.''

A small tremor passed through her hand.

Raimond sighed. ''You are no virgin maid and I—I am no saint, God knows. For your sin and my sins, we will not judge each other. I will keep faith with you in all matters touching our marriage or these lands; you will keep faith with me in these matters as well, and give me sons. Will you do this?''

Within Alyse's mind, long-forgotten voices clamored in conflict. An impossible desire—to touch that other world, to know the life from which her mother had retreated, and to take her own place as a noble lord's wife—struggled against naked fear.

Deal with me honestly, he had said. How could she do so and allow him to discover, mere inches from the queen's treasure, the rotting mass which had been Harald deRançon?

If she dealt with him honestly, Raimond Fortebras would learn that his bride was a murderess.

Behind Raimond, the chapel door moved upon its brittle leather hinges and rested half ajar; if this was a Morston shepherd coming to his lady's aid, he had lost his courage at the threshold. Raimond dropped Alyse's hand; with one fist upon the dagger in his belt, Raimond wrenched the door open to reveal Morston's priest. For a short, precarious moment, the frail figure sought his balance upon the stoop.

Alyse cried out as Raimond reached to steady the man. ''Have care with him—''

Raimond frowned at her white face. ''I seldom butcher old men, even when I find them listening at doors.''

''My lord, he would never—''

The priest's face turned smiling to gaze upon Raimond. ''Peace! My lord, I am Anselm. Father Gregory has told me of the royal decree. Never fear, Queen Eleanor will find us equal to this hasty task. Lady Alyse, Father Gregory had agreed there is no need to wait for banns. You and this knight may be wed within the week.''

"Father Anselm, I have not decided—''

"Good news, my child. Would that your mother, may she rest in God's mercy, could have seen this day.''

Alyse raised her voice. "Father Anselm, we have not agreed to wed.''

Anselm limped slowly past her and gestured towards the low stone altar. "Of course not, my dear child. You will do so after you are wed. Here, in our own chapel. Small and plain, it is, but God's house, nonetheless. No matter, the women of the village will be happy to make it fit for a wedding mass. What matters is God's blessing upon your vows. That I will arrange most happily.''

Raimond could make no sense of the priest's ramblings. Even the lady Alyse could get no proper answer to her half-shouted protests. Was the old man deaf? "My thanks to you, priest,'' Raimond said slowly.

The pale, rheumy eyes turned upon him. "Of course, my lord. I would be happy to hear your confession as well. Tomorrow, after matins?''

"Tomorrow . . . of course. Tomorrow morning.''

Alyse touched his arm. "Father Anselm does not hear your words.''

Raimond lowered his voice. "How does he hear confession—''

"—from this unchaste woman?''

"You twist my words, Alyse. Why do you try to anger me?''

She glanced at Father Anselm's back and spoke again, her voice expressionless. "Father Anselm is my confessor, Lord Raimond. He is Morston's priest.''

"He is also deaf as these stones,'' Raimond declared.

Father Anselm looked up from his inspection of the altar cloth and smiled. He turned back to the altar.

"How can a deaf man mind the souls of these people? You need a younger priest here.''

Alyse's gaze flashed in anger. "My lord, Father Anselm is a good man, devoted to the people of Morston. He would be lost, at his age, were he sent back to the abbey. You must not think of sending him away.''

Raimond looked at her in surprise. She must think him a black-hearted miser if she believed he would send away this old priest when he found a younger man to help with Morston's flock. At Bauzan, Raimond's father kept three priests for the chapel—a young cleric to see to the people's needs, and his predecessors, two ancient men who spent their days in the sheltered sun of the castle garden, playing at draughts after matins.

Raimond returned her hard gaze. ''And who will care for that old priest,'' he said, ''if you shut yourself away from the world at the convent? He would be better off at the abbey, with small duties and decent food.''

''He has decent food—''

''As long as you are here to see to it.''

''What do you mean? Are you threatening Father Anselm?''

''If a warm hearth and the comfort of fellowship at Chilcheton are threats, then yes, I am. Do you have a better idea?''

She made a small, furious gesture. ''Father Anselm belongs here. He has lived here most of his life—''

''—with your mother, and after her, with you to care for him. If you leave this place in my care alone, Alyse, I will make such decisions alone.''

Alyse gasped. ''You are Morston's new lord. You are responsible for my people. You are sworn to protect them. If you do not treat them with justice, God will damn you to everlasting torment.''

''So I understand. But I will not send to St. Ursula's to ask your opinion when I have to make changes.''

Her eyes blazed wide with outrage. ''Changes? The only change we need is to have our men back from Palestine and to have King Richard's tax collectors forget we exist.''

''How,'' he asked dryly, ''shall I bring these things to pass without the help of Morston's lady?''

Father Anselm stepped back from the sanctuary and smiled at them. ''Tell me, my lady. Can the women be spared for a day, now that the shearing is near to finished? I would have them make the chapel clean. After all, we celebrate two happy occasions—your marriage and our good fortune in having a new lord for Morston.''

''Well, Alyse?''

He had won. She was trapped. She could not turn her back on her people.

''My lady?''

''You will allow me to make decisions here?''

''Within reason. I will overrule you only in matters of defense. You will live with me at Kernstowe. It is not far, they tell me. We will be at Morston often enough to manage it.''

He was right. She could not walk away from her people before she was sure he would be a good and merciful lord. Later, when he had tired of her—Later, when she had hidden her crime so well that Hund and Emma would never suffer for it, then she would leave. ''I will wed you,'' she said in a voice that seemed strange to her ears.

''Tomorrow.''

''Tomorrow or the next day.''

''Tomorrow.''

''Father Anselm will continue here?'' she asked.

''You have my promise.'' He was standing over her, waiting.

''Then I will wed you. Tomorrow,'' she said.

Her voice was low, and she spoke in short rushes, as if she had fought a great struggle. Fortebras feared that if he touched her, she would bolt from the chapel. He glanced at the altar. ''Father Gregory will perform the ceremony, and your Father Anselm will assist him. We will not say our vows before a deaf priest, my lady. We will be well and truly wed.''

''The lady Alyse looked as if she had the devil after her,'' Hugo Gerbrai called across the guardroom. ''Your manner isn't gentle enough for that country-bred—'' Gerbrai's jest ended abruptly. He slammed down his wooden drinking cup and crossed the room unsteadily to peer into Raimond's silent features. ''God's teeth, Fortebras,'' he growled, ''you look demon-ridden yourself. What passed between you?''

Raimond looked hard at Hugo's flushed face. His old friend and mentor would have much to say—too much—concerning

Alyse Mirbeau's revelation. He would no doubt counsel Raimond to seize Queen Eleanor's property and return to London, deliver the jewels, and petition the crown for permission to keep Kernstowe and wed elsewhere. It made sense. Perfect sense. But he didn't want to hear it.

"Has she agreed to wed?"

Raimond nodded curtly. The woman's capitulation to his wishes still troubled him. Had she done it to protect her people, or to gain time to recover the queen's property? "Yes. We will wed tomorrow."

Gerbrai's grizzled brows rose in surprise. "I've seen you give more time to a Saracen whore. Are you so eager to bed her?"

The Saracen women Hugo remembered were survivors of siege and battle, two of them maidens who, offered their freedom, had never come to Raimond's bed. No, his bride was like none of those women. She had not seen war in her young life, but she was as wary as a hostage.

Raimond frowned. If his wife continued to look at him as if he wished to murder her in her sleep—if she proved mad—he would ask Queen Eleanor's help in having the marriage annulled once these lands were secure. The dowager queen could do that. She owed him at least that much.

Raimond turned to Gerbrai. "She has agreed. I will wed the lady tomorrow and take her to Kernstowe."

The older man pulled his cloak across his wide chest and reached for the ale jug. "Now, that will be a proper place to lodge. Father Gregory tells me it's a solid stone keep and prosperous enough to have a good fire going in the hall." Gerbrai shivered. "If we stay in this draft-ridden hovel much longer, my joints will seize from the cold. They tell me there is no wine—"

"Hugo, I need you to stay here until I find the queen's jewels."

Gerbrai slammed his drinking cup upon the table. "Then we had better find them tonight, Fortebras. I'm not staying one more night in this ruin. Tell the lady Alyse that the queen has sent you for the gems. Demand that she give them to you. It's a simple thing.'' Gerbrai's face darkened. ''Has she refused to give them into your keeping?''

''No. I'm not sure she knows of them. She said nothing when I told her that the queen had sent me for them.''

''She said nothing?''

''She said she knew nothing of the jewels.''

Hugo scowled. ''Then ask her where old Lord William kept his gold.'' He looked about him in disgust. ''Surely there are few cache places in a ruin like this.''

''I will ask her again—in time.''

Hugo lowered his drinking cup. ''Has this woman got you in retreat? Ask her now, Fortebras. Ask her plainly. If she claims not to know the hiding place, if her parents died without telling her, we'll tear the place apart until we find the jewels.''

Raimond shook his head. ''We might never find the hiding place if these people decide not to trust us. I must win their loyalty before I tear down the keep.''

Gerbrai growled in exasperation. ''My lord Raimond, if you tell these folk that they are free to move to Kernstowe, every man jack of them will be crossing the moors by sunset.''

''A fortnight, Hugo. I want you to stay here a fortnight while I claim Kernstowe and make a plan. No one here will starve, old friend. I'll send supplies tomorrow.''

Raimond turned his gaze to the large table where three Morston women were setting out a meal of cold mutton and fresh bread. He would provide for all of Morston's folk in his own way, even if it meant taking them all to Kernstowe before he demolished this cold, decaying keep. He would do nothing, though, until he had settled his nervous, troubled wife at Kernstowe. ''You will keep watch here, Hugo, until I return. Then we will move quickly. If we need to pull the keep down, the task won't be hard. There's not a solid wall in this place save what's left of the old earthworks.'' He frowned at the rafter beams. ''One good blow, and the weight of the chimneys will take the walls down.''

Gerbrai snorted. ''Folks who build with poor timber should be content with a fire pit. They will thank us to build them a single good byre from the ruins.'' He growled at the empty ale pot. ''This cold place will make me an old man before my time. Ask your lady again. She must know something. Ask her where her father would hide a treasure, if he had one, and spare me these damned drafts. Is the Lady Alyse such a termagant you can't compel her before you're wed?''

Raimond did not answer.

CHAPTER FOUR

Hugo Gerbrai dipped a wooden ladle into the first tub of Morston's bride ale and sniffed in disdain. "Water," he muttered. "Water run through an old ale pot for taste. May your marriage, Fortebras, be more fortunate than those who must drink your health with this swill." He frowned at the sky. "A cold, wet morning for a paltry wedding feast. No need to cover this barrel if the cursed rain begins again—the drink is too thin to ruin," Gerbrai growled. "Here—taste it."

Raimond pushed the ladle aside and gestured to the small party of Bauzan men tethering the pack horses outside the bailey gate. The two youngest men-at-arms were carrying their saddlebags from the byre, where they had slept and guarded the mounts.

"When you find my lady's saddle," he called, "try it on the bay mare—"

Gerbrai's fist descended upon the trestle, sending a sudden shudder through the ale tub. "Not my horse, Fortebras. Take young Gareth's mount, not mine. If you must leave me here in this starving hovel, I will need to hunt to eat." Gerbrai glanced up the hill toward the byre. "Gareth! Where is the man? Hiding his mare from us both, I vow. We did not come to this place to—"

"—starve. Hugo, I have said I will send supplies to this place as soon as we reach Kernstowe. Tomorrow—this same day, if all goes swiftly—I will send you all I can. You there—boy. Wat, is it? Is that your lady's saddle? You're dragging the leather—" Raimond rescued the wooden saddle and frowned at the faded paint upon the once-decorated bows. He twisted the cracked leather girth in his hands and easily wrenched the strap from the base. A cloud of moldy dust fell from the seam. A kitchen maid bearing a bowl of cold mutton backed away from the grit, muttering in the strange speech of the Morston shepherds. Wat sneezed.

Outside the gate, eight Bauzan men led the riding beasts to drink from the stream which ran beside the earthworks. The water was high today, swollen by the rains, running swift and muddy to cascade over the cliffs into the sea. The men-at-arms looked up at Raimond's bellowed demand, unable to hear his words over the rushing of the water. Gareth was not among them.

Raimond pushed the ruined saddle back into Wat's arms. "Find Gareth. The young one with the red beard. Tell him my lady—my wife—will use both his saddle and his mount."

The child hesitated. "Will you take me, too?"

"No, only the lady Alyse will come with us."

"I will ride with her."

Raimond frowned. "You may come later, with your mother."

Wat looked down at his feet. "She died," he said. "On the hill."

"Where?"

"On the big hill, where Lars died."

Raimond hunkered down to see the boy's face. "Was your mother from Poitiers?"

"No, from here. The lady Alyse taught me to speak your tongue. Will you take me with you?"

He looked away from the boy's reddened eyes. "Not today. Now, go find Gareth and tell him to bring his horse." He rose and turned to Gerbrai. "I will send the mare back with the pack animals tomorrow."

Hugo sighed. "I have a better plan. Gather these people

together and bring them with us. Leave this place to the gulls and let these people earn their bread at Kernstowe. Tear down this so-called keep before the roof beams collapse, find the old queen's—''

''Go carefully,'' Raimond muttered.

Gerbrai broke off and followed Raimond's gaze to the open door of the keep, where Emma stood watching them. ''Your lady's old nurse has a sour look to her this morning. She was not pleased to find my pallet outside your lady's chamber last night.''

''The women left the chamber?''

''The old one opened the door. Gave me a few ugly words and retreated. I could hear her speaking with your lady after that, but they stayed within. Couldn't hear their words.'' Hugo sighed heavily. ''Secrets. Damned secrets. Fortebras, when this is done I will have no more of the Plantagenets' doings. As your father says, to be trusted by the Plantagenet brood is to be cursed. And these women, your bride and the old one, have been cursed as surely as the rest of us.''

''And to break the Plantagenets' trust is the way of fools. My father said that as well, Hugo. You speak too freely this morning. The ale has loosened your tongue.''

''This poor place didn't have enough ale to loosen the tongue of a magpie, let alone celebrate your wedding. This is a thirsty place, Raimond. You will send ale from Kernstowe? There is no well in this ruin, and I will not drink that river water at my age—''

''I will send all that is needed here. Smoked meat, barley, and wine—if I find it.''

Gerbrai's face lightened. ''The priest said there is a cellarful.''

Raimond frowned. ''What is taking the lad so long?''

''You will not stay and eat this great feast the women are dragging from the back of the storage huts? That mutton was fresh when you were still in Palestine, Fortebras.''

''Keep a curb on your tongue, Hugo, and listen. Gareth will stay at Morston with you. Alyse will use his horse, and I will send it back with the pack animals this day. My lady leaves her woman Emma here—to put her possessions to rights, she says. More likely to watch over you and Gareth. You will need to look about discreetly, at first. If you find nothing, we will begin an open search when I return from Kernstowe.

"The lady Alyse still has not spoken of what is hidden here?"

"No. In truth, she has spoken little to me this morning."

"She had much to say yestereve, in the chapel, I vow. More than you cared to hear—"

"What say you?"

Gerbrai drew back. "Fortebras, you have your father's deadly look at times—wild enough to make a man spew his guts in fright."

"What said you, Hugo?"

"It is no secret that you and the lady Alyse did not meet in peace, and that you both came forth from the chapel with faces to curdle the blood of a black wolf. Do not gainsay me— young Erec saw you. You look scarce better this morning." He shrugged. "It may be no mischance that I stay here, well away from your courting and bedding of that hard-eyed lady. Yes, I'll stay here, and right gladly—if you send supplies."

Raimond looked away. He had not told Gerbrai of Alyse's angry revelations. For the first time in his life, he would hold secrets from his father's trusted sergeant. To hold inviolate the honor of his viper-tongued, unwilling wife, he was learning the ways of deceit, and he liked it not.

"The supplies, Fortebras?"

"You will not starve, Hugo," he said again.

Gerbrai saw Gareth lead his mare past the empty shearing pen, his petulant lower lip pulling his face into a semblance of his mount's expression. Raimond sighed. "I'll make sure the lad has his horse back. Take care of him."

"Have a care for yourself. I do not want to have to send word to your father that you survived the Holy Lands only to fall prey to a bad-tempered woman."

There was a final procession of kitchen maids bearing dark bread and mutton to the three short trestles beside the ale. Behind them, dressed as Raimond had seen her yesterday in the chapel, came Alyse Mirbeau, balancing a short plank laden with roasted chickens. She set the cold fowl beside the mutton, and after a short, frowning inspection of Fortebras' good tunic, crossed the yard to stand before the chapel door. The priest from Chilcheton appeared beside her, and Father Anselm hurried to join them. From the serving maids and the village folk emerging from their huts there arose a chorus of excited shouting in that undulating tongue the common folk used. The Bauzan men watering the horses at the stream came running, their short swords half drawn as they pounded into the bailey yard.

The lady Alyse, her face colored with anger, raised her voice over the din in an outraged command. The high-spirited shouting ceased as Raimond roared a swift order and the Bauzan men sheathed their swords.

Hugo Gerbrai dropped the ladle back into the ale tub. "I think that was your wedding procession, young Fortebras. We had best join your lady bride now, before a fight breaks out."

"You will witness our vows, Hugo?"

"Aye, I will. And I will relate all that I see to your father, when I see him next. Smile, Fortebras. You don't want these villeins to think you fearful."

The untidy crowd parted for Raimond and Hugo as they crossed the yard to mount the low step at the chapel door. Raimond reached for the lady Alyse's hand and brought it to his lips. "Speak to them in their tongue," he said. "Tell them that we will wed and go to Kernstowe this day. Tell them that I will send the pack horses back with food and supplies before nightfall, and that Hugo Gerbrai will stay here in my place until I return." The small hand resting upon his arm trembled briefly, then withdrew. "Say those words to them, Alyse."

She nodded and began to speak. There was a thickness in her voice when she began, and for a moment Raimond feared that Alyse would weep and cause the people to distrust him. She hesitated and coughed; when she raised her eyes again to the faces clustered about her, Alyse had slowed her speech and there was calmness in the rhythm of her words. Then she was silent.

"You told them?"

"Yes. I told them all you said." There was a stiff smile upon her face, a false expression of contentment which her darkened eyes betrayed.

Raimond drew her hand back to rest upon his arm. "I thank you, my lady." Her fingers remained where he had placed them, rigid and cold "Do not fear me," he whispered.

She gave no sign that she had heard him.

He drew her with him to face the two priests. "Wed us now, in Frankish words that my own men may understand. They will witness our vows."

The Chilcheton priest nudged Father Anselm, who stepped forward and raised his arms to silence the murmuring crowd. "People of Morston, men of Bauzan," he said. "Yestereve, in this holy place, your lady Alyse and Lord Raimond of Bauzan declared that they were betrothed. There need be no banns now—"

"There need be no banns," continued Father Gregory of Chilcheton, stepping before Father Anselm's widespread arms, "as the Lord Raimond is known to the dowager Queen Eleanor to be a bachelor knight of good family with no blood ties to the lady Alyse Mirbeau to prevent this marriage. As Father Anselm has affirmed, there is a lawful betrothal between them. Lord Raimond, will you speak your vows?"

He filled his lungs and spoke loudly, so that the fidgeting crowd would hear him over the sound of the sea and the loud rush of the stream outside the yard. "I, Raimond son of Rannulf of Bauzan, take the lady Alyse Mirbeau as my wife, under the laws of God and the crown. My goods and lands I will share with her, and my sword will defend her." He paused and looked at the faces of his father's soldiers. "I give the lady Alyse this estate of Morston, which I hold from King Richard, as her dower land. It shall be hers as long as I and my heirs hold it." There was a rippling murmur among the Morston folk as those few who understood the Frankish tongue repeated Raimond's words to the others.

There was a telltale brightness in his bride's grey eyes as she stared down at her hand upon Raimond's arm. She did not raise her face to look at him, but gave a low sigh and a whispered word which he did not catch.

"Will you speak your vows, lady Alyse?"

She did not hesitate. "I, Alyse, daughter of Philip of Mirbeau, take Raimond deBauzan as my husband under the laws of God and King Richard.''

There was a moment of silence. Father Anselm drew open the chapel door, and stepped aside for the bridal couple to enter. Hugo Gerbrai and half the Bauzan men stood with their lord and his lady wife and a few Morston shepherds as Father Anselm crossed to the small sanctuary and began to say the mass.

Raimond saw his wife's servant, Emma, among the few elderly shepherds sitting upon the stone bench set against the wall for the old and infirm. As he sank to his knees beside his bride upon the newly swept flagstones of the chapel, Raimond saw the old woman's eyes upon him. At his side, Alyse was pale and still. Her eyes never wavered from the holy cross before which she had sworn, only hours earlier, that she was no fit wife for Raimond deBauzan.

He reached for her hand and closed it within his own. Alyse looked at him in swift surprise, then stared again at Christ's cross above the altar.

She did not take her hand away.

Alyse Mirbeau rode from Morston in her dead mother's gown and mantle, perched cautiously upon a soldier's saddle on a borrowed horse. In the company of strangers—keen-eyed, heavily armed men, of whom the most daunting was the knight she had married three hours ago.

It had been a brief but decent wedding mass, as befit a lady without living kin and a knight with no family in the country. Early that morning, Alyse and the two kitchen maids had killed and roasted seven hens and put out the last of the smoked mutton for a small wedding feast. Then Alyse had put on her wedding clothes—the last from the old chest from Poitiers—and walked the short distance to wed at the door of the chapel where she had begun, just hours before, to know the mind of the stranger who was now her husband. That stranger had appeared in a fine black tunic beneath his crimson pourpoint and leather hauberk—garments fine enough to show respect, but plain enough that she felt no shame to stand beside him in the last of her mother's good robes.

The bride ale had lasted less than an hour, the trestle tables swept clear of their meager burden by many hungry hands. Raimond had drunk her health and had left her side only once to speak with the insistent child, Wat. He had bidden Alyse to give the boy a leg of chicken, and had torn a large hunk of bread from the dark loaf before him to place it in the child's hands. Then he had turned from her to speak to young Wat in low, unhurried words. For a brief moment, Alyse had hoped that Raimond would permit the child to come with them, but he had not changed the decision he had made in curt, careless words earlier that day. She had strained to hear what he had said to the boy, but Raimond had pitched his voice too softly to be overheard. Obviously, he had begun his search for the queen's treasure by interrogating the most credulous soul at Morston.

Soon after, her lord husband had turned back to take her hand and call together the men who would ride with them to Kernstowe. In the confusion of good wishes, farewells, and teary embraces, he had kept his hand beneath her arm, drawing her through the small crowd of Morston people to set her upon a bay mare and lead her up the hills to ride east. If she had rebelled and tried to delay their leaving, he could have seized her and dragged her with him. So she went willingly, cutting short Emma's last embrace. "Do not anger him, my lamb," the old woman had whispered. "Do what he demands. Promise you will not cross him."

When the road to Kernstowe lay before them, her husband left the small column of riders and pack animals to ride a short distance up the side of the tor which separated Morston's steep valley from the moors. He turned to spur his black horse towards her; his voice carried above the rising north wind.

"Is that where you found the body?"

Alyse grabbed the high saddle bow and barely kept herself from slipping down the side of the broad-backed mare. A moment later, a large hand closed upon her arm to stop her fall. She settled her sheepskin boots together again within a single stirrup and accepted the reins from Raimond's palm.

He raised his hand to point toward the tor. "Is that where your shepherd died?"

Alyse nodded. "There, at the base. He must have stumbled near the top."

He made a small gesture to the men behind him and turned his horse once again toward the steep, grassy rise. As the small party followed the path skirting the tor, Raimond's powerful gelding lunged up the short climb to the stone slabs at the crest of the hill. Man and horse circled the massive granite outcropping and disappeared down the western face of the tor.

A short time later, her husband was once again at Alyse's side. "The slope is not steep enough to kill," he said.

Alyse silently agreed. When they had brought old Lars' body back from the tor, she had thought the same. She had asked his widow, as they had sat vigil over the body that night, if Lars had spoken of strangers, or enemies. Of course he had no enemies. Morston had no enemies. No living enemies—

Raimond was watching her face as if he could see her imaginings. "Were there signs of beasts upon him?"

Alyse focused upon the yellow gorse blooms below the tor and willed her darker thoughts aside. "No. His body was broken, but not mauled. Lars must have fallen. He was an old man." An old man with keen blue eyes and a strong, wiry frame—

"Not too old to watch the sheep. Your people are disturbed by this death."

They had reached the end of Morston's valley coombe, and saw the moors stretching pale and green before them.

"Your smith has been missing since last year. Your people still speak of his disappearance."

Wait. Slow the breath. Master the voice. "You were not idle last night," Alyse said at last. "You have been lord here for one night and one morning, yet you know the shepherds' gossip."

"Yes. Such talk is important."

"You understood their speech?"

"No. Father Gregory spoke for me and for them. It is odd-sounding speech, much like Breton words. I doubt I will learn it easily."

"There is no need for you to learn. I will tell you what they say."

A small smile crossed Raimond's face. "You must teach me to speak with them. I cannot defend this place or Kernstowe unless I know the common talk. The herders' tales are useful." He twisted in the saddle to look back again at the tor. "I will not have any death on these lands dismissed without questions."

Alyse dragged a long, silent breath before she answered. "Nor would I."

He turned his gaze back to her. "Enough talk of death, my lady. This is our wedding day. I would not see you so pale." Once again, he reached toward her. She started as the warmth of his hand brushed her cheek; a slow flush began at his touch and flowed to her breasts.

He frowned again and thrust his hand back into its heavy gauntlet. "Go easy, Alyse. Do not shrink from me."

Alyse glanced back at the Bauzan men. They followed at a short distance, too far back to hear her husband's words.

The cold wind of the moor rose to send her mantle fluttering across her chin. Raimond caught the thin wool and pushed it back over her shoulder. "If you continue to flinch at my touch, lady, our marriage bed will be an unhappy place."

Was his tall body as warm as his hand had felt? When they came together this night, would she feel that heat within her— Alyse raised her eyes from his well-muscled thigh and put the insistent images from her mind. She would need her wits about her this night, when she bedded with this man, who would take her body and demand her secrets as well. In the privacy of the bedchamber, there would be none to protect her from him. The man whom the soldiers called Fortebras could kill her with one careless sweep of the sword arm which had earned him the name.

Emma's warnings had been wise. Do not anger him. Do what he demands. Alyse bowed her head. "I have made my vows. I will not cheat you of the—coupling."

"There will be more than just coupling."

She felt the blood leave her face. Already he had begun to torment her.

Do not anger him. Do as he demands.

"That was not a threat," he added softly. "It is a promise a woman should welcome."

It was impossible to stop her hands from shaking. "I need no promises. I will honor my marriage vows without pretty words."

Beneath her, the mare tugged at her tightly-held reins and snorted. Raimond brought his mount still closer. Alyse looked up to find him watching her, his mouth still curved in a slight half-smile.

"My lady, I will honor your wishes. It shall be a simple thing between us. Just coupling, as you have said. Like the otters in that pond." He pointed north, to the dark line where Kernstowe's forest began. "Or the deer in the wood. As you have said, there is no need for pretty words first. Come then, Alyse—" His gloved fist closed over the reins above her hand. "Which will it be, the bushes beside the pond, or the woods beyond?"

"You are mad—"

A hawk's sudden cry pierced the clouds.

DeBauzan released her hand. "You agree then, lady, that we do have need of words. And time." His smile deepened, then disappeared. "You shall have them both." He rose in his stirrups and looked ahead, towards the dark tower barely visible on the horizon. "Now tell me," he said, "what you know of Kernstowe. They told me there is a stone keep within earthworks. Is there a palisade?"

She began to speak of her husband's lands, grateful that he had not continued to torment her with talk of the marriage bed. The north wind came again, carrying the heavy green scent of the moor. Alyse's voice rang strangely loud in her ears. She realized, in a moment of confusion, that she could no longer hear the sea. For the first time in a year—those long months she had not dared to leave Morston—the low beat of the ocean's force was not with her. In place of the sea's slow hammer, Alyse heard the wind, her heart's drumming and the surge of her life's blood thrumming in her ears. Her heart's beat grew louder as she listened.

Her husband's dark blue gaze did not leave her. For a brief moment, Alyse believed that he heard that swift pulsing too.

* * *

The Bauzan men were hard-faced and high-spirited soldiers. The sound of their jests rose above the disciplined, rhythmical chink of bridle iron as they rode. Their leather hauberks and broad swords were clean but imperfect from use, and their cloaks, new and densely woven, shed the misting rain from their shoulders.

One mile before Kernstowe, Fortebras summoned the men to ride close behind him. They took lances from the bristling sumpter packs; the one who spurred forward to ride beside Fortebras raised a crimson banner with a whorled black sunburst sewn upon it. Alyse now rode in the middle of the small band of heavily armed men; two soldiers leading the pack horses fell behind the tightly bunched riders.

They rode faster now, and did not speak. The muffled ring of iron hooves upon moss-covered stones and the sibilant motion of broadswords in their scabbards were the sounds of horsemen well prepared to meet any resistance to their lord's claim to the late deRançon's lands.

Alyse clung to the high-fronted saddle with both her hands and prayed that their arrival at Kernstowe would be unchallenged. She gave silent thanks that deBauzan and his men had not chosen to arrive fully armed at Morston yesterday. If they had, her people would have scattered in fear.

The grey clouds opened before the rising north wind, sending cold sunlight to touch the lance-points and helms surrounding Alyse as she rode. For the first time in her life, she had traversed the moor between Morston and Kernstowe without first crossing herself to ward off the ancient, ghostly horsemen who sought the unwary traveler. Fierce as they were, the Wild Hunt would not dare prey upon the Bauzan warriors or any in their company.

The clouds lowered again and spat rain as the small party of riders reached Kernstowe. A single watchman above the stout timber gate made no move to question them as they passed in a tightly-ranked group through the narrow gap.

Alyse gave up her desperate grip upon the saddle front and

tried to flex her benumbed fingers. The muddy hem of her mantle lay cold and heavy upon her boots.

"I am Raimond deBauzan," her husband bellowed across the rain-spattered bailey. "Your new lord. I have been given these lands by Queen Eleanor in the name of King Richard. I would speak with the warden."

The watchman descended from his perch and glanced towards the grey-streaked walls of the keep. Behind him, three open-mouthed serfs stood unmoving beside an empty wagon. A piglet wriggled out of a pannier and trotted unheeded past their feet.

The rain became grey sheets driven by the wind. Alyse slipped her feet from the stirrup and looked down at the water flowing across the hard-packed earth.

"No, my lady." The man beside Alyse called a terse warning over the sound of the wind. "We stay mounted until my lord tells us to move."

Alyse thrust her cold swollen hands under her cloak. "When did he tell us that?"

The man did not answer. He had turned from her to watch Raimond's broad back. The gatekeeper broke and ran for the keep. The serfs had disappeared.

Raimond and his men waited in silence relieved only by the heavy rain and the protests of the truant pig.

Why were they waiting? Alyse knew that there were none within the keep, or without the tower, who would dare stop this man whom the soldiers called Fortebras. Surely he could see there was no guard. No, her husband was waiting to take Kernstowe with some sort of ceremony, and he was willing to have her perish of lung fever in order to do it.

Rolf Nevers appeared at the entrance to the keep, pulling the sleeves of his tunic down to his wrists. With an alacrity that surprised Alyse, Nevers moved his portly frame from the shelter of the gateway and approached deBauzan. The rising wind and the snapping of the sodden banner hid Nevers' first words from Alyse. Then her husband had dismounted and turned back towards her.

The men at arms nudged their horses aside as Raimond reached Alyse and drew her down from the mare. He clamped her hand onto his broad forearm and drew her along with him, back to the incredulous Nevers. "My lady wife, Alyse Mirbeau of Morston."

Nevers' eyes widened. "Alyse?" He saw deBauzan's dark frown and made a slight gesture of conciliation. "—Lady Alyse. You are wed?"

"Yes. This morning."

DeBauzan's arm hardened beneath her hand. "My lady needs a fire and warm clothes. Will you tell my men where to stable the horses?" He reached to Alyse's throat and pulled her hood closer together, and swore softly when her teeth began to chatter. He lifted her easily, ignoring her gasp of surprise, and splashed across the bailey yard to the keep. Behind them, his men were leading the pack horses forward.

Alyse glanced past deBauzan's shoulder and saw the small pig trot stiff-legged past the confusion and out the bailey gate. To freedom, away from the waiting knives. To brief freedom and then death, Alyse predicted, on the grey moors.

There were servant girls in the great hall, a teeming, noisy bunch of them clustered before the broad wall-hearth with its carved stone hood. Beyond them, through a narrow opening in the thick wall of the keep, was the passage to the timber-built kitchens. Raimond saw with approval that the heavy oaken door, nearly as thick as it was wide, could be battened shut in time of siege. He strode to the hearth and set his wife on her soaked boots before the fire. Twenty paces away, the serving maids hovered uncertainly near the passageway to the kitchens.

Rolf Nevers' voice sounded within the group of murmuring women. There was silence for a moment, then the murmuring rose to excited exclamations. Nevers emerged from the cluster. "My lord," he said. "These women will take your lady wife to the lord's—to your sleeping chamber and give her dry garments."

Alyse shuddered beside him, and sneezed. Three women, each of them dressed more warmly and fitly than Alyse, came forward to take her up the narrow stone stairs. Raimond saw the curious looks and smothered smiles on the faces of the remaining women and felt a rush of anger. Alyse of Mirbeau, daughter of an ancient but unlucky family of Poitiers, trapped in poverty through Henry Plantagenet's marital strife, had no clothing to match the modest finery of Kernstowe's serving wenches. Only her manner, and her fiercely proud carriage, and her fine, hard-set features were testament to her noble blood. The poor, cold home Alyse had left this morning and the once-rich rags she was wearing were also a testament—to the dowager queen's neglect of her loyal waiting woman's family.

To be trusted by the Plantagenet brood is to be cursed. Rannulf deBauzan had taught all his sons that lesson. All but one had managed to remain unnoticed by that royal nest of vipers.

Raimond turned his gaze upon the sweating face of Rolf Nevers. "I saw two sentries," he said. "Where is the rest of the garrison?"

"They left, my lord. Gone to Biddaford to serve Lord Granavil a year ago. There were few travelers upon the road last summer, and the small tolls would not pay so many men-at-arms." Nevers paused and drew a shallow breath. "My lord, will your men begin to take toll fees?"

If there had been tolls to pay on the small roads east of Normandy, Raimond might never have seen his father's lands again. "No," he said. "These lands are rich enough, without tolls. But I must have a small garrison here."

"Of course." Nevers' tunic laces were tied askew below the trembling pink chin.

Raimond managed not to smile. "Father Anselm told me you can read," he said. "And I told him that in that case he need not come with me to confirm to you my charter to hold these lands. You will read the charter first, and then tell me if you will continue here, to serve me."

They went together to fetch Raimond deBauzan's strongbox from the sumpter packs.

CHAPTER FIVE

Alyse remembered the two serving maids who followed her up the twisting stair and across the wide stone passageway between the sleeping chambers.

Three summers past, when Morston had possessed a wagon sturdy enough to cross the moors to Kernstowe and two full sacks of fleeces to burden it, Alyse and her mother had accompanied William on the first stage of his journey to Dunhevet to sell the wool. They had stopped before Kernstowe's walls to sit in the long columns of shade and drink the old Lord Harald's ale while William and the steward Nevers had arranged the purchase of a fine team of oxen for Morston's fields. Maud and Beda had brought the ale and tarried at Nevers' side, resplendent in new, unpatched kirtles of pale green linen.

Alyse had been too shy to speak to the maids on that long-ago day, and they had had no reason to notice the shabby daughter of the reclusive lady of Morston. Now they regarded her with open curiosity as they held open the door of the largest sleeping chamber and waited for her to enter.

"It smells of must," Alyse said. The tall canopy shrouded in broderie-bordered wool seemed to move in the draft from the door. This was deRançon's bed, and there was no way beneath God's great heavens Alyse would sleep in it.

Beda looked pointedly at the mud-soaked hem of Alyse's mantle. "The sheets are clean, lady Alyse. Clean enough."

Beside her, Maud twittered.

Alyse turned on her heel and crossed the cold slate floor to stand outside the second chamber. "My lord and I will sleep here," she said.

Maud's smile disappeared. "Lady Alyse, this is not the lord's sleeping chamber. It is smaller—"

"It is big enough." Alyse pushed open the door and waited while Beda and Maud, visibly disturbed by Alyse's demands, darted into the chamber and emerged with their arms piled high with clothing, and spots of rising color upon their faces.

"Leave them in the chamber," Alyse said. "I will choose what I need. Only a shift and kirtle." She followed their gaze to her clammy boots. "And shoes." The maids stood together in the doorway, blocking their new lady's view of the room.

If she did not assert her will this day, she would never gain the respect of these Kernstowe women. "Well?" Alyse demanded. "Do you understand? Put them back in the chamber."

Beda coughed and murmured, "These are not for you, my lady. They are our own—they were given to us."

Maud hissed at her companion, who lapsed into a red-faced silence. "The lady deRançon's clothes are in the storehouse," she said. "We will bring the chests."

Alyse looked beyond them into the bedchamber—to a wide, rumpled sleeping pallet drawn near the hearth. The women had missed two fine chemises thrown carelessly over the settle.

Alyse remembered Rolf Nevers' carelessly laced tunic and understood the maids' distress. The lord of Kernstowe had been absent for two years, and Nevers had allowed the serving maids to use the sleeping chambers in the keep. The women had not dared to use the lord's chamber; they had left it closed but had taken the other, and made a fine lovenest for the warden. And, Alyse guessed, had taken their rewards from the late Lady deRançon's clothing chests.

"The great chamber is larger," Maud said. "The new lord must use it. We will clean it, lady Alyse, by nightfall—"

"I want this one," Alyse said.

Beda sidled back for the chemises.

Alyse pointed to the pallet. "I want clean linens here and dry clothing, as I have said." She saw with intense longing that there was a wooden tub beside the banked hearth. "And bring water. I will bathe now."

She had managed to speak with authority; the maids heeded her words. After one last attempt to interest her in the larger chamber, Maud and Beda had shrugged and backed down the stairs, leaving the evidence of their sleeping arrangements behind in a large heap outside the smaller chamber's door. Alyse wondered where Nevers and the maids would continue their liaisons—would they eventually find their way into the larger chamber now?

From the stairs, there was the sound of Rolf Nevers' voice rising in alarm, and a woman's high-pitched weeping. It would be some time, Alyse thought, before the warden and the kitchen maids would dare to resume their rutting within the walls of the keep. From the sound of their voices, they would sooner sleep in the fields than risk angering their new lord, Raimond deBauzan.

Three clothing chests, each half-full and suspiciously free of dust, stood open outside the chamber door, their flat oaken lids tipped up against the stone wall. Had she been alone, Alyse would have taken up each kirtle and chemise, each layer of carefully folded mantle, and marveled at the richness of the lady deRançon's robes. Under Beda's curious gaze, Alyse made short work of choosing a kirtle and drawing slippers from the corner of the first chest.

She had waited until the kitchen lads had emptied all but two of the water buckets into the bathing barrel and had shut the door upon Maud's offer to tend the kettle. Alyse's new, precarious authority would shrink to nothing should Maud catch sight of the threadbare chemise Alyse had worn from Morston.

Carefully, soundlessly, Alyse lowered the wooden bar into its brackets across the chamber door. A moment later, Maud's voice came through the panels, asking whether the lady Alyse would like more water heated in the kitchens.

"No," Alyse called. "Leave me now." A warm bath would have been better than the tepid water which Alyse would heat with the single small kettle beside the hearth, but an hour's solitude was more welcome still.

She spread her damp clothing on the bench before the fire, and hesitated only a heartbeat before casting the ragged chemise into the flames.

It occurred to Alyse, as she lifted the bar and pulled the door open, that her husband might not be pleased to spend his first night at Kernstowe on the pallet in this smaller sleeping chamber. And that she, more than Rolf Nevers and the serving maids, had reason to fear his displeasure.

Across the passageway, Maud stood sulking with two empty buckets at her feet.

"My lady?" There was no mockery now in the maid's voice. Her cheeks were pale beneath reddened eyes; her gaze upon the smooth stone floor. "I waited to empty the bath, my lady."

"When you finish, bring clean linens to the great bed-chamber."

"It is clean, my lady. We—none of us would have dared to use the lord Harald's bed."

"Make it ready. My lord husband may prefer it." Alyse hesitated at the top of the stairs. Within a few short hours, Raimond deBauzan would lead her back up these steep, tightly spiraled steps and turn, of course, to the larger chamber.

She turned back to Maud. "And when the chamber is ready," she said, "close the door upon it. Leave the other open."

If deBauzan wished to sleep alone when he was done with her, he would find the larger bed in the lord's chamber ready. Alyse would not follow him there, no matter how he might rage at her. There were, she knew, some things more terrifying than the scowl of the stranger who was her husband.

Raimond deBauzan watched the flames warming Kernstowe's great hall and gave thanks that he had come to the end of his journey. Since Acre, he had traveled hard, never sleeping in the same bed more than one night. At his family's stronghold at Bauzan, Queen Eleanor's mercenaries had allowed Raimond less than an hour to speak with his enraged father and frantic mother in the crowded hall of Bauzan before demanding that he ride north in their company.

At last, that long journey had ended.

The hot, potent vapor of the spiced wine in his goblet held the scent of Poitou's vineyards. Raimond sighed in contentment. "This is fine drink, Nevers. Your late lord was not content with this country's ale."

"No, Lord Raimond. He sent to a merchant at Biddaford harbor each year before the Yule feast, and bought a wagonload of casks."

"And you have kept them with care."

"Yes, my lord." Nevers met Raimond's gaze and flushed. "That is, the last of the wine was stored against Lord Harald's return. Most of it. There is an accounting—"

Raimond smiled. The warden was a nervous man, and given to small lies. Nevers' nervous fidgeting and the high color upon his face made him a poor liar. The man would learn, in time, that he would prosper only if he answered his new lord's questions with the truth.

"If you have drunk the wine, then say so. Surely your late lord Harald would not have begrudged you a few barrels of wine in many years of waiting for him."

"I—we did use some of it, after the harvest was done. And at Christmas. There were weddings, too. Three—no, four—"

"Peace, Nevers. You saved the finest, it seems. This is the richest I have tasted since—" He paused. "It has been years since I have had such fine drink."

"Your men told me you were many years in the Holy Lands, and only lately returned to Normandy."

"Yes, and crossed to England after reaching my father's lands. It has not been an easy homecoming."

"Were you with the king, then, when he sailed for home?"

"Yes, until Corfu. I lost him there."

Nevers' color was high again. "Then you did not see him captured?"

With difficulty, Raimond kept his anger from his face. "No,

I did not. I was with him when he left Corfu's harbor and had to turn back in the storms. The ship had been damaged and there were other delays. King Richard left Corfu again in secret, with a few men who, like him, put their trust in a local crew with a stolen ship. They were wrecked soon after, in Istria.''

"He was captured there?"

"No. He traveled over land, trying to outrun his enemies. Some time later, in Duke Leopold's lands, the duke's men found King Richard and the others who had survived the wreck. Now—now no one knows where the king is confined.'' Raimond drank deeply and summoned a serving maid to fill the goblet again.

Nevers held out his cup to the maid. "And you, my lord? Did you follow the same route he did?"

Raimond did not want to remember the months after Corfu. Led by a brigand more infamous than the one King Richard had trusted, he had discovered the king's wrecked ship, and had heard the confused tales of survivors traveling north and west. He had followed a long, tortuous route pursuing the rumors and half-myths which had sprung up in the wake of King Richard's disguised and foolish party. At last, he had abandoned the search when his questions had seemed more likely to endanger the king than to find him.

"I searched for him. I, and many others. We came too late."

Rolf Nevers gestured to the strongbox upon the table. "And then the king's mother sent for you?"

Yes, with forty armed predators worse than any savages he had seen in those far lands—Raimond drew a breath. "Yes, she wanted to hear what I had learned after Corfu."

"And to give you these lands, of course."

"And to give me land." The steward was asking too many questions. Raimond pushed his wine cup away. Would there never again be a time when he could end his troubles, forget caution, and drink deeply of wine and all the pleasures that could make a man forget the bloody images that haunted his waking hours? This night, with Nevers watching him through narrowed eyes, with the lady Alyse Mirbeau barricaded up in the sleeping chamber with those smirking, noisy maids scurrying about, was not the time for Raimond to drink deeply of the late Harald deRançon's fine Frankish wine.

Raimond stretched his legs beneath the table and turned his attention to the Bauzan men gathering around the table. With their help, recovering and returning Queen Eleanor's treasure would be child's play compared to the hardships he had faced these past years. Once his last duty to the Plantagenet's mother was done, he would be free. He had lands now—his own lands at last. And a keep with fine Norman wall hearths. A warm fire and strong wine were his to enjoy.

There was a bed for him, and a lady to warm it.

Raimond heard a small sound behind him. Alyse Mirbeau was standing on the first of the deeply curving stairs, dressed in crimson robes, her dark hair shining in two braids woven with narrow, deep red ribbons.

He rose to his feet and offered his hand to the frowning, beautiful woman who was his wife. Without hesitation, Alyse placed her fingers upon the fine cloth of her husband's sleeve and walked with him to the long table.

The kitchen maids were determined to impress their new lord. They brought roast capons, each bird three times the size of Morston's scrawny hens, and venison. And wine—good, strong wine from Burgundy which made Alyse's face flush and gave her the spirit to stare boldly at her husband. He turned to meet her gaze and smiled. She smiled back.

Rolf Nevers, too, had lost his nervous manner. "My lord, how is it that the duke Leopold dares keep our king to ransom?"

"The Austrian would have lost his nerve before now, had he acted alone. But now the emperor himself has taken King Richard into his keeping and imprisoned him elsewhere. It is the emperor who demands the ransom."

Nevers gave a soft whistle. "Henry, the Holy Roman Emperor?"

"The same. King Richard's ransom must be paid or he will never have his freedom. There is no ruler in Christendom who will protest Henry Hohenstaufen's actions."

"Count John will not protest."

Raimond grimaced. "Count John will not gain England's throne by these troubles. The Emperor would never kill Richard Lionheart. He would not dare to harm the king, but he will keep him prisoner as long as he wishes. Forever, if Philip of France influences him."

"Even an emperor should be shamed to treat any crusader in this way."

Raimond shook his head. "The Austrians had no love for King Richard. At times, there was more strife within our camps than on the battlefield. Even on the day we took Acre, there was some squabble about King Richard's men and the Austrian banners atop the city walls. Months later, when Conrad of Montferrat was killed, the Austrians were quick to accuse King Richard of the deed. By the time he reached Leopold's lands, the rumors were everywhere. The king was traveling in disguise when they captured him."

Nevers drained his goblet and gestured to Beda to fill it. "A Christian king imprisoned by another—it is a terrible sin. But at least he lives. Our late lord Harald was not so lucky. He was lost to us, and we never had word of his fate."

Raimond nodded. "Queen Eleanor said that deRançon disappeared before he reached the Holy Land. Was there no one traveling with him to tell the tale?"

Beside him, Alyse shifted. This talk of armies and ransoms could not interest her. Raimond covered his wife's hand where it lay between them on the trestle bench. She did not pull away.

Nevers cut a plump leg from the capon and placed it upon his trencher. "No, lord. He left two seasons after the others. He had hoped to get a child on his lady wife, but God was not willing. So Lord deRançon took the cross and followed Richard's army."

"His wife? I did not know he was wed. Where is deRançon's wife?"

"Dead, my lord. She died, poor lady, a month before Lord Harald left."

Raimond felt Alyse's hand stiffen beneath his own. He began to stroke her fingers. "God rest the lady's soul," he murmured. "Your late lord traveled alone, then, in his grief?"

"Yes. I think he heard God's voice one day as he rode out

hunting, and he left before evening, though it was midsummer eve and the feasting had not begun. He told me before he went that he would ease his soul in the Holy Lands, and gave me orders—the same as I showed you today, my lord. He told me to keep Kernstowe for him and promised, most surely, that he would return, however many years it took. Three times he swore it, and charged me to keep his lands safe. Told me to pay the king's tax and send men-at-arms if the crown raised an army here. And he commended us to Count John in his absence, as if—"

"Go on."

"As if he believed he might be lost, for a time."

"Or forever," Raimond said. "He may have seen his fate. Some men do, when they go to war." He remembered Nevers' earlier words. "He was Count John's man?"

"Aye. We sent to John Plantagenet and to the dowager queen when a year had passed. He had not come to Windsor, they said. There was no word of him."

"Had he intended to go first to Windsor?"

"He did not tell us. He rode from here that same day, to the west. We thought he was going to leave orders at Morston as well. But he did not."

"Did he not, Alyse?"

She pulled her hand from his. "My lord?"

Raimond smiled. His wife had not been following his speech with Nevers. No doubt, her mind was upon the long hours to come within the darkness of the bedchamber. It would go easier with her if they passed an hour or two in speech together beforehand. Raimond filled her wine cup and pushed it towards her. "My lady, we were speaking of deRançon. Did he not ride west to Morston to tell you that he had taken the cross?"

Alyse reached for the cup. "No. He did not tell us." She lowered her gaze. "At Morston, we learned of it many days after he had left."

Raimond turned back to Rolf Nevers. "When did he go?"

"Two years ago, on midsummer's eve," Nevers said. "I remember I asked my lord if he would stay to spend midsummer night at the bonfire, as he always did. But he said his heart was too sore with grief for his dead lady. He would have passed your bonfires that night, lady Alyse, for he rode west along the Morston track.''

"He might have seen them," Alyse said.

"We never heard from him again," Nevers said. "Not here, not at Morston, not at Chilcheton.''

"A sad tale," Raimond said. His lady wife must agree. She had gone pale again. Her face was as white as it had seemed in the chapel when she had told him—

Of her lover. The lover who would not return.

Raimond turned back to Nevers and asked him how the roads were between Kernstowe and the markets at Okehampton, and listened absently as Nevers embarked on a detailed description of the market and the two heavy wagons which needed repairs.

Beneath Nevers' droning voice, Raimond considered Alyse's sudden pallor. Of course—his wife's lover must have been deRançon, a man grieving for his dead wife, unwilling to wed Alyse before his mourning was complete. A man who had taken the lady Alyse's honor and then abandoned her for the crusade.

Raimond had heard a sad tale of a widowed knight riding alone into oblivion. If his suspicions were true, the late lord of Kernstowe had first eased his grief with the orphaned, defenseless Alyse Mirbeau and had then left her without the protection of marriage.

For which sin that grieving crusader deserved to burn in hell.

Alyse had dreaded those questions since first the Kernstowe warden had looked for news of his absent lord. Lord deRançon rode west over the moor. Why had he not stopped that night at Morston? Had he turned south, toward Chilcheton? Then why had he not stopped at the abbey of St. James? Had he taken a vow not to seek shelter, to sleep beside the road?

Emma had dealt with the questions when Nevers first enquired. No, Emma had replied. Lord Harald was not here. And have you seen our wandering blacksmith? The kitchen crane needs mending and the man has not returned from his journey south to fetch a bride from Dunhevet. Would the Kernstowe smith have a day to spare?

Rolf Nevers had left Morston clearly puzzled, but had not seemed to doubt Alyse's brief denial and Emma's claim that they had been watching the road for Hund the smith to return with his new wife.

Raimond deBauzan would not be so easily deceived.

Alyse murmured an apology to her husband and rose from the table. She waved away the wide-eyed Beda and mounted the stairs alone.

From the bedchamber, Alyse heard her husband's men begin to raise their voices in loud jesting. Among them, Raimond's voice boomed good-naturedly, forbidding them to raise him upon their shoulders to follow his new wife to her chamber. A voice bellowed something about the river, and the lord Raimond's answering laughter was met with shouts of merriment.

The frankly curious Beda had followed her new mistress up the stairs despite Alyse's attempt to dismiss the maid. At the bedchamber, Alyse had turned the girl away and pulled the door shut.

There was warmth and a blaze of light from the small hearth. The people of Kernstowe were not careful with firewood, it seemed. The fire must have been burning in the empty room since the feasting began.

The chamber was warm and the wide pallet covered with good linen. On the settle lay a robe of soft green wool, likely a gesture of contrition from Beda and Maud. The ale-stained rushes between the bed and the hearth had been taken away, leaving the wide planked floor uncovered.

Alyse heard voices from the shuttered embrasures facing the river. She eased open the smallest panel and saw torches lighting a crooked path down the earthworks to the water, to a small bank upstream from the keep.

A dark figure planted a burning brand in the grassy bank and stepped beyond it to the river's edge. The sputtering light fell upon deBauzan's black and crimson robes, then flickered low as he pulled his tunic over his head and flung it past the flames onto the grass.

His body shone bronze in the crimson torch light. Bronze, and gold as well, where his powerful trunk joined muscled thighs. He turned away, and the flames played sinuous magic over his arms as he thrashed into the black river.

A small, noisy crowd of Bauzan and Kernstowe men stood atop the embankment and laughed as two young lads slipped upon the long, wet grass and rolled down the slope, fully clothed, into the river after Raimond.

DeBauzan's shining head moved farther from the shore, beyond the loom of the torches. The laughing crowd pelted down the hill, calling for him to return to face his husbandly duties.

He surfaced then, in a high, glittering spray of water and golden hair, and waded to the bank. He seized his crimson tunic and began to rub the water from his body. The planted torch blazed high again, and the flames licked brighter still upon his well-made body and his thick nether parts, now the object of that unruly crowd's bawdy shouts.

Raimond shrugged his mantle over his broad shoulders and raised his head. A flash of blue beneath that gilded brow found Alyse's figure at the firelit embrasure. She drew back behind the panel.

With a gruff word, Raimond turned his men's attention to the two drunken lads struggling to wade their way back to the riverbank.

And Alyse closed the shutters upon the night wind.

He came to her much later, fully dressed with his pourpoint over his arm. Beneath his doublet, he wore a black tunic she had not seen before. His hair was tousled, and still damp from the river.

Her husband stood in the doorway and smiled.

"They made this chamber ready," she said.

He looked over his shoulder at the shadowed doorway to the larger chamber and brought his blue gaze back to her.

She wished he would speak. "My lord, this chamber will be warmer in the mornings. I prefer it to the other."

He pushed away from the grey stone frame. "Are you troubled by ghosts, Alyse?"

Ghosts. How did he know—he could not know. "Ghosts, my lord? There are none here."

"Then why will we not sleep in the lord's chamber—deRançon's chamber? Do you think he still walks there?"

"Yes," she said. And realized, as she had spoken, that it was not a lie.

"Then we will remain here. We will have no ghosts with us this night." He was close enough to touch her now. Alyse could feel her knees tense, ready for flight. With all her will, she resisted the overwhelming urge to run.

He looked down at her bare feet. "You are cold. Get into the bed, then."

She could no longer feel the soles of her feet beneath her. She felt as if she floated, immobile, inches above the floor. To take a step would be to fall. "I am not cold," she said.

The half-smile returned. The firelight caught the whorls of damp-curled gold about his face as he glanced at the pallet. "If this bed is not to your liking, then we must deal with the ghosts in deRançon's chamber."

"No—that is, this bed is good enough for us. For me, that is. You are the new lord and may have the best—"

He laughed. "It is good enough for me, Alyse. It is as fine as any I have been offered these many years." He looked again at her feet. "This may be time for a gift."

She had not noticed the saddle pack in the corner shadows, and her husband's great broadsword upon it. He placed the weapon beside the chamber door and lifted the bar into place.

Alyse flinched at the sound. Raimond made a small gesture. "Caution is a good thing, Alyse. I do not know these people." He turned back to the sumpter pack. "Nor do you, I think."

"I know them well enough."

"You do not trust Rolf Nevers, do you?" His face was turned to the shadows as he unlaced the leather pack.

She moved closer to the fire and placed one hand upon the stone hood. Her feet were prickling upon the cold floor, as if she had been standing for hours without stirring. "Why do you say that?"

"You and the others at Morston were starving—or close to it—and Nevers did not know. Two meals for my ten men took the last of your stores. It is two months or more to the first harvest, yet the granary—''

''The granary?''

''Your granary at Morston,'' he continued patiently, ''was all but empty. You, my lady, were wearing rags and hauling fleeces when I came to Morston yesterday. You had not enough people to do half the work still to be done with the shearing. Yet you had not sent to Nevers for help.''

He pulled a large bundle from the sack and walked toward her. ''Your family held their land from the lord of Kernstowe, and Nevers was his steward as well as warden, as far as I can see. This is a rich place, Alyse, and could have eased the hunger at Morston. The supplies I sent back to your land this day will not be missed from Kernstowe's storerooms. Yet, you stayed holed up with your people in that cold place, risking their well-being and your own by your silence. Why did you not ask for Nevers' help?''

''We had enough for weeks to come. I would have sent word to Nevers when the time came.''

He shook his head. ''Had Nevers given you offense? Were you afraid to come here?''

There was another question behind his words. Her husband's darkened eyes were focused upon her, compelling her to tell him. Sweet Mary, mother of Jesus, Raimond deBauzan was asking if Nevers had debauched her.

''No! He gave me no cause to mistrust him. I—''

''My lady,'' he broke in, ''you must tell me which man gave you offense. I need to know.'' He set the formless bundle at her feet and straightened again to tower beside her. ''I do not wish to imagine, each time a man defies me or crosses my will, that he does so because he bedded you and believes my claiming you is unjust. Nor do I wish to watch your eyes when you avoid speech with a man and imagine it is because he had you, madam. It will be easier for us both if you tell me now—who was the man who took your honor?''

''I will not speak of him.''

''God's bones, Alyse—''

''You said you would not reproach me.''

''This is not reproach. This is a question.''

"I will not tell you."

Raimond muttered something Alyse could not understand as he knelt before the bundle on the floor. His hands worked slowly, carefully, to remove the thin cords which held it together. Alyse released the breath which had begun to burn in her chest.

He was not angry. She had refused him, and he was not angry?

Raimond began to pull a layer of heavy cloth from the bundle. "Calm yourself. I will not ask again." He looked up at her and shook his head. "Do not fear me. Must you shrink away from me each time we disagree? It is not necessary." He turned back to his task. "I do not use my fists to speak for me. Nor do I ravish every woman within my reach."

"I am your wife."

He made an impatient gesture. "Even a wife. I see no reason to treat you worse than I would a camp-follower. I am home from the wars, Alyse, and sick of fighting. I will have peace in my bedchamber. Now stand back."

The cloth unfolded and turned beneath his hands.. Alyse saw that it did not conceal a gift within its folds. It was itself the gift—a piece of silken velvet the size of a trestle table. It glowed with countless colors, impossibly rich.

Raimond cast its brilliance upon the floor before the fire and watched as Alyse fell to her knees beside it and stroked the deep, soft surface.

"Sit upon it."

"Oh, never. It is so beautiful."

"You are meant to walk upon it, or sit on it, if you wish." He took her hand and drew her towards him. The wondrous cloth was like the finest fleece beneath her knees.

"It is a Saracen cloth, Alyse. The Turks and the Saracens weave them for their houses and for their tents."

She could not take her eyes from the intricate profusion of colors beneath her. "You won this as a battle prize?"

"No. Montbazon, my mother's cousin, gave it to me at Windsor, before I began the journey here. He had seen the manner of my leaving Palestine. The only thing of value I had left when I took ship at Acre was my life. And I was so full of wounds that I valued my life but little, that first week on ship.''

''You were wounded?''

He shrugged out of the doublet, then pulled the black tunic over his head in a swift, smooth motion. The bronze she had seen at the riverbank was gilded with thick, shining body hair which glowed amber in the firelight. It covered his wide chest, showing darker in the hard valleys where his muscles met ribs and flat belly, shining brighter on the ridges of his muscled flesh. Across both, dark and bright, were traced wide swathes of white, scarred flesh; upon his shoulder, a jagged red patch had only recently healed.

She gasped and touched him, before she thought better of it, on the thick muscle above the angry flesh. He covered her hand with his own and drew it down, to the center of his chest. There were golden flames moving within the depths of his eyes. ''I am your husband, Alyse. Do not make me wait.''

''My lord,—''

''Raimond. In this chamber, I am Raimond.''

''I have not—I will not refuse you. I will keep my vows.''

He raised her hand to his lips and kissed the center of her palm. Alyse drew a breath and felt her spine stiffen. His lips moved over the calluses at the base of her fingers. He would not permit her to pull her hand from his grasp.

At last, he released her wrist. Her knees were slightly parted, nestled upon the softness of the Saracen cloth. A vision of Fortebras' golden pelt against her breasts sent an involuntary cry from Alyse's lips.

He traced a gentle line from her chin to the neck of her chamber robe. And waited.

She placed her hands upon the lapped cloth. ''I will disrobe for you, now.'' The words came out in a breathless rush.

His gaze passed swiftly down her body to her trembling knees and back to her eyes. ''If it please you, Alyse. Tonight, we will do what pleases you.''

''Do not speak in riddles. Tell me what you want.''

He slid his hand beneath her crossed fingers and smoothed the robe from one breast. ''You know the way of this, Alyse. You have had a lover. Show me what you want. I am a man like any other. As patient as any.'' His fingers brushed the soft underside of her breast. ''No worse than most.''

He kissed her then, full upon her mouth, and covered her breast with his palm. And moved in a small, slow, maddening circle upon it.

She heard a hoarse, reverent oath as he moved his mouth down the pulse of her neck, down to where his broad, warm hand held her breast to his lips.

Her knees sank deeper into the velvet beneath her, and parted. She felt his arm behind her shoulders, steadying her, holding her fast as his mouth suckled upon her. The hard, muscled arm behind her back pulled her closer, made her arch against his golden head, against the strong, sweet pull of his mouth.

He was very large, and surrounded her, supported her completely. There was no need to keep her body still beneath him, no need to keep her balance. She could not have moved if she had tried. She was—helpless.

The fire flared and hissed beside them. Somewhere in the distance, a heavy door boomed shut and voices made hoarse with drink grew louder.

In that moment, he moved his lips back to the base of her throat and stopped, breathing hot against her neck as she tried to still her trembling. Raimond drew back and caught the fallen cloth of her robe within his fist to bring it to cover her once again.

He rose and walked to the embrasure from which she had watched him at the riverbank. He reached for the loosened shutter and turned it shut.

''Why?'' she asked. And sank weakly upon the cloth. ''Why? Do you not want me?''

''I want you, Alyse. But I will not take you tonight.''

The blood pounding in her ears was fainter now. She could think now. Her husband—her overwhelming, golden husband—had released her from his embrace of power and pleasure.

His chest rose and fell in deep, swift breaths. The golden fire flames still shone within the blue darkness of his eyes. There was no indifference in his gaze.

"I see," she said. "You fear that if you got me with child this night, you would not be sure it is yours."

"Should I fear that?"

"No," she said. "I told you I am not with child. I—It was long ago that I—sinned. And I—"

"—will keep your vow. All your vows. I know. But not tonight. I do not bed women who fear me."

"I am willing."

He shook his head. "You are not. I tasted the fear upon your flesh." He raised his hands to the lacing of his chausses and flexed them slowly, as if surprised to see the tight fists they had formed. Then he stripped the garment from his body and Alyse saw his manroot grown large in arousal. He drew the coverlet from the wide pallet and knelt upon the bed. "Come here," he said.

Had he decided to take her, after all? Sweet Mother Mary, she could not summon the courage to walk towards that vision of potent desire. Alyse rose to her feet and began to roll the precious Saracen cloth.

"What are you doing?"

"I will put it upon the chest in the hall. I—we could hang it on feast days."

"Leave it. It is meant to cover the floor." He stretched along the far side of the bed and pulled the linen cloth over his lower body. "We will sit on it each night, before the fire. If you wish."

"Yes—perhaps."

He sighed. "It is my gift to you. Do as you wish. Keep it for feast days if that is what you want."

"No. Thank you. I will keep it here."

"Then come to bed."

Alyse crossed the room. She placed one knee upon the pallet and reached for the coverlet.

"Your robe, my lady. You forgot to remove your robe."

She looked at the twisted sheet which covered him and saw that his arousal had increased. "You said—"

"Surely you do not sleep in clothing. It is unhealthy."

There was humor in his voice, but none in his eyes. He looked up at her with the same thoughtful expression she had seen in the torch light at the river's edge. And she knew, as she gazed upon her husband, that she would not protest if he turned and took her now. His thick mane of hair, his powerful, scarred chest, and his arms were golden in the firelight. He was a gentle, powerful man.

He was her husband.

The half-smile appeared again; he sighed and turned his broad back to her.

Alyse hastily dropped her robe and pulled the sheet over her body as she slid into the bed beside him. She waited, breathless and still.

"Sleep," he whispered. "I will not touch you—tonight."

The silence was unbearable. "Thank you," she said in a small, careful voice.

He sighed. "This is not kindness, wife. A man who forces an unwilling woman to take his—his weapon between her legs might find, at sunrise, her dagger between his ribs."

A moment later, he turned to her and peered at her in the firelight. "I made a jest, Alyse. It was a jest. God's bones, will you not stop your shrinking and quaking? Now sleep, or I'll— sleep, damn you."

CHAPTER SIX

Raimond did not sleep, nor did his lady wife. She had stirred twice, so slowly and cautiously it had almost seemed to his war-tuned senses an act of stealth. Her breathing—so shallow and quiet she might have been smothering—disturbed him even more.

Now she lay stiff and straight as a corpse, with her eyes closed tight and the sheet wadded between her hands over her breasts, as if she feared he would take it from her. With each small breath she took, the sheet moved slightly, lewdly, so delicately that he could see no motion, shifting a hair's width back and forth across his tortured body. Across his aching manhood.

Once, when the fire had died to embers, he had thought of the river, and decided to cool his throbbing body in the dark water. He had pushed himself up on one elbow and had seen that her eyes were screwed shut and that her breathing had ceased completely. She was like an over-stretched bowstring, ready to break at his slightest touch, his softest word.

He had settled back upon the bed and waited too long to hear her breathe again.

By St. Magnus' eye-teeth, he should have taken her hours ago and ended her fearful waiting. Yes, he should have taken her. Twice. Once, to show her not to fear him, and again, more slowly still, to make her faint with pleasure. Then, by the saints, she would be sleeping deeply, and caring not whether the sheet moved from her pretty breasts.

She smelled of flowers. She should, for her lips and the peaks of her little breasts were the color of young roses, as small and tender as the earliest blooms. His heart had tightened—aye, more than his heart had stiffened—when he had tasted one of those pulsing sweet flowers. The color of her body, starkly white against the dark glory of her hair, had glowed beneath his touch into a hue more delicate than any floret.

He had been near to desperate as he had held her this night, near to thrusting her down upon the soft, infidel mat and weighting her body with his own. But she had shuddered, fearful in his arms, and the hot desire had fled from his mind, but not from his body. His hungry flesh had cared not that she had begun to struggle. Indeed, his arousal had grown harder when she had done so.

It had taken all his will to leave her unravished. Tomorrow, he would begin again to bed her. If she still feared him, he would find another woman to ease him, to give his wife time to accept him. It would not be a Kernstowe woman, for bedding with another so soon after marriage would shame his lady. No, he would ride south, to that market town of Okehampton, and find a woman there.

But first, he must deal with the matter of Queen Eleanor's treasure. Find it and take it to Windsor, to the court. There would be women there, women he had known before he had left for the Holy Lands—women of subtle lusts who craved what his wife did not.

But none of them, none that he could remember, had a body where flowers bloomed upon whitest snow.

It was well past dawn when Raimond awoke from his shallow sleep. The morning sun streamed through the arrow-slits in the eastern wall to warm the oaken pallet-frame. Alyse had been right about this chamber—the first light would take the chill from this chamber even in the cold months, when the sun moved to the south.

Raimond moved past his sleeping wife to find his chainse and tunic on the cold floor. He dressed quickly, lest Alyse awake to see his half-aroused body in the morning light. She had seemed nervous of his body and shy to look upon it in the firelight yestereve. Or had it been the sounds of merriment from the hall below that sent that sudden shiver of fear through Alyse's body? She was different from the other women who had taken him into their bodies—those ladies had not needed the darkness of night, nor the silence of the bedchamber to allow their desires to flower. A firelit alcove above a hall filled with boisterous revels, a sunlit meadow within earshot of the hunt—no place was too risky, too unlikely for the eager widows and sly young wives who had invited Raimond's lust when a stolen moment was possible. No, they had sought his body with a daring zeal which at times had surpassed Raimond's own healthy passion.

Alyse was different from those women, though there was no good reason for her to be so timid. She was no virgin. She must have felt hot desire for her anonymous lover—deRançon, most likely—to give him her body without marriage.

Was she still grieving for the man? It had been two years, Raimond calculated, since deRançon had left. Two years in which Alyse's hard life must have shown her that deRançon, however persuasive, had not been a good and considerate lover to leave her without protection. Surely, by now her grief must have been tempered by that knowledge.

Or was the lady Alyse cold by nature? Raimond's breath stopped as he remembered her response to the touch of his lips upon his wife's breast. She had been close to completion in that confused moment before she had tried to draw away from him.

Raimond smiled. No, the lady was not cold. Her first lover, whoever he was, may have been clumsy. The reason for her reluctance could be as simple as that. His smile broadened. He would not be her first man, but he would, perhaps, bring her first woman's pleasure. He looked again at his sleeping wife. Soon, my lady, you will have your true wedding gift. Something new to you, but ancient as a Saracen song.

Alyse stirred. By St. Olav's sacred breath, Raimond muttered beneath his breath, he must leave the room before he fell upon his wife and spent himself upon her sleeping body.

His boots lay beside the door, muddy and still damp from yesterday's rains. He reached into his sumpter pack and drew forth new ones, a gift from Montbazon at Windsor. With a hollow thud, Queen Eleanor's coffer rolled out of the sack, its linen wrappings tangled with the boots. Raimond cursed under his breath. Even here, in his bedchamber in the presence of his sleeping wife, Raimond felt the influence of that overbearing old woman as though she had followed him to Kernstowe, demanding that he deal with her treasure before he wooed his young wife.

He pushed the small coffer against the wall, amid the scattered contents of his saddle pack. It was a morning gift—so Queen Eleanor had said. The dowager's gift for Alyse was nestled within a small coffer of silver-banded cedar—the mate, she had told him, of the casket in which Isabelle Mirbeau had carried her lady's treasure into hiding at Morston. Show the coffer to your bride, she had instructed Raimond, when you are well and truly wed. If Isabelle's daughter has seen the other, she will recognize this coffer and know that her new husband has my trust. And she will tell you, if she knows, where the other is hidden.

Raimond had suggested a more straightforward way to convey Eleanor's royal wishes. No, the queen had replied, a letter was not possible. More than impossible—a letter would be dangerous.

Queen Eleanor had pushed the coffer into Raimond's arms, cutting short the questions which had smoldered in his mind since that day.

Raimond cursed again and dropped the empty pack over the coffer. He would give the damned thing to his wife today, after she had awakened, and hope that by nightfall she would be finished with her raging or trembling or whatever else she would do when she saw the cursed box.

For now, he would leave her to sleep. If he could coax her, this night, to accept him, she would need to rest beforehand.

Alyse heard her husband kick aside his boots and rummage through his saddle packs. Then there was cursing, and more cursing, and a solid thump as he kicked his possessions toward the wall and threw the pack down atop them. Then he picked up his sword, unbarred the door, and left. There was a small scraping sound, as if he had started to open the door again, then nothing but the silvered murmur of the river which curved close beneath the unshuttered embrasures.

She waited a moment to be sure Raimond was gone, and wrapped her robe about her as she crossed the room to find her clothes—the late lady deRançon's clothes. Alyse would wear the crimson kirtle once again this morning, and hope that her own was dry enough to use by evening.

The rich cloth slid easily over her head and fell in warm folds down to her calves. The most handsome of the robes which had remained in Constance deRançon's half-emptied clothing chest, this garment was soft and new—far too good for everyday use. Alyse's own gown would be better for days spent working within the keep; she would demand that Maud or Beda or some other woman wash her kirtle and dry it before the fire.

She gave the red wool one last caress and began to fold the bedrobe. The robe she would keep until she could manage to make one of her own, for she needed some way to keep deBauzan's eyes from her body when they were in this chamber together. Sharing a chamber—and a bed—with a large, virile man presented dilemmas she had never imagined.

He had been kind, last night, to leave her in peace—if peace indeed it was, to lie in the darkness nearly touching his long, powerful body and hearing his deep, slow breathing. Remembering the feel of his firm mouth, his wicked tongue upon her breast.

He had felt her fear, tasted it upon her flesh, and he had released her. In that moment, her relief had mingled with another kind of fear—the suspicion that he could read her mind. If he could sense fear so quickly—for indeed, she had been at the point of surrender before fear of his body's strength had seared her mind—then what else had he learned from her unspoken thoughts?

Had Queen Eleanor sent her a sorcerer to wed?

Alyse placed the robe on the settle and looked in dismay at her husband's muddy boots and the snarl of smallclothes tangled with the laces of his sumpter pack. Would a sorcerer be so careless with his clothing?

Raimond had mounted the narrow, twisting passage to the battlements above the sleeping chambers. Kernstowe was a fine, solid keep with a long view in all directions. The river bordered the eastern wall, flowing south towards the far distant market town of Okehampton. To the north, beyond Kernstowe's southern-tilted fields, lay the forest, rich with game and graced with three springs, one of them a holy place, Nevers had told him. And to the west beyond the fields were the moors he had crossed yesterday; black-green pools and large, moss-covered boulders lay scattered, as if by a giant's mischief, across the pale grey tracts. The small rock cairns which had guided them around the low ground and bogs stretched in an erratic pattern, wending towards Morston. Where Morston should be, there was only dense, dark mist covering the land and the frigid sea.

Alyse would never pass another night in that cold place, if he could manage to keep her away from—

Then the hair upon his arms stood stiff and erect, and his danger-sense came over him. He had already drawn his sword and bolted down the first steps of the spiral backbone of the keep when he heard his wife scream.

Their chamber door was closed and the passageway deserted. The larger room, the one Alyse had refused, was dark and empty. From his sleeping chamber, Raimond heard a brief, guttural sound and the sharp crack of breaking wood. He raised his sword and kicked open the door.

She was alone, standing with fragments of pale wood and a snarled silken cloth at her feet. By the thin silver straps which still vibrated from the broken base, Fortebras recognized the ruins of Queen Eleanor's coffer. The queen's gifts to Alyse, the samite veil and broad golden band, lay torn and warped among the fragrant cedar splinters.

She looked at him with tear-glossed hatred. "How did you do this? How could you have done this?"

The cold wings of fear brushed the back of Raimond's neck. His wife was more than distraught. Here was more than guilt. Here was—

Her wide, staring eyes were upon his sword. "Whatever I have done, it is not as cruel as this torment. Use your weapon— end this game—and be damned to you."

It was madness. Here was madness.

In that moment, Raimond did not care whether his wife had taken Queen Eleanor's damned jewels and had cast them into the sea. The queen's devious choice of morning gift had sent his bride straight into deathlike terror.

He lowered the sword and placed it upon the pallet. "What torment?" He walked slowly, speaking low. "This is—this was the queen's wedding gift to you."

She stepped back. "Wedding gift? It is not that. I know it, and you know it."

Behind him, a confusion of voices, boots and steel welled up the stairs. Nevers reached him first, breathing hard. "My lord, I heard—"

"Leave us," Raimond snarled.

"Is there—"

The Bauzan men had sheathed their swords. Young Erec stepped back, pulling at Nevers' arm. "Come away. My lord said—" The serving women pushed past him, straining to see past Raimond into the chamber.

His gaze upon Alyse, Raimond pushed the door shut behind him, upon Nevers, the serving maids, and their questions.

He stepped around the ruined veil. "You were not meant to find it alone. I was to give it to you, to say that the casket is much like the one your mother took away from Salisbury. For the queen."

She drew a quick breath and began to shake. He took her arm and pulled her to the settle. "Sit," he said. "And listen."

"It is not the one—"

"No, this is not the one your mother took away for safekeeping. How could it be? This is—this was its mate."

She wove her fingers together and made of her hands a white-boned tangle. "And you were to show it to me and discover whether—"

"Whether you recognized it. I believe we must agree that you recognized it."

She looked up bleakly. "Damn you, Raimond deBauzan. Damn you—"

He knelt before her, but did not dare touch her brittle hands. "Listen to me, Alyse. Tell me the truth. Did your mother keep it safe? Or did she lose the gems? Did she need to sell them?"

Alyse shook her head.

"Do you have them?"

"No, my lord." Her answer was a cry of pain.

With effort, Raimond controlled his voice. "If they are gone, Alyse, I will send word to the queen that they are lost—that you knew nothing of them, and that we searched and could not find them. It was many years ago, Alyse, and your parents are dead. You will not be blamed."

"She will be angry."

"It does not matter. When did she last send word to your parents?"

The surprise on her face was genuine. "Send word? She never sent word. It would have been too dangerous."

Her words did nothing but add to his confusion. "Who thought it was dangerous?"

"My mother."

"King Henry has been dead these past four years. What danger was there for Queen Eleanor if she sent for her jewels once her husband died? Did the queen not send word to your parents when she was freed from Salisbury?"

"No, but—"

"But what?"

"They went to her when the king died—when she was freed. They went to Windsor."

Christ's bones, had Eleanor taken back her jewels and forgotten them? Was the aging queen, who continued to order the lives of King Richard's subjects, beginning her dotage? Was this coil of half-truths and confusion a result of Queen Eleanor's poor memory? Raimond lowered his voice to a whisper. "And they gave her the casket?"

He saw her hesitate, as if tempted to agree. "No," she said at last. "They did not see her. You must know that. She had left for France, with King Richard. To see her son's army assembled. My parents returned to Morston."

"And the jewels?"

She shook her head.

"Alyse?"

"No. I have not seen them since. Do you want me to swear it?"

She looked as if she would swear that the jewels were at the bottom of the ocean, if that would end his questions. And follow them there, when she had the chance.

"No," he said. "I believe you." There was only so much this woman could stand. And he would be damned if he would push her over the brink again in aid of Queen Eleanor's schemes.

"What will you do?"

"Search Morston for the gems. If I find them, Queen Eleanor will use them to ransom King Richard."

"And if you don't find them?"

"Nothing can be done."

"Will she take your land away?"

Raimond winced. His wife had gone right to the marrow of his fears. He rose and pulled her to stand beside him. "No, Alyse. She would not take back these lands, so soon after she gave them to me. Not without a reason she could make public. She will let me keep these lands for a time, perhaps for all time. Queen Eleanor is an old woman, Alyse; she may forget her disappointment. If she does not—there are not many years left to her to show her anger.''

''My mother loved her, Raimond. She said the queen would remember her loyalty for all time.''

And that same queen had let her loyal woman die hungry in a hovel at the end of the world. Raimond took his wife's hand. ''Alyse, try to forget the cursed gems. I will try to find them, and I will deal with the queen. This is no longer your burden, Alyse. Let it go.''

After a time, she lowered her eyes. ''You cannot know how—'' Alyse stiffened and pushed him away.

He did not release her. ''Know what, Alyse?''

She drew a shaking breath. ''You cannot know—how great a burden I may be.''

''You are my wife.'' Raimond began to smooth the crimson linen beneath his hands. ''And if a burden, a sweet one.'' *And from this day, the only burden you will carry, my lady, shall be my sons.*

She colored as if she had heard his thoughts, but her eyes remained as troubled as before. Raimond drew her with him to open the door. Rolf Nevers and the maids still waited, their eyes staring wide above pale cheeks. Raimond advanced, pulling Alyse beside him, and stopped before the steward.

''My lord, is all—''

Raimond cut off the question. ''Nevers, is there a saddle here, a woman's saddle for my lady?''

''A saddle? A saddle?''

''Answer me.''

''Why—yes, my lord.'' Nevers wet his lips. ''Lady Constance, God rest her soul, had a fine saddle.'' He looked beyond Raimond. ''My lord, is something amiss—''

Raimond stepped between his wife and the steward's gaze. ''And the grey mare I saw there? Is she docile?''

Nevers took a step backward. ''I rode her myself to Okehampton last month.''

''Then make the beast ready.'' Raimond frowned at the three anxious faces in the passageway. ''Go then. All of you. Go now to put a meal on the table and that saddle on the mare.''

He turned back to Alyse. "We will ride the borders of Kernstowe today."

Nevers had retreated to the stair, pushing Beda and Maud before him. Alyse looked over her shoulder at the shattered coffer upon the chamber floor. "I cannot go with you. There is much to do here—"

"Leave it," he said. "We will close the door and go down to eat. I will stand here until you agree."

"Then I will come," she said.

Her husband's demand was god-sent. It would be necessary, when the time came, to return quickly to Morston. If Alyse learned to manage Nevers' mare today, and saw where the saddle was kept, it would be easier to leave unnoticed to make her solitary trip across the moors.

In recent years, Alyse had seldom tried to travel by horseback, for her mother's saddle had not fit upon the broad backs of Morston's two remaining horses—placid animals trained to the plow and wagon. Two summers ago, when heavy rains had ruined her crops, Alyse had traded the beasts at Okehampton for extra grain.

Yesterday, as she had tried to keep a decent, modest seat on a man's saddle on that huge mare borrowed from deBauzan's man, Alyse had realized she had forgotten what little skill she had possessed. Three nights from now, she would need skill and steady hand to reach Morston in time to bring the queen's coffer to light.

Her husband had been lying to put her mind to rest when he made light of the consequences of telling Queen Eleanor that her jewels were lost. There would be trouble for Alyse, and for Raimond as well. And if the queen believed he was lying to her, Raimond might lose his life.

Alyse had no choice. She must put aside her fear, and free the coffer from its loathsome hiding place.

On the three occasions Isabelle Mirbeau had taken the coffer from its first hiding place, she had allowed her daughter to look within, and had described each gem and spoken of its provenance. There were not many, she had said, but they were irreplaceable, and dangerous in the hands of the queen's enemies. Alyse's persistent, childish questions asking how the queen's enemies could harm her with one of those small jewels had been dismissed unanswered.

As the years passed, Isabelle said more. It was dangerous to send messages to the queen, even after she had been released from Salisbury keep, for her enemies might intercept a letter and come looking for the cache. Nor could Alyse's mother leave the jewels at Morston unattended, for they were irreplaceable, of importance beyond telling. Finally, Isabelle and her family must not call attention to themselves or to Morston in any way, even when desperate for grain following a bad harvest. Only in obscurity would they and the queen's treasure remain safe.

There had been speculation and confusion when King Henry died and Queen Eleanor, on behalf of her royal son the new king, sent to Kernstowe's lord to forgive the king's tax upon Morston, in gratitude for Isabelle Mirbeau's faithful service to her queen in her early years of imprisonment.

Isabelle and William of Morston had greeted deRançon's news with joy but had subsided, days later, into frightened silence. There had been no letter for Isabelle, no word from the queen to send for the coffer. Were they to take it to her, now that she had her freedom?

At last, William and Isabelle took their secret—the small chest they had kept hidden beneath their bedchamber hearthstone—and traveled to Windsor to give it back to the queen. They had not dared to write to her before they began their journey, of course. It would have been too dangerous.

They arrived too late to see the queen; she had left for France, ignorant of their coming. William and Isabelle, weary and disappointed, had brought their burden back to Morston.

There had been fever that winter in the market towns. When William brought his lady back to Morston, the doom sweat was already upon his face; he had watched, fretful and helpless, as Isabelle and Alyse put the coffer back in its hiding place before the hearth and heaved the large flagstone back over the cache with great difficulty. When Isabelle fell ill and followed her husband to the grave some weeks later, Alyse did not know where to send to the queen, nor would she have dared break Morston's long silence in that way.

She never imagined, in that last summer of innocence, that it was already too late for caution.

CHAPTER SEVEN

DeBauzan carried his swordbelt beside him as he led the way down to the hall. The stone stairs were nearly the same height, but uneven enough to cause a stranger—an invader—to slow his steps. With approval, Raimond saw that the fifth step above the hall was higher than the rest, the first tripping place for any assassin who managed to enter the keep.

He turned to offer his hand to Alyse. She glanced at the sword he held at his side. "Will you come armed, each morning, to the table?"

"Until I know the minds of the people of Kernstowe."

She nodded slightly and took his hand. "What will you say to them? About my—about what happened."

"Nothing." Across the hall, the younger scullery girl dropped a heap of trencher bread upon the table and darted back into the kitchens. The Bauzan men were gathered at the table, speaking in low voices as they waited for their newly married lord. "And you say nothing, my lady. For if you answer their questions, you will say more than you should. Let the serving maids imagine, if they will, what I did to cause your screams." He smiled. "It is past time that those trulls gave you the respect they owe you."

A small smile flickered and vanished. "And I will have their respect for wedding a beast?"

His wife's voice was steady, but upon his palm. her hand trembled. He closed his hand over her fingers. "No, they should not respect you for that. But when they see you sit beside the beast at table and share his bread without fear, there will be an end to their sly looks."

The smile returned. And remained.

Raimond caught his breath. When she smiled, there was such beauty in her face that his blood ran hot in his veins. With regret, he dismissed the thought of taking his wife back up the stairs to coax her smile into delight. Even if he turned his back upon his men and took Alyse back to their chamber, the sight of the splinters of that cursed box and the old queen's gift would cool his lust.

He turned his gaze back to the table. "Come, then. Sit you beside me, close beside me, and think no more on Queen Eleanor and her gift. My men are watching. Do you want them to think I put a frown on my wife's morning face?"

Rolf Nevers came late to the table and took his place below the Bauzan men. "The mare is ready, my lord. The saddle is cleaned and set out beside the stable door."

"How far is Dunhevet?"

"Along the road south of here—a half-day's ride, my lord. Are you and the lady Alyse—"

"No, the lady Alyse will ride with me around the borders of Kernstowe. Erec will ride to Dunhevet today." Raimond dismissed Erec's half-formed question with a small gesture. "I will send you on your way this morning, Erec. You will take a message to Dunhevet."

"To the assizes?" Nevers drained his ale cup. "To the assizes, my lord?"

Raimond turned to the steward. "On a private matter. Is there an assize in session at Dunhevet?"

"No, my lord."

Nevers' face had paled again. Had he feared that Raimond would bring him to a court of justice to account for his small liberties in his late lord's absence?

Across the table, Alain had begun to tell what he had heard, the night before, of the fine whores—twin sisters, they said—who had a house near Dunhevet's market place. Erec cast an apologetic look in Beda's direction and turned to hear Alain's words.

Beside Raimond, his wife's eating knife dropped to the table. "My lord," she said, "are you sending your man to Dunhevet for the whores?"

Raimond smiled. The controlled outrage in Alyse's low voice told him that she would not take kindly to losing his attentions to a skilled woman of pleasure. He leaned across the table. "Erec. Alain. Your talk of whores is an affront to my lady wife. You, Erec, will take my message to Dunhevet. Alone, you will ride fast enough to go there and back this day, if you ignore the whores. You, Alain, will remain here to learn silence and discretion."

Raimond picked up Alyse's small knife and placed it above the trencher. When Erec discovered that he must deal with cloth merchants at the markets, his face would lose that silly grin. If the lad managed to find cloth worthy of the lady Alyse, only then would Raimond reveal the purpose of the trip to his curious wife.

Dunhevet. A fortified town where accused criminals were kept, the assizes held, and the king's justice done upon the guilty. A trading place close by the castle walls, where a market day might end with the hanging, in the late afternoon, of a thief. Or a murderer.

There was no reason to believe that deBauzan's message had anything to do with the assizes. He had drawn the young knight Erec aside in the far corner of the hall and spoken to him quietly, pausing only once to look back at Alyse with a slight frown. There was no reason to believe that he suspected her of—

If she thought the word, she might speak the word. And one look at her face would rouse her husband's suspicions.

Alyse rose from the table and walked to the kitchens. She had learned, in the past two years, that idleness was her enemy. When she stopped moving, sat still and silent with her thoughts, the people of Morston worried that some great affliction had come upon their lady. So she had kept busy and put an end to the questions that might have led to rumors, and to questions from the king's deputies at Dunhevet.

The kitchen was crowded with foodstuffs and noisy with the chatter of many voices. Alyse stood at the door and saw, upon the long tables, more bread and cheese than Morston had consumed in a summer month. Beyond the main room, in the passageway to the storage huts, hung enough smoked meat to feed Morston's people through the next winter.

Maud saw her first, and approached with no trace of her earlier tartness. She followed Alyse's gaze. "You wish to count the hams, my lady?"

"I—yes," Alyse said. If she did not take charge now, she would lose her advantage. "The storage huts. Show me where you keep the smoked meat."

Maud glanced over her shoulder. "My lady, that's all there is. Lord Raimond sent the rest to Morston yesterday. Twelve hams and three bags of milled wheat." She frowned and began to count upon her fingers. "Three casks of ale, we sent. Two baskets of apples. Wine for Lord Raimond's two men at Morston—"

It was impossible to speak.

"We will replace it, my lady. There were more pigs last fall than we expected and the harvest was better than—" Maud looked past Alyse's shoulder and clasped her hands demurely before her bodice. "My lord," she murmured.

DeBauzan's hand settled carefully upon Alyse's arm. "Come, Alyse," he said. "Come ride with me."

Raimond fitted the late Constance deRançon's saddle upon Nevers' mare and helped Alyse climb upon the elegant perch of inlaid wood. The sun shone warm in the shelter of the high bailey walls as Alyse took the reins in her hands and waited for her husband to lead his tall black destrier from the stable.

"He's called Shaitan." DeBauzan smoothed a crimson cloth onto the glossy, broad back and turned to lift the high-bowed saddle into place.

"Wat told me you named him after a Saracen devil."

"I named him to frighten the liver from my rivals," deBauzan said. "And to keep small lads away from his hooves."

And from his enormous head, Alyse hoped. She tucked her arms close to her sides and hoped that the beast would not turn his muzzle towards her. "You brought him back from Palestine?"

DeBauzan's laugh was short and bitter. "I had no horse by the time I reached the ships at Acre. I had barely enough silver to buy passage home. No, Shaitan is a Norman horse from my father's lands. Gerbrai and the others brought him to me when they followed me to England."

He swung up onto Shaitan's back and pulled on his gauntlets. "You have no gloves," he muttered. "You will be cold."

Alyse smiled. "It is warm here. Even at Morston, where the sea brings the cold, I had no gloves." The grey mare followed deBauzan's black through the bailey gates. From the watchtower, the young knight Alain waved to her.

DeBauzan headed out between the flat fields towards the narrow road which led south. "My blood is thin from the years in Palestine," he said. "This is a cold land, and your Morston is the worst of it."

The image of the torchlight upon deBauzan's golden body in the cold river came to Alyse. She spoke before she thought. "Last night—"

He laughed. "A cask of wine and the prospect of bedding a beautiful woman heats the blood as nothing else."

They had reached the end of the fields. To the west lay the grey moors, and to the north the dark forest. There was no one near in the vast stretch of lands surrounding them. Only her husband, speaking of wine and lust and blood. The road was far below her, beneath the massive hooves of the mare. Alyse clutched the saddle bow and looked down at her hands, away from the open spaces.

"Alyse."

It was impossible to look up. She shut her eyes and tried to still the swirling.

"Alyse." He had moved the black beast closer and placed

his hand upon her arm. "Shall we ride towards the village, now?"

She raised her head. Her husband and the large black horse were a wall between her and the dizzy spaces beyond. "Yes," she said. "The village."

She took the reins and lifted them. Beside her, deBauzan had not moved. "This is no ambush, Alyse."

"My lord?"

"I did not bring you out here to force you to couple with me." He pointed across the heath. "Yesterday, on the moor, I was speaking in jest."

"I knew it, my lord."

His hand moved to cover her knotted fingers. "Then do not strangle the mare. She's a gentle beast, and easily frightened."

He rode beside her down the edge of the barley field. She began to remember how she had managed her mother's palfrey so long ago, in the richer times when Morston had possessed two saddle beasts and enough grain to feed them.

The village lay south of Kernstowe's fortifications, between the river and the grain fields. "The fields we passed are yours, my lord. The Kernstowe folk owe you one day in seven to work there. The crops are yours alone." Alyse pointed farther south, to a row of long, narrow plots stretching from the river to the Dunhevet road. "Those are the people's fields."

"How many families?"

Alyse shook her head. "Rolf Nevers will tell you. I know little about these folk."

Raimond turned to her in surprise. "Morston is a short four miles from here. How is it that you know so little of Kernstowe?"

"Every day spent away from my own fields meant less to eat when winter came."

Her husband muttered a short, angry oath. They rode in silence to the edge of the village and began to pick their way through the sprawl of wattle huts and cattle folds.

Raimond had little English and no knowledge of the people's strange Celtic speech. Alyse spoke to them for him, and told her husband, in the resonant accents of her mother's Poitevin French, what Kernstowe's people had answered. The lord's own fields were rich with grain, they told him, and his cattle kept well as their own, carefully marked with the late deRançon's brand. The lord's sheep, they told him, were west of the narrow fields, in summer pasture at the edge of the moor.

Raimond nodded as he heard the accounts and managed a few words of farewell to add to Alyse's speech.

"How long did you and Father Gregory spend with the shepherds at Morston?" she asked as they rode north towards the edge of Kernstowe's cultivated land.

"An hour or two. I had Father Gregory bring them to the your guardroom and gave them ale."

"I did not know."

"No, you were sulking in your chamber with Emma." He ignored a small sound of exasperation. "It would be better for you if she were here, I think."

"Yes. I have no one here."

"Only your husband, Alyse."

"I mean, no one that I knew well—before."

He laughed. "You were wrong to leave your woman Emma at Morston. I will send for her."

"No. Please do not. As I said this morning, she will stay at Morston a fortnight more."

He gave her a swift, curious glance. "Would she not wish to come here? She prefers Morston to this place?"

"She will see the wool cleaned and baled before she comes."

Raimond raised one eyebrow. "Your Emma did not seem to be a likely woman to deal with new fleeces," he said. "She had the look of a fine lady, not familiar with hard labor."

"She will manage," Alyse said.

"Then she may help me when I go back to Morston to look for the queen's property."

"Oh. Yes—she might remember hearing something of it." She placed a careful smile upon her face. "When will we return?"

"I will go there tomorrow or the next day. Hugo Gerbrai has been searching since yesterday. When the supply horses return today, there will be news."

"If he hasn't found them, will we leave tomorrow?"

"I will go to Morston. You will stay here."

The mare sidled away from deBauzan's black. Alyse gathered the reins. "I would like to come with you."

DeBauzan smoothed the mare's neck and muttered a word to calm her. "I want you to stay here, Alyse. You must be sick to death of Queen Eleanor and her box of trinkets. And I would spare you the sight of the confusion our search may cause."

She kept the smile in place and hoped that he would not see the veins in her temples throbbing with dread. With effort, she smoothed her voice into a semblance of courtesy. "You wish to open walls and pull up floors?"

"If I must, I will. I won't do so until we have looked in all possible cache places. Do not worry, Alyse. I will have the damage repaired—if it is necessary." He drew a long breath and continued. "This may be a time to consider Morston's future, Alyse. For the sake of those living there, it may be best to bring your folk to Kernstowe after the harvest. From what I have seen, there is enough good land still uncultivated for your people to farm here. It would be easier than trying to keep Morston's two small fields producing."

"Are you saying you will abandon Morston?"

"No, the church would remain, and the keep, after repairs. I am saying that there is not enough good land for farming. A few shepherds could remain, and their families could use the better field for their own."

"My lord, you promised me Morston—the care of Morston—if we wed. And now you propose to send all but a few of my people away—"

"—to richer lands near a strong keep where they could take refuge if war comes. It will be your decision, Alyse, but I ask you to tell your people what I have said. They may see the virtue in my plan, even if you do not."

"But there will be many more of them—far more than you would wish to bring here—once the men return."

"What men?" Raimond frowned. "Have some of your people taken to the woods?"

Alyse flushed. "Of course not. Morston's folk are hardworking and understand the law. The men—forty of them, my lord— were in Palestine. Soon they will return, and where will they earn their bread? Before King Richard's war, they kept sheep—

large flocks, back then—and they were clearing a third field near the—"

"Palestine? You sent shepherds to Palestine?"

"If you bellow again, my lord, those men in that field will think—"

"They may think what they will. Do you tell me, madam, that Morston's shepherds took the cross?"

"Yes."

"Your mother's husband sent them?"

"No. We—he had no choice. DeRançon sent them. They went willingly, my lord, for the bishop told them—"

He made a harsh sound. "I know what the bishop would have told them. That they would all die martyr's deaths and their sins would be forgiven. And if they lived, they would return with gold."

Alyse nodded. "They all wanted to go. DeRançon picked the strongest of them."

"And sent them with the army to keep the livestock? This is a strange tale, madam."

"Will you let me speak? They were no longer shepherds, my lord, when they left. DeRançon's sergeant had trained them as foot soldiers. Some were archers, and some learned to use a spear."

"And how long did the Kernstowe sergeant train these warrior shepherds?"

"A fortnight." Alyse saw anger rising upon her husband's face. "They had to leave after a fortnight," she added. "The sergeant went with them."

"And deRançon stayed behind, with his garrison to keep order here?"

"The soldiers left, they say, after Lord Harald went away. The maids told me last night. Are you sure," she asked anxiously, "that you did not hear of Morston's foot soldiers in the Holy Lands?"

"No." He clenched his fist upon the saddle bow. "Let us hope, Alyse, that they were stranded along the way, and never made it to Palestine. If so, there is a chance they still live."

"Or they might have been among the last to leave Palestine and even now, they may be on their way—"

"No," he said harshly. "Only the best trained infantry survived the early fighting. At Acre, and on the road to Jaffa—" He glanced at her horrified face and cut off his words. "Your lord deRançon," he said at last, "should rot in hell for sending them. He deserved to die—"

Alyse felt hot nausea rising in her throat. "What are you saying—you cannot know—" she began. She clapped her hand over her mouth to stop the words from coming.

"To send your shepherds to do a soldier's work after a fortnight's training, your Harald deRançon was a fool. A stupid, greedy, fool who sent herdsmen rather than soldiers to King Richard's army to honor his obligation to the king. Or dishonor it, as God would see it." He took her hand from her face. "Does it pain you, Alyse, to hear me speak of your lord deRançon thus?"

"You say they must have died—all of them? They did not have a chance?"

"Alyse, a knight spends his childhood learning the use of arms—"

"Yes, but the men-at-arms—"

"Men-at-arms must be trained as well. Warfare is not a simple matter, even for the strong." He hesitated and spoke again in a lighter tone. "As I said, Alyse, the Morston men may have been left behind in Sicily. The armies were there for months before they took ship. There was a large fleet, but most of the ships were small. Those shepherd lads would have been the last to win a place on those boats. They might have been left behind. They may be there still."

"Do you believe what you say, Fortebras?"

Raimond sighed. "I hope it is true." They rode on in silence near the thick forest at the edge of the barley field. Raimond turned his horse into the trees. "We will eat there, in the shade, and speak no more of these heavy things."

He tied the reins to a young hawthorn and helped her slide from the saddle to the ground. He slung a leather bag over his shoulder, and walked with her to the deep shadow of a twisted oak. They sat upon the thick roots which snaked above the mossy ground.

Raimond offered Alyse a hunk of bread and cut a piece of

cheese. "There is a place here for your Morston folk, if you want them to come. Even for your Father Anselm, if the Morston wind becomes too hard for him. Nevers tells me the chapel beside the keep has not been used since the last priest died, and the village priest speaks only Latin and the local tongue." He passed the wineskin to Alyse. "Will you speak with your Morston people after the harvest is in?"

"I will speak to them." The wine was strong and as warm as the sun upon Kernstowe's fields. Alyse shrugged her mantle from her shoulders and sat back against the trunk of the great oak. Beside her, the summer light shone through the golden fire of Raimond deBauzan's hair.

In the distance, the villeins called to each other across a half-grown field and cornered a black-fleeced ram. They chased it clear of the young barley shoots and returned to repair the damaged rows.

Beneath the sound of her own laughter, Alyse heard her husband's voice. She stopped to draw breath.

"Why your family, Alyse? Why were they chosen?"

Laughter ceased. "My lord?"

"Was it William of Morston the queen trusted with her jewels, or was it your mother the queen chose to watch over the treasure?"

"My mother had been imprisoned at Salisbury with the queen. She was Queen Eleanor's chosen companion."

"And before that? Was she at Eleanor's court in Poitiers?"

"For a time. Her mother—my grandmother—lived at the queen's court for the last years of her life."

"Your grandmother was the queen's waiting woman?"

"From her youth. She was with Queen Eleanor when they were young, and Eleanor went north to marry King Louis. Even in Palestine, she served her—"

"She was in Palestine with Eleanor? At Antioch?"

Alyse smiled. "Yes, even at Antioch. She spoke of little else, when she was old. My mother had to silence my grandmother when she began to prattle about the scandal. The queen was not pleased to be reminded of the night her first husband dragged her from the palace at Antioch and sent her home." Alyse broke off and laughed. "My mother once said that Queen

Eleanor chose her to bear the burden of hiding the jewels as revenge upon my grandmother.''

Raimond shrugged. ''Those stories were no secret. My uncles were there at Antioch, in the service of King Louis, and brought home tales of Saracen lovers and the queen's abduction by her own husband to bring her back to Christendom. They told me, when I was a lad, that King Henry showed the greatest courage of his life when he dared to wed King Louis' cast-off wife; Queen Eleanor had the reputation of a termagant, even in her youth.''

''She trusts you because of your uncles, Raimond.''

He opened his eyes and smiled up at the sky. ''No, my uncles were Louis' men, and the queen loved them not. If I believed she had sent me here because of my family, I would have feared to wed you, Alyse.'' Raimond reached for the wineskin and settled closer to his wife.

They ate the bread and cheese, and spoke of fields, shepherds and crops. Although they had sat within an arm's reach of each other, Raimond did not touch Alyse. Only when they walked back to where the horses grazed in the sunlight did he put his hands upon her to lift her into her saddle.

He did not know, and Alyse would never tell him, that they had sat only a few yards from the small spring where two summers ago Harald deRançon had pushed her to the ground to violate her.

She had not remembered the place at first. And when the afternoon shadows had lengthened and the green depths of the forest had darkened, she had recognized where they were.

At that moment, she had sat up and begun to place the remains of the bread and cheese in the pannier. Raimond had raised one golden brow and proffered the wineskin. ''Lady wife,'' he murmured, ''this is not a day for haste.''

There was something in Raimond's gaze which stopped the panic, which gave her the strength to look away from the deep woods and take the leather flask from her husband's hand and drink the dark, rich wine within.

Harald deRançon's ghost was losing its hold upon her. Even if deRançon's shade walked here at Kernstowe, it would not come for her. Not now, while Raimond deBauzan was at her side.

CHAPTER EIGHT

They rode back along the forest's edge, keeping to the shade of the ancient oaks, turning their mounts in a serpentine path among the trees. Across the fields, the stones of Kernstowe's keep shone as roughened silver in the bright sunlight.

Raimond frowned. "It is a solid place. Richer than I had expected. DeRançon prospered here."

"You knew him?"

"No, but I heard the tales. Years ago, the old lord deRançon joined his cousins to rebel against King Henry in Normandy; he was exiled here, never to return to France under pain of death. Odd that he was given a large keep such as this one." Raimond turned his gaze upon Alyse. "Did he collect heavy tolls from those who took the road south past here?"

"Not from Morston folk. But there were stories of travelers forced to pay silver."

"And the last deRançon, the young one?"

"I do not know."

"He had a taste for good wine. How did he pay for it?"

"I do not know." Alyse lowered her gaze to her hands upon the saddlebow. Saint Mary Magdalene, let him stop these questions—

The grey mare whickered and sidled away from the green

shadow of a young hawthorn. "Look to your hands," Raimond said. "You still hold the reins as if you would pull the beast backward." He reached for the bridle and leaned from his saddle to murmur a calming word to the horse. "There," he said to Alyse, "Leave the leather looser and let the mare move her head freely. It is safer for you both."

"I know that," Alyse snapped. "I will not forget again."

He released the bridle. "You must ride every day until you learn," he said. "But you must not ride alone."

"I have no wish to ride alone."

At her side, Raimond was silent. Alyse saw that his mouth curved in the half smile she had begun to recognize—half courtesy, half mockery. "The river is just ahead," he said. "We will take the horses down to the shore to drink." He narrowed his eyes against the full sunlight. "The water will be warm."

"I do not swim," Alyse said.

"But you are happy to watch those who do."

She slid from the saddle before he reached her. "The noise brought me to the shutters last night. You and your men were shouting loud enough to rouse the deaf. I but looked to see who was drowning."

He laughed and led the horses down the riverbank. "I had no interest in rousing the deaf. I would have been content simply to rouse my wife."

Yesterday, she would have turned away to hide her smile.

Today, she laughed. "No doubt you will try again, my lord, with more noise. And—and brighter torches."

For a moment, he did not move. When he turned to see her flushed face, the half-smile upon his lips had broadened into surprise and cautious joy. And the promise in his eyes was no longer subtle.

Alyse wanted that promise. She wanted to feel his touch. By sweet Saint Morwenna, she wanted this tall golden man who was her husband.

There were three days—and three nights—before midsummer's eve. Would it be all she would ever have of him—

In three days, Kernstowe's people would build the midsummer bonfire. Until that time, Alyse could accept this man as husband and sleep in his arms. For three nights, she might pretend that she was a bride beginning a lifetime of unshadowed happiness, rather than a woman who must leave her husband, perhaps forever, when the summer fires flared high.

He had moved to stand before her, to stroke her cheek with gentle fingers and speak low into her ear. "Handsomely said, my lady. But tonight, we will have only the chamber fire to light our bed. As for the noise—I can manage that, I think."

Alyse flushed hotter still as she looked into her husband's eyes.

"This night," he said, "we will begin with that fire within the chamber hearth. But one day, my lady, when you know my body as well as your own, I will bring you as many torches as you wish, and you will know how long and hot our love games may grow."

Alyse felt the heat of a thousand flames upon her cheeks, and an exquisite melting sensation within her body. If this man chose to begin their first lovemaking here, upon the riverbank in the bright light of day, Alyse would lie with him upon the grass as eagerly as any wanton. The long grass was soft and sweetly green. Already she could feel its silken blades upon her legs.

Raimond glanced up at the battlements of the keep, where a small group of men were prodding the stonework. "Why," he muttered, "did I set those folk to repair the defenses today?" With a word of regret, he dropped his hands. "I fear, Alyse, that if I touch you again, I will take you where we stand. And those men will mortar their beards to the battlements before we're done." He drew a long breath. "Still—"

"My lord," Alyse said, "the horses have wandered down the bank." Her husband smiled in regret and went down to the river.

Five sumpter horses, stepping smartly beneath their empty packs, and two mounted men were approaching Kernstowe. One of the riders followed his own erratic course behind the pack animals, balancing a red-haired, wriggling bundle before him on the saddle bows.

Alyse shaded her eyes against the low sun. "Do you see—is it Wat? He must have persuaded them to bring him. It must be Wat. There's no other child who looks so—it is Wat. Raimond, may he stay here? I'm sure he will be useful somehow."

Raimond led the horses up the grassy bank to stand beside her. "Useful? Do you think so?"

"Please, my lord—"

Raimond shrugged. "I expect him to be useful. I sent for him this morning, when you first refused to bring your woman Emma here. I hoped you would be pleased, or will you say that Wat, too, must stay at Morston to finish the shearing with your hardworking Emma? Wat could catch the beasts and Emma could freeze their rumps to the spot with that odd stare of hers."

The image of Emma at the shearing pen sent Alyse past all dignity. Tears ran from her laughter-closed eyes as she touched Raimond's smile with her fingertips. Laughter ceased when Alyse felt the smooth heat of her husband's mouth.

Raimond's smile broadened. He caught her trembling hand and brought it back to brush his lips a second time.

A distant squeal of recognition from the baggage train rang across the field. Raimond released her hand. "Here he comes—here to see that you have not been devoured by the moor goblins and to reassure you that Hugo has not yet eaten the last of the sheep. You are content?"

"Oh yes, my lord. Wat? Wat—"

"He can't hear you from here."

Neither did she hear her husband's words. Alyse had managed to climb upon Nevers' mare and urge her into a lumpish trot towards the approaching company.

From the foot of Kernstowe's earthworks, Raimond watched his wife aim her unenthusiastic mount down the road to the moors. Her dark braids fell free from their heavy coil to fly and bounce upon her slender shoulders. He could not hear the words his wife exclaimed as she reached the last rider and the boy, but the sight and distant sounds were all he had hoped they would be.

Alyse took the child before her upon the saddle and turned the mare back to where Raimond was waiting. She managed to guide the beast well, despite the urchin's efforts to balance his bundle of clothing between the horse's ears.

"Behold, Lord Fortebras, your new squire," Alyse said.

"He wriggles too much to be my squire. Shaitan would think him a small worm among the apples and eat him in one bite."

"Your horse will not eat me. The lady Alyse said so."

"Then it must be true."

"And I speak your tongue, Lord Fortebras—as well as any Frankish child at Kernstowe. Lady Alyse and I," said the child with a small dignified gesture, "practice the Frankish tongue every day."

"It is true," Raimond said, "that there are no Frankish children here who speak more skillfully than you."

"Then I will be your squire," Wat said.

Raimond had sent for Wat to keep his lady from loneliness. He had seen Alyse's subdued looks last night as the kitchen maids and the men at arms had laughed and teased in the great hall. She had seemed to know very few of the Kernstowe castle folk, even the skilled workers who should have traveled to the smaller estate when needed.

"I do not know their names," Alyse had said when Raimond had asked her the ages of the tradesmen listed in Rolf Nevers' roll. "And I don't know which is the wheelwright."

"You have no wheelwright at Morston. Did you not bring the Kernstowe workers to help you repair the wagons?"

"No," she had repeated, plainly irritated by his questions. "If a wheel needed mending, one of the men took it to Kernstowe and brought it back repaired."

"You took the wheels across the moor rather than bring in extra people to help you?"

"That is exactly what I have said."

"And after your blacksmith went missing, did you walk your animals across the moor to have a shoe replaced?"

"If we had to. We have only two oxen. We never needed the smith very often. Have you forgotten," she said, "that you have married a poor woman?"

"No," Raimond had replied. "But I had not realized I had married a lady hermit—archoress."

He had summoned his men, and out of his lady's hearing had sent a rider from Kernstowe to catch the supply train to Morston and bring back with him Wat, the young boy who had tried to follow his lady across the moor.

Raimond had expected the young orphan lad, devoted to Alyse and as curious as only a boy of seven years could be, to be the first, easy link between the people of Kernstowe and their new mistress.

By late afternoon, the boy Wat had trotted through every storehouse and hut in Kernstowe, asking questions of those he found within and causing enough confusion to bring his exasperated mistress rushing to find him. By evening, Alyse was speaking without awkwardness to all the Kernstowe people who lived within the palisade walls.

She had been nervous, though, when Erec had returned from the broad road to the south. Alyse had visibly bristled when the young knight had cantered through Kernstowe's gates and announced that the business in Dunhevet had gone quickly. "My lord," she had asked sharply, "is your business in Dunhevet to remain a secret?"

"It is an important matter," he had replied, "concerning my lady wife."

She had set her mouth in a rigid line and fallen silent. Raimond had taken the saddle pack from Erec and presented his large-eyed, silent wife with three bolts of cloth.

Alyse had seemed relieved—extraordinarily relieved—as if his gift of cloth had released her from some terrible dread, or serious worry. He was pleased, then, that he had acted quickly to provide her with clothing of her own; he had not realized how much it would mean to her.

When she had thanked him and turned her attention to the cloth, he had caught the drift of a muttered oath—some obscure comment about markets and the justiciars' court. He had begun to ask her what she meant, but Alyse had turned abruptly to summon Beda; within the hour, the women had begun to fashion clothing from the soft, deeply green wool in the first bolt.

Beda and three other women had followed Alyse up the winding stairs to her bedchamber to cut the cloth and begin to sew the first gown. Raimond had followed an hour later to find all four women in his chamber, surrounded by cuttings of wool, stitching in the waning light below the window embrasures. Young Wat was stretched upon the Saracen floor cloth, idly pulling a singed scrap of cloth through the embers in the hearth.

Raimond had asked, then, if there was no better place to sew, but had retreated when the women had met his question with mild surprise and one quickly muffled giggle.

Having retreated from the bedchamber, Raimond's next move had been to ensure that young Wat would sleep as far as possible from the upper level of the keep. Alyse seemed disposed to coddle the child; this was reasonable, within limits. And those limits stretched across the threshold of the sleeping chamber. By night, by God, his chamber was his own—his and his lady wife's.

Darkness came after an eternity of waiting. "Where did Wat sleep at Morston?" Raimond asked carefully as he took his place beside Alyse at the table and pulled a platter of cold meat before him.

"In the keep, near the kitchen hearth. Flyta, the cook, and Enid her daughter looked after him."

"We will take him to the cook, then, and see whether his wife will let Wat sleep in the kitchens tonight." Raimond drew a long breath and added cautiously, "It will seem more familiar to him for the time being."

Alyse gave her husband a look that told him she understood what he was attempting to do. "I will speak with the kitchen maids. And—I thank you, my lord, for bringing Wat here. He has no family, and I had worried that he would be too much for Flyta to manage, when I was gone."

"We will see how he finds life here. If he is unhappy, I'll take him back to Morston in two days' time."

"You are going back?"

"I cannot postpone the search."

His wife heard his words with no sign of distress, as if this morning's anger and horror at the sight of the queen's gift had never happened. She nodded her head, then drew a short breath, as if she had remembered something. "Will you not stay here until the third morning, past midsummer eve? It is the lord's place to light the great bonfire, and to taste the first ale, and to begin the dancing. The Kernstowe folk drink the lord's health as the fire grows. They would think it a good omen to see you here that night."

Raimond shrugged. Alyse was staring at him with a strange intensity in her gaze, waiting for his answer.

Rolf Nevers had said something last night, something—

Then he remembered.

"Was it midsummer's eve," Raimond asked, "when Harald deRançon left this place to begin his journey?"

His wife's face was pale, and determinedly calm. Her hands were upon her lap, hidden by the trestle top. "That is what they told me," Alyse said. "They said that Lord Harald left at midsummer, and never returned." She set her mouth in a brittle smile. "And now you have come to them in the same season. It would bring good fortune to them all if you were here to begin the revels."

Revels. Feasting and pleasure. On that night, more than any other, a maid would see no offense in a man's desire. "On midsummer's night," Raimond said, "a man might find his lady willing, his waiting done." He picked up his goblet and swirled the firelight and shadows within the dark red wine. After a moment, he raised his gaze again. "Tell the people that I will go tomorrow and return by midsummer night."

She shut her eyes briefly; the slight tension around her whitened lips vanished as her color deepened from ivory to faintest rose. She spoke softly and distinctly for his ears alone. "Stay here with me, Raimond, and midsummer will come early for us."

It was all he could do to keep from touching her, from carrying her to their chamber and asking her to make good the whispered promise in her words, the invitation in her eyes.

If she took him this night as her true husband, if she showed him the honest passion he saw now in her gaze, it could well be more than three days before their passion cooled enough for him to return to Morston.

He set the goblet upon the table and pushed it gently aside. To stay with Alyse, to tarry here until that night of summer fires when he would drink the first of the ale and throw the first torch into the bonfire, would delay the search at Morston. It would mean Queen Eleanor would wait three days longer for her treasure, or for Raimond's message of regret, whichever it was to be. And Richard, King of England and of Normandy, might languish three days longer in the Emperor's prison.

"It is only three days, my lord." In his bride's voice, Raimond heard a calm and determination he found nigh miraculous. Somehow, during their ride along Kernstowe's boundaries and back to the river, the lady Alyse had come to desire his touch. What had he said, what had he done to change her heart? "And three nights," she added.

His wife's face had turned the color of a young rose. Her eyes were still upon him. "Do you want me to stay, Alyse?" he asked

She did not hesitate. "Yes."

Was it desire alone which made his wife speak so boldly? It occurred to Raimond, in that moment of silence between them, that her intention might be to prevent his search of Morston, to delay his discovery of the jewels or of her duplicity. But she had not asked him to take her with him, nor had she tried to return alone to her former home. It was possible that her offer to him was as innocent and clear as her wide-set eyes. And he could not bear to wait.

"Then I will stay, my lady," he whispered, "until midsummer morning."

His wife looked down at her hands. "Thank you, my lord."

Raimond felt the blood pounding in his temples. His manhood throbbed beneath the heavy cloth of his chainse. Never before had he been in such great desire that he had wished to touch a woman in an unmannerly fashion in the presence of others. He spread his hands upon the table and tried to turn his thoughts from the bedchamber. The image of that room as he had last seen it, filled with chattering women and bits of cloth, was almost enough to send his desire from him. Alyse was wearing a red kirtle. The scraps of cloth covering the pallet bed had been green. "The cloth, Alyse—"

"Yes?"

"Have they—have your women finished sewing?"

"Nearly so. Maud promised a green kirtle by morning." Alyse looked up and understood what her husband was asking. "She will complete it here beside the great hearth, my lord. There, beside the fire."

Raimond saw a folded green cloth upon a bench beside the kitchen passage. The women would not need to return to his sleeping chamber. "Good," he said.

"The other cloth is very fine, Raimond. Your man, the one who fetched it from Dunhevet—"

"Erec."

"Yes, Erec. He chose very fine cloth, some of it too good to use here. It would be ruined within days if I wore it."

"Have the women use it to make you clothes for court."

"But I will not need—"

"You will. When I go to Queen Eleanor, you will come with me." He shook his head. "Do not say no, Alyse. Whether we bring her jewels or"—he lowered his voice—or bad tidings, you will come with me to receive her thanks."

"She will not thank me if we do not find her coffer."

"You have spent your life in that cold place for her sake. She must thank you, Alyse, for that. At least for that."

"The big man who cooks—"

"His name is Barden, Wat."

"Barden said he would leave me a honey tart for morning. Is it there on the table?"

They had gone to the kitchens to see Wat settled on a plump feather tick beside the hearth. Alyse had spoken to the child softly and tucked a woolen blanket around his shoulders.

"It's there, Wat. See you wait until morning to eat it, or you will have a belly ache."

"I will wait."

When she rose, Raimond took his wife's arm and drew her

to the far end of the kitchens, where the firewood was stacked beside a door open to the evening breeze.

They crossed the yard to where a deBauzan man stood atop the small platform over the gates. The barricade bar was out of place and the gates slightly ajar. Raimond made a brief sign to the sentry as he lifted a flaming torch from the iron bracket and guided Alyse through the gap into the darkness without. They made their way slowly between the cultivated field and the rough exterior of the palisade, and turned north, to walk upstream along the river's edge.

The warmth of the night caressed Alyse's face. The cold sea winds which had kept Morston's people close by their hearths each night did not reach this far inland. At Kernstowe, only the deep, swift river could chill the summer night. Raimond took her hand and started down the riverbank.

"We are not going back?"

"Not yet," he said.

"I heard you tell the sentry to bar the gate at nightfall," Alyse said.

"So he shall. And open it when we return."

"He will wait for us?"

"Yes. Do not be afraid for your modesty, Alyse. He will not see us at the river."

Alyse stumbled and felt Raimond's hand close tighter upon her arm. "I think I have a stone in my slipper," she said. He planted the torch into the soft earth and pulled her down upon the grass. His hands sought her thin leather shoe and slipped it from her foot. "There, my lady. The stone is out." She looked at him in confusion when he rose to his feet and took up the torch once again. "A little farther," he said , "there is a place where we may lie upon the riverbank."

"Where you were last night—where you bathed?" There had been torches upon the grassy bank, and her husband's large, golden body with the amber ripple of firelight upon it. She pulled back. "They will see us from the keep."

He held the torch high and drew her with him to walk along the sweet grass above the river. "We will walk upriver—where they will not see us."

Raimond left the torch burning behind them and led her into

the darkness, where an ancient willow spanned the riverbank and the shallow water which pooled beside it. He opened the thick curtain of leaves and they passed through; the green wall closed behind them; the distant torch was only a mottled glow among the delicate shadows of the willow fronds.

She had not noticed that he had carried a cloak from the kitchen. With deliberate care, Raimond spread the garment upon the soft earth within the shelter of the willow. Slowly, he loosened the belt of his scabbard and placed his broadsword beside the cloak.

"If someone should follow us here—"

"No one will follow, Alyse. There are sentries, men I trust, far up the river and to the west. We will be alone here as long as we wish to be."

"They will know what we do."

"There is no shame in what we do." He drew her close and found the laces of her kirtle front. "You have promised midsummer this night, wife. We will lie here, under this tree, if it please you."

Beyond the deep flow of the river, night birds called to their mates. At the water's edge, the wall of green tracery moved in the silent breeze, dipping into the shallow pond gilded by the distant torch fire. "It pleases me," Alyse whispered.

Beneath Raimond's broad hand, the ribbons binding the crimson kirtle were loose, but he had had not yet pulled them free. "We are far from the light, and there are none to hear us." Alyse felt the silken slide of the laces and the sudden night air upon her skin. Raimond's lips brushed past her mouth. "We will join here, lady, or we will not—as you choose. But first," he breathed, "I will learn your body, and you will know mine." He drew the kirtle softly down, past her breasts to the curve of her waist.

"I cannot see you," she whispered.

He laughed softly, and she gasped as his breath warmed the peak of her mounded flesh. She cried out softly when he lifted his mouth from her. "We will begin in darkness, this first night. You took a fright, I think, when you saw my scars yestereve."

"It was not your"—good God, he had lowered his mouth again, and had begun to move his lips upon her breast, as he had done last night—"scars." He moved away slightly, and she saw, in the mottled dimness, that he was pulling his clothing from his body.

Then he was with her once again, pulling her against the length of his hard body. Deftly, gently, he turned her against him so that his massive arousal pulsed upright between them, warming the flesh of her belly as he pushed her kirtle down past the curve of her hips.

"Not my scars? Then what frightened you?" he murmured into her mouth. He kissed her long and deep, moving against her, warming her flesh with the hot length of him. Beneath her trembling limbs, Alyse felt the earth turning beneath her, moving slowly round under the canopy of fine shadows.

Raimond's arms closed about her. "I will not harm you." She sagged against him, whether from breathlessness or desire, she did not know. "Do you not believe me?" he muttered.

"I believe you."

His mouth moved to her sensitive ear. "Then what do you have to fear?" he asked again.

"I—I think you know."

Against her cheek, she felt his lips curve into a smile. "I have never harmed a woman, Alyse. Not with my arms, nor my fists, nor with—any part of me." Raimond caught her in his arms and sank with her onto the softness of the cloak. He covered her and lay carefully upon her, warming her flesh with his long body, moving with thought to spare her the burden of his weight.

Between her legs, his rod pulsed hot and thick with desire. One slight movement, one brief push from his powerful body would lodge his manhood within her.

Alyse closed her eyes and lay motionless. He had said he would not harm her. He had never harmed a woman. He would not harm her. Not with his arms, not with his—

"There is a thing I would have you do to give me pleasure."

Alyse opened her eyes. Though she could not see his face in the darkness, she felt the warmth of his mouth upon her lips.

"I would have you breathe, wife."

"I am breathing."

"Not enough to please me." With a muttered oath in a

language Alyse did not recognize, Raimond rolled upon his side, pulling her with him to rest facing his warm chest, their legs still entwined, his manhood still warming the softness where her thighs had opened.

"Do you think I take pleasure in women half fainting from dread?" He took her hand and placed it upon the hard length of his rod. "I will tell you now, my lady, that you have only to begin weeping, or hold your breath until you swoon, and this weapon you fear will not find pleasure between your legs."

Beneath her palm, his flesh grew harder still. Alyse snatched her hand away. "If you spoke the truth, my lord, men would not violate women. Do not lie to me."

He took her hand again, and began to stroke the sensitive places between her fingers. "The release a man feels with an unwilling woman is like scratching the bites of vermin. But with a willing maid, it is like nothing else. Like finding a well of sweet water in the desert. Or finding a mount when you have been unhorsed in battle, or—" he broke off.

"And you have given up unwilling women in order to seek the kind of pleasure you get finding a stray horse?"

"Yes. Not as you said it, but—God's blood, I have told you I lack a courtier's words. By Satan's brows, I—"

He slid his hand into her hair and pulled her face against his mouth. With a delicacy which belied his angry outburst, Raimond coaxed her lips to open to him, to the skilled invasion of his tongue. His hand upon her breasts was an exquisite torment, moving in slow caresses too soft to bring her the release she sought. With a small cry, Alyse fell back upon the soft folds of the cloak, drawing her husband with her.

He moved carefully, wonderfully against her, bringing a sweet fire to her womb. His kisses upon her face were fleeting; the pressure of his loins upon the heat of her desire was firm and unyielding. His mouth moved upon her cheeks, as if savoring each detail of her features, while his body moved slowly, strongly against her throbbing mound.

Once again, she cried out in incoherent longing. As in a dream she felt her legs move apart, drawing slowly past the rough warmth of her husband's hardened thighs. When at last he moved his hand to cup her hot desire, she arched to meet him. His voice was hoarse. There was a question. "Yes," she breathed. "Yes. Please. Yes."

He came into her in one swift movement and lay heavy upon her loins. His mouth moved across her forehead, finding the cold sweat upon her face. "Do not move," he whispered. "Wait."

Her lips opened, but would not form the words she needed. She shifted beneath him, and felt him pulse within her. He shuddered, but did not move from her body. "If you cannot—if this pains you," he muttered, "I will go."

"Go where?" she managed to ask.

"Into the river."

He felt her shake and started to withdraw.

"No," she gasped, as the laughter surfaced from her oddly aching chest. "No, please—" and gasped again as he moved within her, driving them both across the soft woolen cloak upon the ground.

Then there was no place for words, only low, hoarse cries as she strained to meet his increasing need, his thrusting against her hot flesh. He was within her, deeply and completely within her.

He muttered something intelligible and brought his broad hands to lift her and roll her with him, bringing her to lie upon his heaving body an instant before he came against her womb, spilling his hot seed within her. Drawing her soft cries of pleasure into his hungry mouth.

He brought her through the willow fronds to the river and held her in his arms as the dark, swirling water and his gentle hands laved the sweat and passion from their bodies. After a time, he waded back to the shore, back to the fading light of the torch. As he walked, Alyse pressed her face against the wet roughness of his chest and began to laugh.

"If you laugh, madam, I will think you mock me." When she laughed harder, Raimond turned back into the water. "And I will drop you in the river and let you make your own way back." He laughed and let her slip lower in his arms. "Madam, you are losing your body servant."

"Stop," she gasped at last. "I would ask—"

He held her at arms' length. "Quickly then, before I drop you."

"—would you have stopped, Raimond? Would you have stopped and gone into the river if I had asked you?"

He set her on her feet in the shallows and moved his hands to the curve of her hips below her delicate waist. "I would have tried, Alyse. I would have tried." His hands moved lower to stroke her pale thighs. "But now that we have come together, now that I have lain with you, it will take something colder than the river to kill my desire." His hands moved upward to caress her damp cheeks. "Do not send me from you, Alyse. Already, I lack the strength to let you go."

CHAPTER NINE

On the second night, Raimond brought Alyse once again to the great willow at the riverbend, well north of the place where the current swept past Kernstowe's keep. At the moment when he saw their leafy shelter ahead in the moonlight, when he had stooped to plant the blazing torch in the soft mud bank well clear of the tree, he had heard the sounds. A soft drag, a hesitant rustle—they came from the north, beyond the tree.

There were watchmen to the north, where the river emerged from the dark woods, far from the outlying huts of the peasants who had chosen to live beside their fields. The sentries were loyal men of Bauzan, and knew better than to come near their lord and his wife without warning them of their approach. Nor would they leave their posts without reason.

Raimond turned back to wrench the burning brand from the earth.

Alyse laughed softly. "My lord, leave it. If it falls into the river, we will find our way back by the moonlight." She placed a timid hand upon his arm. "Do you see? The moon is already rising, near full."

He looked north, into the moon-cast shadows. His wife had not heard the sound, that slight disruption in the pattern of the night creatures' calls. Only a war-hardened knight who had spent long, wakeful hours in enemy darkness could sense the approach of a skillful man attempting to move unheard.

For a brief moment, Raimond considered calling out to the sentries, raising the alarm. But his instincts told him there was only one man in the shadows to the north, and a man alone would be more easily found by stealth. When captured, the intruder would likely prove to be one of the village folk intent on snaring small game in the forest.

Raimond raised the torch high and slid his free hand along the soft swell of the kirtle over his wife's hip. On his other side, his broadsword rode sheathed against his thigh. If they were attacked, the torch thrown into the assailant's face and the sword quickly drawn would finish the man. He turned to his wife. "Come, Alyse. I have a mind to call the sentries in early tonight."

She frowned and looked past him into the moon-dappled darkness. "Is something wrong?"

He drew her close and began to walk back to Kernstowe's rough walls. "Young Erec and Alain were both trying to catch Beda's eye this afternoon. They were ready enough to watch the river for us last night, but they will begin to quarrel if they spend another hour out there."

"Why did you wait until now to call them back?"

Raimond patted her rump and shifted the torch into his left hand. "To be honest, wife, I had a sudden thought to offer you a new bedsport. A pleasure that would be better learned upon a soft mattress than upon the hard ground. Are you willing, my lady?"

They had reached the bailey gate. Raimond struck the heavy wood with the pommel of his sword and raised the torch to signal the watchman.

His wife's eyes were warm in the dancing light; the small shadow where her brow curved was not fear, but curiosity. After two skittish days, Alyse had begun to feel safe, and Raimond did not wish to destroy that hard-won peace. Only if the sentries found evidence of an enemy at the river would Raimond tell Alyse why he had brought her back to the keep—and darken his wife's memories of their first night beneath the canopy of the willow.

"Lord Fortebras?" The guard at the gate and his fellows had guessed why Raimond deBauzan had posted the extra sentries upstream and to the west in the early night hours. The fellow was plainly curious to know why Kernstowe's lord and his wife had returned after so brief a sojourn at the river.

Raimond sent Alyse before him with a sly stroke of his hand down the curve of her hip and a whispered promise in her ear. When his wife had passed through the door of the keep, deBauzan turned back to the guard. "Blow the horn and set the torches into the signal place. And when the sentries return, tell them to search the riverbank. There was a man there, between the keep and the two men to the north."

"My lord, no one left after you. I did as you said—"

"I believe you. It may be one of the villagers, hoping to snare waterfowl. Whoever it is, bring him into the bailey yard and keep him until morning. If he is armed, summon me when they bring him in."

He stepped from the shadows and moved down the riverbank to the willow tree. In the distance, a single torch moved back to Kernstowe, back to the safe walls.

He had come too late. The Mirbeau bitch was safe, for now, surrounded by her husband's garrison within the great keep. She would sleep beside her warrior husband, who cared not that he had married a bawd—an unclean she-animal who had mated with another.

A man of honor should have killed the lady when he had first discovered she was a whore. Such a man as had let her live would kill her, eventually, when he tired of her bed. It was bound to happen before harvest time.

When he returned, he would discover what the common folk knew of their new lord's disposition towards his lady whore— how close the hard-faced knight had come to tiring of the woman. If the new lord let his wife live, but ceased to watch over her, it would be possible to find her alone.

She would not live long after his return.

He had learned of the marriage yesterday when he had reached Dunhevet. It had been hard to hide his anger, but he had dared not strike the cloth merchant's lad so near the marketplace. It would have caused talk.

He had turned north, afraid that the tall knight and the Mirbeau woman might have moved beyond his reach. But that dark-headed whore and her lust-struck lord seemed in no haste to leave Kernstowe. The trull had not told her husband, then, the thing which would have sent the new lord pounding to Windsor on that black devil horse.

No, he had not expected the woman to tell her husband that he had married a murderess. If, one morning, that lust-crazed knight found his woman strangled by the river, he would never, by cunning or by sword, discover why she had died. By then, there would be no living soul who could imagine the true purpose of her death.

The sudden call of the sentry horn and the flaring blaze of light upon the watchman's tower roused the distant sentries into noisy speculation.

He hurried his steps to reach the oak grove, and passed into the deeper darkness.

Alyse found the Bauzan knights still at the great table. Wat was with them, hovering near the youngest two who were playing a game of draughts. Engrossed in the game, the lad did not notice when she passed the table. Alyse spoke with the serving maids and retreated to the bottom stair. Behind her, she heard the two players answer Wat's rapid questions as they moved the pieces.

The watchman's horn blew twice. The two young knights pushed their game aside and walked to the door of the keep. Beside her, Alyse watched Wat toy with the draughts; he yawned and climbed into her lap.

A moment later, Raimond was beside her. "The kitchen lads will bring water to our chamber."

"At this hour? What will they think?"

"They may think we want to bathe." Raimond absently stroked his chin. "And what shall we do, wife, while we wait for them?"

"My lord, I do not think—"

He laughed deeply. "Nor do I. Cry peace, Alyse—I would not shock the serving folk. Let us stay here at table while they work."

The two young knights sauntered back to their game. The one called Erec, who had traveled to Dunhevet for her cloth, was smiling as he watched the kitchen lads sidle through the door with water buckets. "Did they know, my lord, when you took these lands, that you would drain the wells with your bathing?"

"If we have a drought, Erec, I will leave you here in charge. For, by St. Magnus' great toenail, the wells would be in no danger from you."

Another voice spoke from the gaming board. "Get you to Palestine, Erec, if you would find a craving for sweet water and bathing. Your lord had a bellyful of dust and precious little water to wash it away in the Holy Lands."

Alyse took her place beside Wat and stroked the boy's bright copper hair. "Is it true," she asked her husband, "that in Palestine there are no trees, and no rain?"

"There are trees, small ones, which smell of spices in the heat. There is rain, too, but not as here. When it comes, it floods the earth for a time. Then there is no more for months."

"But near the sea, is it not the same as here?"

"It is a different sea, Alyse. Warm as a queen's bath should be, and more blue than the sky. And clear. You could see an anchor two fathoms below your ship."

Alyse looked up in surprise. "Two fathoms?"

"Or more, when the water was calm. It is true, Alyse."

"And the Saracen devils, how did they look?"

"Much the same as Frankish knights. Dark faces. Different armor, different swords."

Wat looked up. "Father Anselm said that their teeth are pointed and their eyes glow red in battle."

"They are men, Wat. Their eyes are as ours, and in battle"— he rose to his feet and crossed to the hearth—"In battle, they were no more red than we were. But their blood—" he kicked the end of a log back into the blaze. "Their blood," he muttered, "is red. As red as ours."

Wat looked up in alarm. "Lady Alyse? Why is the lord angry?"

"Hush, Wat. He is not angry."

Raimond turned to face them. "I am not angry, boy."

The kitchen lads, empty buckets in hand, had come down the bottom of the stairs, and stopped to stare at Lord Raimond. Alyse set Wat from her lap. "Go to bed, now." She slipped from the bench and walked to her husband's side. "My lord, the water is ready. Shall we go to our chamber?"

He moved his fist from the hooded hearth and nodded.

Raimond barred the bedchamber door and muttered a low oath. His wife was skittish again. God's bones, would she enter their bedchamber like a martyr to the sword each time he frowned? If so, she had best learn not to speak of the Holy Lands. The hellish lands. The killing lands.

"Wat did not mean to anger you, my lord."

"He did not."

She had begun her damned trembling again. "Then I did."

He should tell her. Tell her and hope that she would never speak of it again.

The Saracen floor cloth had been carefully folded back from the hearth, and the wooden tub half-filled before it. An iron pot rested upon the lower flames at the front of the fire. "Get in the bath, Alyse, and I will tell you."

She was still shy of him, trying to keep her body from the full firelight. He smiled faintly. "Do it quickly. I will manage not to take you first."

He shrugged out of his tunic and took the time to fold it and place it upon the settle as Alyse stepped into the oaken tub. The slight splash as her sweet body entered the water was the most erotic sound Raimond had ever heard.

She was sitting with her slender knees drawn up beneath her chin. A small linen bag of herbs floated beside her.

He closed his hand about the herbs and smelled their sharp fragrance.

"You are not angry," she prompted.

"No." He placed the bag upon her knees and retreated to

the settle. If he was to speak of anything beyond his bawdy thoughts, he would have to keep his distance. "It does not please me to remember Palestine, Alyse. I spent three long years and much blood in that place. Now I would forget."

She drew the herbs below the surface of the water. "The young knight—Erec—told Wat that you won much honor in Palestine. That King Richard declared your bravery and loyalty were without equal."

Alyse lifted the fragrant cloth to the valley between her breasts. Raimond closed his eyes against the temptation before him. "Erec was ever wont to see giants where others see ordinary men."

"He said you saved King Richard's life last year."

He drew a long breath.

"Fortebras?"

"It would please me, wife, if you would call me Raimond. Or husband. Or my lord, if all else fails. Fortebras is the name I heard upon battlefields. No other—for years."

She nodded. And waited.

He gestured to the puckered scar upon his shoulder. "I took a dagger here. A dagger intended for King Richard, at Acre."

"In the fighting?"

"No, after the city was taken."

Alyse gasped. "Who dared to do that?"

"A cutthroat came out of the dark one night as I walked with King Richard and a guard upon the battlements. The assassin escaped; Richard's men searched but never found him. It could have been any of the people of Acre, they said. Any one of the thousand—"

There was brandywine beside the hearth, and two goblets. She shook her head when he brought the first cup to her. He shrugged and returned to the settle. "I was sorely wounded, to the bone, and in a fever for days. They told me later—"

"What did they say?"

"They told me later that King Richard's temper had grown worse as the days had passed and the assassin was not found. He decided to quit Acre, but the prisoners—" he opened his eyes and looked into his wife's wide gaze. "There were prisoners. Warriors—many hundreds of them. And their wives and

children. Richard would not free them, and Saladin was slow
to bring ransom. After the night the assassin struck, the king was
mad to leave Acre. And he did—before the ransom arrived.''

"And the prisoners?"

Tell her. Tell her quickly and she will know not to speak of it
again. He closed his fists before his face. "Cut down. Beheaded.
Every one of them. Hostages—the men, and their women and
their children. It took three days to do it. I heard the—the
sound of it, but thought it a delusion of fever. It was when the
army moved and they carried me from Acre on a litter that I
saw it. Saw them. So many of them.'' He shut his eyes briefly.
"Their bodies covered the earth."

She was absolutely still. "King Richard ordered them
killed?"

"It was his right. The ransom money was late and the army
was ready to march to Jaffa." He gave a curt, harsh laugh.
"Queen Eleanor frets that King Richard will suffer if the ransom
money for the emperor is not ready by harvest time. I have
wondered," he said, "if she fears for him because of Acre. Or
if King Richard thinks of Saladin's late ransom money now,
as he waits in his prison.'' He drank deeply of the brandywine.
"Like as not, they do not think of it at all. King Richard does
not waste his time with guilt. If he did, he would be haunted
like the rest of us."

"Raimond, surely you do not blame yourself. You were not
there—"

"I was not there," he said. "I did not spill their blood." he
said. "But on the road to Jaffa, I began to think that I had
some part in it. I had saved the king's life but failed to kill his
attacker. King Richard could not find him, and his anger against
the people of Acre grew. And I was not there to speak against
his vengeance."

"You were not responsible—"

"There were some of us who could speak sense to him,
when the killing rages came upon him. They were all dead, by
then, except for me. Better I had died before Acre."

"How can you say that? You lived to reach Acre and you
were there to save the king's life. To regret it is—'' her voice
died.

"Is treason," Raimond finished. "I will say this once, Alyse, and will not speak of it again. For this is treason in thought, if not deed. If I had seen the future, I would not have stopped the dagger."

"King Richard is the greatest of all Christian lords—"

"Richard Plantagenet is the greatest of all Christian warriors. A hero. But as a king—as a lord, he fails his vassals—bleeds them dry and turns from them to wage war for Rome." Raimond picked up his tunic and folded it as he spoke. "Even John, young weasel that he is, would have been a better duke for Normandy. And a better king for this starving country."

"You would have Count John take his brother's place?"

"I said, wife, that I would not speak of the matter again. Do you hold my life—and your own—of such small value that you would twist my words into plain treason for all to hear? God's blood, woman, I was a fool to tell you my thoughts."

Alyse shrank back, sending a shallow wave in motion before her white shoulders. "I need not tell your words to others," she said. "Anyone who cares to hear your thoughts need only to sit in the hall and listen to you bellow."

His wife's words were brave, but her eyes had widened in dread. Her white breasts were as still as—

He knelt beside her and took the wet herbs from her hand. "You are doing it again. Does it not make you ill when you refuse to breathe?"

"I am breathing."

"Do it plainly, then, so that I may see." He lowered his voice. "I have had enough of war and bloodshed and Plantagenet lords. I will have peace, now, and raise my sword only to defend my lands. There will be no more treachery, no more daggers in the night. No murder."

The water had gone cold. His wife shuddered and drew herself against the oaken barrel staves.

Raimond touched her cheek. "Alyse, you must not fear me. It was the vision of Acre that came upon me, and brought those foolish words that could lose us all we have. You will help me forget, wife. You, and these lands." He moved his hand down her slender throat and below, where the chill water lapped her fair breasts. She was still beneath his palm.

He covered her cold mouth with his own and brought color to her face. Her breast moved, then, within his hand. "We will not speak of it again," he said. "It is not a fit tale for the innocent."

She whispered against his neck.

"Tell me," he said.

"I am not innocent," she said.

He brought his hand back to her face, and touched her mouth. "You are innocent, Alyse, of the sins which blight lives."

She shook her head. The drops which fell upon his fingers were warm. She was weeping.

"Damnation." He brushed the tears from her face. "Do you weep for the maiden's blood you spilled before we wed? I swore to you, Alyse, that I would never shame you for it. God's bones—after what I have seen—after what I have told you—your sin is as nothing. Beside the spilling of lifeblood, beside treachery, it is nothing. You are innocent, wife, in my eyes. And in God's."

Alyse had wrapped herself in a linen cloth and taken the brandywine he had brought to her. Seated upon the settle, near the warmth of the hearth, she watched her husband pour the kettle of hot water into the chilled bathwater and strip the chausses from his body to take his turn in the tub.

She drank from the cup and watched her husband lower his large frame into the steaming water. She welcomed the lust that began to curl within her body. Lust would take her mind from the past. From fear of the future.

She had nearly told him, just now. She would have told him, had he not declared himself Count John's man. What would he do, if he discovered she had killed a man loyal to John Plantagenet? How long would it take Raimond to guess that her tears this night had been for more than her lost maidenhead? How long would it be before he guessed—

It did not matter. This was the last night. One last night before midsummer.

And later? After tomorrow, would there be more nights with

this man? Would he ask her—would he permit her to return, after—

"Drink again, Alyse. Drink it all. I want no long faces in our bedchamber, wife."

She lifted the goblet once again, but did not drink. She must not cloud her mind this night. She had already come close, too close, to telling her deadly secret to this man.

"Can you not smile, Alyse? We have done with the past— or nearly so. In a few days' time I will return to Morston to look for the old queen's coffer. Then, whether I find it or not, within a fortnight we will go to Windsor."

"No, I—"

"Yes. We have spoken of it before, Alyse. We will go to Windsor together, that you may see the dowager queen. Your mother served her faithfully, and the queen will thank you for it." He looked at her through half-closed eyes. "You are so damned skittish, wife. I am offering you a chance to see your mother's lady, the queen, and you are frowning and chattering your teeth. You will find much to amuse you at Windsor, once you are there. All women want to see Queen Eleanor's court."

"I do not."

"Your mother lived at court for years, did she not? And your woman—the mule-faced nurse—dresses as if she still serves the old queen. That woman—what is her name?"

"Emma."

"I will bring her back with me from Morston. She will travel with us, tell you what you need to know. From the looks of her, she never forgot how she lived at Eleanor's court. She will put your fears from you."

He rose from the water and moved to the fire. He stretched powerful, golden arms to the flames and brushed the droplets of water from them.

"Have the women begin to make clothing for you, from the bolts you thought too fine for Kernstowe. By the time I return from Morston, you must be ready to leave."

He turned, then, to face her—a tall, powerful shadow before the flames, the moisture steaming from his body in a radiating amber glow. Alyse clutched the linen cloth to her breasts as her husband moved towards her. The firelight moved upon his body—no longer a smoking shadow, but a man of massive frame, sinews, scars, and soft, gilded pelt. And manhood, already swollen in desire.

He knelt before her and took the cup from her hand. And from her other hand, he took the bunched cloth shielding her body from his own.

"Roses," he said. "You smell of roses."

"I smell of the herbs."

He pushed the linen down to her lap and slid his palms up to the softness under her breasts. "Do not gainsay your husband, my lady. You smell of roses." He brushed her lips with his mouth. "And you taste of roses." His lips moved lower, to the blushing flesh cradled within his hands. "Roses, my lady. Blooming as I taste them."

She passed her hands above his head, and cradled him to her yearning breasts. "You said—"

He stopped. "What is it, Alyse?"

"You said you had no words to please a woman."

His soft laughter was hot upon her. "I do not speak in poet's words, wife. I speak what I see. What I taste."

His hair was damp between her fingers, thick and amber-dark from the water, moving slowly from side to side as he tenderly worried her pleasure-teased flesh. She realized, after a moment, that the hoarse breathing she heard was her own. And that she clutched his head to her breast with hands made numb with trembling.

His hands closed upon the rumpled cloth upon her thighs. Her arms dropped to cover them, seeking to keep the linen in place.

"No," he whispered. His blue gaze was upon her face, demanding what his words had not yet claimed. "Let me do this." He lifted her hands to his mouth, kissing each swiftly before placing her fingers upon his shoulders. "For there is another rose, my lady."

Then his hands were upon her thighs, smoothing them apart as he lowered his mouth once again to breathe warmth upon their trembling. "Open to me," he whispered. "Bloom for me, Alyse."

And she did, at his first hot touch, in a flowering of pleasure between her violently shivering limbs.

He held her until she had done, then drew her down upon him, slowly filling her with hot manhood as she brought her face to rest against the hard-straining muscles of his chest.

He pulsed within her, bringing her once again towards completion. She rocked against him, and felt a new bloom of sweetness as she took him deeper within her. "Slowly, my lady. Go slowly, or you will do yourself harm." He held her still against him. "We have this night, and many others. There is time to go slowly, Alyse."

He had begun to sweat as he held her quiet against him, waiting for her body to relax around his hard desire. This time, he would not know that she wept. She pressed her face against the damp thickness of his golden hair, and cried in sorrow for what she must do after the dawn.

And mourned the passing of this night which would be their last together.

"Is it near your woman's time?" he asked.

Alyse drew the damp cloth from between her legs and flushed deeply. She dropped it into the cold bathwater and pulled her chamber robe around her. "Why?" she said in irritation. "Must I tell you when to expect it, and each time it begins?"

Raimond raised himself upon one elbow and looked across the rumpled linen coverlet and the clothing scattered from the pallet clear to the bathing tub. "It would help," he said. "Are you near your time?"

"No," Alyse said. There was a catch in her voice, and the corners of her eyes were flushed pink, as if she had been crying.

Raimond was sure she had been. In the midst of their passion, when he had tried, with the last of his self-control, to gentle his wife's own movements to be sure she would not be harmed by their lovemaking, she had been weeping against his chest.

They had reached completion as they had begun, with Alyse upon Raimond's wide-spread thighs, Raimond's back against the heavy wooden settle with his wife's slender body drawn against his chest. With his manhood still pulsing inside her,

Raimond had carried his lady to the bed and lowered her gently to rest on her side. She had slept briefly, her limbs still entwined with Raimond's own, while her husband watched her sleeping face and brushed the drying salt tears from her face.

In the past two nights, he had seen her look at him with an innocent wonder which told him that Alyse was discovering, for the first time, the joys of passion. Her first lover had not given her joy; Raimond would wager his lands on that. And he had enough pride in his skill at love games to believe his wife did not think upon her first lover when they coupled. Why, then, was she weeping this night? She had insisted their long lovemaking had not harmed her; from his experience and her own words, he had believed her.

It must be her woman's time that had set her to weeping.

His brother Ivo had told him about these strange moods of women four years ago, before Raimond had left for Palestine. After five months of marriage, Ivo had begun to spend time in the hall of a night, sometimes three or four nights together, drinking strong brandywine and avoiding his bedchamber until his drinking companions were long asleep. He had told Raimond, one night, that he had learned a thing about women that the two brothers, in all their years of happy swiving with the village girls, had never known. Having tempted his younger brother to wager a new tunic against a gold coin that there was, indeed, something Raimond Fortebras did not know about women's ways, Ivo had proceeded to tell of his young wife's tearful rages if Ivo said aught to anger her near her woman's time.

"Have you not heard her?" Ivo had asked. "One day she rages, the next she weeps. It matters not what I say to calm her," Ivo said, "for any word from me makes her angrier still. But when her woman's time is passed," he added, "she is once again the sweet lady I wed."

"You have lost the wager." Raimond had said. "This is your wife's own oddness, not the way of all women."

Ivo had sighed. "Our father told me I would have found the same with any village girl, had I taken her to live with me.

When our lemans feel thus, he said, they do not let us come
to them, so we never know. With a wife in your bed each night,
you learn such things.''

Raimond had frowned into his cup, trying to remember the
last time the widow Herlissa had turned him away. ''You are
serious? Father said it is true?''

''I swear it, Raimond.''

Raimond had shrugged, and pulled his tunic over his head.
''You have won,'' he said as he handed the garment to Ivo.
''But I hope I never find the truth of it for myself.''

Alyse had wakened. Her husband was looking upon her face
with a crooked smile, muttering something about wagers.

''Who is Ivo?'' she asked.

His smile deepened. ''My brother,'' he said. ''My wise
brother Ivo.''

Within her woman's passage, there began a throbbing which
was not her own. They were still entwined in intimacy, as if
their lovemaking had not yet ended. And the pulsing heat of
their joining was no longer her husband's alone. She shifted
her hips to allow him to come over her.

Raimond's large, warm hand stopped her before she turned,
and drew her leg back over his body. They lay facing each
other, upon their sides, as his manhood grew greater and the
pulsing grew into a gentle motion resonating through their
bodies.

Every slow, skillful motion of her husband's long body drew
her closer to the flowering of passion. She strained against him,
and cried words of supplication against the hard strength of his
sheltering arm.

''Not yet,'' he whispered. ''Sweetly, Alyse. Go slowly, and
we could do this until dawn.''

''Now,'' she cried, pushing away the hand which kept her
from moving against him. ''I cannot wait.''

''You can. A little longer—'' His words ended abruptly
as she sank her teeth into his arm and lunged against him,

demanding with her body what her incoherent cries had asked.

He gasped and turned her beneath him, coming down upon her in one great thrust which sent them past the threshold into a crimson frenzy of joy.

CHAPTER TEN

Alyse awakened before dawn in the shelter of her husband's arms. She had been dreaming of the moor, and of a wind so strong it had kept her from Morston, sweeping her back to the safety of her bedchamber in the keep. A wind so fierce that she had no choice, no thought but to return to her husband's side, leaving her burdens behind her, upon the road to the sea.

For one radiant moment after she opened her eyes, Alyse still dreamed, and believed she would never need to return to the place where she had killed deRançon. But the sound outside the embrasures was the swiftly flowing river, not the wind; Alyse knew, in the stillness of the bedchamber, that her dream had ended.

Fortebras—Raimond, she must call him in their bedchamber—stirred and stretched his long body against her. Even in slumber, he held her carefully, circling her tenderly with those powerful arms made hard with the use of war axe and sword.

She would remember him this way, sleeping with a small smile of satisfaction upon his face, after a night in which he had taken pleasure in giving her joy. Gently, she touched the golden pelt upon his chest, where it curled beside the darkness of her tousled hair.

His hand closed upon hers. "I have a wanton wife. Wanton

to the point of heedlessness.'' He brought her fingers to his mouth and kissed them. ''Sleep, Alyse. If you rouse me now, neither of us will be able to walk this day.''

A moment later, he turned to look at her. ''Speak to me, my lady. Are you well?''

''I am well.''

''You do not sound well.'' He sat up and frowned at her. ''Are you hurt? I should have stopped before the last—''

She pressed her fingers back against his lips. ''No, Raimond. I am well. I was dreaming, and woke from it too soon.''

He lowered his head again. ''Dreaming? Of what?''

''The wind. Will there be a storm today?''

He rolled his head toward the embrasures and listened. ''It is still as a midsummer morning should be, Alyse. There is no storm.'' She felt his breathing slow and deepen beneath her cheek.

No storm, no wind to keep her from this day's deceit.

She lay quiet, with open eyes, until dawn. Thinking of the moor.

There was no work done at Kernstowe that day, save the gathering of wood for the bonfires. Here, with many hands to do the work, the shearing had been finished in the week past, before Raimond had come to claim his land. This midsummer day, shepherds brought their newly lightened flocks back to the meadows south of the keep and joined the farmer folk in building the bonfire. They dragged broken axles, rotten timbers, and kindling from the pile within the bailey yard and loaded it in a sturdy wagon to pull it to the western edge of Kernstowe's cultivated land, where the fields ended and the dark moors began.

The bonfire was to be larger this year, in honor of the new lord. Kernstowe men took a second wagon north to bring fallen deadwood from the forest, down the sloping fields to where the high, conical mass of wood rose beside the heath. Then the kitchen maids claimed the cart to haul a large wooden tub, larger still than the lord's bathing barrel, to rest apart from the firewood, to hold the freshly brewed ale.

In late afternoon, when the wooden tower had risen high above their heads, they feasted. Lord, lady and common folk sat at trestle tables set at the end of the barley field, overlooking the closely stacked firewood. Raimond and his men had been well content to join in the building of it; they had stripped the tunics from their sweating bodies and wedged the heaviest logs to support the tall mass of straw and wood.

When night fell, the people secretly wagered among themselves to predict how long their lusty new lord would wait before taking the lady Alyse back to the keep to bed. For Lord Fortebras would surely not take his wife into the pale green fields or into the dark woods to plow her this night, as a common man and wife would do, as many unwed maids and their lovers would do.

He made a fine sight, their new lord, as he raised a great burning brand above his head and heaved it high atop the dry wood to give life to the midsummer bonfire. The drums and whistles began to sound, and the people of Kernstowe moved to surround the flames.

The lord's men had joined in the circles to dance as the summer fire blazed brighter. Lord Fortebras watched for a time, and called for the cart to bring more ale.

Wat was too young to stay for the dancing and the revels after the fire was lit. The lady Alyse had told him so, but promised that he would have a special task, a squire's task, after the bonfire began to burn.

She found him soon after the dancing began, and waited with him at the edge of the firelight as the ale wagon rumbled from the darkness to stop beside the tables.

"Lord Fortebras is there, Wat, beside the dancers. Do you see him? Go to him now, and give him this cup to drink. Tell him that I have gone back to the keep. That I wait for him in the keep. Can you remember that?"

"But you aren't at the keep, you're here."

"I will be, Wat. Go and tell him."

"Why don't you tell him, Lady Alyse?"

"It is a game, Wat. A midsummer jest. Walk back to the

keep with Lord Fortebras, and go to the kitchen and stay there. Can I trust you to do this, Wat?"

"Of course. This is not difficult."

"Then tell me what you will do."

Wat had sighed and repeated her orders. "I will take this ale to my lord and tell my lord that you have gone to the keep to wait for him. And that he must take me with him to the keep—to the kitchen. And I am to go to bed." Wat reached for the ale.

"Be careful, Wat. Do not spill it."

"I know."

"And do not drink from it. It is not for you."

"I know."

"Go, then. Wat—"

"Lady Alyse—you are making me spill the lord Raimond's cup."

Alyse released Wat from her hasty embrace and wiped her eyes. "Go then, Wat. And be a good lad."

It was the worst of her plan, involving young Wat. But she had no choice. Anyone older would wonder at her orders and ask why she did not wait for her husband.

Raimond would be impatient to find her missing, and angry when he did not find her in the keep. He would question the child, but he would not harm young Wat. He was a fair man, and would not turn his temper against the boy.

Her belly twisted in fear. Raimond would not be harsh with the child, nor would he punish the driver from whom she would cozen the horse and cart when the ale had been unloaded. He would blame neither of them. His anger would be for his wife.

Alyse turned back to the wagon. Three unsteady figures were sliding a deep, open barrel from the cart; too many willing hands at the task sent a quantity of ale rippling over the rim of the vat to fall upon the firelit earth.

She waited until they had leveled their burden and moved away from the wagon. Raimond was beside the bonfire, a tall black figure backlighted by the flames. Alyse allowed herself one last look at the man who had given her his name and had shown her, in three nights at her side, that his warrior's ways and blunt manner were but the outer shell of a fiercely tender soul.

Her eyes began to sting as she turned from the firelight. When next she met Raimond deBauzan, there would be nothing but contempt for her in his face. Of all the grief this night would bring her, the loss of her husband's trust would send the sharpest pain.

Raimond had begun to look for his wife among the circling dancers. She had left his side to see to the ale wagon, promising to bring back a tankard before the thirsty revelers began to empty the tub. When next he looked, he could not see her.

Little Wat from Morston had found him then. The boy had pressed the cup into his hand and repeated his lady's coy message. Raimond guessed that there was more to Alyse's promise than the simple words the lad recited. More, he hoped, than the young urchin could understand.

He drank of the ale and dashed the rest into the darkness.

"You did not like it, my lord?"

"I have drunk enough this night."

"It wasn't as good as the first barrel."

Raimond laughed. "You were tasting every batch? And what did the lady Alyse say about that?"

"She said the last one wasn't for me."

"I imagine she did," he agreed.

Wat had finished by repeating the most immediate part of the message—that the Lord Fortebras was to bring him back to the keep and safely to the kitchens. They had left, then, to stroll down the narrow track between the barley field and the meadows, toward the empty tower.

Wat had been unwilling to hasten their walk, as he obviously relished having his lord's company. He asked how long he must wait to begin to train as his lord's squire. And he won Raimond's distracted promise that his duties would begin when they left upon their journey to Windsor to see the old queen. Wat had a strong wish to see the fabled Queen Eleanor. She would be dressed, Wat claimed, in a robe of silk sewn with two hundred precious jewels, and she would be as old as the stones on the tor above Morston.

Raimond had humored the child, and slowed his steps to allow Wat time to ramble on. Halfway to the keep, he saw that the upper chambers showed no light. It was deserted, as it must be once each year, when the bonfires drew the Kernstowe folk out to the night's revels.

Only the sentry's torch was visible.

Raimond quickened his pace. The bedchamber was at the far side of the keep, overlooking the river to the east. He would see the firelight soon, when he drew nearer.

Wat's speech had slowed and moved erratically from one thing to another, and the lad's steps were uneven to match his speech. Raimond lifted the boy to his shoulders and quickened his pace.

The chamber was empty, the hearth cold. Raimond lay down upon the broad pallet and waited. Had Alyse planned some game, some mischief in the echoing keep? In their three nights of lovemaking, there had been brief moments when she had become playful. It would please him well if she had come far enough to permit more extravagant love games. Or better still, to initiate them herself.

His body tensed pleasurably at the thought. How long would she tarry, his half-shy, half-daring young wife? He lay quietly, waiting for her to surprise him in the summer darkness.

But she did not come, and the keep remained as silent as it should be on a midsummer night. She should come soon. By now, she must be ready.

If she was preparing for a night of lovemaking, was she bathing? And with the kitchen maids gone, she would have no one to help her draw the water. Had she gone down to the river?

The river. Raimond lunged to his feet and pulled on his boots, cursing the time he had waited. Remembering the sounds he had heard in the night past, near the willow. Cursing himself for not telling his wife why he had brought her so suddenly back to the bedchamber last night, leaving their trysting place unvisited.

He did not stop to bring his men from the distant bonfire. With his naked sword in one hand and a torch in the other, Fortebras bolted past the sentry's frightened questions and ran to the river, calling her name.

She did not answer.

He searched the riverbank, but found no sign of his wife, no kirtle discarded on the grass. And then, his torch held above his head and his heart sickened within him, he walked in the shallows, splashing through the black water, hoping that he would not find what he most feared.

I do not swim, she had said. And she had not dared go into the river, save at his side. In his arms.

His men came, summoned by the terrified sentry. They searched as well, their voices quiet and grim as the ale left their heads and they saw that the lady Alyse was not to be found.

Raimond left two of them at the river and took the rest back to the keep, where they burst into the kitchen to find Wat asleep upon his pallet, surrounded by crumbs of honey cake.

At the sight of nine armed men, hard-faced, dripping river water and mud upon cook's fresh-scoured floor, the child had begun to cry. "I took two, my lord. Only two cakes. The lady Alyse said they were for me."

Raimond turned to the others. "Search the keep," he said. "and the storehouses and the cellars."

And when they had gone, Raimond knelt beside the large-eyed child. "I cannot find the lady Alyse," he said carefully. "You must help me find her. Did you tell me all she asked you to say?"

Wat nodded once.

"Tell it again, then. What did the lady Alyse tell you to say to me?"

"That she was waiting for you in the keep. It was a game, my lord. It is permitted to lie when you are jesting."

"Did the lady Alyse say she lied?"

The child nodded faster. "It was a jest. She was there, behind the horse when I told you."

''What horse?''

''The cart horse. She told the cook's son who drove it that he could join the dancing. She sent him away, then, to dance with the others. She told him she was tired, and wanted to go back in the cart.''

''She took the cart?''

''No, my lord. She was hiding behind it. It was a hiding game, she said.'' The boy looked up and began to weep. ''It was a jest, my lord. I did not lie. I did not mean to lie.''

Fortebras drew a long breath and set his teeth into the flesh behind his lip. ''You did not lie, Wat. You did as your lady asked. It was a jest.''

''You are not angry?''

''No. Go to sleep, Wat. You have done nothing wrong. It is the lady Alyse who is—jesting—with me. It is a game, between us. Nothing but a game.''

Erec had returned, breathing hard. ''My lord, she is not within the keep. Shall I go back to the river?''

Fortebras rose and turned his face from the boy. ''No,'' he said. ''Call the men back. We will ride west to find her.''

''I'll tell them.''

''And warn them to arm themselves.''

Erec paused at the bailey yard door. ''They have their swords with them now, my lord.''

''Tell them to arm themselves well.''

The young knight turned back incredulously. ''Has your lady wife been taken, my lord?''

With difficulty, Fortebras kept his voice low. ''Tell them what I have said.'' And he turned back to the dark hall. To find his war axe.

With the pack animals, it had taken three hours to cross the moors. With one large plow horse and an empty cart, the journey should have been half as long.

Alyse had waited until she had seen her husband walk out of the firelight with Wat, slowing his long stride to accompany the boy back to the keep.

She had turned, then, to lead the cart horse west. To the

moor, away from Kernstowe, beyond the firelight. It was as if she had stepped off the steep side of the tor at nightfall, into the darkness, beyond all that was familiar. Destroying, with each unsteady step, her lord husband's trust.

She had not dared return to Kernstowe's stable to find Nevers' grey mare. Fortebras had placed four sentries on watch this night, and they would have seen her take the beast through the gates.

A short distance along the track, she had taken the halter reins and climbed into the two-wheeled cart. The horse had tried to turn back, had stopped and refused to continue west. She had climbed down again and begun to lead the beast, moving along the jagged track from cairn to cairn, finding the white stones as they shone dimly in the rising moonlight.

She knew that she should let the stubborn carthorse go, for she would travel faster without the skittish animal, but there was a chance that the beast would become docile once they had traveled far enough from the stables at Kernstowe, and continue west while she rode in the cart. And, she admitted to herself, she was reluctant to leave behind a warm-blooded companion, however much trouble the beast might cause.

Alyse was afraid of the moor, and always had been. There were creatures upon it, cold, long-dead beings who would not allow mortals to witness their swift passage over the moorlands. They rode their red-eyed mounts behind black hounds, moving over the ground a man's height above the earth, soaring high and fast over the moonlit stones. Looking for mortal prey.

The shepherds called them the Wild Hunt, and took care to keep to their huts and campfires when they heard the host of the damned coming near. If you did not look upon them, the shepherds said, you might survive their passing.

Alyse had begun to dream of them, after the night she had done murder. DeRançon had been with them, looking upon her with his wide, dead eyes. Calling to her that she, too, was damned and fated to pass eternity upon the cold, barren lands with the savage rush of hunters, steeds and hounds.

The first time it had happened, she had awakened in terror. It had taken all her courage to walk to the arrow-slit overlooking the new granary, where deRançon lay under the earthen floor.

What had she expected? To find the door flung open and the blue ghost-fires within? Emma had heard her and bidden her back to bed, had reminded her that all would be lost if Alyse appeared, to even the simplest folk at Morston, to be haunted by that granary.

It had been hard enough to face them that midsummer morning after she had done murder, to appear unconcerned as Father Anselm rambled on about Hund the blacksmith leaving to join deRançon in the Holy Lands. Emma had dismissed the deaf priest's words as the delusions of the aged, and the Morston kitchen folk, preoccupied with their aching, ale-poisoned heads, had forgotten. And Father Anselm, in the way of the very old, had sensed their disbelief and ceased to speak of what he might have seen in that pre-dawn vision, after the moon had set.

Alyse and her aged nurse had been cautious, aware that the smallest hint that deRançon might have come to Morston that midsummer night would mark the beginning of curiosity, and later discovery of their deed. The blacksmith Hund, the only other who knew the truth of that night, had disappeared and never sent word to them.

Emma had stopped Alyse's distraught search for the man. Hund would not betray them. Had he not fled in fear that he would be blamed for concealing the death of a noble lord? Wherever he had taken refuge, Hund would never speak of what he had seen that night.

Alyse had made a plan. What had been done within the deserted walls of Morston one midsummer night could be set right a year later, on the next summer solstice eve. Once again, the people of Morston would abandon the keep and their houses and would be gathered upon the tor, tending the bonfire. They would not notice their lady and her woman returning to Morston across the dark fields. Nor would they ever know the grisly work their lady and her ancient nurse would do that night.

But it had stormed, that next midsummer night. Only the young and the foolish had remained at the bonfire once the rain had begun to drum down upon them. They had returned, then, to drink their solstice ale crowded in the guardroom, and had taken their midsummer pleasures in the shelter of the storehouses and sheds. Alyse had watched with churning disgust in her throat as two laughing shadows had retreated into the granary—seeking their privacy, all unknowing, over deRançon's unholy grave.

So Alyse had waited for the next midsummer night and prayed for clear weather.

She had not imagined that the queen would demand her treasure before then, after all the long years of silence. Or that the queen would remember her long-neglected waiting woman's child and send a husband for Alyse. Or that the husband would be a knight who craved honesty and hated murder above all else.

Alyse was holding the reins too tightly, twisting them through her fingers and piercing the skin of her palms with her fingernails. She forced her fists to open and ease the leather straps.

The horse pulled the reins from Alyse's sweating hands, and shied from the tall cairn marking the halfway point between Kernstowe and Morston. Alyse cried out and grabbed for the leather strap as the beast moved from her, backing the cart into the boggy ground beside the rocky track.

DeBauzan had told his men nothing beyond the fact that he was searching for his wife. He had said nothing of Wat's message, nor had he reminded the others of the intruder he had heard moving upon the riverbank the night before. He could not bring himself to speak the only sense he could make of Alyse's contrived flight from Kernstowe: his wife's first lover—the lover she had obviously craved to the point of folly—must have come to take her from Raimond. Why else would Alyse leave her home in stealth?

Alyse had gone to meet her lover after suffering her husband's lust for three long nights—first with acquiescence, then with a skillful sham of passion that had seemed to match his own desire.

Raimond's hand closed upon the hilt of his sword as he turned to glare at the line of riders behind him. He did not want them here. He wanted no one near when he found Alyse and her man—whoever he was. Whatever he was.

If Alyse's lover was a knight with men of his own to defend

their flight, Raimond would need his own men to confront
them. If her man had come alone to take Alyse, Raimond would
send his own men back to Kernstowe, to the revels. Where
they might be fortunate enough to find an honest bawd among
the women to satisfy their lust without deceit, never knowing
that they were more fortunate in their bed partners than their
lord had been. They were all, even the ones who paid their
lemans, more fortunate than their well and truly deceived lord
Fortebras.

He wanted Alyse and her lover alone.

He would kill the man. Quickly, lest his blood-lust lead him
to commit savageries. And then—

God only knew what he would do then.

The horse would not turn back towards the cairn, and the
cart was too heavy for Alyse to push it free of the bog. As
Alyse worked to free the harness from the shafts, the thick
gorse beyond the mud moved whispered once, then bent over
the shining black surface of the mire. Alyse stopped and listened, her heart drumming wildly.

It was the wind. The wind had begun to blow from the north.

As in her dream, the gusts came stronger, racing across the
narrow track, whistling around the cairn, sending droplets of
mist into Alyse's face. Unlike the place she had seen in her
dream, the moor stretched too far behind her to allow a quiet
turning back to Kernstowe—she was halfway to Morston and
she had been gone too long to return in peace. And there was
a task awaiting her at Morston, a task that old Emma would
never manage alone. They had one last chance to set right all
that threatened them.

She cursed and tugged at the halter until the horse moved
forward upon the narrow road. At the cairn, Alyse held the
reins and scrambled halfway up the rocks to slide onto the
beast's broad back.

She could see the Morston bonfire before her, smaller than
the Kernstowe flames to the east. It was close enough to see
the rhythmic flare and flattening of the blaze as the northern
gusts blew over it.

The high whistling came again, and the horse turned back to the road, to the west. Alyse held its mane and braced her feet upon the harness straps. And gave thanks to God that the beast was with her, that she was not in this dark place alone.

The wind stopped, as suddenly as it had begun. Alyse opened her eyes and saw the next cairn ahead. Morston's fires seemed closer now. Alyse slapped the horse's rump and urged it forward.

Then the cold blast came again, harder than before, finding its way around and through the jagged cairn. The whistling grew louder, and more shrill to Alyse's ears. Beneath her, the horse swerved and threw its head back in sudden fright. Alyse let go the halter line and clutched the mane in both her hands. And lost her footing upon the harness strap.

Raimond saw the beast first. It ran straight to them from the west, shying from the torches when it was nearly upon them. There was lather upon its thick neck, and broken harness slapping its heaving sides. The halter was twisted over its ears, the reins tangled in its heavy mane.

Erec caught it and pulled the halter straight upon the horse's broad head. "It must be from Kernstowe, my lord. It was heading there."

It had to be the cart horse. "Lead it behind you."

"My lord, do you think—"

"Bring it with us." And he had turned Shaitan back to the moor road. Fear was turning his guts to a writhing mass of pain. Somewhere ahead, there had been violence—the twisted harness was evidence of that. Was she lying ahead, beneath a ruined cart?

If she had come to harm, he would kill her lover slowly. Limb by limb.

CHAPTER ELEVEN

To walk across Morston's moor in the darkness was foolish. To heed the panicked voice within her mind, to begin to run towards the distant bonfires, would be fatal. She would lose her way, or stumble from the path into one of the dark, shallow pools concealing the bogs from which a lone and unseen traveler would never emerge.

The moon had risen above the blowing mist. Its thin light fell upon the distant cairns marking the track which skirted the hazards of the moor. Within two short hours, the moon would be down and the path would vanish in the darkness. The moors would once again become a deathtrap for those who traveled by night.

Even had she dared to quicken her pace, Alyse could not have run far on her bruised and lacerated legs. Less than an hour ago, the wind had sent a high-pitched vibration through the largest cairn—the white stone heap which had looked so like a standing man—and the cart horse had shied and run. Alyse had risen from the road a moment later to find the horse vanished and her knees throbbing nearly as painfully as her scraped palms.

It had taken all her resolve to walk past that tall cairn, for the sharp, keening whistle changed pitch with each rise and fall of the northern wind. As she passed, the sound died into a soft, growling huff.

If she had not fallen from the horse, she would have given up then, and allowed the frightened animal to carry her back to Kernstowe; she might have abandoned her last hope of reaching Morston in time to conceal her crime. But she had fallen, and she was alone in the wild land, closer to Morston than to Kernstowe.

Alyse walked west, and did not look back.

They found the cart by the side of the track, half submerged in the black water of a wind-rippled pool. DeBauzan had forced Shaitan into the muddy shallows and jumped from his back to heave the cart on its side. The undulating tangle of dark tresses streaming on the surface of the water between the wheel spokes had proved to be weeds. He had crushed them in his fist and called for Erec's lance; he had cursed and raged, leveling the wooden staff again and again beneath the surface, as he had done with his sword in the river at Kernstowe only an hour ago. A lifetime ago.

His men had called him back from his frantic search to show him what their torches had found at the shaft of the cart. There was no trace of harness leather there, they told him; the leather straps must have been untied. And the wall-eyed, skittish cart horse still wore the long traces dangling from its harness.

The lady Alyse, they told him, must have freed the horse herself. She must be somewhere near, trying to walk back to Kernstowe. She might have strayed from the road. They might have passed her in the darkness.

Raimond splashed out of the pond and mounted Shaitan in silence. He did not deny that his wife had taken the cart, nor did he acknowledge the silent questions upon the puzzled faces watching him in the torch light. They would know the truth soon enough. Too soon.

"We will ride west," he said.

"My lord, she might be—"

"We go west," he repeated. "And the next man who speaks will find my dagger through his tongue."

*   *   *

Morston's fire looked larger, now. The mist had lowered and taken the color of the flames, spreading a diffused crimson glow across the horizon.

Alyse was nearly home. The small, crescent-shaped pool which lay close beside the road shone clear in the faint glow from the Morston blaze. It was the first of the moorland ponds, less than a mile from the tor which rose above the settlement.

She had not expected to hear the distant pounding of the sea so soon. It was faster, unsteadier than she remembered it. The irregular buffeting of the wind must have sent a strange, ragged surf upon the coast to make that sound.

Alyse stopped to listen. Had she mistaken the direction of it? She turned, and staggered back in astonishment. The bonfire at Kernstowe, which should have been only a faint point of light behind her, was too large. Too high. It should—

It was moving. Undulating, separating into tongues of flame which crossed and re-crossed as they grew larger.

And the pounding was not the sea.

Behind her were horsemen, riding fast, their torches flaring through the low blowing mist. She began to run.

The drumming came louder. There were voices, hoarse cries rising in a confusion of sounds over the whining cold wind.

She lunged off the road towards the low bushes at the pond. Cover your eyes, the shepherds had said, and the hunt may pass above you. Their breath is a cold fire to freeze the blood and turn your eyes to ice. If you see them, you will see no other thing in this life.

The pounding stopped. The wind had stopped. There was the sound of one horse, one mortal horse moving slowly with a heavy, inevitable pace over the moss-covered earth.

Alyse raised her eyes and opened her mouth in a choking, silent scream. They had tricked her. Mortal sounds from a devil horseman had drawn her to gaze upon the face of hell's hunters.

There was only one. The torch it held threw a yellow flame, but the eyes of the horse and its unholy rider glowed red in the demon light. As did the naked sword at the rider's side.

* * *

His wife had been alone when he had sighted her on the road ahead. She had been only a shadow, a swift image bolting from the track into the high bushes.

It could be a trap. Her lover might have hidden himself first, leaving her to draw her husband off the road. There could be men hidden beyond her, waiting for him to follow.

Raimond's mouth twisted in disgust. Only a white-livered coward would risk his lady's life in this way. In the rage which came upon him, Raimond Fortebras ceased to care how many armed men awaited him in the darkness. He would kill them all. He needed to kill them all. And he needed to do it alone.

And if his wife was alone, or had only her lover awaiting her in the darkness, Raimond wanted no witnesses to this betrayal. He stopped, then, and watched. There was no movement in the moon-defined bushes. If there was an armed party, it was some distance from her.

He turned and called to his men. "Go back."

Of course they did not. They rode toward him, shouting questions as they raised their swords.

"My lord, have you found her?"

"Ride back now, damn you."

"My lord, have you found her?"

"Go back," he roared, "or by Satan's prick I will slay you all myself."

They stopped before they reached him. He heard young Erec's voice tell the others that he had seen a woman run from the road. There were other voices, then, speculating on the game the lady played. A dangerous game, to anger her lord.

They began to turn their horses east.

Raimond watched, his sword in his hand, until the last of them had turned away from the pool. They rode slowly, speaking among themselves. The lady had gone too far, even for a midsummer jest, cozening Lord Fortebras beyond wisdom. There was no laughter among them.

The voices grew more distant still. Raimond waited until he could hear them no more, and rode slowly down to the water.

Alyse was crouched not far from the road, among the bushes.

He was nearly upon her before he saw the moonlight upon her white face. If he had had any doubt of her guilt, the terror he saw in her features would have killed his hope.

His wife raised her face and there was a terrible sound, a hoarse death rattle from the mouth of the living. Raimond hauled Shaitan's panicked, tossing head back to the woman, and brought the torch low to illuminate her features.

She turned, then, and clawed through the bushes to flee him, sobbing as her desperate movements and the heavy wind tangled her hair through the branches. She began screaming, then, and thrashing faster through the gorse, dragging leafed twigs from the branches behind her, stuck in the wild confusion of her hair.

"Do not move," he shouted.

She stopped and stood panting in the brush. She had turned her head as far as she could, but her eyes were looking past him. There was no focus.

He dismounted and moved toward her. When he raised his sword to cut the tangled branches from her hair, she did not wince or cower. Or understand.

"Where is he?" Raimond demanded.

Her gaze came to him then.

"Where is he," he repeated softly.

"In the granary."

"At Morston?"

She closed her eyes.

"Waiting for you?"

She began to weep. He planted the torch in the ground and sheathed his sword. With his dagger, he began to cut the branches which had entrapped her. She had shuddered once, then waited in rigid panic as he finished freeing her.

From the movement of her fingers to her neck, he knew that she had thought he had raised the dagger to slit her throat. And with shame, he remembered the killing rage which had possessed him as he had searched for her. The rage had gone, but his task remained. For his own honor. She had none.

He took her arm and pulled her from her tangled shelter. "I will kill him," Fortebras said. "I will kill him tonight."

She looked at him in amazement. "But he is dead."

"He will be."

"He is dead."

She spoke as if she believed her words. He had seen men-at-arms in this state, after a battle, in the heat of Palestine. His wife's mind had fled, leaving a walking husk which understood little. He spoke slowly, then, and tried to level his voice. "Alyse. I will take you to Chilcheton, to the priest. To Father Gregory. You will stay there until you know whether you are with child."

She began again to weep.

"And if you are not with child, you will be sent—"

She cried out then, a hoarse demand he could not comprehend.

"If there is no child, I will send you to—"

"No. Do what you will, but end it there, at the abbey."

Did she believe, after this night, that there could be more between them? "Madam, it is ended now."

"My lord, please. It must happen at the abbey. Not at the assizes. Not by—hanging—"

Raimond felt the hair upon his body rise and prickle. She was mad. His unchaste wife had lost her reason.

"You will do it. Please. Your sword—use the sword. Please—not by hanging."

Black rage returned. "You plead a noble man's death for your lover? Rest your mind, madam. I will not take the time to hang the coward. He shall die under my sword. And you, madam—you shall watch him die."

She put her ruined hands over her face and shook her head slowly. Her whispered words rose to a hoarse cry. "No more. I cannot understand. He is dead. He is dead. He is—"

She was mad.

Or she believed, somehow, that her lover must be dead.

Had the man died before this night? Had an old grief, not present dread of a lover's death, taken Alyse's wit, and caused her to wander these dangerous moors?

He would ask one question more. He owed her that much.

"Alyse, who is dead?"

Alyse slowly lowered her hands. "DeRançon," she said.

"He is gone, Alyse."

She shook her head. "He is there—in the granary."

He saw that she was shivering. "DeRançon is dead. No one knows where he lies."

"He is there. I put him there. And I was going—" She raised her eyes and looked at him without expression. "He is in the granary. I will find him there tonight. I must do it tonight, when the bailey is empty."

Raimond felt bile rise to his throat.

Madness took many forms. But never, even in the battlefields of Palestine, had he known any soul, man or woman, so obsessed with a dead lover that she would open a grave and—

Raimond felt the hot sting of tears behind his eyes. This frightened woman was his wife, and she was mad. What path did her crazed mind take, when it wandered foul? He closed his throat against the bitterness rising within his gut, and asked a last, terrible question. "Alyse," he whispered. "tell me what you must do tonight."

And she told him.

He slashed green wood and branches from the copse beside the pool and set them around the guttering torch. She sat silently beside that smoking fire as he brought water in his upturned helmet for her to drink. Then he dipped the hem of her wide sleeve in the helm and bathed her face.

"How did deRançon know what you kept at Morston?"

"He did not know. He knew only that my mother and William had raised their hearthstone and—"

"Slowly, Alyse. Go slowly."

She hesitated. ". . . On that day, when they heard the queen had been freed, William and my mother raised the stone and took up the coffer. They left the next morning, to seek Queen Eleanor. They found her gone when they reached Windsor— gone to find a bride for Richard and follow him to Sicily. My parents came back with the queen's jewels and buried them again. We did it in secret, but there was talk."

"And deRançon guessed what they had?"

"Not at first. Then, a few months later, the queen's letter came to Kernstowe."

"To Morston, you mean."

"No, Kernstowe. She had remembered us and sent word from Aquitaine that Morston should be spared the second taxes for the crusade. DeRançon was told he would be forgiven Morston's share of the tax. Then he knew that my mother had done something for Queen Eleanor. And he remembered the talk of the hearthstone."

"And he demanded that William tell him?"

"By then William had died of the fever. And my mother soon after."

"And deRançon came to you to find what was hidden?"

She pushed away the cloth. "I told him I knew nothing, that William and my mother had not moved the hearthstone a second time, but I could see he did not believe me. He became angry—"

Raimond waited, but she did not go on. "Alyse, was deRançon the one? Did he force you?"

"He was the one. He did not force me."

"He was your lover?"

"He was—we were to wed. He had the right to take me. He had the right."

Raimond moved closer and closed his hand over her arm. "How did he die?"

She tensed as if to run, then drew a long breath and looked into his eyes. "I killed him. And buried him. When the bailey was empty, on midsummer night."

"In the granary."

"Yes."

It might be true. "You did it, Alyse?" Raimond felt her pull away. "You did it alone?"

"I was the one who did it. When he—when he died he fell into the dry well, where I had hidden the coffer. They helped me—" She covered her mouth as if to hold back a sickness. "They brought stones to fill the well."

"Who helped you?"

She sagged in defeat. "Emma. Hund. They only helped. Please—they did no wrong."

"Alyse? Why did you do it? Because he took you?"

"He had the right," she said, as if reciting a lesson she had learned only imperfectly. "It was later—a fortnight later—he came to Morston to look for the queen's treasure."

"He knew of it?"

"He knew there was something. He did not know what it was."

"How did he know, Alyse? Had you said something?"

She shook her head. "He knew. Somehow, he knew."

"And you knew you had to move the coffer."

She closed her eyes. "He was planning to bring men to raise the hearthstones first, and if he found nothing, to dig under the ruined wall. Emma heard this from the serving women. On midsummer night, when the keep was empty, we kept Hund back from the bonfires. There was to be a new grain shed built over the dry well."

He remembered the unseemly clutter of sheds and store-houses in the bailey, south of the keep. "In the middle of the storehouses?"

"Yes. The old sow had rooted under the cover and had fallen into the well. We had to cover it better, and we needed the granary." Alyse shuddered. "It was half-full."

"The granary?"

"The well. It was half filled in with stones when I—when it happened."

Raimond covered her hand. "You put the coffer into the old well?" he prompted.

"Yes, and we had covered it with earth. We had begun to fill the hole when he came."

He moved his hand slowly up her arm, as if to awaken her from a dream. "And he tried to dig it up?"

"No. I said—I made him think we had just begun to dig. I said we intended to hide my stepfather's gold."

"And he did not believe you."

"He did not believe me. He knew we had little wealth, nothing worth hiding so well. So he put his sword to Emma's throat and demanded to see what we intended to bury."

Raimond's temples began to pulse in anger. "The man needed killing. You did no sin."

Alyse shook her head.

"He was armed, and Emma was in danger. How did you do it?"

"With the spade."

"It is not easy to kill a man with a spade."

She winced. "It was not easy."

"DeRançon had a sword. You were lucky, Alyse, he did not kill you first."

"He kept Emma under his sword. He told Hund to stop me."

"The man was as stupid as he was evil. He deserved to die twice. Why did he imagine Hund would defend him?"

"He was our lord. Hund's lord, and—mine. I killed him, Raimond—"

He caught her hand and held it tight. "And you buried him there, In the well?"

She nodded. "It was past midnight, and the people would begin to return at dawn. There was no time."

"To bury him?"

"To get the coffer. The hole was half filled when he fell. I—I took Emma back to the keep while Hund buried him. The coffer was beneath him. It is still there beneath the—beneath him."

Alyse looked into her husband's eyes. "I was a coward, Raimond. I could not risk getting the coffer that night. And I never had the courage to get it since. Not until now."

"Now that I threatened to tear down Morston to find it."

They sat in silence.

She drew a long, hoarse breath. "Will you wait, Raimond? Will you wait until I am gone before you open the well?"

He looked at her in astonishment. "Until you go? What do you mean?" And watched helplessly as his wife began again to weep.

"Come," he said. "You may weep later, if you must. Now, we must move quickly. Does Emma wait for you?"

The sound of her weeping grew louder. He seized her hands and dragged them from her eyes. "Alyse," he rasped. "have you done all you did, and have you come this far, only to stop and sit under this bush weeping the night away?"

He rose to his feet, and pulled her with him. "If you do not stop your sobbing, wife, all of Morston will hear you. And then how will we manage to ride past the bonfires unseen?"

"Unseen?"

"I see no reason to tell your people what happened."

"I killed him, my lord, and let him lie in unhallowed ground. For this, Count John will want vengeance. When he hears—"

"He shall not hear, Alyse. You did no crime. You needed to kill deRançon as much as a man needs to kill for his lord on the battlefield. There will be no more talk of crimes and vengeance."

"If you hide this deed, and we are found out, you will suffer too."

"We will not be found out."

"And if we cannot bring the coffer out before the people return to Morston?"

"Then we will keep them out, by God. They will stay out, on my orders, until we have done."

"But they will imagine—they will talk."

"They will not speak of it."

By God they would not. For he would kill them all, if he needed to, to have their silence. His wife had suffered enough under the burden of Queen Eleanor's trust.

CHAPTER TWELVE

Raimond Fortebras left the fire burning beside the shallow lake, and took his wife in his arms upon Shaitan's back. The destrier grew skittish as they neared the end of the moor, and sidled away from the track where it turned east, where the great tor stood over Morston and the sea. Raimond held Alyse close to him, for he had seen her fear of his mount.

He looked down at his wife's white face, and saw in the moonlight that she was still and calm; she did not seek to steady herself as Shaitan tossed his great neck and worried the bit. Raimond understood that stillness: in her frightful visions this night, Alyse had seen such things that the danger of falling beneath the hooves of a mortal beast no longer held terror for her.

The bonfire was upon the peak of the tor, blazing within its jagged stone circle. The night was half gone; Raimond knew that the young among the revelers would have begun to slip away in pairs to begin a dance more ancient than the pattern they had woven around the flames.

"Where do they go, when they leave the fire?" Raimond whispered. "Back towards the keep?"

"No. They go onto the moor," Alyse said. "But never far. They are afraid they might see the dead who walk there."

Moments later, he dismounted and led Shaitan from the track, skirting the loom of the high flames, moving slowly to find solid ground between the small pools and thickets upon the barren land. Shaitan turned his massive head and snorted as he sensed the presence of those few revelers who had wandered away from the tor. Raimond clamped his hand over his mount's nostrils; the well-trained war-horse kept silent as he bore Alyse past the distant rustlings and laughter in the crimson half-light.

When they had completed a wide half-circle around the tor and heard the sea before them, Raimond swung up again upon Shaitan's back and pulled Alyse into his arms. She turned to look past his shoulder to the dancers on the hill.

From the ocean side, with the heavy sea mist blowing past the base of the tor, the stones seemed to shimmer, to turn before the flames which backlit their ungainly bulk. The fire-limned shadows of the dancers moved faster as the whistle and drum quickened their beat.

Through the heavy wool of the cloak he had wrapped around her, Raimond felt his wife's quick, gasping breath. She, too, had seen the illusion of Morston's stones moving with the flames.

Raimond pulled her back against his chest. This was a strange, wild place whose people were more foreign to his own Norman soul than he had first imagined. How much of Morston's ancient, primitive history had Alyse learned in her years upon this land? Had her mother managed to give Alyse, born under the enlightened sun of Poitou, enough of her own history to keep her from believing the Morston folk's stories of devil creatures roaming this land?

Or had the people of Morston given Alyse their ghosts as well as their loyalty? She spoke with these farmers and shepherds as easily as she used her Poitevin French tongue; the slight hesitations in her speech, and the hint of husky, guttural inflection when she spoke to her people were present even when she spoke to Raimond in his own tongue. She was a part of this land in a way he never would be; the tales of the dead hunting the living were as real to Alyse as Raimond's own childhood stories of brave and bloody deeds had been to him.

Alyse believed that Harald deRançon's shade haunted this

place, and watched for her in the night. Raimond made a silent vow to bring his wife away from these moors into the world her mother had known, the world from which Queen Eleanor's demands had exiled Isabelle Mirbeau and her innocent young daughter.

The green barley shoots were pale in the moonlight as Shaitan's wide hooves crushed a straight path through the field, moving towards the few dim lights upon Morston's seabound promontory. Raimond cast a long, sweeping look around him; Alyse had been right—no one among the revelers had come back to the fields. Only through the crooked bailey gate, gaping open on this midsummer night, did he see a sign of human presence.

As they drew nearer, the postern torch revealed a Bauzan soldier, Gareth, slouched in stupor at the side of the listing gateway. The young knight awakened with a muffled shout and half drew his sword.

"Go easy," Raimond called.

"Who is there?"

"Fortebras." There was a rapid scrambling noise as Gareth rose to his feet and pulled his cloak from the damp grass. His head was bare of helmet, his hair rumpled from sleep. "Where is Hugo?" Raimond demanded.

Gareth let his blade fall back into its scabbard. He craned his neck to see past the dark cloth enveloping Alyse's still body. "Courting," he said; the young knight made a brief sound of mirth.

Raimond pointed at the tankard resting against the frame of the bailey gate. "Spill the ale before I spill your brains for a drunken sentry. Find Hugo, and bring him here."

The young knight staggered back, upsetting the ale cup before his groping hand could seize it. "My lord, I do not think—"

"Do not think. Bring Hugo."

Gareth caught sight Alyse's face, deep within the folds of Fortebras' cloak. "Your lady wife is ill? What has happened?"

Raimond swung down from the saddle. "Find Hugo and bring him here, or you will have no need of questions or answers until doomsday, Gareth. Bring—Hugo—now." He reached up to lift Alyse from the saddle. "My lady, I will take you to Emma."

When he spoke to her, his voice was tender, as gentle as his bedchamber speech had been.

Gareth returned to the gate. "My lord, Hugo is with Emma. That is, they are together. In the keep."

Raimond lifted Alyse down and turned her face toward his chest, against his fine velvet tunic; it was his wedding tunic, worn again this midsummer night. Darkened, now, by the night mist and the oily smoke of the brush fire they had left to burn down. Alyse smelled the spicy scent of the green wood and sighed in contentment. Her husband's arm tightened about her shoulders.

"Then stay here," he growled. "We will find them." Raimond inclined his head toward the dim light beyond the chapel. "Who else stayed behind?"

"The priest—Father Anselm."

Alyse heard her husband's oath rumble low beneath her ear. "It can't be helped," he said at last. "Go to the priest's hut and keep him there."

"What can't be helped? The old priest is asleep, my lord."

Raimond's next curse was both clear and venomous. "Then it should be a simple thing to keep him in the hut. If he wakens, keep him there with—I care not how you do it."

Alyse was aware, from some place far above her husband's moonlit features and her own shivering body, that she wanted to tell her husband's young knight that a torch near Father Anselm's hut would awaken the old priest. She wanted—

But the time for such concerns had passed. Her burdens were gone, now. Raimond had taken them from her, and would deal with them as he saw fit. The secrets she had carried were now his—passed to his broad shoulders. Leaving her lighter. Free to float higher still.

She looked down and saw her husband lift a slight, rigid body wrapped in his dark cloak. And from a great distance, she heard him begin to shout Emma's name. Again and again.

* * *

When she came back, there was more shouting. Hundreds of shouting throats, ringing in great echoing waves about her in the sleeping chamber at Morston, waxing louder as the echoes came closer together, contracting into three bellowing voices.

The warmth around her moved and shifted. And then there was light.

And Emma's voice.

"Her face—her poor face. And her hair has been—"

"Silence, woman. Blankets. Hot water. Now."

Emma's words receded and another voice spoke in a harsh rumble. "Leave her, Raimond. If we are to do this thing before dawn, we must begin now."

Alyse heard her husband snarl something she did not understand. A curse she did not comprehend. She must ask him, one day . . . .

"—and tell them anyone who comes past the bailey gate before I permit it will be cut down where I find them. Get the young fool Gareth from the priest's house. Tell him to close the gate. Keep those drunken sots outside the bailey until I give him leave to let them in. And keep the priest in his chamber. Or I'll hang them both on the gates and—"

"My lord, she's waking."

There was another oath, a short, hoarse word muttered at her ear, and the sound of Emma weeping.

Alyse opened her eyes. Raimond was at the door, his eyes vivid blue within his muddy, soot-darkened face. He spoke again the words that she had heard at the small fire he had built upon the heath to warm her. "By dawn, there will be nothing left to link you to that coward. No one will see us. No one will know but Hugo."

Hugo Gerbrai cleared his throat. "And Emma," he said.

Raimond frowned. "And the smith, wherever he is. If he ever speaks of what he saw, I'll find him and cut his tongue out."

Emma made a small sound of distress. Raimond narrowed his eyes. "Emma, you will come with me and show me where—where it is. Hugo, stay with my lady until Emma returns. Do not leave her alone. She must not be alone."

And Alyse knew then that Raimond understood. That he

knew how easy it would be for her to float free, and stay in that silent place she had found above them, beside the cold midsummer moon.

Alyse sat up and dragged the heavy blanket around her shoulders. "You wish your lord had never come here—had never wed me."

Hugo Gerbrai turned his grizzled head from the arrow slit and looked at her in astonishment. "You are my young lord's wife. I have never said aught against you."

"But you did not like the marriage," Alyse continued wearily.

He gave a small, incoherent grunt.

"What will happen to Raimond, if the—if deRançon's death is discovered? Will they blame him for keeping it secret?"

"Blame him? No. But they will use it against him—send him on some other hopeless quest to some godforsaken place. And he will not dare refuse them."

"The king's councilors?"

"The king and his accursed family. His mother, the old queen, uses men as counters in her games, and forgets the ones who fall from the play. There are plenty more foolish young knights to do her bidding. And the brother, Count John. There's a poisonous young ferret—too dangerous to follow, too close to the throne to punish. When this matter is finished, my lady," he growled, "see that young Fortebras takes you to Normandy, to his family at Bauzan. If he's lucky, you will both be forgotten for a time. It's the most you can hope for, once the Plantagenet brood has decided you might be useful to them."

He drew a sharp breath and turned back to the embrasure. "Your pardon, lady Alyse. Your mother was one who did not manage to be forgotten."

"No," she whispered.

"She had little choice, mind you, once the lands were taken."

"You knew her? You knew my mother?"

Gerbrai shook his grey head. "No, but I saw her once at Barfleur, when the old queen and her ladies took ship for

England, when King Henry was sending them to live at Salisbury."

"You were there?"

"Yes, I watched the fleet go. Your mother—it must have been the lady Isabelle I saw, a young woman much like you, with a babe in her arms—was with Queen Eleanor. The wind was strong, a storm rising, and they did not want to go. But the king sent them across the water. He might have hoped the queen's ship would founder, and end her scheming for all time."

"And drown the child who would become your lord's inconvenient wife?"

Hugo made a vague gesture. "I did not say that."

Alyse sank back upon the pallet. "I did not lie to harm him. I thought I would find the coffer alone and never tell him what I had done."

"Some day, someone would have found the body, lady Alyse, here on my lord Raimond's lands."

"I would have confessed what I had done to protect him from the king's justice."

Gerbrai snorted. "If you want to protect him, my lady, go with him to Bauzan. Take the jewels to the old queen at Windsor and ride on to the coast. If there is trouble about deRançon or these lands, your lord Raimond will need his brothers' swords beside him. Remember that, my lady."

"I will remember."

When she opened her eyes, Emma was there with a cup of steaming brandywine. Strong drink from Kernstowe, Emma was saying. Sent by Lord Raimond in the wagons on the first day. Drink it and speak, Emma said. Speak to me.

"He knows everything. He knows what deRançon threatened, and what we did, you and Hund and I," Alyse whispered.

"You told him," Emma said. "And now we are in his hands. He will decide—"

"He said that we would not suffer—"

"He said that you would not suffer, Alyse. He blames me.

I can see it when he looks at me. He is angry, Alyse. What will he do?''

"He is more than angry. But he said—''

"What happened to you, out on the moor with him? There were dead leaves, Alyse, in your hair. As if he had dragged you, poor lamb, upon the ground.''

"He did not hurt me. I ran from him, into the bushes.''

"Did he beat you when he found you? There are women at court, Hugo says, who want such treatment from a man. One of them once took Lord Fortebras to her bed. She was one of many he had. Hugo told me.''

"He did not hurt me.''

Alyse saw a shifting, flickering glow from the arrow slit across the chamber. "Where is Raimond?''

"Where do you think he is? You are not to look, he said. You are to stay here, in the bed, and wait. Or he'll have my head on a—''

Emma was too slow to stop her. Alyse threw herself from the bed and pushed past the frail barrier of Emma's arms. And reached the place where she had stood so many nights, looking out over the granary shed. Hoping, each time she had returned to her vigil, that there would be nothing to see. No shadows, no movement, no grave light rising cold and blue to flow beneath the shuttered door.

There were shadows, now—two of them—heaving and stabbing long-handled spades in the streaming yellow torch light. The sound of their steady, rapid excavation was audible over the rhythmic thud of the sea.

"Come away, Alyse. He will see you, if he comes out.''

"No matter.''

Alyse wanted to call to him, to bring him away from that terrible place. She did not want him to be there when the light reached deRançon's rotting corpse. She wanted him far away, distant from the granary shed and the deed it concealed.

He had come from the great world outside this haunted place; he had brought, despite his stern warrior's demeanor, warmth and joy to his marriage bed. And he had shown her tenderness beyond her early dreams of courtly love.

To know her husband was down there in the crude shed

above that hasty grave, uncovering the ruined face which had occupied Alyse's dreams of terror, must mark the end of an idyll. For now Raimond deBauzan was to be part of the memory which Alyse had hoped to conceal and forget.

One of the shadows threw its spade aside and lowered itself to kneel upon the ground.

Alyse ran to the privy pot and knelt beside it, holding her hair back from her sweating face with trembling hands. But the sudden nausea ceased, and left a heaving pain in its place. It was her heart, hurting as it beat.

The moon was down when Raimond Fortebras came out of the granary. Emma had taken Alyse's place at the embrasure, describing what she saw in brief, strangled words. And Alyse had sat straight-spined upon the bed, her face turned to the hearth. Waiting.

When Raimond returned to this room, he would have the queen's jewels in his hands. Soon after, he would leave for Windsor. For this royal task, he no longer needed her help, willing or not.

Her husband had said she would not face the king's justice, and she believed him. He would leave her behind, at Kernstowe or at St. Ursula's convent, when he rode east. Raimond Fortebras, son of the great lord of Bauzan, would not bring to the court at Windsor a wife who had deceived him, a wife whose night terrors had horrified him. A wife who had done murder.

They had had four days of wedlock. One of fear, and three of passion. And now, a night of grisly revelation. Having seen the decomposing ruin of the man Alyse had slain, would her husband bring himself to look upon her as he had before?

Alyse sank back against the wall and closed her eyes. It was the end of waiting. The end of the watching her mother had begun and never ended while she lived.

She had promised Hugo to send Raimond home, to safety in his father's Norman stronghold. It would not be difficult to persuade him to go.

* * *

Raimond came to her an hour later, his steps so slow that she did not recognize the sound. It was not the stride of a man eager to return to his wife. Of course he was not eager. He had seen it. He had seen—

He opened the door and stepped into the firelight, wearing a tunic she did not recognize; the sleeves of it were clean, and there was no sweat upon the fine linen cloth. He had not worn it, then, when he had—

Alyse closed her eyes briefly to banish the vision.

She looked again to her husband. He had washed in the hour she had been waiting. His face was clean and shaven, and his hair darkened by the water it still held. Alyse wondered whether he had bathed in the stream outside the bailey walls.

His hands were clean. There was no trace of soil anywhere upon him. The pain in Alyse's breast began to diminish. She had not realized, until this moment, how she had dreaded that he would come to her with traces of deRançon's grave upon his hands.

The coffer was under his arm, wrapped in a clean cloth which Alyse recognized as a piece of William of Morston's old woolen mantle, given last year to the kitchen maids.

Raimond looked at her with an expression she had not seen before. Not the revulsion she had dreaded, but something else. There was tenderness there. And pity.

He turned his gaze from her to the woman in the shadows near the door. "Emma," he said, "leave us."

Emma opened her mouth as if to object, then snapped her jaw shut; she glanced at Alyse and shook her head slightly, then she walked out the door. Raimond closed it behind her.

"Alyse," he said softly, "I would like you to look at the jewels."

She stared at the cloth stretched over the coffret and swallowed. "You found them," she said.

"I found the coffer." He began to unwrap the cloth. "It is clean, now. But you need not touch it, if you do not wish to. I want you to look within."

The bands of silver had blackened and the once-fragrant

cedar wood had turned darker still in its time under the earth. The silver clasp had broken, leaving a bright edge of white metal.

Raimond had opened it before he had brought it to her.

He set the coffer upon the floor, at her feet, and raised the lid.

Alyse remembered the three golden arm bands and the dragons' ruby eyes set within the queen's brooch. She recognized the long silver chain, now as black as the coffer's twisted bands, bearing a tiny pearl in the center of each heavy link. There were ten gold coins beneath the dust-caked pieces that lay uppermost, and two small silver rings.

"Is this as you remembered?"

"Yes. There is dust—" She closed her mind to the dust. And to its possible origin. "The pieces were cleaner, before. They were—they do not seem to be damaged."

He was watching her as if he expected her to say more.

Alyse spoke again. "There is no damage I can see, Raimond. Queen Eleanor will be pleased when we—when you take her treasure to Windsor."

He sat back on his heels and raised his open blue gaze to her face. "This is no treasure, Alyse. Surely you know that?"

"What do you mean?"

"You know this is not a treasure."

She looked up. "I do not understand. There it is, before you. I will—I will ask Emma to clean the pieces before you take them to the queen."

Raimond drew a deep breath. "Alyse, there is not enough here to warrant Queen Eleanor's interest. She told me that the coffer your mother took from Salisbury contained gold and jewels which would make a great difference in King Richard's ransom." He let the lid drop back into place. "There is barely enough here to ransom one knight in his armor, Alyse."

He was wrong. This was treasure. This was more gold, greater riches than Alyse or her dead parents had imagined possessing at Morston. "This is—this is all there was. I saw it before, when I was a child. I remember every piece. When I was four years old, my mother let me touch them all, before we hid them beneath the new hearthstone of this chamber. The arm bands, the rings, the—''

And she realized, then, what he was asking. ''Are you saying that I took something from the coffer? That I stole from the queen?''

His gaze was blue, unblinking, and hard. ''No,'' he said at last. ''I am not saying that. I am saying that this is not a treasure, in Queen Eleanor's eyes. The queen wears as many jewels by day in her poorest demesne. My own mother wears jewels of greater worth at Eastertide. There must have been more here, Alyse, to warrant your mother's spending the rest of her life in this place to conceal it.''

''But she did—''

''There is not enough here, Alyse, to have tempted Queen Eleanor to send me here to fetch this coffer. She told me, Alyse, that what was in this coffer would speed King Richard's release. What I see here is of little worth.''

Alyse rose and walked to the arrow slit. ''It is all there was. That was all there was when I was four years old and saw my mother put the casket into the hiding place. And it was all there when I took it down there—when I took it to the dry well. Do you believe—''

Beneath the embrasure, Hugo Gerbrai, barechested and filthy, emerged from the granary and threw his torch aside. He wedged the door shut.

''I believe you,'' Raimond said behind her.

Alyse watched Hugo cross to the gates and raise the massive bar. He and Raimond had worked quickly. When Morston's people began to return from their night beside the bonfire, they would find nothing amiss. They would never know why their lord had closed the gates to them.

''You left him there?''

Raimond did not answer.

Alyse turned and saw that his eyes once again held that strange expression. Moments ago, she had imagined it was pity. Now—

He rose to his feet and walked towards her. When he rested his hands upon her shoulders, he did so with care, as if he feared some sign of the night's grisly labor still remained upon him.

"It is unhallowed earth," she said. "He will not lie easily until it is blessed."

He drew a great breath and tightened his hands upon her, as if to hold her from the wall. "Alyse, he is not there."

"You took—you moved—it?"

"There was no body. No bones. Nothing."

"How could there not—there would be—"

"Alyse, there was nothing. DeRançon was not there."

He would not permit them to leave her alone. He had summoned Emma first, and had demanded that she find a kirtle and robe for her mistress. He had watched with impassive eyes as Emma had drawn the damaged green cloth from Alyse, leaving her only her torn wedding shift, and had bathed the scratches upon her arms and legs.

When Alyse had been covered with Emma's blue kirtle and wrapped in her faded rose mantle, deBauzan had added the last of the stack of firewood to the hearth and dragged the settle to face it. Only then, when Alyse sat facing the warmth, had Raimond beckoned Emma to the thin dawn light wavering through the arrow slit and had opened the coffer.

There had been a low, murmured exchange which ended when Emma, pale and protesting, had retreated to Alyse's side.

"Alyse, tell him I would never have taken a single thing—"

Raimond stopped Emma's words with a single gesture. "I have not accused you of theft, woman. Stop your weeping and tell me what I asked. When you left Salisbury with Alyse's mother, the lady Isabelle, did you see what she took with her in this coffer?"

Emma's chin had begun to tremble.

Alyse sat up slowly. "Tell him, Emma. He needs to know this."

The old woman nodded. "I saw."

"Was there something more? Did you—did Alyse's mother, her stepfather—did anyone take something from this casket to conceal elsewhere?"

Emma shook her head.

Raimond thrust the coffer into her lap. "Look at the pieces. Tell me whether something—even a small thing—is missing."

"Please, Emma, tell us everything you remember." Alyse said.

"I did not steal from this. Would I have betrayed Queen Eleanor, and your dear blessed mother—"

Alyse put her hand on Emma's shoulder. "Lord Raimond did not say you stole," she said, her eyes compelling her husband's silence. "He wants to know what these things are."

"Well," the old woman began. "The coins are here. Ten, as before. And the armbands, the gift of a suitor—a great bear of a man from Normandy, she told me. She was a girl unwed, then."

"You speak of Queen Eleanor?"

"Yes," Emma said as she tilted the coffer and swept the dust aside. "See how the silver has darkened? The ring with the blue stone she never wore, the chain with the pearls from the Holy Land was a gift of her uncle the Prince of Antioch. She will not be pleased to see the silver so black and the rings covered in—"

"But you notice nothing gone?"

"Nothing, my lord. Nothing I can remember. Is it true, Lord Raimond, that you found no—nothing more than this coffer?"

Raimond took back the small casket. "Hugo awaits you in the kitchen."

"There was no body, my lord? How is that possible? He was—"

"Be silent, Emma. Hugo will tell you." There was no anger in his eyes. And when he spoke, there was no accusation in his tone. "Emma, there is no longer a reason for you to remain here. Hugo will take you to Kernstowe tomorrow."

"Why, I cannot just—"

"Be ready," he said, and turned to Alyse. "My lady, the dawn is here. It is time to go back."

She looked at the rough floor. "My lord, I am content to stay here."

"And I will not permit you to do so. We will return now, Alyse, and stop the rumors before they begin."

He offered her his hand. His blue gaze forbade her to refuse it.

"Your men—and the people at Kernstowe—they know I ran away."

"They will know what I tell them," Raimond said. "Now come, Alyse. It will be easier if we leave now."

Emma moved between them and caught Alyse's hands within her own. She made a small sound of disgust. "Let her stay here, my lord, until her face heals and her hands are whole again. If she returns now, the people will think—"

"Be silent," he demanded. "The people will think what it pleases me to tell them. They will hear that the lady Alyse led me a hot chase to Morston, thinking to amuse me. I followed—searched for her. And—" Raimond looked down at the coffer in his hands. "I found it was nothing but a jest. A midsummer jest."

CHAPTER
THIRTEEN

They set out under the late dawn sky, as the people of Morston began to return from the tor. Between the barley rows and the oats, clusters of bleary-eyed women and men of unsteady gait came in a ragged line from the dying bonfire across the fields to the sea.

Raimond guided Shaitan down the narrow space between the fields and halted near three old men whose thin voices were raised in a vigorous, gesticulating argument. "What are they saying, Alyse?"

The peasants heard his voice and stepped apart to bow their heads in hasty respect. When Alyse drew the hood of Fortebras' cloak from her head, the rapid talking began once again. The oldest of them called to her and pointed to the ground.

Alyse smiled. "They say a group of thieves or vandals crossed the barley field last night, crushing two rows of the crop. They say the trail leads to Morston keep, and they expect the kitchens are stripped and Emma's throat slashed in her sleep."

Raimond laughed. "Your farmers have the souls of courtiers, Alyse. Tell them that it was, as they have already guessed, their new lord, not a pack of brigands, who crossed the barley field. Tell them Emma is in good health and that you know exactly what was in the kitchens when you left.''

It was good to hear her laugh. She spoke Raimond's message and waved farewell as Shaitan moved on. A few steps later, he pulled on the reins to avoid a cluster of women walking towards them upon the track. Raimond did not need to hear the words to guess the questions.

''Tell them we came by night to join their dancing upon the tor but we were too weary to stop.''

Before Alyse could speak, the shepherd's wife Hawise and two kitchen maids approached and made mock pitying sounds as they touched the woolen cloth of her kirtle. The other women laughed.

Raimond muttered a Frankish farewell to them and rode on. ''They think I ride you too hard of a night and leave you too exhausted for midsummer dancing?''

She looked back over her shoulder. ''How did you know?''

''Some thoughts,'' he said, ''sound the same in any tongue.''

From the cluster of tall stones upon the tor, they saw the fire's last, thin smoke rising to darken the sea mist above. There was a dark crimson glow at the foot of the largest monolith, the youngest ashes resting upon the site where Morston's long-dead fathers had built their ancient bonfires.

Raimond turned Shaitan's head to the path which skirted the high sides of the hill and turned in the saddle. Behind him, he saw the people of Morston watching them, standing silently in the rough green field. And he knew, then, that Alyse had been right. The small settlement so precariously lodged over the sea must continue; the weather-burned faces he had seen on this day's dawn would not willingly leave this ancient place.

Alyse sat across Raimond's lap as he guided Shaitan at a cautious pace along the twisting path marked by the cairns. They passed the broken branches and scattered ashes where Raimond had found her, beside the deep bog. A mile later, the overturned cart appeared, still half-sunk at the edge of the black-green pool. The ground beside it had been churned into mire by the mounts of those who had searched for a survivor beneath the heavy, broken wheels. Raimond turned his face from the site of his desperation.

The sun was visible now, and the night mist was burning clear of the grey land. The smoking place where Kernstowe's bonfire had died down was a short distance before them, sharing the horizon with the ringed trestle tables and the dark battlements of the keep beyond. Soon, the palisade wall would be visible, and the sentry would see them approach.

And the questions would come.

As if he had sensed the turn of Alyse's thoughts, Raimond hauled on the wide leather reins and brought Shaitan to halt at the last cairn. An arrow's flight ahead, the moor ended and the cultivated fields of Fortebras' new lands began.

"There will be questions," he said.

"What I told you is true," Alyse said. "Raimond, I told you what happened. I struck him—twice. And he died, bleeding from—"

"No, Alyse. Do not think upon that night. Keep your mind free to get through this morning." His arm tightened around her. "We will speak of that—that question when the time comes," he said. "There are other matters to answer this day. When we appear, my men will ask about last night. Say little to them; if possible, tell them nothing at all."

Raimond let the reins fall across Shaitan's neck and smoothed the dark tangles away from Alyse's brow. "I will tell them what they must believe: you wished to join the revels at Morston. I refused to take you across the moor at night. You were stubborn; you took the cart and left Wat to tell me to seek you."

He looked down at her and frowned. "Your face is scratched. Tell them you fell from the cart horse. It is true enough, I think."

"It is true. And if they do not believe that, and ask whether you were angry and beat me—"

"It matters not. Tell the Kernstowe people what you wish. My men will not ask; they know I do not beat women."

Shaitan moved beneath them, turning to face the wind still blowing from the north.

Raimond put his hand upon the wool-wrapped coffer in Alyse's arms. "Say nothing of this. When we reach Kernstowe, keep it beneath the cloak and take it to our chamber. Put it in the linen chest.''

''Raimond, I told the truth. I took nothing from this chest. And deRançon was there. He was there. He was dead when I left—''

''Alyse—I believe you. Put it from your mind. This morning, you must think of nothing but last night's doings, and an explanation for them. If you think of—the dead, all who see you will know something more is amiss.''

''But if he lives, Raimond—if he lives, and he returns—''

''He put his steel to the throat of a woman, Alyse. For that he will die when I find him. He will not come near you, be he alive, or a walking corpse. I will not leave you unprotected. But for now, put him from your mind.'' He looked back to the dark bulk of Kernstowe's keep on the horizon. ''Now can you act the chastened wife? The sentry has seen us.''

By nightfall, the coffer was well hidden, unnoticed in the general excitement of Lord Raimond's return with his foolish wife. The serving maids had asked no questions, but Alyse later heard them in the kitchen, speculating about her fall. She must have fallen into a thorn bush, they agreed, for Lord Raimond's fists would not leave such marks. As to how the lady Alyse came to be tossed into the bushes, they had much to say. If her husband had sent her flying into a thicket when he found her, it was no more than she deserved. Only four days wed, and leading her husband on a cold chase to the sea, when the lady should have been content to bide in bed, where she belonged of a night . . . There were other women, they agreed— many other women—who would not treat a fine, lusty man in such a way, however strong his temper might be . . . .

Alyse had found Wat stirring a kettle of pottage, glorying in his importance in the absence of Maud, who had gone back with an aching head to her bed in the loft above the north storehouse. Wat greeted her with a wide smile. ''I knew Lord Fortebras would find you. Is it true he tossed you in a holly bush for lying?''

''Wat!''

"Um. Not for lying, for jesting. Is it true he picked you up and you flew right over his shoulder like a bird?"

"Wat, that is a silly story. My face is scratched because I fell off the horse."

"Erec said you had the cart."

"Well, I lost the cart and rode the horse. And I fell off."

Wat stepped down from the stool he had been using to reach the rim of the kettle. "Lady Alyse, when you play the game again, you must take me. I can make a horse go where you want him, and you cannot. Hund said you frighten them when you hold the lines so tight."

"And who is Hund, who knows the lady Alyse's only fault?"

Raimond had followed her into the kitchens. He had been close at hand since their return to Kernstowe, oblivious to the general opinion that he was freshly besotted after an encounter on the moors with his wayward wife. He had fueled that rumor himself, allowing his men to speak uncorrected when they murmured of their lord's obsession with the lady Alyse.

Wat smiled up at his lord. "Hund is the smith."

"Walther is the blacksmith."

"No, Walther lives here. Hund was our blacksmith at Morston."

"The one who left?" Fortebras' voice was level, his expression calm.

"He went away a long time ago. He didn't say good-bye to me."

"Was he in haste?"

"Father Anselm said so. He said Hund went crusading with the lord deRançon."

Alyse put her hand upon Raimond's arm. "Father Anselm knew that Hund wanted to learn armory. When he—" there was a warning flash of blue in her husband's narrowed eyes. "When he went away, Father Anselm thought that he must have gone with deRançon."

Raimond's face showed no expression. "Perhaps he did." He turned back to Wat and brushed the top of the boy's wild, bristling hair. "What your friend Hund said is true, I fear. The lady Alyse seems to have a lot of trouble with horses. What you said is very sensible. When my lady next decides to wander, go with her, lad. Manage the horses and bring her safely back to me."

Wat gazed back with an expression of complete devotion. "I will, my lord."

"And no more jests. We must keep my lady wife safely with us."

"I know, my lord."

"And remember, Wat, you are too young—"

"I know, my lord. I am too young to know when I may tell a lie, even in jest, to my liege lord. I will remember," Wat said.

Alyse's eyes had begun to water in the steam wafting from the pottage.

Because he did not want to leave her alone, Raimond insisted that Alyse remain with him in the great hall when Rolf Nevers brought out the Kernstowe strongbox and the vellum scroll upon which he had marked the wool money and taxes for the past three years.

She had listened in disbelief as Raimond had claimed a large sum of gold from the strongbox for their journey to Windsor.

"You have managed these lands well, Rolf Nevers. Few stewards in the kingdom would have kept this much treasure safely for an absent lord."

There was a faint flush on Nevers' thin nose. "Fair words, my lord. I but did my duty, as I have sworn."

Raimond nodded. "I will not forget your honesty, Nevers."

Alyse gestured towards the stack of coins. "We will not need so much, my lord. My parents took only a few such coins when they made their journey to Windsor."

Raimond flashed a warning look over Nevers' head. "There will be expenses if we stay at court," he said. "You will need better clothing, as I have said. In the weeks at Windsor, you will need to buy more."

"Weeks? How can we spend weeks there? We must be back here for the early harvest. If we leave this week, that gives us only—"

"We do not leave this week. We will travel in August, after

the early harvest. Nevers will manage the great harvest very well, as he did these two years past.''

There was an intensity in his eyes which warned her to say no more.

Rolf Nevers looked up from the scroll. ''If my lord wishes to take a large sum to Windsor, it is his right. There will be more gold—much more, my lady, when the wool has been sold. Have you decided, my lady, when to bring your wool from Morston? I will send it to Dunhevet with our own, if you wish it. Just as we did last year . . .''

And the talk turned to supplies for Morston and the sale of fleece wool. Alyse toyed with the nearest of the stacks of gold coins set aside for Raimond's use. Kernstowe was a rich demesne, richer than she had imagined.

And its new lord was taking the price of a small army with him to Windsor. He had said nothing of the ransom tax which Kernstowe and every other estate in the land would have to pay.

Alyse remembered Raimond's warning looks and fell silent. And remained silent when her husband asked Rolf Nevers to give him parchment, pen and ink.

She doubted, then, that the heavy pile of gold beside the strongbox would make its way into Queen Eleanor's ransom treasury.

Raimond put the coins which he had set aside for Windsor into a soft leather bag and placed it in Nevers' strongbox. He took the parchment and ink to the sleeping chamber, and returned to lead Alyse to the hall for a cold meal in the company of his men-at-arms.

The first moment of awkwardness ended when Raimond, smiling placidly beneath a cold blue gaze, thanked his men for their forbearance the night before. ''As any of you could have told me,'' he drawled, ''as many of you tried to tell me, my lady was indulging in a jest of her own devising, leading me away from the last ale pot to clear my head on the moor. I had been too long away from such games, and followed in bad temper.'' He looked down the table, stopping to look carefully into each man's eyes. "I trust you returned to Kernstowe early enough to find your own pleasures waiting."

Erec clutched at his ale cup as the grizzled man beside him sent an elbow into the young knight's ribs. "Some of us had been already halfway into our"—he glanced at Alyse and coughed—"into our revels, my lord, when you summoned us. When we returned to Kernstowe, young Erec here found his— someone waiting at the bailey gate, sitting on her sweet— forgive me, my lady—she was sitting beneath the sentry post."

Erec's downy face reddened as the table shook beneath the drumming fists of his comrades.

"The rest of us, " the soldier continued, "were not so lucky. If I were a younger man, my lord, I'd say we should begin again tonight, bonfires and ale, and hope that we might each find ourselves a—your pardon, Lady Alyse—a good end to the night."

Raimond groaned in mock distress. "You will beggar me with the firewood and the ale. If I were a younger man, I might agree. As it is, between last night's ale and this morning's early rising, I will count myself lucky to manage the chamber stairs this night. Ask me another day, Guy, when I've not spent the night on the moors with my lady woodsprite here."

He rose and extended his hand to Alyse. "Come, my lady, and give me your arm up the stairs."

The well-meant laughter which followed them up the stairs was for Raimond alone. By speaking as he had, he had drawn attention from Alyse's scraped face and darkened eyes. The men-at-arms had been reassured and deceived by their lord's determinedly clumsy humor.

They did not see, as Alyse had seen, that his eyes had remained as distracted and cold as before. The brilliant blue which had so startled her when Raimond had come first to Morston had darkened to the color of the ancient silver rings in Queen Eleanor's coffer. Opaque, cold, and troubled.

Alyse found a small table beside the bedchamber hearth; Nevers' parchment and ink waited upon it.

Raimond barred the door and pushed the table closer to the heat of the fire. "It is from the empty sleeping chamber."

Alyse touched the smooth wood of deRançon's table. Everything in Kernstowe had once belonged to Harald deRançon; why should she feel aversion to only those things which had been placed in his bedchamber?

The carved wooden legs of the piece were heavily incised with a spiraling, serpentine design which seemed to writhe fitfully in the light of the fire. Alyse turned her back to the light.

Raimond spread the parchment across the surface. "I will take it back when I have finished writing."

"Tonight?"

"If you wish."

"Why did you bar the door? You will need a scribe. Nevers will write for you."

Raimond shook his head. "I am a second son, Alyse. I was taught to write before the King Henry's bishops realized that my future did not lie with the church."

Alyse smiled. She imagined the young Raimond deBauzan would have disrupted even the most tolerant religious order. "And how did you convince them of that?"

He smiled back. "My father took me to Avranches when I was seven years old; King Henry had called a council with the papal legates, and my father was one of the Norman lords he took with him to watch for treachery."

"Was there danger?"

Raimond's smile broadened. "Not from assassins. Only from me, when I saw one of the pope's messengers pinch my mother's serving maid; later that day, I set a candle beneath his bench."

"Was it—"

"Yes," he said. "What would have been the use of an unlit taper?"

"My lord, you were a terrible child. But loyal," she added, "and a defender of women at a tender age."

"Aye, tender of age, and tender of rump as well, after my punishment was done. I would have appreciated a little mercy from the woman I had avenged, but alas, she was the one told to carry me from the room and give me a whipping.'' He laughed. ''I was a sorry lad that day, but I had managed, all unwitting, to save myself from life as a cleric. Between the legate's lust and the maid's pretty bosom, somehow I escaped the abbey. King Henry himself declared that I was not the stuff of which churchmen are made.''

He placed his hand upon her belly and smoothed the soft wool of her kirtle. ''When our sons are born, I doubt there will be one among them with a churchman's nature. Will you be content, Alyse, to raise warrior sons?''

Her laughter stopped. ''I would be content, my lord, to be with you long enough to have sons. I pray I will be.''

''And who would take you from me?''

''Raimond—''

His embrace was sudden and strong, his lips hungry for her mouth. ''No one shall speak against you. No one shall harm you. And no one, living or dead, shall take you from me. Believe it, Alyse.''

Beneath that fierce blue gaze, one could not doubt that Raimond Fortebras would defend her with his life. ''I believe you,'' Alyse said. Almighty God, she prayed, protect this man from our enemies. Living and dead.

Then Raimond's hands were upon the laces at the neck of her kirtle. ''The parchment has fallen,'' Alyse whispered slowly.

He placed her hands upon the wide, dark cloth of his tunic. ''Then let our clothing follow it. Of a sudden,'' he whispered, ''I know I will not finish that letter before the moon rises.''

Raimond stared at the blank parchment before him. ''This matter of our lands and the queen's jewels becomes more tangled each day.''

''It was never simple,'' Alyse muttered. She was swathed in her warm bedchamber robe, sitting across from her half-naked husband at the serpent table.

He reached for the quill and dipped it in the vial of ink. ''No, it was not. And it became still more difficult when you hid the truth from me.''

Alyse returned his level gaze. "I meant to return to you, with the queen's jewels. And I would have stayed, if you had wanted me."

He wrote a single line. "But you did not trust me with the truth."

"It was not my decision alone. There were three of us, Raimond, at risk. I know—we all knew—what happens to murderers and those who help them. They hang. Witches come by night and take the hands. What is left hangs until it rots."

Raimond stared at her with unreadable eyes. "I do not want you to speak of hanging," he said at last.

Alyse was the first to look away. "It frightens you?"

"It frightens you. I see that you are in great need of brandy-wine, Alyse."

"Do not jest with me."

He found the flask beside the hearth and poured a large measure into the silver wine cup. "I never jest about brandy-wine, Alyse. Drink."

She needed a clear head if they were to speak of murder and hangings. "No. Thank you."

"Yes. Drink it."

She lifted the cup to her lips but did not drink.

"You imagined I would drag you to Dunhevet and watch while the king's justiciars accused you of murder. You and Emma and the blacksmith."

"You hate bloodshed. Do you not remember, Raimond? In Morston's chapel, when I told you I was no maid, you said my sin was an innocent one. Not a great sin, you said. Not like the spilling of a man's lifeblood. You said you left such atrocities behind you, in Palestine."

His mouth twisted slightly.

"You came here," she continued, "to live a peaceful life. Away from those blood-soaked fields. Had I had only my own fate to consider, I might have risked telling you—risked finding that I would disgust you. But I had Emma to think of. She did nothing, Raimond, but help me conceal what happened. She is blameless. I was the one who did it. I picked up the spade—"

"God's bones, Alyse. Sit down and be silent."

Her heart had begun to hammer again.

Raimond reached to level the cup in her hand. "Do you believe that I—that anyone—would see what you had to do that night as a sin? Think, Alyse. He was an armed knight threatening two women and an unarmed serf. If you had gone to Chilcheton and told Father Gregory—"

"—he would have written to Count John," Alyse said. "DeRançon was Count John's man. He said as much just before—"

"What did deRançon say?"

"He said Count John would not be surprised to find we were hiding gold from the queen's court at Poitiers. He said John believed his mother was keeping back from him the wealth he needed."

Raimond sighed. "Of course the dowager queen keeps her gold from John. If John had money enough to hire an army, his brother would return to find his kingdom gone. That is no secret, Alyse. A great number of English lords believe that keeping John solvent is a sensible course. If King Richard does not return, those lords will be in the new king's good graces. Count John has a hundred such benefactors. He did not miss deRançon among them."

"If it had been your neck, and those of two of your people, in danger—would you have risked telling anyone? In time, a rumor might have reached Dunhevet and Count John's men—"

Raimond leaned forward. "No, I would not have risked that. But I would not have believed a husband would declare his wife a murderer and see her people hanged with her."

"Bloodshed and treachery, Raimond. You hate them both. I did them both." She lifted the cup and took a deep swallow. It burned down her throat and behind her eyes.

When she blinked her eyes open, he was smiling. "You and I, madam, are going to breed fine sons together."

"And when you give them their first wooden swords, you will tell them tales of their bloodthirsty mother."

"Even so." He took the cup from her hands and set it beside the roll of parchment. "We must make a plan, tonight. There must be no more talk of sons, madam, until we agree upon our course.''

His eyes were no longer dark. The firelight shone within them, just as it had on their wedding night. Azure blue fired with golden flames—Alyse stiffened. ''The gold,'' she said. ''What will you do with the gold you set aside?''

''You do not want robes for court?''

''It is so much, Raimond. How will you use it? It is a great sum. I saw Nevers' face.''

Raimond began to write again upon the parchment. ''Let Nevers believe that we will spend it upon court finery.'' He looked up and smiled. ''And so we shall use some of the gold.''

''And the rest?''

He shrugged. ''We may need it to leave England.''

''Because of deRançon?''

''Possibly. But he is not a threat to us now, Alyse. If he lives, he has reason to remain hidden for some years. With his family's history, deRançon could not risk having King Richard discover that he had tried to take Queen Eleanor's property and slit the throat of one of her Poitevin ladies.''

''What history? His father was one of many Normans who rebelled against King Henry. There were many of them, and so many years ago—''

Raimond shook his head. ''Did you not know the rest? The old lord Geoffrey deRançon rebelled against Richard in Normandy. His half-brother, your first lord Harald deRançon, was given this land and told that he and his son must never return to Normandy or his older brother's lands at Taillecourt. If his heir angers King Richard, not even Count John will be able to save him. Did your parents not know that the deRançon lords have lived with great caution, these past years, if they lived at all?''

There had been signs, but she had not recognized them. The old lord deRançon, red-faced and furious that Nevers had turned back from the swollen river and delayed by three days the delivery of Kernstowe's annual tribute to Count John. The younger deRançon, eager to send more footsoldiers than King Richard had demanded for his army embarking for Palestine. And keeping his own well-trained men at Kernstowe, always on guard. "No," said Alyse, "my parents did not know. But my mother knew little of war and rebellions, save what little she understood of the struggle in which my father died. Her second husband—"

"Your stepfather, William?"

"Yes. He was never a man of the court, and knew less than my mother did of the quarrels of the great lords."

"If he had, he might have questioned Harald deRançon's right to take those untrained farm lads from Morston to send them to Palestine in the place of his own army." Raimond turned back to his half-filled page.

Alyse sat down and placed her aching head in her hands. "If he fears the king so much, deRançon must be hiding, waiting to see whether King Richard will return."

"Or he may be dead."

Alyse shuddered. "His body was gone."

"Your smith may have taken the body away to conceal it where no one could find it."

"Why would he do that?"

Her husband frowned. "He may have feared he would be accused of the deed. If you had decided to denounce Hund, the justiciars would have dug up the dry well and found no body. And Hund would have been saved."

"I would never—Hund knew I would never—"

Raimond looked at her with narrowed eyes. "You doubted that you could trust your own husband, Alyse. The serf may have feared you would some day tell of deRançon's death and let him pay the price."

She had imagined that Hund had fled from Morston in panic, overwhelmed by the horror of what he had seen that night. It had never occurred to her that Hund might fear she would send after him, to blame him for deRançon's death. "Merciful God," she whispered.

"DeRançon may not have died that night. If the man had stirred after you and Emma left, while Hund was alone with him in the granary, would the smith have had the courage to finish deRançon?"

"Kill him? No. Hund is a gentle soul. He would never kill."

The broad hand which covered Raimond's jaw did not quite

conceal the widening smile which showed behind his fingers. "Then Hund is not as fierce as my bloodthirsty wife."

"It is wrong to laugh, Raimond."

He straightened his face, but his eyes glowed brighter still. "Some day, Alyse, when the danger is past, we will speak of that night and you will smile. I swear it."

When the danger is past. "Do you believe deRançon lives?"

The light vanished from Raimond's eyes. He shrugged. "If he lives, the snake may be waiting to come back to claim this land. If King Richard falls and John becomes king, deRançon will expect John to give him back the land. If this happens, we will be ready." He ran his hands through his hair and glanced at her.

"Then there is no danger while King Richard lives."

Raimond sighed. "There is a much greater danger, Alyse. John and his supporters are but cubs in the presence of an old, fierce lioness."

"Queen Eleanor?"

"When she sees how little gold, how few jewels we found in that coffer, she will be angry."

"Emma said there was nothing more in the chest when my mother took it from Salisbury."

Raimond nodded. "I know—I believe Emma. I believe you. But the dowager queen is old, and her memory may have turned strange. She expects that I will bring her great riches from her cache at Morston. Enough to bring Richard back soon, she told me."

He gestured to the parchment roll. "I have written to my father, Alyse, to ask him to offer us refuge if Queen Eleanor accuses us of treason."

"Treason?"

"Yes. For to hold back in the matter of King Richard's ransom is treason."

"We might be accused—"

"Our future, Alyse, lies in the hands of an old woman sick at heart over her son's imprisonment. Her memory may have deceived her."

"And if we say we never found it?"

"She will send others, then, to tear Morston to the ground

and sift through the smallest pieces. She will guess that we have found it. We have no choice but to take what little we found to Windsor and give it to her.''

He gestured to the serpent-legged table. ''But we will not go until Lammas, when the first ransom money will be taken abroad. By then, my brothers will be ready to help us.''

''And Kernstowe? Your lands?''

''I may lose them. There are other lands where a man with a good sword arm is needed, Alyse. There will be a place for us.''

''But not in England.''

''If this goes badly for us, not in England. Never again.''

CHAPTER
FOURTEEN

Two days after midsummer, Alain of Pilat and his young cousin, Erec, said a hasty farewell to Beda, the serving maid, and set off for Normandy. With them, in a bag concealed beneath Erec's new tunic, were letters from Raimond deBauzan to his father, Lord Rannulf, and to Lord Rannulf's firstborn son Ivo, heir to the Bauzan lands.

Of his father's answer, Raimond held no doubts. Nor did he fear that his brother Ivo would fail to support him if Queen Eleanor's unwanted confidence in him turned to distrust. His only worries were of timing, of planning his appearance at Windsor early enough to reassure the queen of his good faith, yet late enough to allow his kinsmen time to put their considerable influence in place to protect his lady wife.

Twice, during the weeks he waited for Erec's return, Raimond came near to leaving Kernstowe with Alyse and his remaining eight men. In three days of hard riding, they could reach the far coast to sail for Normandy. Each time, Raimond had decided against flight. It would take only one small rumor, one royal courier's report that he had seen Lord Raimond deBauzan riding straight for the southern ports, to raise the dowager queen's suspicions and turn her thoughts to the possibility of treason.

No, the safest course was to wait until help was in place and then to take the cursed, paltry jewels to their careless owner, and pray God that the gems of Queen Eleanor's memory had not grown in size and number with the passage of the years.

Nor would he tax the queen with tales of Harald deRançon's perfidy. This was no matter for royal justiciars, but a debt Raimond would settle himself, and risk the consequences. When he put the former lord of Kernstowe under his sword, most would believe Raimond had done it to keep his lands. If he was lucky, he would manage to take Alyse with him into hasty exile. If his luck failed, he might pay for deRançon's life with his own.

Each day he waited, Raimond prayed to God that deRançon was already dead.

On the third day after midsummer, Raimond left Kernstowe before dawn and returned after noon with Hugo Gerbrai and the young knight, Gareth. Behind them, upon the wool sack in Morston's heavy cart, was Emma des Roches and four chests of clothing.

Gerbrai swung down from his horse and eyed the keep of Kernstowe with obvious relief. "Now here is a fit place to house an honest knight." He turned to see Alyse emerging from the storehouse door. "Your pardon, Lady Alyse. But my old bones do not love that cold, windy ruin. It is a place for younger men than I."

"Take care," Raimond said behind him. "My lady wife has a temper that would send you straight back to the coast without tasting the feast this night."

"Feast? By Christ's eyetooth, how I have longed for a proper feast. The wenches at Morston—again, your pardon, my lady—hardly know what to do with decent food when it is given to them. Why, just last week I brought them a fat young hart from the woods north of the fields, and they ruined it. Cut the meat with the grain, if you please, and treated it just as they do mutton. Boiled it with their damned bitter roots until it was naught but broth. Now, if they had roasted it and prepared a sauce—" he stopped and squinted into the low morning sunlight streaming past the portal of the keep. "By Saint Peter's great foot, who is that? Can it be the skinny young knave I sent from Morston these days past?"

Wat giggled and brushed the crumbs from his new tunic. "You will like it here, Sir Hugo. The kitchen is very big and there are three women and two lads to cook. There is something different every day. And they are very clean. Maud is pretty and she gives you bread whenever you want it and—"

Raimond broke into Wat's litany. "Well, there you have it, Hugo. Will you manage here, while we are at Windsor? Keep the sentries in place and the fields in order, and you may spend the rest of your time making up for your lean days at Morston."

Wat drew a breath and began again. "Last night there was pork and the last of the dried apples from last year. It will be even better now that the lady Alyse's dresses are made; Maud and Beda don't have to sew in the afternoons and they can be in the kitchens all day. That's where they are today, for your feast . . ."

Raimond turned from the piping voice and took Alyse's hand. "Hugo has agreed to take charge of Kernstowe. Gareth will take charge of Morston when he goes back tomorrow. And we will go to Windsor, when the time comes."

It was impossible, in the soft morning sun, with Wat and Hugo and William looking on, and her husband's warm hand covering her own, to be afraid.

The dagger gleaming across Raimond's palm was thin-bladed, its richly incised hilt small enough for a woman's hand.

"Take it," he said. He slipped it into a rigid leather sheath and placed it in Alyse's hands.

"Is this what women at court are using? It is too long, I think, for an eating knife."

"The women at court have them. They wear them within their sleeves, or beside their waists, beneath a cloak when traveling. This is not an eating knife, Alyse."

He had been dark-eyed and moody since bringing Hugo from Morston. After the first jovial moments of reunion, even Hugo had lapsed into what would pass, for Hugo, as a time of quiet.

"Something is wrong," Alyse said. "Tell me."

"We must be careful."

She smiled. "If there is one thing about which we have agreed since our wedding day, Raimond, it is that we must be careful."

He was frowning still. "Tell me," she said. "I promise not to run screaming into a thorn bush. I am beyond that, now. I hope."

His mouth twisted into what might have been a smile. "Running across the moor is out of the question, Alyse. Alone, you will go nowhere." He set her from him, at arm's length. "I found Father Anselm eager to talk, this morning at Morston. I tried to make him understand that this autumn your freemen and serfs would be given the choice of remaining where they are or coming to Kernstowe. He understood, and began to list those who might want to leave. And those who had left already. Among the last was Hund, the smith. Father Anselm told me that Hund had left Morston two summers ago. With deRançon."

Alyse sat down. "It is not possible."

"Then why did the priest say it?"

"Father Anselm knew that Hund wanted to learn to make fine armor. When he disappeared after—that night—Father Anselm began to say that deRançon had offered Hund a place with King Richard's army in Palestine, and that Hund had traveled with deRançon. It was helpful that he believed that, for it lessened the questions asked after Hund disappeared."

"He told me, Alyse, that with his own eyes he saw Hund leave two years ago, on midsummer night."

"He never said that to me."

"This morning, he asked whether I had seen an armorer or blacksmith of Hund's appearance with King Richard's army in Palestine. I questioned him. He did not hear the words, I think, but I made signs as well, and the priest began to speak of what he had seen. On midsummer night two years ago, he said, he had been awakened by torch light near his window."

Alyse sucked in her breath. "It is the only way to waken him, for he can't be roused by noise. He feels the light near him, and he looks to see whether the dawn has come."

"Well, he wakened before dawn that night. He saw Hund

ride close by his hut, carrying a torch. Leading a packhorse with deRançon's harness upon it and its pack heavily laden for the journey.''

Alyse sat down. ''The horses. Emma and I looked for them the next morning, but there were no horses. We thought they had wandered back to Kernstowe, and feared there would be questions. But Nevers never mentioned them.''

''If deRançon thought to come upon you by stealth that night, he would have left his saddlehorse and the pack animal outside Morston's gates.'' Raimond rested his hand upon Alyse's shoulder. ''I believe he lived, Alyse, and compelled the smith to help him. He must have promised—he would have promised anything, at that time. And he would have told your blacksmith where to find the horses to carry him away.''

''But the next morning, the grave was closed, the earth level and the empty bins covering the place. Hund had done as we had told him.''

''If deRançon lived that night, and if he was not wounded too badly to reason, he must have had the good sense to know that what he had attempted was treason. He had threatened a family trusted by Queen Eleanor, and had tried to steal her treasure. For all he knew, half the gold King Henry's army missed in Poitiers might have been at the bottom of that well. He had reason to hide, and to wait to see what tales came out of Morston. It suited him, perhaps, to leave the Holy Lands unvisited. He must have asked Hund to fill in his false grave.'' Raimond's mouth twisted in a cold smile. ''In that, the knave proved a sensible man.''

''But where would he have gone? Do you think Count John would have sheltered him all these months?''

''Even John would not have given shelter to a man who had threatened the daughter of Queen Eleanor's loyal lady.''

''Then, if he still lives, where would he be?''

The half smile disappeared. Raimond began to play idly with the hem of Alyse's new shift. ''Do you not grow weary of these questions, wife? Would you not prefer to hear what the Saracen ladies wear beneath their silken gowns?''

Alyse stopped her husband's questing hand. ''I would prefer to hear the answer to my question, Raimond.''

He sighed. "The knave may have died later of his wounds. More likely, he lies in a grave far from here, and Hund was too frightened to return to you." Raimond's voice darkened. "His shade will surely come to dwell with us, wife, if we speak of him again. It is a thing I have learned to do, Alyse—to keep the ghosts of vanquished enemies from my bedchamber. I would have you do the same."

"I ask your forgiveness, then."

Raimond drew his wife into the shelter of his arms.

"I wish you had never come to this place," she said.

"And never taken you to wife?" he chided.

"Even that. If this matter goes wrong, you will lose your honor, and live in exile."

"In some place where the summers are warm, and a man does not need to hire a merchant ship to have wine for his table? I have told you before, my lady, that it would be no hardship with you at my side."

Alyse smiled and blinked back tears unshed. "I will be with you, my lord husband."

"Then you will need to learn, my lady wife, what the Saracen ladies wear beneath their silken gowns."

She brought his hand back to rest upon her thigh. "Tell me, Raimond."

His hand closed upon the thin linen of her shift. "I will show you."

There was witchery in his touch, strong enough to send her thoughts from the future. For that long summer night, all questions ceased.

When July brought the summer heat, the sleeping chambers within Kernstowe's mossy grey walls remained cool. Emma, pleased to leave Morston's cold comforts behind her, now shared the larger chamber with Beda and Maud. By day, the three women sat in the sunlight beside the western embrasures and sewed court robes for their lady Alyse. By night, they slept on pallets against the walls; none of them had wished to use the bed of the dead lord deRançon. Nor did Maud and Beda imagine that the sharp-tongued, exacting Emma, late of Morston, had her own reasons for leaving that wide bed unoccupied. Lord Raimond and the lady Alyse would, they speculated, want to move to the western chamber when the winter snows began.

Raimond deBauzan and his lady wife kept to their bedchamber by night. Long after the three women in the western chamber had settled into their pallets in the soft summer darkness, they would hear the sound of their lord and lady speaking behind the thick oaken door. That door never opened, now, between dusk and dawn.

Since the lady Alyse's midsummer folly, her husband had not taken her to the river, to walk by torch light seeking a place where lovers might spend the sweet early hours of the darkness. Maud had slipped away, one night, to meet the cartwright in the bailey yard. There had been a bad moment when the sentries—there were three of them, now, since that midsummer night—had found them at the gate and had fallen upon them in the darkness, pinning the startled Alaric to the ground until the torches were brought to illuminate his features.

Summoned from his bed, Lord Raimond had questioned them both, ignoring Maud's embarrassed claims that they had planned only the briefest look at the river. He had dismissed them with a short rebuke and repeated his recent orders—no one was to enter within Kernstowe's walls between dark and dawn. If Maud wanted to see the river by night, he said, she and the red-faced cartwright would be obliged to leave before dusk and to occupy themselves until dawn. For the bailey gate would open for no one by night.

Young Wat heard the kitchen maids' complaints and approached the lord Fortebras with an innocent but complete account of the maids' distress that they could no longer go with their lovers to the half-grown fields. Lord Raimond had laughed, and the lady Alyse had smiled as well, but they would not relent.

The bailey gate stayed closed and guarded from dusk to dawn.

It was just after dusk on Lammas night that a sentry's heavy fists upon their door awakened them. The lord Fortebras' men were back, the sentry bellowed through the door. They were outside the palisades, awaiting Lord Fortebras' permission for the men-at-arms to unbar the gate.

Raimond pulled on chainse and tunic before grabbing his sword in its scabbard and lifting the bar from the chamber door.

Alyse sat up. "Why your sword? Is it not Alain and Erec, returning from Normandy?"

"Very likely."

She reached for her chamber robe and thrust her arms into the deep, soft sleeves. "You have doubts?"

"Stay here. I will bring their news back to you."

"You are worried." Alyse found her shoes in the moonlight and crossed to the door.

Raimond touched her cheek. "Not worried. Cautious. I will make sure they are alone."

"And if they are not?"

"They should be alone. If they are not, they are bringing more men from my father. Or—"

"Or what?"

He rammed the leather strap through the buckle of his sword belt. "Or they were noticed by the queen's men. Or John's men. Or both."

"They would tell you now, before the gates open."

Raimond smiled thinly. "Never doubt the ability of the Plantagenets and their brood to compel men."

Alyse frowned. "Never. They sent you to wed me."

He laughed at her displeasure and gave her bottom a solid pat. "They compelled me to come here, wife, but they do not compel me to want you beyond reason. That I do freely, Alyse."

The hammering at the door began again. Alyse followed her husband's broad shoulders down the narrow, winding stair and across the deserted great hall. She stood inside the bailey gate as Raimond vaulted up to the lookout platform and hailed the men below.

Moments later, the gates swung open; two mud-encrusted mounts with dark-garbed riders trotted into the yard and headed for the stable troughs. Erec and Alain, unrecognizable beneath the grime of their journey, walked stiff-legged beside their tall lord to the great hall to quench their own dusty thirst.

When Alyse returned from the kitchen with a jug of ale, the two men had removed their capes and pulled small bags of letters from their tunics.

"Thank you, Lady Alyse," Erec said. He buried his mouth in the cup she poured him and looked up, smiling, to wipe his face on his darkened sleeve.

"Were you seen?" asked Raimond in a low voice.

"Only at Dover. A courier from the queen was on the same boat, and asked questions."

Raimond cursed. "What did you tell him?"

"That you were sending news of your marriage to your father and brother, telling them of your good fortune and lands, asking their blessing upon your lady wife."

"And?"

"What, my lord?"

"Did he believe you? Did he question your haste?"

"No, my lord. He did not mention it."

Another curse broke the silence. "The queen does not hire simpletons to carry her dispatches. There will be questions."

Alain made a small gesture. "I doubt it, my lord. The courier was loud as a magpie and as prone to speak. He was carrying a summons from the queen to Hubert Walter, who was in Caen."

Raimond raised one brow. "That messenger will not last long in Queen Eleanor's service, if he does not learn discretion. What else did he say?"

"He was to wait and return with the bishop. He was not to return without him."

"Another fortunate man, to be blessed with Queen Eleanor's demands."

"My lord?"

Alyse laughed and drew Alain's gaze to her smile. "Your lord told me that Bishop Walter returned from Palestine half-dead from arguing the terms of truce with Saladin's advisors. He said that Hubert Walter wanted nothing more than a few years of peace."

Raimond nodded slowly. "My lady remembers well. So much for Walter's peace, poor wretch."

Erec reached for the ale pot. "There are many such, according to the courier. He asked us whether you and the lady Alyse had started your journey to Windsor. Said he heard the queen expects you before harvest time."

Raimond covered Alyse's hand upon the table. "She does. Obviously, she does not trust me to treat her waiting lady's daughter as well I should, and she intends to question my lady herself. Well, wife, will you come with me to Windsor to give the queen your good report?"

The sudden, slight pressure of his hand reminded her that the young knights, though weary from their journey, were regarding Raimond with open curiosity. She swallowed quickly and smiled. "Well, my lord, that depends. We will visit the clothing markets, I think, before I see the queen. My report will depend upon the splendor of the headdress you will buy for me."

The letters from Normandy brought a smile of relief to Raimond's face. "My brother Ivo and a large party of men from Bauzan will be at Canterbury in one week's time. If they go to Windsor, it may raise Queen Eleanor's suspicions, but a pilgrimage to Thomas Becket's tomb following safe deliverance from Palestine will cause no comment."

Alyse smiled back. "From my mother's tales, Queen Eleanor will not think well of any knight who prays at Thomas Becket's tomb."

"True enough, but she cannot afford to make her opinions of him public. If she did, she would be a very lonely woman indeed." He held the second letter in his hand. "My father writes that my cousin Montbazon, the one who delivered Queen Eleanor's summons to me at Dover, will be at Windsor, and will be advised to take care for us. If there is trouble, he will send word to Ivo."

It was arranged. If there was trouble, the combined efforts of Raimond's kin would see them safely out of England. Once their absence was discovered, Queen Eleanor's displeasure would descend upon all who had helped them.

Raimond had tossed the letters onto the settle. "What is this, Alyse? Tears, now that our escape is made possible?"

She shook her head.

He took her in his arms. "You'll be safe, Alyse. I swear it."

Her tears were staining his tunic. She drew back and began to brush the droplets from the cloth. "I know you will keep me safe. But at what price to your family? Your brother, your father, his cousin Montbazon—what will happen to them, if they shelter me?"

He smiled and began to brush the salt from her cheeks. "They will be sheltering both of us, and gladly. This is not the first time the men of Bauzan have felt the Plantagenets' displeasure. Indeed, we have never been dainty of their opinions, if the cause warrants plain speaking and quick action. Believe me, wife, of all the causes for which you might weep, this is the least necessary."

"I do not believe you. You have married trouble, Raimond. And your family may suffer for it."

"My family," he said, "will manage very well. In all the years since they came south to Normandy, they have never had an angry king's army at their castle walls."

"No king has ever been as angry as Queen Eleanor will be, if she thinks I stole King Richard's ransom jewels."

"Armies avoid besieging my father's keep because they know it is well defended. Believe me, wife. If it comes to trouble, my kin will survive the dowager's displeasure."

CHAPTER FIFTEEN

In the weeks she had passed at Kernstowe, the aged Emma des Roches had lost the slight tremor which had plagued her at Morston. Her cheeks had bloomed and her eyes shone clear after nights in a warm pallet far from the pounding of the sea. The silken rags she had worn at Morston had disappeared, and in their place were new garments, sewn from the finest cloth in Dunhevet's markets. Her speech had gained new authority.

It was that last improvement Raimond regretted. He sank back in his chair at Kernstowe's high table and remembered not to place his boots upon the newly scrubbed boards. The serving maids had long since carried away the remains of the morning meal, and the passageway to the kitchens was deserted. From the bailey yard came the sounds of the Bauzan men at arms readying their mounts and weapons for the daily practice which Raimond now required and which he should be leading at this moment.

Raimond closed his eyes. "Madam, has my lady wife not warned you to speak quietly, if at all, of Morston's service to the queen? Did you keep her grace's secret all these years only to shout the history of it through the walls of this keep?"

Emma raised an ivory fist. "I will shout louder still if you take that poor child to Windsor without me."

"That poor child is my lady wife, and near twenty years of age. Alyse has agreed that you will stay here."

"And who will deal with Queen Eleanor? My poor Alyse, who has no knowledge of the court? You, my lord, with your rude speech—"

"Madam, if courtesy is your concern, have a care for your own words."

"—will have you both in disgrace before your packhorses reach the royal stables. I will speak properly to Queen Eleanor, and remind her that the coffret was but half full when she gave it into our keeping those many years ago—"

Raimond sighed. "Madam, I will give the queen your greetings and your message. But you will stay here, with Gerbrai."

"And if the queen turns against you—"

"If the queen is angry, I have the means to protect Alyse." Raimond lowered his voice. "You will be safe as well. Hugo will know what to do. You will go south with him in the wagon, disguised as a merchant's wife, and sail for Normandy, where you will travel to my father's house. Alyse will be waiting for you."

"And who will comfort my lady Alyse if you must take her to Normandy, dragging her along roads she has never seen, and across the water? What will you do if her fears come upon her—"

"She fears the sea?"

"Not just the sea. All of it."

"All of it? Speak plainly, madam."

Emma made a small sound of triumph and lowered her hand to the table. "You do not know? Of course you do not know. You do not know the first thing about Alyse—"

Raimond dropped his own fist to the boards with a dull thud. "Tell me. Now. What fears?"

She sat back and placed her hands carefully upon her lap. "Alyse has feared the roads, and open places, since the day we brought her out of Salisbury with her mother and William. She gave such mighty screams for a child so small, we thought her voice would break."

"What did she fear?"

"Anything outside the walls of Salisbury. Alyse had not

been outside the fortress since she was a babe in arms. We had to pry her little hands from the fortress gates. She covered her eyes halfway to Shaftesbury, and never spoke after that. She was silent until we reached Exeter.''

"She was only a child. Now Alyse is a woman grown—she crossed the moor alone, at night—''

"You brought her to Morston in a death-swoon. How will you get her to Normandy, traveling with rough men?''

"Alyse knows she is safe with me.''

"You will fail her.'' The woman fell into a narrow-eyed silence, her wrinkled mouth moving without speech. She drew her mantle close about her, as a winter traveler might have done.

Raimond softened his voice. "When this journey is over, when the danger is past, where do you want to go?''

"What do you mean?''

"You may stay here, if you wish. Or follow us to my father's lands, if we flee. Or do you wish to return to Poitiers?''

"Never.''

"Your family—Alyse's family—''

"Gone. They are all dead. The old king Henry killed them when he put down the young princes' rebellion.''

"Alyse's cousins were turned out of Mirbeau, but surely they can be found?''

"You will find them all at Mirbeau, my lord. In their tombs in the crypt. The last of them died when the king's army came to Poitiers.'' Emma pursed her mouth into an expression of disgust. "Take her to see them, my lord, should you get as far as Poitou. Her dead are all she has left, in this world, thanks to Henry Plantagenet.''

"She has me,'' Raimond growled. "And, God help me, I will be enough.''

"You wanted lands and peace, my lady told me. You will not have them if you anger the queen.''

From the kitchen came the sounds of the maids returning to their labors. Beda appeared in the passageway, a bundle of kindling in her arms. Raimond rose to his feet. "The lands may be lost, and peace may end,'' he said to Emma. "But I will not fail my wife.''

* * *

Erec and Alain went to Dunhevet soon after, and came north along the river track leading three new mounts, a bay gelding and two black mares. Raimond offered Rolf Nevers his pick of the three, and took his steward's own grey mare for the lady Alyse.

Nevers seemed eager to give up the mare. "Indeed, my lord, she was not mine. I never used her until the lady Constance was—until she died. And afterward, it would not have been good to leave the mare to pasture. She is a valuable mount, and it seemed better to use her, keep her used to the saddle—"

Raimond stopped the man's breathless words with an angry gesture. "Nevers, I do not begrudge you the use of the horse. By Saint Peter's great nose, I tire of your excuses for the use you made of Kernstowe when you were without a lord. You kept it well, you saved the gold in trust, it matters not that you drank a few casks of wine, that you used the mare, that you used the serving maids, as they were willing. Have I not told you I am pleased with your stewardship?"

Nevers looked at the ground. "Yes, my lord."

Raimond turned to go. "Then choose one of the three new mounts and use it—and learn to save your words of repentance for matters of importance." He looked again at the steward. Was there something about the mare? If Alyse was to ride the beast to Windsor, there must be no question of its soundness. "The mare—"

"Yes. Yes, my lord." Nevers had not lost the fearful catch in his voice.

"The lady Constance used the mount?"

"Yes."

"It seems a docile beast. Was the lady Constance pleased with her?"

"She said so."

Something in Nevers' voice made Raimond turn back again. "How did the lady die?"

"In her sleep, my lord. One morning she was dead. That was all."

She had died at deRançon's side. In his bed. In the room where Alyse refused to sleep.

With effort, Raimond kept his voice low. "Had she been ill?"

Nevers dropped his gaze to his boots. "No, my lord. She had miscarried of two babes, but that was years before she died. My lord Harald—Lord deRançon was sure she must have been riding too fast, and injured herself being jostled about upon her mare the day before, and died because of it. She was not strong, the lady Constance—"

"Did she ride alone?"

Nevers looked up, misery in his eyes. "She rode with Lord Harald. But she had no mark upon her, my lord. I doubted— we all doubted that it was the fault of the mare. The lady Constance ate her evening meal and went to bed and in the morning, Lord Harald found her dead. It—"

"Speak."

Nevers drew a shallow breath. "It might have been the fever, come quickly upon her."

"What fever?"

"William of Morston had died the week before, and the lady Isabelle a few days later. Our priest had gone to help bury them. Only a fortnight from then, he buried our poor lady."

"Where is this priest? I have seen no priest here."

Nevers looked even more miserable. "He was old, and had pain in his bones. Lord Harald sent him back to the abbey at Chilcheton, where he prays for the lady Constance's soul."

Raimond dismissed Nevers and led Shaitan from his stall. He would ride alone this day, and think upon what Nevers had revealed. Had deRançon poisoned his wife, or smothered her in order to clear his way to wed the newly-orphaned Alyse? Had he turned to murder to claim Morston's lady and the rumored treasure? If he still lived, would the man return to this land to conceal, with more murders, the coward's acts he had committed?

He threw the saddle across Shaitan's back and reached for the girth. He would not yield to rage. Not until he had deRançon before him, within the reach of his sword.

Raimond cleared his mind of all but the matter of Harald

deRançon's possible return. He put from him the image of that faceless wife-killer riding across the moor to Morston to demand Alyse's hand, and to lie with her without marriage vows. With effort, he turned his thoughts elsewhere—to the nearly empty coffer, to the granary walls, and the hut in which Father Anselm had slept.

He rode out through Kernstowe's gates and turned Shaitan to the west, where Morston's small tor was barely visible across the moor. The tor—

Raimond pulled Shaitan to an abrupt halt. The shepherd's tales he had heard that first night, in the Morston guardroom, took on a darker cast. Two people had died on the hill, at the bottom of a slope which a child could manage easily. Wat's mother, a young woman herding swine, had died last summer. And the old shepherd Lars had fallen and died only days before Raimond had come to Morston. From the tor, a man could watch all that happened within the cluttered bailey yard at Morston and in the fields—

Shaitan shook his head and sidled from the track. Raimond lifted the reins and turned south, to ride past the demesne fields where the Kernstowe villagers were scything the early-ripened oats. The two who had died at the tor had probably fallen, perhaps frightened by a far-roaming wolf from the forests.

If he did not control his thoughts, Raimond would begin to see deRançon's hand in every foul deed in the duchy of Cornwall. It was enough to know what the man had done to Alyse in the weeks before he had disappeared. For that, deRançon would die the coward's death he deserved.

"Raimond, there is much to be done before the first harvest begins here. How can I—" Alyse climbed down from the storage hut loft and shook the dust from her kirtle. "How can we ride out each afternoon and leave my tasks undone?"

"Easily. You walk through that door and to your horse. You mount the mare and—"

"Do not jest, my lord." Alyse fixed her husband with a withering frown. "You do not know what it is to starve. When you have God's bounty at your hand, it is a sin to leave it untended.''

It was impossible to resist. Raimond reached for the bounty concealed beneath his wife's bodice and set about tending his good fortune.

Alyse's cry of outrage subsided into a murmur of pleasure. Her hand caught his wrist and pushed it to her waist. "Do you mean to take me now?" she whispered. "Or will you wait until the lads bringing the wagons are through the door to gawk at us?"

Raimond smiled. "As I said, wife, we will ride out this afternoon. If you get your mare to move quickly, we'll be far down the river path before I ravish you."

She glanced back at the confusion of empty grain troughs and baskets in the loft. "Raimond, the harvest is important—"

He sighed. "And what I have to teach you is even more necessary."

"I am not jesting."

"Nor am I." He stepped back and drew her with him toward the door. "There are some things—other than love games, Alyse—you must learn before we leave for Windsor. I want you to handle your mount so well that you need not think before you guide her. I want you to face the open road without fear, to ride without holding the saddlebow as if you would wrench it from the saddle. I want you to learn to use your dagger so quickly that it will be something more than a weapon for a man to wrest from you and use against you." Raimond caught his breath. "Do not look at me so, Alyse. This is necessary."

"You must think me a useless creature," she whispered. "Good enough for your bed, perhaps, but a burden in all else."

"You speak of burdens? By all that's holy, you have borne and hidden more burdens than a woman should know. It is time, Alyse, that you allowed another to carry a part of them." Raimond turned her face to meet his gaze. "No one will starve, not here nor at Morston. The Kernstowe harvest was rich last year, and it shall be again this year, whether we are here or not. The burden that you were born to bear, that I vowed to bear, is to find Queen Eleanor at Windsor after Lammastide and give her the damned coffret. And I cannot make the journey if each mile I fear I will lose you should I have to leave your side.''

She drew a long breath. ''I see.''

He drew his fingers along her cheek. ''I must not lose you, Alyse.''

She blinked twice and turned to the door. ''Then I had better learn how to mount the mare without losing the reins.''

Each day after he led his men in practice at arms, Raimond deBauzan rode out from Kernstowe with his wife. Each day they took a different direction; once, when the summer's heat was at its peak, they forded the river downstream from Kernstowe and rode east, and turned back when the sun was low in the sky. Every day they followed the same practice: Alyse always rode first, guiding her mount along the chosen path. Raimond rode close behind her, speaking only when Alyse was unsure of the direction. Later, they would ride side by side, letting their mounts find their way home.

On the last day of heat, after they had stopped to eat bread and cheese, Raimond had begun to teach Alyse to strike a man with her fists. ''This is useless,'' Alyse had said. ''Try as I will, you are too swift for me. And when I manage to strike you, my hand hurts and you never falter.'' She rubbed her fingers and smiled slowly at her husband. ''I liked our games yesterday in the meadow much better.''

''Yesterday in the meadow, you showed much skill, my lady. When you can defend yourself as well as you play at love games, then we will go back to the meadow.''

Alyse sighed. ''Then there will be no more afternoons of pleasure, Raimond. I will never have the strength to overcome a man.''

''But you will have the skill to disable him.'' Raimond drew his dagger from his boot. ''Put this in your fist, and strike as I have taught you to do, and you will wound an attacker. Do it quickly—across the face, if you can—and run. On the road to Windsor, you must carry the knife I gave you, and use it in this way.''

Alyse looked at the bright steel upon her husband's palm. "I could not."

Raimond smiled. "You may need to. You may not have a spade at hand."

Alyse looked away.

Raimond's smile did not falter. "Come, Alyse. Pick it up and use it on that sapling oak. There may be time for the meadow later." He offered the glittering hilt upon his hand, and she reached to take it, but he moved from her in a swift and soundless motion.

She threw up her hands. "Must I learn to steal daggers as well as attack with them?"

He pushed the hilt towards her. "Take it and hide it in your boot, as I taught you."

Alyse sighed. "I learned that well enough yesterday. What I need—"

But he was not heeding her words. He was looking past her shoulder, to the river road. Alyse turned and saw three riders moving slowly north. Their surcoats were white—unearthly white, with blood red marks upon them, fluttering in eerie contrast to the rich green and gold of the harvest fields.

"Who are they?"

"Trouble."

"Raimond, what are they?"

He looked at her then, and his expression softened. "Not the Hunt, Alyse. Not the Wild Hunt. They are Templars."

Alyse tucked the knife into the secret fold within her boot. "I never saw one before—never thought to see them here."

"Nor did I." Raimond picked up Alyse's mantle from the long grass. "They will have seen us in passing. We should not keep them waiting."

"They may not stop at Kernstowe. They may be heading up to Biddaford—"

"No." Raimond led the horses from the river and helped Alyse mount. "They will stop at Kernstowe. And we must greet them as if we have nothing to hide."

"They are Count John's men?"

Raimond shook his head. "They answer to no lord of this land. They have estates in every part of Christendom, but they give their allegiance only where they see fit. And they reveal their reasons to no man.''

He brought Shaitan up beside the mare. ''If there is a Christian king they may be expected to support, it is Richard Plantagenet. His mother, too, may have their allegiance.'' Raimond smiled briefly. ''She gave them rich lands at La Rochelle, and the use of the harbor. Thus she knows she may trust them—until they receive a richer gift from one of her enemies.''

''Will they know—''

''No. Do not imagine that they know any of Queen Eleanor's secrets.'' Raimond lowered his voice. ''If the dowager had believed she could trust the Templars to deal with our task, she would have chosen them to come here in my place. No, they will not know the tale, but they may be acting upon her orders.'' He reined Shaitan to a halt, and reached for Alyse's hand. ''Stay by me,'' he said. ''Stay near me, and do not fear. They will not mean me harm, for I fought beside them at Acre. And beyond.''

He put his spurs to Shaitan, and motioned Alyse to follow. The three riders heard his bellowed greeting, and turned their mounts to wait.

''At last,'' Raimond murmured, ''we have found men whom Maud and Beda do not try to cozen.''

Even with their white and crimson surcoats cast aside, and their black tunics blending with the shadows of the hall, the Templar knights would not be mistaken for any other men. Above the long, sun-bleached beards, the Templars' features were dark, as severe as their warlike reputations. Their hair was shorn short, whorled unevenly by the mailed helmets they had put aside at Kernstowe's gates. They ate sparingly of their meat and drank little wine.

Hugo Gerbrai was the only Bauzan soldier who spoke freely with them; they answered his blunt talk and tired jests with solemn, cold courtesy. To Alyse, they said nothing beyond greetings and brief thanks for their meal. To Raimond, they said they wished to discuss, after the meal was done, the payment of King Richard's ransom tax.

Alyse put her hand upon Raimond's arm. "Please, my lord. Do not jest about them. They will be offended."

He covered her hand with his own. "Soon, you must go to our chamber and wait for me there. Nevers and I will speak to them about the ransom tax. They would not expect a woman to have interest in those matters, and you might rouse their suspicions if you stay."

"Raimond, you will be careful—"

"Go now."

The Templar knights rose as Alyse left the board, and Raimond gestured to Beda to come forward and clear the trenchers. As Alyse mounted the stair, she heard their low voices behind her and the sound of Beda's footsteps hurrying back to the safety of the kitchens.

"I paid the ransom tax at Dunhevet, my lord." Nevers glanced from deBauzan to the dark faces opposite him. "My lords." He turned back to Raimond. "In June it was, my lord. A week before you came to Kernstowe. A fourth part of the gold and another sum equal to a fourth part of the value of the stock. And another sum equal to the value of the unharvested grain, as well as I could judge it." The steward's voice rose higher. "The deputies at Dunhevet were pleased, and I returned with their good faith—"

If the man continued to speak, he would undo them all with his fearfulness. "Well done," Raimond broke in. "You did as I would have instructed you."

Aimery Mauleon turned his pale eyes upon Raimond. "I will come to the matter which brought us," he said. "Parthon, Lessire and I have settled near Bolaventore, on the moors south of here. We heard rumors, deBauzan, of a treasure found on your lands at Morston."

"Treasure at Morston. Indeed." Raimond willed his voice to remain amused. "And have you seen the place?" He picked up his wine cup and gestured across the table. "My friend, if you find treasure in that miserable place, you will deserve the sorcerers' repute the Saracens gave your order. Have you seen

Morston?'' Had young Gareth babbled of the night his lord shut his people out and dug out the granary by torchlight?

Mauleon hesitated. ''No. Nor will we, until we come south again from Biddaford.'' He leaned forward. ''I know your reputation, deBauzan. Your word on the matter is enough. You found no treasure at Morston?''

Baubles. Trinkets. An old woman's delusions. All those, but no treasure had rested within the warped coffret. ''No,'' Raimond said. ''There was no treasure.'' He drank again and offered the jug of wine to Mauleon. ''I dug out the old well,'' he added. ''Dug it right down to the harder rock, where I found the bones of a pig. There was no water. And no treasure.'' He shrugged. ''If you wish to look, I will give you half of what you find. And a fourth part to the ransom tax, of course. Where did your rumors tell you one should look?''

Mauleon hesitated. ''It was a pilgrim who told me,'' he said at last. ''A simple man who had heard talk of it at Dunhevet. He knew only the name of the place. Nothing more.''

Raimond smiled. ''I heard the story from a shepherd lass of Morston who said it was in the well.'' He shrugged. ''It must have been a holy well, in ancient times. Such stories are common in these lands.''

Mauleon sat back. ''We will look when we return from Biddaford.''

''Are you collecting the ransom tax there?''

The Templar shook his head. ''Count John's deputies have done that. We bring Queen Eleanor's greetings to Lord Granavil and her request that he attend her at Windsor.''

''I see.''

Mauleon smiled. ''You and your lady wife will leave for Windsor soon?''

Raimond smiled back. ''Of course. My lady's mother was the dowager's waiting woman in Poitiers. I vowed to bring lady Alyse to Windsor after Lammastide.''

Mauleon pushed his cup aside. ''When our messenger goes back to Queen Eleanor, he will tell her you and your lady have not forgotten.''

Raimond filled the cup and placed it back beside Mauleon's hand. ''We have not forgotten.''

* * *

"It is the queen who sent them," Raimond said.

Alyse rose from the settle. "Will we give them—"

"No. Nor should you speak of it."

She sat down again. "I doubt they will listen at the door."

"Never doubt their cleverness. If there is a way to hear through stone walls, they will know it." Raimond shook his head at the wine Alyse had poured. "No more. I drank deeply in the hall, to show Mauleon and others that I had no fear that the wine would lead me to tell them something I would better hide." He pulled off his tunic and stretched his arms before the fire. "They asked whether we found treasure at Morston."

Alyse covered her face.

Raimond brushed her hands aside and placed his palms upon her cheeks. "I told them I had heard the story, and had dug out the well. I told them to look, if they wished. I doubt that they will trouble themselves."

"Why did they ask? How did they know?"

"A pilgrim on Dartmoor told them the story," Raimond whispered.

Alyse trembled beneath his hands. "How long—how long ago?"

"I did not ask. If I had shown interest in the pilgrim himself, they would have had questions of their own."

Alyse closed her eyes. "Do they suspect us?"

Raimond kissed the lids. "They came with a message from Queen Eleanor." His lips moved down to take hers in a feather-light caress. "She reminds us to come to her after Lammas."

Alyse opened her eyes and drew back. "Does she not trust you? Why did she send them? A single messenger—"

Raimond sighed. "A single messenger is not Queen Eleanor's idea of a royal spokesman. When she sent to Bauzan to require my attendance upon her, she had a mercenary captain and forty former bandits deliver the invitation. Mauleon and his fellows are but lambs by comparison."

He stood up and began to lower his chausses. "There is another problem."

Alyse rose to her feet. "Tell me."

"As I told you, I drank many cups of wine to show Mauleon that I had nothing to hide." Raimond took her hand and drew her to the pallet.

"And you spoke carelessly?"

Raimond drew the coverlet from the bed. "No. I spoke with great care. I spoke so cautiously that one of the queen's courtiers could have done no better. I begin to think I would manage well enough, if I cared to join a queen's court—"

Alyse sank down to the pallet. "The problem, Raimond. What went wrong?"

He stretched out upon the linen covering, and yawned. "I drank a little too much to ravish you, wife."

She collapsed beside him. "That—that is all it is?"

He raised a lock of her hair and turned it about his finger. "Here you were, waiting for me. Fearing what the Templars would ask, fearing what I would tell you when I returned. After such a time, a woman needs a good swiving to sleep." He smiled. "I am lazy with wine, Alyse. Much too lazy to rouse us as I should. You will have to do the work this night."

Alyse turned and answered his smile with her own. "I should thank you, husband, for your labors these many nights."

"Yes. Thank me. All the night long."

Alyse moved over him, and hovered delicately above his growing lust. "And if we lie abed until noon, who will deal with your long-faced Templars?"

He slid his hands through her hair. "No man, even a warrior monk, would expect me to rise before noon after a night with your beauty."

She placed a hand over his lips. "If those men can hear through stone walls, my lord, you must learn to be silent. Or I'll not swive you."

He nipped her fingers and pulled her down upon him. "Then do not take your lips from mine, wife. Keep them there, and I'll be silent. All night long."

"Only there, my lord?"

He made a dark sound, deep within his throat. "I have wed a witch."

She slid from him, and traced fluttered promise upon his throbbing manhood. "Remember, husband. Silence. Not a single sound—"

"Witch," he whispered. Again and again.

CHAPTER SIXTEEN

The sound of stumbling footsteps and the ring of chain mail against stone awoke Raimond deBauzan. Alyse stirred and nestled her face against his shoulder. It must be past dawn; they had slept late, as Alyse had—

Raimond's eyes opened upon absolute darkness. Someone had tripped upon the stair. Had fallen, in the night, upon the odd step above the hall, the assassin trap built into the stairs—

He was at the chamber door, his sword in his hand, before the scrambling steps halted at the other side of the oaken planks. A solid thud jarred the door.

"Raimond—"

"Alyse—stay where you are," he whispered.

A second dull blow shook the door, then the sound of iron upon the wood. With one hand, Raimond slipped the bar from the door and stood back, his sword in both fists.

The intruder fell into the chamber in a confused tangle of limbs, weapon, and mail. Raimond raised his sword.

"Move just once and I'll—"

"—Fortebras. Lord Fortebras—" Erec's words were a panicked, breathy echo of his true voice.

Raimond let out his breath. He did not lower his sword. "Speak, you pox-faced idiot. Are you alone?"

"You must come, Lord Fortebras. To the bailey gate."

If the young simpleton had called him by any name but Fortebras, the lad might not have lived to croak those words. Raimond made a sound of disgust. "Erec, if you ever again—"

"Please, Lord Fortebras. They are at the gates, demanding that we open them. Please come quickly, before they—"

Raimond pulled his tunic over his head and gave up his boots for lost in the darkness. "Who is it?"

"The Templars. Mauleon and the other two."

He picked up his sword. "What do you mean? They slept in the hall. How did they get outside—"

"They are in the bailey. They want to leave and told Alain to open the gates. We told them you would not allow it. They are mounted and ready, Fortebras, and have threatened—"

Raimond shoved Erec out into the passageway. "Bar the door behind me, Alyse. Keep it barred. Open it for no one until I come back."

There was no life in the hearth fire, not a single ember which she could have coaxed into a blaze. Alyse sat upon the Saracen cloth, her back against the settle front, gazing across the chamber in the direction of the barricaded door which stood between her and the passageway.

Twice she had crossed the room to slide her hands across the bar, to be sure it was in place, and stumbled back to the hearth through the blackness. Through the barred shutters of the embrasures high above the river came the sounds of horses and distant voices—none of them Raimond's.

She found her kirtle upon the settle and put it on, and slid her feet into the boots she used for riding. The dagger Raimond had given her was in its place, within the hidden fold of sheepskin against her right calf.

Alyse did not know how long she had waited. There was no moon outside the shutters, no way of knowing how long she and Raimond had lain together, sleeping while far below them in the bailey yard, the trouble had begun. Please let Raimond come back. Merciful Saint Morwenna keep him safe.

The Templar knights were leaving in the black hours of night. It made no sense. Why would they—

A faint line of red glowed beneath the chamber door. Alyse slipped the dagger from her boot and shrank against the settle front. There was no sound, no footsteps. Only the brightening, yellow rim around the door. Someone had come in silence with a torch to the other side. Alyse closed her fist around the dagger's hilt.

"Alyse."

It was her husband's voice.

She ran to the door and pushed up the bar. It clattered to the floor as the golden loom of Raimond's torch flooded the chamber.

The figure at the door did not move. "Have I come back to face the assassin I trained?"

Alyse looked behind her, then back to Raimond.

"I am naked, wife, beneath this tunic. And you have your dagger pointed at my nether parts. You have a complaint?"

She tossed the knife aside and threw herself into his arms. "I thought—"

"I know." He pulled her against him. "I found no danger— it was a simple thing, in the end. Just Mauleon and his men eager to be on the road before dawn. Alain and Erec held to my orders, and would not open the gates without my word."

"Mauleon? Why did he leave? He must suspect—"

Raimond drew her into the chamber and shut the door behind him. "Mauleon and his men suspect nothing, Alyse. They were showing their Templar training, rising long before dawn as if they were in Palestine, traveling in the cool of the night."

"Why do that here?"

Raimond set the bar in place. "To show how little they value a warm pallet and other comforts. It is a form of boastfulness, Alyse. Nothing more. This is how they keep all Christendom in awe of their discipline." He set his sword beside the door and threw the torch upon the hearth. "Stiff-necked bastards."

"They nearly cost Erec his life."

"Erec nearly cast it away, hammering on the door without speaking his name." Raimond sank down upon the pallet. "And I was too ready to cut him down." He sighed. "We are like sheep for the slaughter, Alyse. Penned up here, waiting for the worst. Next time that young fool Erec comes upon me suddenly, I might run him through before I think.''

''Raimond, it was not your fault.''

He shook his head. ''And you, my lady wife, might draw the dagger I gave you and slice off my balls if I startle you.'' Raimond took her hand. ''Alyse, it is time we left. Let us set out early for Windsor, and tarry along the way, if it pleases us. It would be better than waiting here, expecting trouble each time a traveler comes upon us.''

''You want to leave now? So soon?''

''Within the week. Within three days, if we can be ready. I don't want to be here when Mauleon and his men return from Biddaford and begin to search Morston.''

''They will wonder why you left so early.''

''Then they may ask me, when they reach Windsor. By then, we will have nothing to fear from Mauleon. Our lives will be in the hands of Queen Eleanor.''

They left Kernstowe at dawn on a late August morning with six men at arms and two packhorses as large and swift as their fine saddle mounts. They took with them Wat, who rode perched before the lady Alyse until they reached the wide road outside Dunhevet. A party of wool merchants making their way east fell in behind them; by noon, three riders had passed them on their way west. After the noonday halt, Raimond placed Wat upon the broad panniers of the first packhorse, where the child fell asleep.

As he watched the road, Raimond wished he had taken them all—Alyse, Hugo, Emma, the Bauzan men still left in the Kernstowe garrison, and the small party with him now—straight south to the well-provisioned fishing boat Erec and Alain had bought secretly with Bauzan gold at the coastal village of Secoma on Rannulf deBauzan's orders. The vessel waited there, ready for Raimond if he needed a swift, furtive end to his time in England.

And for the hundredth time that day, Raimond reminded himself that Queen Eleanor's informers had followed him to

Cornwall. If the three Templars who had descended upon Kernstowe had sensed that Raimond and his lady wished to flee the country, they would have brought the wrath of the Order upon them, and taken them to Windsor in chains. It would be safer—far safer—to deal honestly with Queen Eleanor if he could.

At nightfall, they slept outside Dunhevet in an old timber hall, upon straw bolsters set out for them by the tenant and his silent wife. Alyse and Wat slept near the corner farthest from the door, with Raimond and his men close beside them. In the center of the room were the embers of the long fire pit, the smoke of them rising to a wide opening in the beam-braced roof. When the rain came at midnight, it spat through the smoke hole onto the glowing ashes, and cut through the hissing steam which rose in moonlit columns.

Two Bauzan men sat awake until the darkest hour of night, and sought their rest only when Erec and Alain took their places.

Alyse slept fitfully, waking often to slip her hands into the woolen cushion upon which she rested her head, to touch the cloth-wrapped coffret which Raimond had given into her keeping. She was to place the cushion with its hidden burden into her saddlepack each morning, and rest her head upon it each night, whether in an abbey hostel or a city inn.

She had protested, that morning, that the coffer would be safer upon Raimond's saddle. He had helped her up onto the mare's back and tied the bag beside her. "You must have it, Alyse. If we should meet brigands or Count John's deputies"—his smile broadened—"or both, in the same skins, my men know that your safety comes before all else."

Wat had bolted from Kernstowe's keep, resplendent in a crimson tunic of new cloth. "Are you leaving without me?"

Raimond had beckoned him to his side. "Come here, lad, and check the mare's girth. If you're to ride with us, you must check your lady's saddle when she mounts each morning. And do not tarry so long over your meals. If you fatten too much, the horses will founder before we are halfway to Windsor."

Together, they had watched young Wat give a casual tug to the saddle girth and slip back to the Kernstowe kitchens in search of Beda. Raimond had swung into Shaitan's saddle and nudged him close to Alyse's side. "Remember," he murmured. "If we should meet treachery upon the road, and if you must leave your mount behind, forget the cursed box and save yourself''—he frowned at the sight of Wat balancing a basket of Beda's fresh honey cakes across the bailey yard—"and the young brat."

"Thank you for bringing him," she had said.

"You will have one familiar face with you."

"And another very beloved one," she had added.

Raimond's smile had broadened, and had not wavered, even when Wat tipped the honey cakes into the pannier which held his lord's best surcoat.

Wat stirred in his sleep. Alyse pulled his woolen blanket over his shoulders and raised her head to find her husband. He was stretched across the rushes beside Wat, blocking Alyse and the child from the other sleeping forms. In the moonlight pouring down through the smoke hole, she saw that Raimond lay facing the ladder the tenant and his woman had used to climb into their sleeping loft. His sword, silvered by the moon, lay ready at his side.

At dawn, the small party woke to the smell of oat pottage and bread. They ate quickly and forded the wide river below the manor hall. By full light, they rode east up to the great moor which spread as far as Alyse could see. This was no grey wasteland where the eye could mistake land for cloud; it was a vast, roughened plain which offered rocky crags and stones raised by the ancients to mark the way. It was possible, in this windy scrubland, to look upon such features, one by one, and close the mind to the vastness of the open space.

By midday, when they stopped to rest and eat the hard Kernstowe cheese from the packhorse's panniers, Alyse had begun to look at the far horizons with more curiosity than fear.

Raimond sat beside her, watching young Wat skip back and forth across the level stone width of the road which stretched into the distance. "We will travel easily, these next two days," he said. "The road is like this all across the moor, right through to the Templar settlement."

"They made this road?"

He shook his head. "The knights said the track was here before they came. Miles of it, level and dry. At Dover, I found such roads between the coast and London. My cousin Montbazon believes the ancient warriors of Rome sent their workmen to build it."

Alyse laughed. "Father Anselm told me that Rome is a rich place. Why would they come here to build a road?"

Raimond shrugged. "In Palestine, there are such roads as well. And fortress towns where the Romans lived in the time of the Christ. Montbazon might be right."

"It is so far."

He lay back upon the late summer moss and looked at the sky. "One day, you may wish to see the far lands. Once you reach Windsor's court, and London town, you may want to see more." He toyed with the hem of her mantle. "You may cross the sea to Normandy, one day."

Alyse stroked his arm. "I know that we may need to go across the water to Normandy if Queen Eleanor is displeased with us. I will do it, Raimond."

"And if the queen still holds us in honor, and if we may choose freely where we will go, would you cross the water with me to Bauzan, to my father's house?"

She turned his face to gaze upon her. "I will go with you to the very edge of the earth," she said. "You have only to ask me."

They slept upon the open moor that night, in a coarse woolen tent which shut out the moonlight, but not the sounds of foxes and the distant plaints of wolves. Raimond lay beside Alyse, with her head upon his shoulder, speaking of small matters— the loose shoe on the big bay packhorse, the need to buy a wheel of cheese at the next settlement. He had turned to her and begun to stroke her kirtle from her shoulders when Wat's small voice came through the double fold which closed the tent.

"He is afraid of the night sounds," Alyse whispered.

"Erec and the others will keep him safe."

"He has never slept out of doors."

Raimond kissed her shoulder. "He will learn."

"He will keep them all awake. Not just the sentries, but all of them."

He rolled away, upon his back. "You will fret until we bring him in to us," he muttered.

She touched his cheek. "We can hear him, husband. Will the boy and the others not hear us?"

"Why do you think I brought this fine tent with us?"

"Are all men as loud as you when they take their pleasure?"

He pulled her palm to his lips and placed it upon his chest. "I will be quiet, wife. Very quiet."

"As quiet as you kept that night the Templars came to Kernstowe?"

He shrugged. "Just as quiet."

Alyse sighed. "Why do you think Mauleon and the others left in the darkness? I think they could not sleep with your bellows in their ears."

Raimond sat up and breathed a kiss upon her shoulder. "I remember that night very well." He laughed. "I was silent. I played your game, my lady, as best I could."

"My lord, you were as quiet as a bull with his head in a wool sack."

Gentle fingers brushed her lips. "I have a cruel wife."

There was a rustling behind them.

Raimond turned and lifted the tent flap. "You cannot sleep here."

"Erec said I move about too much to sleep near the fire."

"Then move to the other side."

"The wolves eat boys."

"They eat boys who move about the camp, disturbing their lords."

Behind him, Raimond heard the slither of cloth pulled to cover soft, exquisite limbs. And a muffled giggle.

He sighed and pulled Wat's bedroll through the opening to rest at his feet. "Make one sound, just one peep, and I'll put you out to plague the sentries."

"I will be quiet, Lord Raimond." Wat chortled into his bolster. "Very quiet."

Raimond closed the flap and fell back upon his bedroll. Beside him, Alyse shook in silent laughter. He threw an arm above his head. "Some time soon, my lady, we will find a proper bedchamber."

She rolled over and nestled her head upon his shoulder. "Where will we find one? You said that most country lords sleep in their own halls, with their people. You said there were few—"

"Believe me, wife. If there is a private chamber to be found between here and Windsor, we will have it."

At their feet, Wat in his short bedroll hiccoughed and curled into sleep.

By noon, they had reached the highest part of the moor, where a rough granite tor rose high above the windy levels. South of the rocks, in a shallow bowl of arable land, the Templars had built their settlement. A single keep rose out of a cluster of buildings, as grey as the tor but skillfully built to present a smooth surface to an enemy's grappling ladders.

Around the keep, in neat rows, lay the Templars' living quarters—long, low halls built of undressed stone, shaggy with lichen and moss.

Raimond pointed to a low ridge above the keep. "We will pitch our tent there," he said. "Just inside their sentry line."

Alyse looked up to the rock-strewn heights, and back down to the orderly houses of the Templars. "Will they not have a pilgrim's hall where we could stay?" She smiled in mischief. "Or a chamber for us?"

"Not here. In a settlement this small, the Templars will not have a hall for women and their protectors. I would have to dress you in Will's clothes to get you in there, wife, and risk gaining a reputation as a lover of young men."

Alyse laughed. "Then look to your reputation and spend another night in silence, Raimond." Her smile narrowed. "In truth, I would rather not spend a night under their roof, my lord. This is Mauleon's settlement?"

Raimond nodded. "It must be. We will set our camp up on the hill, and come back down to speak with the preceptor and take the evening meal. Before dark, we will go back to the tent.''

''What will I do with the coffer?''

''We will set a man to watch your horse. There is little danger of thievery here. The knights may be greedy, secretive, and even blasphemous, if the rumors run true. But they are not thieves.''

Out of respect for Raimond, the Templars tolerated Alyse at their board, but could not hide their eagerness to see her leave the hall. She ate in silence, listening to the brusque exchanges of questions and evasions between the aged, black-eyed preceptor and Raimond. From the little she understood, there seemed to be distrust on both sides concerning King Richard's misfortunes on his journey home from Palestine.

Raimond ate quickly, and took Alyse up the hill before the sun had begun to set. Wat and the Bauzan men, seated too far below the preceptor's bench to merit questions from his sergeants, tarried longer with the plain bread and marrows the Templars had offered.

They walked up the slope, leading their horses behind them in the low sunlight. Behind them, within the narrow embrasures of the round chapel, candles shone as the Templar monks began to assemble.

''Why are they living here?''

Raimond made a dismissive gesture. ''Pilgrims. They are here to give aid to pilgrims. That is what they say wherever they settle.''

Alyse looked around the small circle of fields within the valley. ''There are so few of them here, if they tend their fields properly they will have no time to protect pilgrims upon the road.''

''If they can find any pilgrims in this remote place.'' Raimond pointed to the far side of the valley, and to the rocky outcropping which dwarfed the settlement. ''There are many more of them up there. Sentries, some of them, and many others upon the tor.''

''I see no one.''

"Look again. They have left off their surcoats, and wear black." He wound Shaitan's reins around his hand and started up the steep upper hill. "Do not look too long. They are the devil's own agents when sifting rumors and uncovering the business of those they watch, but they like not to attract the curiosity of others."

They tethered their horses to a stake driven before the tent, and sat waiting for the rest of their party, watching the black shadows move upon the far slopes.

CHAPTER
SEVENTEEN

They passed him on the road.

Three miles west of the abbey, in plain daylight, the Mirbeau wench and her great ox of a husband had passed him on the road without so much as a glance. Preoccupied, it seemed, with the sight of the abbey roof rising high in the distance. Anticipating, of course, a comfortable night spent in the abbot's fine guestroom with the abbot's finest brandywine to warm them as they sought the comfort of the abbot's fine guest bed.

He saw them too late to leave the road. Such an act would have provoked the thick-skulled warrior's suspicions and resulted in discovery. So he did not leave the road, but lowered his head as his brown mule passed their fine mounts and pack horses.

They were traveling earlier than he had expected. He did not like surprises. He could not afford surprises.

The loud, irregular knocking of his heart grew painful as they drew near.

The road was narrow. He felt his knee brush against the big knight's mail-clad leg. He jerked the mule to the side of the road—too conspicuous, that, but unavoidable—and muttered a word of apology.

It was not acknowledged. They had not heard him. They had not even turned their heads to see him bring the mule back to the track. If they had, they would not have recognized him, nor would they have seen him as a threat to them.

They rode on, knight and lady, men-at-arms. Only the untidy urchin perched upon the first sumpter horse had even glanced back.

The man on the mule continued west, head bowed, breath contained, until he could hear them no more. Then he kicked the animal around and followed.

Slowly. Well behind their dust.

He did not need to keep them within his sight. He knew where they were going.

The bed in the abbot's guest room rested upon oaken feet carved in the shape of hawks' talons. Above the soft feather mattress and the linen cloth to cover it, three woolen blankets had been spread. The broderie edges of the cloth were worked in designs of many colors, more intricate than the small square of altar linen Isabelle of Mirbeau had brought with her to Morston. At Kernstowe, the great bed left unused in the lord's sleeping chamber had not been so magnificent.

Alyse drew her hand across the finely woven coverlet and moved it back to level the slight depression. "The abbot must be very rich to offer his guests such a bed," she said.

Raimond shrugged. "The abbot is rich because he has such a room to offer his guests. He is obliged to offer safe haven to any traveler; many will pay well to sleep separate from the pilgrims. And they pay too much to have this particular chamber."

Alyse snatched her hand back from the coverlet. "Then let us ask for another. We do not need this fine a place."

Raimond caught her hand and brought it to his lips. "We will go nowhere, my lady wife. We will enjoy it soon enough and well enough to warrant the price."

Alyse drew her hand across the clean line of his jaw. "Raimond, a simpler chamber will do. Any room, as long as we will be alone, will please me. That will be costly enough. We do not need—''

His teasing mouth found her fingers and bit delicately. ''The abbey is crowded with travelers, not all of them honest merchants. None of the other chambers is as easily defended as this one.''

Alyse smiled. ''Then we must enjoy it.''

''I promise you.'' Raimond kissed the soft arc of her wrist. ''We will.''

Laughter slowed, and became a soft moan of pleasure. Alyse caught her breath as she felt the warmth of Raimond's hands move to the laces of her kirtle. ''Will you send Erec away?''

Raimond shook his head. ''He will be outside the door until nightfall, then Alain will take his place. Even here, we will take no chances.''

''Then you will sleep with your sword on the bedpost and your eyes half open.''

''I have slept with my eyes half open since we were wed.''

She slid her hands beneath his tunic and stroked the golden pelt upon his chest. ''For fear of your bloodthirsty wife?''

''Indeed.'' His voice lowered to a satisfied growl. ''And to enjoy the sight of her pretty body in the firelight.''

Beyond the barred door, voices sounded in the hall. With a muttered oath, Raimond began to retie the kirtle. ''Someone has come to plague us.'' The laces tangled beneath his fingers. ''When this journey is over, wife, we will never travel again.''

She brushed his hand aside and pulled the laces straight with swift efficiency. ''Remember, my lord, that you wish to bring me to Normandy after Windsor. And to Poitiers, and to Rome next, you said.''

He smoothed down her skirt. ''I was wrong. We will find a good inn, hire a room and live there until next spring.''

''With Erec and Wat waiting in the hall?''

''I'll offer them to Queen Eleanor for her next schemes.''

Outside the door, Erec spoke briefly. There were heavy thuds, scraping and splashes before the voices subsided into distant murmurs. ''The bath,'' Alyse said. ''I sent Wat to ask for bathing water.''

''Lord Raimond,'' Erec called from the passageway, ''they brought the barrel. They are gone to fetch more buckets.''

''Tell them to come back after supper.''

''Raimond, I am covered with dust,'' Alyse said.

He sighed in mock dismay. ''Peace, wife. By St. Magnus' elbow, I'd not bed a dusty lady. As God and the abbot know, we've already paid enough for this chamber and a dozen hot baths as well.'' Raimond frowned. ''I'll put the coffer out of sight. It wouldn't do to have the kitchen lads walk out of here with the old queen's treasure.''

''Hush, they will hear you outside the window.''

''Thieves with an eye on abbey guests will be prowling elsewhere. We may have the best chamber, but we are not the richest travelers here.'' He shoved the coffer under the bed. ''The closer we get to Windsor and London, the more ridiculous we are, guarding that box with our lives. When we go to the abbot's hall for our meal, look about you, Alyse. There are some merchants' wives here this day who might disdain what we're bringing to Queen Eleanor.''

''And there are many who would value them,'' Alyse said. ''When I was a child, I thought that coffer contained all the riches of the Orient.''

''Only the Orient?''

Alyse smiled. ''Emma said only the Pope had a greater treasure.''

He smiled back. ''If the Holy Father has less than this collection of baubles in his treasury, the next campaign to Palestine will be a short and miserable campaign rather than a long and miserable effort. Let us hope, Alyse, that the Pope is not as rich as Emma believes.''

''There is something unholy about what you just said.''

Raimond glanced at the door and back to Alyse. ''Don't repeat it to the abbot, not until the bath is done.'' He kissed her slowly, thoughtfully. ''Not until this night is done.''

Alyse stretched her arms above her head and smiled again. ''Not until then. The abbot will never know that the knight to whom he has given his best chamber has vowed his sons will never see the Holy Lands.''

He placed his hand upon her flat belly and smiled. "If you would talk of sons, Alyse, we must—"

There was more knocking at the door. Raimond lifted the bar and stood aside as the abbot's servants entered, dragging a large tub behind them. They returned to the door to bring water, their gazes turned away from where Alyse waited beside the bed. The last of them, a stolid, burly fellow with his Benedictine hood pulled over his lowered head, lingered long over the tub, emptying his bucket in a long, slow drizzle. The edge of the hood nearly concealed his sidelong glance at Alyse.

Raimond stepped forward to block the man's view. Even a cloistered monk must have desires, he mused. What man could wish to turn his gaze away from Alyse? She was a vision of grace as she stood in the low sunlight which streamed across the abbey fields into the carved stone embrasure.

The monk, poor man, was making a slow business of emptying the bucket.

With a brief but courteous gesture, Raimond sent the monk from the room and stood shaking his head. There went one poor wretch obviously unsuited to the celibate life.

And Raimond Fortebras gave thanks to God for that day long ago at Avranches when a rush-seated chair, a tall candle, and an angry papal legate had conspired to show Rannulf deBauzan that his second son had not the makings of a priest.

The great hall declared the abbey's wealth, its walls decorated with vivid colors, its hearths embellished by fine carved stone. The guests of the abbot, as richly dressed as Raimond had predicted, sat at long boards laden with more food than Alyse had seen in one place in all the years of her life.

Raimond and Alyse ate among the Bauzan men at one end of a linen-covered table, and spoke briefly to the mercer who brought his three daughters to sit at the far end of the board.

Alyse watched Alain reach across the table to offer wine to the maids. "Erec would bolt from his sentry post, could he see how his cousin is passing this hour."

Raimond laughed. "Alain would bolt from the table, could he hear the thoughts going through the mind of that father. The man is troubled by Alain's interest in the maids. Do you see him stare at Alain's tunic as if he would know the cost of it? He wishes to know whether Alain has lands of his own to inherit, but he hesitates to ask, for fear of scaring the lad clear of the trap. He knows that he risks letting a young fox into the dovecote if he allows Alain to look at his daughters, but the young whelp is well spoken and might be worth the trapping.'' Raimond tilted his head. ''Watch the old man's face. It's not any easy thing, gambling a dower against an unknown knight's inheritance—and the chance that Alain will have all three maidenheads without wedding any of them.'' Raimond smiled. ''It's good fortune for the man that we spend only one night here.''

The girls were as colorful as spring flowers, wearing silken veils edged with the hues of their kirtles. Alyse longed to touch the shining cloth. ''They are very grand, the ladies and their father.''

''He might be rich, but not grand enough, I think, to dower the girls with land. He will offer gold to their bridegrooms' families, and hope that the maids will gain land and a noble name by marriage.'' Raimond cast an amused glance down the table. ''If young Alain is canny, he will keep his new friends in ignorance lest the father decide to abduct him and force him to wed the oldest girl.''

Alyse followed his gaze. ''The blond one? She is very beautiful.''

''Beautiful, yes. And wearing half her father's wealth upon her fingers.'' Raimond shrugged. ''Still, Alain could do better.''

The splendor of the night dimmed. Alyse looked down at her own hands, softer since Raimond had taken her from the rigors of life at Morston, but still darkened from the sun, bearing calluses which would never disappear. Beside the merchant's daughter, Alyse was an awkward, horn-fingered hag. But Raimond deBauzan scorned the rich maid as a bride for young Alain.

Which woman would Raimond deBauzan have chosen for himself, had Queen Eleanor not forced him to wed a landless woman?

Alyse placed her hands upon her lap, where the table hid them from sight. Raimond had never shown her, in word or deed, disappointment in her lack of dower and influence. In return, she would try to make him a good wife, and not disgrace him among the rich and powerful men—and women—they would find at Windsor.

A brown-garbed monk with his hood pulled close around his face began to clear the board of the hard bread trenchers, sweeping them into a pannier at his side. Another joined him to bear away the great joints of mutton and the many platters of goose bones picked clean by the hungry travelers.

Raimond poured wine into their cups. "Drink again, Alyse. We will need the warmth. The passageways in this place are as cold as Morston at noon." He glanced a second time. "Are you tired?"

Alyse reached for the goblet with a hand whose ugliness she had learned only moments ago. There would be many fine ladies at Windsor with white, soft hands. Hands that Raimond knew well.

Creeping back to her chamber, avoiding the color and glitter of the merchant's splendid family, would do no good.

She raised her head. "No," Alyse said. "I would like to stay a little longer."

A black-haired man dressed in crimson robes moved to a small bench in the corner and picked up a great wide fiddle. A pleased murmur rippled through the hall; across the room, a young soldier called out a wine-loudened greeting. The musician smiled to himself and placed the fiddle upon his legs.

"Where is his bow?" asked Alyse. "I have never seen such a large—"

Raimond turned to his wife in surprise. "There is no bow. He plucks the strings. Have you not seen—"

"That is no harp."

"He plucks them from above. Have you never heard—"

"Shh," Alyse cautioned. "He is going to play."

As the young trouvere began to tune his instrument, sounding the strings one by one, Raimond watched his wife's eager face. There had been no music at Kernstowe, other than the villagers' whistles and drums. When Emma had come across the moor from Morston, bringing Alyse's treasures with her, there had been an small vielle with two strings missing, and a bow, tangled within its broken horsehairs, which had warped in the years it had rested unused. Was it possible that Alyse Mirbeau, granddaughter of one of the fallen lords of Poitou, had never heard the music of that country's trouveres?

Alyse had taken Raimond's hand when the strings sounded, one by one, in a cascade of colored tones. But when the young musician drew his fingers across the strings to sound the first rich chord, Alyse had gasped in pleasure.

Raimond forgot his earlier plan to get his wife back to their chamber as soon as possible after they had eaten. He tried to slow his rising lust for Alyse, a difficult feat as he watched her eyes grow wide above flushed cheeks. The harmonies and rhythms of the trouvere's music built, grew more complex, and filled the great hall with a long, plaintive song from the ancient courts of Provence.

They sat silently, hand in hand, long after the last of the wine had been drunk, as the young man's fine, light voice sang songs and lais of courtly love. As the trouvere began the last of his music, Raimond saw tears streaming down his wife's face. "Do not be sad," he said. "If you like, I will find you a jongleur as skilled with the words, with a voice as sweet as this man's, and give him enough silver to keep him with us to play for you."

She tightened her grip upon his hand. "It's not that he is ending his music," she whispered. "It is the song he sings that makes me weep." She drew a long breath. "My mother sang that song, every day of her life. But never with this music as well." She wiped her cheeks. "Oh Raimond, now I know what she heard in her mind as she sang. She remembered this—she remembered how the strings had sounded when first she learned the song—"

The young man let the last chord sound unstopped until it died within the hushed corners of the hall.

Raimond gave him a silver coin and words of thanks. He returned to take Alyse's arm and walked with her toward the darkened bedchambers, past the smaller hall where the abbot's servants were setting out the used trenchers and the remains of the meat before the poor who had gathered during the guests' rich meal. The discarded bounty of the great hall was enough to feed the twenty ragged folk who crowded about the small table.

A toothless woman with wide, vacant eyes called out a bread-stuffed greeting as they passed. A heavy-set monk silenced her babbling with a harsh word. Raimond nodded to the hag and drew Alyse along the dark passageway. "The abbot's charity is impressive, but his servants must curdle the food with their manner."

Alyse nodded. Had the paupers gathered in the little hall heard the voice of the trouvere from the larger chamber? Even the destitute might ease their souls, for a time, hearing that music.

In her mind, fragments of the music still played, but the sound of it had begun to soften and to dim. By tomorrow, the echoes would be gone.

Alyse passed Erec, on guard beside the door, with only a slight nod of her head.

"I can see," Raimond said as he coaxed the embers of the small hearth into a warm blaze, "that I must not let you linger with both wine and music of a night. You will be too moved, madam, to give your husband the smiles he craves."

"Would you—"

"Would I what?" He brought her to the hearth and began to breathe kisses upon the softness of her neck.

"When we go home, will you bring a trouvere to play"— she gasped in pleasure as his hand found its way beneath her kirtle to caress her breasts—"to play for us?"

"Madam," Raimond murmured, "I will find two of them. One," he continued as he freed Alyse from her surcoat and placed it aside, "to play for us in the hall each day. And another—"

Alyse cried out softly as he drew her kirtle from her and knelt to kiss the gentle curve of her hip.

"—and another, my love, to play outside our bedchamber door each night until the moon rises." Raimond shrugged his tunic from his shoulders and stripped his chainse from his loins. He rose to his feet and stepped free of the last of his garments.

"Will you love me as well, Alyse, with music in our hall, or will you take me with only half your heart, and the other part lost in the song?"

He moved to her, then, and took her in his arms. Between them, against her smooth belly, his manhood pulsed hot and grew harder still. "Do you imagine," she said, "that my mind could be elsewhere when you are touching me as you do now?"

A hoarse growl of desire rose from his throat as she pressed her slender body against him. "And what of you, my lord? Would music outside our chamber door keep your mind from lovemaking?"

He caught her hand and brought it between them, to close around the aching thickness of his rod. "Do you think," he muttered, "that I could keep any part of myself from you? A hundred trouveres in song could not change that."

She held him in her hands as she slowly sank to her knees and dragged the silken fullness of her hair across his throbbing length. Upon his belly, he felt the warmth of her breath. "When you do this to me, my lord, I cannot hear anything but the beating of my heart." She bowed her head and kissed the flesh of his desire. "Is it the same with you, husband?"

In a flaring moment of urgent, hot need, he raised her to her feet and lifted her to take him as he stood, and lowered her upon his staff as he held her close against him. "It is the same," he said.

And as she clung to him, as he began to move within her, she went beyond the echoes of the music, and forgot the sound of the strings. There was only the rushing cadence of her pulses beating their own wild song against the surging golden body of her husband.

Raimond woke to find the bolster beside him cold, and Alyse gone from the bed. She was standing beside the wide-flung shutters, holding her hands before her, turning them from front to back in the moonlight.

He sat up. "I had a Breton nurse who believed the light of the moon would harm a woman."

Alyse started and lowered her arms. Her hands curled beside white, moon-washed thighs.

Raimond smiled. "She was wrong. It gives beauty." He stretched out his hand. "Come back to bed."

She began to raise her hand, but lowered it quickly and slid into the bed beside him. He reached for her wrist. "Is something wrong?"

Alyse pulled her hand away. He captured it again, and traced her palm.

"It's—"

He began to stroke her fingers, one by one, in lazy succession. "What?"

"It's as rough as your own, my lord."

Raimond laughed. "The moon has taken your wit."

She snatched her hand away.

The laughter died. "Why are we lying here in this soft bed, with no urchin at our feet to keep us from our pleasures, and wasting the night away as we consider the scars upon our hands?"

"Was I the one who fell swooning asleep when satisfied?"

He pushed the tangle of tresses from her face. "I have wronged you," he sighed. "I thought I had left you so well pleasured that you would sleep soundly past dawn." His hand strayed down to her breast and hesitated. "Instead, I find you roaming about the chamber, fretting under the moon." Raimond gathered her close to the warm length of his body.

She reached for his shoulders and drew him nearer still. "Then let us begin again. Perhaps you will do better this time."

"Twice more, then, for good measure." He growled in contentment. "Come closer, wife. Your hands feel good upon my back."

CHAPTER EIGHTEEN

From the abbey back to the London road, Raimond led his party along a narrow track through the marsh. Alyse's mare picked her way carefully behind Shaitan, following the path which wandered across the watery valley below the abbot's fields. Tall banks of reeds, top-heavy in the light breeze, moved in long waves beside them as they made their way back up to the solid ground of the well-traveled way.

The road was more crowded now. When they had gained the top of the long, gentle slope east of the abbey, Wat looked behind them and tugged at Alyse's sleeve. "Look," he said. "The fierce monks from the moor—the ones with the bad food."

In the distance, beyond the uneven column of pilgrims, farm wagons, and mounted travelers, were four Templar knights riding two abreast, their vivid crimson crosses aligned in perfect symmetry. Their horses, rangy bays with black markings, seemed as well-matched as their riders' surcoats. Two black packmules followed upon short leads.

"Raimond, have they followed us?"

He did not look back. "Mauleon and his companions are not among them," Raimond said. "They had camped upon the abbey fields; I saw them strike their tents this morning as we left.''

Alyse looked away. Even at a distance, their cold, impassive faces disturbed her. ''They were not at the abbots' tables last night.''

Raimond made a sound of disdain. ''They preferred their own cold camp. They avoid comfort before the eyes of outsiders—and hold other orders in contempt for soft living. If the Templar knights had appeared in the hall last night, Muchelney's abbot would have sent his people scrambling to keep back the finest dishes and the Languedoc wine.'' He smiled. ''Those poor souls in the paupers' hall would have dined well.''

''The abbot fears them so much?''

He shrugged. ''The abbot has a reputation for rich living, and those stiff-necked Templars carry tales.'' Raimond cast a long glance behind him. ''See the monk on the brown mule just before them on the road? He's one of the abbot's servants, I think. He's shaking so hard I can see his chin wag from here. The fellow can't wait to get off the road and let them pass.''

Alyse looked back. The broad-shouldered monk was indeed afraid, riding with his head bowed low, nudging his mule into the muddy reeds beside the road. The Templar knights rode past him without a glance.

Raimond shrugged. ''I have heard tales, though, of the riches the Templar knights keep within their own preceptories. When they reach London, those four will dine well enough with their fellows. In secret, as they do all else.'' Raimond looked ahead and saw a long stretch of flat, dry track. He made a gesture to his men and lifted Shaitan's reins. ''Can you persuade that mare to pace faster, Alyse? Let us put some distance behind us.''

Upon her lap, a wide-eyed and frowning Wat shifted and grasped the saddlebow. ''Yes, Lady Alyse. Make her go faster.''

By late afternoon, their party was well ahead of the other travelers who had passed the night at Muchelney's abbey. The merchant and his daughters had set off west to Exeter, leaving Alain in a thoughtful, distracted state which amused Erec as he tried to goad his cousin into speech. The Templars and the timid abbey monk had fallen far behind the press of local harvest workers and mounted travelers who crowded the road behind Raimond and Alyse.

The land had become an erratic pattern of fields and pastures and hedges overlooked by fortified manor houses on the low rises above the road. The timber huts bordering the London road were small and close upon the track, with only woven vines and thin palings to keep passing cattle from ravaging the gardens. Already, there were horses tied outside the larger, more solid huts where more prosperous travelers had bespoken an evening meal and a place in the sleeping loft.

Raimond turned in his saddle and looked at the column of travelers behind him. "We have lost our Templar shadows, Alyse. What say you to another night in the tent?" He pointed to a gentle slope above the road. "There is a good stream running through the pasture, and nothing bigger than sheep to trouble us. I will buy us a meal and the use of the field, if the tenant is willing."

Although they watched the road as they made their camp, none of the Bauzan men sighted the Templar knights passing in the last hours of daylight. But in the dark before the moon rose, a campfire appeared to the east, less than a mile down the road. It flickered brightly upon the next gentle slope, a distant reflection of the Bauzan party's warm blaze. "It might be pilgrims," Alyse said.

Raimond had returned from speaking with the three men he had set to early night sentry duty. He stepped into the tent and placed his unsheathed sword on the earth beside the bedroll. "There was no one camped there when the sun went down," he muttered. "And the track was clear of travelers. If it is the Templar knights, I'll have an end to this game of theirs."

Alyse sat up and smoothed a blanket over Wat's sleeping form. "Please do not anger them."

Raimond stretched his legs out before him. "They are not ungoverned killers—not in King Richard's country. I knew many of them in Palestine. Though I like not their odd vanity, I understand them well enough. There will be no fight—not tomorrow—but I will warn them off following us."

"Mauleon and the others who came to Kernstowe were acting for Queen Eleanor."

Raimond pulled the bedroll close about Alyse's shoulders. "If this lot are acting for her as well, and they can prove it, I'll ask them to ride with us and be of some use in guarding our camp."

Alyse laughed. "You said they prefer to keep their intentions secret, Raimond."

"They will discover they have failed this time."

Raimond was gone before dawn, leaving Alain asleep outside the entrance to the tent, and Alyse watchful in the darkness. He took no torch with him, trusting Shaitan to pick his way down the hillside to the road. Down the empty track, Raimond rode in the waning moonlight to the place where the Templars had set their camp.

As he had expected, the Templars' fire blazed high as the knights threw the last of their wood upon the flames and used the light of it to bring down their tents, striking the camp before dawn's first light.

He did not need to hail them. They had seen him approach, had watched him with little interest as he came into their camp and tied Shaitan to a scrub bush a safe distance from the fire.

"Raimond de Bauzan," a dark voice called. "You recovered from your wounds."

He turned to see a broad figure emerge from the night. "Payen?"

"The same."

"And a Templar now, for all your sins."

The figure hesitated. "I travel with them, when it suits me."

"Wearing their surcoat, as if you had taken their vows?"

"When it suits me."

Shaitan tossed his head and began to sidle away from the man. Raimond hauled him back to place. "I did not recognize you on the road today. Do you disguise yourself as a pannier pack—or the mule itself?"

"Did you leave your lady's side to speak of packmules?"

"I left my wife in safety, guarded well. And I will keep her safe, Payen. I will kill the man who threatens her. Or frightens her."

"Of course you will."

"Do not speak lightly of it."

For a moment, the fire blazed high. Payen's narrowed eyes shone briefly in the light. "Do not suggest that I travel this road to harm your lady," he said.

"And the others? Are they Templar knights, or do they too wear the cross without right?"

"Anger will not loosen my tongue, deBauzan. Do not provoke me."

"I care not for your anger or your secrets. You may march to London with an army of spies to steal the walls of Westminster itself, for all I care. But do not imagine that you or the others may harm my lady and live."

Two figures beside the fire rose and turned in the direction of the angry exchange. Somewhere outside the loom of the light, the fourth man had to be watching.

Payen raised his hand to point west, to where the Bauzan campfire had diminished into a faint embered ring. "Go back, before my companions hear your insults."

"Tell them, Payen. Tell them what I said."

He turned his back upon the Templar fire and pulled Shaitan's reins from the gorse. As he led Shaitan onto the road, the voice came again.

"Give your warning elsewhere, deBauzan, if you would keep your lady safe."

At her feet, the sleeping forms of Raimond's men ringed the dying fire. Above the camp, and below the tree where the horses were tied along the picket line, two sentries sat hunched within their heavy cloaks.

"My lady?" A groggy voice mumbled from one of the bedrolls.

"Sleep. The sentries are in place." Alyse picked up a half-burned stick and began to prod the embers. Upon the opposite hill, the campfire seemed brighter.

Across the meadow, the sheep moved restlessly. The sky had lightened slightly, enough to show the milling white forms against the far trees.

And Shaitan, mounting the slope in a slow walk.

It was Raimond, riding up the hill. Alyse set down the stick and picked her way past the sleeping men. Halfway across the meadow, she reached him.

Raimond swung down from Shaitan's back and placed his cloak around Alyse's shoulders. "You should have stayed warm in the tent."

"I could not sleep. What did you do?"

"Talked."

He caught Shaitan's reins and placed an arm across Alyse's shoulders. They walked to the picket line in silence. With a brief word to the sentry, Raimond tied Shaitan among the horses. "I'll leave him saddled. It's almost dawn."

Alyse put a hand upon his arm. "Tell me now, Raimond."

He sighed. "If they are on the queen's business, they said nothing of it. They mean us no harm." A thin smile curved his mouth. "Or if they did, they said nothing of it."

"Raimond—"

He drew her to him and smoothed her night-dewed hair back from her face. "Now, do not become angry. I have told you all I learned." He kissed her brow. "I knew one of them. A man I last saw in Palestine."

"A friend?"

"No—not a friend. But I trust him."

"Did you ask them to ride with us?"

"No." He drew her with him toward the tent. "Go back to sleep. I'll give the sentries what's left of the night to rest." He caressed her face. "Go on. I will be watching."

Alyse gave her husband his cloak and stepped over Alain's sleeping form, back into the tent. Wat did not stir as she moved past him to sink down upon her cold bedroll. Beneath her cheek, the jewel coffer was a hard lump within the bolster.

She pushed the cushion from her, and nestled her face down into the flat wool mattress. In only two more days, Raimond had said, they would reach Windsor and be rid of the duty which had shadowed Alyse's life. And sent her husband alone into the night to warn away Queen Eleanor's other pawns.

Alyse closed her eyes and prayed that at Windsor they would reach the end of their troubles.

* * *

It was long past dawn when she awakened alone in the tent. From the resurrected campfire came the sound of Wat's laughter and the smell of food.

She found the Bauzan men sitting around a great wooden trencher filled with smoked meat. The tenant's wife was laboring up the hill with a basket of hot bread and pale cheese.

The horses, unsaddled save for Shaitan, grazed hobbled among the bawling sheep.

Wat thrust a fistful of dried meat into her hand. "We slept late. Lord Raimond said we should."

"Where is he?"

Wat pointed to the top of the meadow. "He watches the road."

"Why?"

"I don't know. I helped him, until the woman brought the food to the fire. Then he said I should eat."

Alyse chose a small loaf from the basket. "I'll take him some food."

Wat settled into the circle again. "He said he will come down later to eat. There is no hurry this morning, he said."

After days of early rising and hurried departures, this morning seemed more a festival day than an urgent journey. Alyse walked through the cold dew to the rocky outcropping where Raimond stood.

He smiled at her approach. "It was a lonely night, wife. When we reach Windsor, we will lie abed until noon the first week." He spread his cloak for her to sit beside him.

"Will we not travel today?"

He looked back down to the road. "Later. We will set out before noon."

"Yesterday, you wanted to travel faster."

"Today, we will wait until yesterday's folk are well down the road. It is sometimes easier to fall behind an enemy than to stay before him."

"We have an enemy?"

"We will know soon enough. If we see any familiar faces

on the road today, anyone who has stopped for a lame horse or to repair a wagon, stay near my side.''

Alyse shivered. "Do you expect trouble today?"

"This near to London, there are fat prizes upon the road, and many thieves to take them. We have good men-at-arms, and we do not display riches, other than our horses and armor, to tempt brigands. Still, it is prudent to fall in with travelers who have not watched us before, people who do not know our habits.''

"And the Templars—have they moved on?"

"They left before dawn." He pulled her to his side and drew the cloak around her. "Your cold summer is ending. This morning is as chill as a winter night in Normandy. If we sleep in the fields again tonight, Wat will weasel his way right into our bedroll.''

"You are softhearted, Raimond."

"And you? Would you put the young whelp outside to sleep tonight?''

She sighed. "At times, I am tempted."

He smiled. "Wat is but a small nuisance compared to the noisy crowds we will find at Windsor. But do not fear—I know of a place at the edge of the king's forest, outside the castle walls, where lovers may find a quiet chamber for the night.''

Alyse drew back to look into his eyes. "You know it well?"

He kissed the tip of her nose. "Very well. We will have a good bed, good food—''

She drew back again. "And will we find a lady—or two—waiting for you?''

Raimond laughed. "The women at court have short memories. I do not expect any of them to remember me.''

"Then you were bedding fools, my lord."

His smile broadened. Raimond turned to take her in his arms, but found his cloak empty beside him

Alyse was striding back to the campfire. She did not give him a backward glance.

CHAPTER
NINETEEN

DeBauzan's party reached Windsor three days later. They had followed an erratic path, using obscure lanes between hedged fields to double back three times upon the London road, arriving well behind the slowest travelers who had first shared the track with them across the Somerset marshes.

For three nights, they had slept far from the good road, building small fires out of sight of the inns and huts where they had bought food in the late afternoon hours. Though mercifully dry, each night was colder than the last, presaging a winter to come soon after the second harvest. With caution learned in Norman border skirmishes, the Bauzan men let the fire burn down to ashes as they opened their bedrolls each night, and slept cold but well concealed under the dark skies.

Within their tent, Raimond and Alyse spoke little each night after quieting Wat to sleep. Although they had slowed their progress toward Windsor, they rose early and rode late, and slept deeply after the long hours of crossing and re-crossing the countryside.

Raimond was restless, and left the tent many times each night to speak with his men taking their turns at sentry duty. Alyse woke each time he left, and lay awake listening for his footsteps to return. Many times she rehearsed in her mind the words with which she might bring Raimond to speak of the women he had known at King Richard's court. But each time Raimond returned to lie down beside her, Alyse kept silent. Her husband's vigilance had cost him sleep, and he needed peace when he took what little rest he allowed himself.

After those days of hard riding and little comfort, Alyse was short-tempered, often irritated by the dust which had settled within the hem of her new mantle to turn the deep green into muddy brown. Her hair was an unruly tangle which she had brushed and braided with great difficulty each night in the dark tent; she was not tempted, as she had been in the early days of the journey, to loose it from her snug wimple and let it rest in a single shining plait upon her shoulder. She thought with longing of the Kernstowe bathing barrel in the warm bedchamber; even the cold stream which had flowed past the earthworks of Morston had been deeper, and more swiftly moving than the brooks and rills where she had tried to wash on the past two evenings.

When the great castle of Windsor upon its hill was visible above them, the Bauzan party joined the crowded throng upon the road and no longer sought to avoid the eyes of fellow travelers. The stream of riders from Windsor passed them slowly, many of them mounted upon well-groomed palfreys with splendid borders upon the trappings.

The women who rode with these parties were dressed in many layers of soft, delicate wool of rich color. As they passed the Bauzan riders, the women's gazes would stray with open curiosity to Raimond's imposing figure, would linger longer than discretion should allow, and then would flicker past Alyse's dusty form with careless disdain.

Two Templar knights had appeared behind them, and three others had passed single-file among the folk setting forth from Windsor. None of them had led black packmules, and none of them had shown any interest in the Bauzan riders. "There are many of them," Raimond told Wat. "Hundreds in this country alone. I doubt these are the knights we saw days ago."

When they were close enough to hear the royal banners

snapping upon the heights of Windsor keep, the track narrowed. The way was more crowded still by the folk from the houses and inns of the village beneath Windsor's walls. The voices of the foodsellers and the shouts of wagonmen turning their draftbeasts into the narrow lanes were as loud as Dunhevet on market days.

Alyse reached to her side to put a protective hand upon the bolster in which she had hidden the coffer. Sensing her fear, Raimond brought Shaitan closer to the grey mare and warned off a tinker who had stumbled too close to Alyse's side.

DeBauzan turned away from this road to lead his party south of the royal settlement, to a small track at the edge of the dark, uncultivated land of the king's forest. A short distance down that track lay the priory where his tired men could rest more easily than at Windsor. And at last, he could offer his wife a chamber with a soft bed and decent food.

The past three days must have been difficult for Alyse; though uncomplaining as ever, she had grown silent and distracted. The sight of the crowds riding forth from Windsor had seemed to annoy her, but though Raimond had been careful to observe each passing face, he had seen no one come close to her saddlebags or give other affront to his wife.

The priory, four low buildings joined into a neat square, lay close beside the king's forest. Within the orchards which bordered the settlement on every side, dun-garbed monks moved beneath the apple trees, carrying deep baskets of fruit to the small carts set beside the track.

"We will sleep here," Raimond said. "Tomorrow at dawn I will send Erec and Alain to ask who is at Windsor, and how the queen fares. We will go up to the court at noonday, if all is well."

Alyse strained for a last look at Windsor keep in the distance before they rode into the priory. "Could we not ride there at dawn? If the queen is present, we might be rid of the coffer by midday."

"And be recognized before we know who waits for us? No, I'll not approach until I'm sure who is there."

"You speak as if you were planning an assault." Alyse said.

"I will approach with more caution that I would plan an assault. I would sooner face an attack by Saracen bandits than take on the dowager queen when she is displeased."

As they passed through the priory gates, the yard cleared of all but a frowning, sweating monk who stood at a safe distance from Shaitan's massive head.

Raimond heard agitated voices behind the refectory door. Some squabble among the prior's assistants was in progress. The single monk willing to greet the Bauzan party was staring at Alyse's skirts. Raimond cleared his throat. "We need lodging for two nights and a dry stable for the horses."

The monk did not budge. "You must speak with the prior, my lord."

Raimond dismounted and moved to help Alyse from her mare. "Tell the prior we'll pay his price," he said over his shoulder.

"My lord, you must ask the prior for rooms."

Raimond took his hands from Alyse's waist and turned to face the monk. "Well, bring him here then. Or take me to find him. My men are hungry, and the horses need care."

"My lord, you may not—there may not be a chamber for you."

Raimond looked about the silent yard and back to the sweat-sheened face of the monk. "What mean you by this foolishness? We need your guest chambers, and we will pay you well." He took Alyse's hand. "Come. We will find the way ourselves. I know this place—"

"So you do." A second voice came from the cloistered passage between the stable and the prior's wing. "And I remember you, Raimond deBauzan." A short, rotund figure in immaculate white stepped from the shadows. Below the hems of his robe, wrists and ankles thin as herons' legs protruded from ungainly bulk.

The first monk retreated to the stable door and ducked inside.

The prior, the quivering, red-faced bolster balanced upon kindling stick limbs, cleared his throat. "This is a decent house now. Prior Thierry died two summers ago, God rest his soul and forgive him for allowing the sins of the flesh to flourish within this holy place. I am prior now, and these walls no longer shelter women. This house will no longer tolerate sin of any kind, deBauzan.''

Four years ago, before Palestine, there had been a clerk who had kept Prior Thierry's accounts, a skinny-shanked creature who had hovered outside bedchambers in the night—Raimond drew a long breath. ''By St. Petroc's warty—''

''Nor do we lodge those who blaspheme in my presence. Or those who were wont to bring women to their bedchambers without the blessing of wedlock. I remember you well, Raimond deBauzan.''

Raimond heard his wife catch her breath as she moved back towards her mare. He closed his eyes and tried to keep his mind from murder. By Satan's prick, did this smirking, jumped-up clerk believe he could drive a man's wife from his side?

Raimond dropped his hand upon Alyse's shoulder and drew her back to him. Speaking slowly, as his mouth had grown numb in fury, he addressed the prior. ''Beg forgiveness of my lady wife, and do not sully her or my family with your puling accounts of what you might remember of—the past. We will have your best bedchamber. I know which it is, priest. Your stubborn ways must not keep my wife from shelter. Or send you early to your maker.''

With a lurch and a scramble, the prior fled back to the cloister walk. He flung a blue-veined arm around a pillar and surveyed the yard. DeBauzan's men slouched in their saddles, unconcerned and only mildly curious. From the back of the group, where Alain and Erec held the packhorses' leads, came a brief snort of laughter.

The prior raised his heavily jowled chin. ''One night. No more,'' he said.

Raimond's gaze did not leave the cleric's face. He said nothing.

''Two nights,'' the prior said. ''And Queen Eleanor will hear of this.''

''Tell her what you wish.''

''This village and this priory are under her protection.'' The cleric loosened his grip on the pillar and warmed to his subject. ''She will not allow lawless knights to offend her subjects.''

Raimond turned and began to unbuckle Shaitan's cinch. "We will take our chances, priest."

Alyse had been shocked by her husbands' brutal words to the prior—so shocked that she had forgotten to bring the coffer from her saddlebag into the chamber Raimond had claimed.

"Wait here," he said. "And do not look at me so. These monks have not the right to accuse—"

"Raimond, I cannot stay here if they do not welcome women. There must be an inn—"

"No."

"Raimond, on the road I saw two—"

He ran his hand through his hair. "Damn that bloated, pox-ridden priest." He stalked out of the chamber in the direction of the stables.

Alyse sank onto the bench before the cold hearth. She was a long way from her homelands, cast upon the hospitality of a house of monks who disliked the presence of women, and in the company of a husband who had uttered blasphemy. What had Raimond—and his women—done to upset the prior so violently? Her husband's words came back to torment her: I know of a place, he had said, at the edge of the king's forest, where a man may bring his lady—

From the open door, Alyse heard Wat's high voice beyond the cloisters, urging the packhorse into the stableyard.

She sighed. Raimond was a kind man, and his greatest gift to her had been to bring one familiar face from Morston on this long, tense journey. God might forgive blasphemy, and past sins of the flesh, in a man so considerate of his lady's happiness.

The prior would be harder to convince.

For the last time, Raimond heaved his wife's saddle pouch over his shoulders and bore Queen Eleanor's coffer into the bedchamber he would share with Alyse. It was the last night they would sleep guarding that small chest with its unremarkable baubles. And tomorrow would be the first night in memory that his wife would seek her bed without the shadow of that burden upon her.

Nor would she feel the shadow of the prior's petulance. Raimond would force the wretch to beg her pardon if he had to strangle the words from the man's sweaty throat.

If there had been any other place as safe as this isolated house with dozens of monks sleeping in the adjoining wings, and wide passageways in which a sentry could watch the door, Raimond would have taken Alyse away before she had heard the words which had set her to thinking of his past sins. But the inns in the village were poor places with thin walls, much frequented by thieves and spies. And within the walls of Windsor, worse knaves lay in wait.

In the great keep, or in the new timber halls which housed the queen's attendants in the upper bailey, Raimond could claim a bed among the scribes, justiciars, soldiers and courtiers who crowded King Richard's castle under the dowager queen's authority. But in that confused nest of ambition, there would be creatures more dangerous than any hazards Raimond and Alyse had faced on their long journey.

Raimond lowered the saddlebags onto the small table beside the door. The priory chambers were cold and bare, and the food would be as plain as the prior would dare order it, but despite the prior's ill humor this place would be a safe haven. And compared to the smiling deceptions of Queen Eleanor's servants, the prior's harsh words were but a small nuisance, and could do no real harm.

Their chamber was small but warmer than the hall, with the last of the low crimson daylight streaming over the abbey's orchard and through the narrow shutters. The evening breeze brought the scent of apples into the chamber, and the smell of newly turned earth.

Alyse was prodding the struggling new fire when Raimond lowered the last of the leather packs to the floor.

"The prior sends regret, and begs your pardon."

She did not look up. "And did he offer you absolution for your words?"

"No."

Alyse dropped the poker. "Raimond, your immortal soul—"

"—will not suffer for my words to the prior. God knows, Alyse, this place harbored women aplenty in the past—"

Were there women at Windsor who knew this room as well as they knew Raimond's body? Alyse turned upon her husband. "Did you bring your lemans to this room, to this bed—"

"What are you saying? Am I to account for my old sins? Deeds done long before we wed?" Raimond crossed his arms and leaned a shoulder against the wall. "All right. What must I tell you? Their ages? Their number? The color of their hair?" His gaze rose to lock with hers. "Their names, Alyse, I will not speak. You must forgive me that much."

She sank back to the bench and covered her face with her hands. "I beg your pardon, my lord. I beg—"

He crossed the room in two strides and knelt beside her. "Do not cry, Alyse. It was years ago, before Palestine, before we wed—"

"You never reproached me," she whispered. "Never once. What right do I have—"

"Do not speak of rights. Alyse, we are—" He rose to his feet and drew her up into his arms. "By St. Peter's great nose, did we not agree to put the past behind us when we wed? That scrawny-shanked priest has troubled you. And now you are crying, and I cannot abide your tears."

Alyse drew a long breath and rubbed her cheek across her sleeve. "And I cannot abide one more hour wearing the dust of the road. Will they bring bath water, or has the prior forbidden it?"

Raimond smiled. "If you will permit me to blaspheme one last time, I will speak with the prior's servants."

They dined in their chamber upon cold meat, bread and a bowl of the priory's apples. At their feet beside the table lay the small bolster which had disguised the coffer during their journey.

"I shall be glad to sleep without that hard lump beneath my cheek," Alyse said.

"And I shall be glad to sleep without waking each hour to watch for thieves."

Alyse picked up the small cushion and began to pull thread from the re-sewn seam. "I would like to see them, one last time."

"The jewels will not have multiplied, Alyse." He sighed. "It would go better for us if they had."

She shrugged and pulled the coffer from its woolen nest. The lid opened with difficulty and fell back upon the wool, hanging by a single hinge. Alyse prodded the dusty snarl of precious metal. "They may be few, but they should at least be clean when Queen Eleanor receives them."

"Why?"

Alyse ignored the question. "I will rinse the jewels in the last of the water—the jewels and the gold pieces too." She reached for the wooden bowl and tipped out the apples.

Raimond pushed away from the table. "Our time would be better spent in that soft bed, Alyse."

She held up a thin golden armband and shook it. "And if there are spiders in the coffer? We cannot take such a filthy, dusty thing to Windsor and—"

"Peace," Raimond muttered. "Here, I'll bring the jug."

The blackened silver chains turned the water murky as they sank to the bottom of the bowl. Fortebras picked up the casket and frowned. "There is no point in bringing Queen Eleanor a trowelful of Morston earth with her treasure." He moved to the window and tilted the coffer.

He grunted and returned to give Alyse a silver band with a dark, flat stone set into it. "Here," he said. "I nearly threw it out with the dust."

Alyse took the ring and wiped it with a linen cloth. "Oh yes. The one Emma said Queen Eleanor never wore." She slipped it onto her little finger and swirled it across the surface of the water. "If you had dropped this little treasure into the orchard, the queen might have forgiven you. It is ugly, is it not?" She rubbed it again. "And the stone is marred."

Raimond shook his head. "As worthless as the rest of these baubles."

Alyse dried the heavy ring and sighed. "I can see why she kept it. The scratches on the blue stone are no accident. It looks as if a child has tried to scratch his name upon it. It must have been Richard. He was her favorite, they say."

He reached for her hand and held it to the firelight. "Or Henry, the heir who died. She doted upon—"

Alyse looked behind her, then back to her silent husband. "Raimond? What is wrong?"

He slowly drew the ring from her grasp. And stared at it without expression.

"Can you read it—is it the dead prince's mark?"

"No." And then he cursed. And cursed again.

"Raimond, what is wrong?"

His gaze had not left the imperfections upon the surface of the ring. "I am weary, that is all." Raimond shook his head. "Alyse, put those things away. They are clean enough by now, I think."

He still held the ring.

Alyse began to draw the silver and pearl chain from the water. "Well, we should both sleep soon." She reached for the linen cloth. "Tomorrow I must not be weary. Tomorrow I will meet her at last."

His head came up. "No."

She nudged him playfully with her foot. "If I spend the whole night without sleep, I will look like a tired hag. If you ask very sweetly, my lord, I will allow you an hour awake in bed. But then I will sleep, no matter how you tempt me." She laughed. "I hope I can sleep. Meeting the queen for the first time—"

"No—not you."

Alyse smiled. "And who else in this chamber is about to meet Queen Eleanor for the first time? I shall wear the green silk tunic and the blue mantle, I think. And if the dust of the road is too much, I will cover it—" She frowned. "Raimond? What is wrong?"

He closed the coffer lid. "You will not go to the queen— not tomorrow," he said.

"You said—"

"—I will go alone to take her the coffer and see how she is disposed. You will stay here in this house—"

"But I want to see—"

"—in this place until I return. I will have Erec find a woman from the village to help you with your court dress while I go alone to Windsor."

"This night? The gates will be closed—"

"In the morning." He grabbed his saddle bag and tore open the leather ties.

"My lord—"

He threw the bag onto the pallet and began to pull clothing from it. "I will return and take you to her later."

"Why must I wait? May I not come with you?"

"It is—how these things are done." He did not look at her.

"What is wrong, Raimond?"

"You will anger me with your questions, wife." He shoved the coffer into his own saddle pouch threw it over his shoulder. At the window, he stopped to glare down at the orchard with a gaze that should have set the trees aflame.

In the past few weeks, Alyse had forgotten how heavily a sense of dread could weigh upon her chest. It was back now—the dread, the heaviness and pain—as Alyse watched her husband at the window. He had treated her well enough—indeed, she had begun to believe he loved her—from the time he had wed her until he brought her out of the remote western lands. Now, within sight of Windsor's walls and the splendor which they must contain, Raimond did not want her with him.

In their days on the road, he had spoken many times about how they would manage their retreat, together, if their meeting with the queen went badly. They would confront her together, he had said.

Why, now, had he changed his mind?

Alyse must have a woman from the village to help her dress, Raimond had said. The women sleeping this night upon the great hill of Windsor's castle would not need the advice of a tradesman's wife. Those women—wealthy, polished and discerning—would look upon Raimond deBauzan with pity should he appear with his awkward, untutored wife whose roughened

hands would tell them all they wished to know of her life before
she had wed. And those women would welcome Fortebras once
again into their beds, their bodies, and into the intricate love
games they played so well—

"I understand," she said softly.

He did not look at her. Never before, when they had quarreled, had he refused to meet her eyes. Now, on the eve of his
return to the Plantagenet court, he had become a silent, angry
stranger.

Alyse turned away. Raimond deBauzan did not want to see
his wife beside the women of the court, to realize what he had
lost through the marriage which Queen Eleanor had forced
upon him.

If, indeed, Raimond considered those women lost to him.

Raimond did not dare to look at his wife. She had ceased to
ask questions—those soft, resigned questions that pained him
more deeply than complaints would have done—but he dared
not turn to face her.

He was frightened. So frightened that his guts might spew.

When still a boy, he had touched danger in many forms, and
had learned to school his face at such times to hide his thoughts.
But now, in the face of this monstrous thing he had at last
understood, he could not speak to his wife to comfort her.

The only help he could offer her was to keep her ignorant
of that which had turned his blood to brackish ice.

His hand closed upon the ring. The blackened ring with its
deeply carved lapis stone could kill them all, if revealed to the
wrong people. All of them—his men-at-arms, young Wat from
Morston—and Alyse. Even Queen Eleanor herself might suffer
if the true significance of that ring came to light.

Why, in sweet Jesu's name, had a Christian queen possessed
such a thing? A symbol of the Assassin sect, the ring and the
promise it carried was a powerful talisman—potent enough to
summon the massed might of those Syrian killers, bringing
them down from their mountain refuge to do the bidding of
the man—or woman—who sent it.

And why, if a Christian queen had come to own such a thing, had she left it in the keeping of her late waiting woman and her husband, a simple knight from the barren lands of Cornwall? And why had she called for it now, when her son lay imprisoned in a far land, accused of murder, vulnerable to the Holy Roman Emperor's justice?

Queen Eleanor must have expected Raimond to recognize the symbol carved deeply upon the lapis face. In Palestine, Christian knights had heard the tales of Assassin tokens and their promises. The storytellers had drawn the patterns in the sand, tracing the ancient signals of vengeance and debt. Queen Eleanor herself must have heard the tales, and must have expected that any man returned from Palestine, having seen the ring, would ask all the questions which now tormented Raimond.

The ring could be a danger to the queen's own reputation—or even her life.

As a young woman, Eleanor of Aquitaine had been daring in love, but cautious in political matters. Now, as an old woman who had lost nearly two decades of freedom following a political mistake, she was more than cautious. She was a skilled mistress of secrecy and intrigue. Why, then, had she decided to risk her reputation by sending Raimond to bring the cursed ring to light—to Windsor, where her enemies as well as her allies might discover this shocking relic of her past?

Raimond stared west, over the tops of the abbey's apple trees, toward the dim haze that had obscured the setting sun. Whatever the queen intended to do with this ring, her secret would not be safe until every living person who knew of the ring and its significance was sworn to be silent. Or lay in the more reliable silence of a tomb.

She might have spared them the danger, had she sent a courier who knew nothing of these signs. Why had the queen involved him? And what would become of Alyse, if the queen moved against him?

The anger came then. A useful anger that would take a man through a pitched battle with no regrets. It would carry him through the next day's trials, God willing.

* * *

Raimond did not touch her.

He was awake; his irregular, shallow breathing told Alyse that he did not sleep. Yet he did not touch her.

Half-fearing that the prior would find the courage to send his servants to attempt to turn them out of the chamber, Alyse had come to bed wearing her chamber robe. Raimond had not seemed to notice.

Never before had he shown her such indifference. Even during her woman's times, he had offered warmth and comfort in his embrace.

She could stand his silent wakefulness no longer. "Do not be concerned," she said. "I will not try to follow you tomorrow."

He turned to her then. "After I go up to the castle, and when Erec returns from the village with a woman to help you, you will dress in your court robes and ride to the inn beside the castle gates. Erec will guide you there. You must wait until I come for you."

"I will stay here. It is quiet. The prior won't mind if I—"

"Damn the prior. This has nothing to do with him. You will wait at the inn. Do you understand? There can be no rebellion now, Alyse. You must do as I say, stay where I tell you to, and tell no one who you are."

She had expected that he might wish to keep her from the eyes of the court. She had not imagined, though, how much his words would hurt. "There is no need for this mystery, Raimond. I never asked you to give up the other women."

The oath he muttered was beyond anything she had heard, even in the Morston shearing pens. He rose from the bed, dragging her with him. "And how," he said, "did you come to believe that I would leave you and bed one of Eleanor's ladies?"

"Not one, Raimond. Surely, not just one."

"By Satan's warty prick, Alyse, this is not the time for jealousy. Where do you get your ideas, wife?"

"Emma told me. She said that Hugo had not told her the half of it. The tales reached Morston, my lord, even before you came."

"How—" his grip tightened upon her arm. "Do not turn from me, Alyse. Who told Emma?"

"We were remote, my lord, but not parted from the civilized world."

"Tell me."

"Why must I—"

"Tell me."

She drew a swift, angry breath.

"Please."

Alyse closed her eyes. "It was a foolish thing. My mother was not strong, yet when she heard that the old king had died, and that Queen Eleanor had come out of imprisonment, my mother and William came to Windsor to give the queen her jewels. As I told you, the queen had left France with King Richard. William and my mother spent some days at Windsor, before they turned back."

She pulled her arm from Raimond's slackened grasp. "They were shabby, my lord, but there were those who accepted them, for my mother's sake. No doubt they heard tales of you then, and brought them home to Emma. She remembered the tales. I did not."

Alyse could not see Raimond's face in the darkness. "Within a month," she said, "both William and my mother were dead of the fever. There had not been much time for talking. Emma must have heard the stories when they first returned."

Raimond reached for her again, and drew her to sit upon the bed. "Listen to me, wife. Before I left for Palestine, I was a young stripling who had been lucky enough to find a few willing ladies here at Windsor and at the court in Falaise. I had won no honors in war, but had some small fame in the tournaments. Nothing more. I was one of a hundred knights of similar reputation. Aside from an small incident when I was a child in Poitiers, even Queen Eleanor had little reason to remember my name. Yet you say Emma heard tales of me at Morston. Why would your parents have carried them? Why would Emma have remembered them?"

Alyse shook her head. "I know not. Why does it matter? They never spoke your name to me. It was Emma who said—" She sighed. "I am sorry, my lord. Emma must have been confused. It was on midsummer's eve at Morston, and you were in the granary, and I was upset, and Emma was frightened—''

"Who is she?"

"My lord?"

"Emma. What was she, before she came to your mother?"

"The queen's servant. The wife of a landless knight who died at Antioch, during King Louis' pilgrimage. Emma and my grandmother had gone with Queen Eleanor to the Holy Lands, but left soon after they reached Palestine. They returned to live at Mirbeau afterwards."

"They left the queen after she quarreled with her first husband at Antioch? Why did they not stay with Queen Eleanor?"

Alyse sighed. "Emma never said. She would speak of it to my mother, though never openly, in my hearing. The queen had been angry with both Emma and my grandmother, for a time. I am sorry, Raimond. I do not remember the stories. Does it matter?"

He lay back upon the mattress and pulled her to his side. His touch upon her cheek was a fleeting brush of warmth. "I have told you of my uncle who was with King Louis' army on that crusade. He ended his days in Antioch, in the queen's service. Emma must have known both your kin and mine, Alyse, in the year of Queen Eleanor's scandal at Antioch."

Alyse sighed. "The scandal. The old stories, of the queen's love for a Saracen knight? The queen's wish to divorce King Louis and stay with her lover?" She made an impatient gesture. "They were all lies, of course. She divorced King Louis years later, and there had been no lover in Palestine. It was just a story, like the songs about the queen poisoning the maid Rosamund and—'' Alyse drew back. "Raimond, do you believe she is angry still? Was there something in those stories—''

"No." He sat up and took her hand, his manner much more gentle than his voice. "No, the stories were foolish songs, stolen from brothel ballads from ancient days. Do not speak of them at Windsor, and never in the queen's hearing. Promise me—never."

Alyse laced her fingers through Raimond's grasp. "I promise, Raimond. I promise you." For a brief moment, she thought he would take her in his arms again. But he pushed her down upon the softness of the bed and drew the coverlet over her shoulders. "Sleep now," he said.

His touch was too brief. Alyse caught his hands between her own. "Love me," she said.

When at last he spoke, his voice was unsteady. "I am—" Raimond slipped his hands from her grasp and traced the corners of her lips. "It has been so long."

Beneath his fingers, her mouth curved. "Only three nights, since the abbey."

His hands shook as he pushed the robe from her shoulders. "Three nights taken from us."

She tried to see his features in the darkness. "Are you angry? We will have many more nights."

Raimond buried his face in the curve of her neck. "I pray we do."

Alyse opened to him, and urged him, with touch and breath and words, to take her quickly. He moved within her, tempering his haste with a brief question muttered against her opened lips.

"Do not stop," she whispered back. "I have been waiting, too."

They found their pleasure within brief, powerful moments and lay sated in a tangle of sheets, limbs, and the confused twist of Alyse's robe. Raimond rolled onto his back and pulled Alyse to rest upon his chest. "Next time," he said, "you will have something more than a rutting animal with you."

She pulled the sheet free and brought it up to cover them. "Then next time, I must remember to be delicate," she murmured.

When she opened her eyes, the bed was cold beside her and Raimond was standing at the shutters, staring into the orchard. Twice again in the hours before dawn, she woke to see him there, unmoving and silent in the chill autumn moonlight.

CHAPTER TWENTY

At the gates of Windsor Castle, Erec had recognized a sergeant-at-arms from the Norman stronghold at Falaise, an aging mercenary soldier who had crossed the channel, believing the pay and the lighter duties at Windsor's garrison would bring more comfort than his duties on the continent. Old Rollo had said he arrived five months ago, in time to see Hubert Walter, that churchman so skilled in diplomacy he had almost talked old Saladin out of Jerusalemtown, ride past these gates to convince the king's young brother, John, to hand over Windsor Castle to the dowager queen's besieging army.

Since that day, life had been good for the men of the garrison. No more trouble from Count John, no surprises in the sentry walk aside from the constant comings and goings of the old queen and her advisors. Within a few weeks, the workmen on the walls would finish repairs to the damage from last spring's siege, and the castle would be as secure as any place on God's earth.

Rollo had seen the queen arrive three days ago, weary and in grim humor, much as she had been all summer. She had been in Londontown, where she had seen the first of the king's ransom money stored in the crypt of St. Paul's church.

Then yesterday, Queen Eleanor had sent for Bishop Walter

to come back to Windsor. The word was, in the garrison, that within the month twenty men would be chosen to take the bishop to Mainz, where King Richard was confined.

Eric had bought Rollo one last tankard of ale before he had returned with his news to the priory.

It seemed there was no reason to delay. Raimond deBauzan rode to Windsor's round tower in the late morning, keeping Shaitan well clear of the mason's buckets which scraped the walls and gyrated on their lines in the rising wind. In his mind, Raimond had repeated many times what he was to say; now, he knew the words so well he was in danger of tripping over them. And that he must not do.

The sentries at the portals of the queen's long hall in the east bailey had let him pass with few questions. That was a flattering sign, on the surface. Thinking deeper, it was a bad thing. As he had suspected, Queen Eleanor's people must have been watching him as he had made the journey from Cornwall, following at a distance, allowing him the space and time to do the honorable thing unimpeded. The Templars had watched him upon the road, but there may have been others as well. Any one of them would have been ready, Raimond suspected, to move in with naked steel for his throat if Raimond had failed the dowager queen in intention or in deed.

Queen Eleanor was not alone when Raimond followed her guard into the audience room. A few steps into the large chamber, he saw two young men standing near the empty throne, their hands upon their weapons. The dowager queen, who had sharper, more subtle weapons at her disposal, awaited him at the far hearth, out of the young men's hearing.

She looked at the wadded wool cradled in his arm—his deliberately encumbered sword arm—and smiled. Of a sudden, her face lightened and the years which had shadowed her eyes seemed to diminish.

"You have succeeded," she said.

The two guards at the throne had not stirred. "There is something I must tell you," Raimond said.

She smiled again. "It will wait, I am sure, until they bring us wine."

"No, it cannot."

There was a small cough from one of the guards.

"You manner is rough, Raimond deBauzan, after a summer in your new lands. They have taught you discourteous ways." She made a small signal to the men across the room.

"I know what I have brought you, your grace," he said. "But Alyse my wife does not, nor does her old nurse Emma. There is no danger—no danger, your grace—that your secret will be compromised by those two women, or by my men, who know nothing of this coffer."

"Indeed."

"In truth, your grace. I am the only one who knows— who could guess—what Isabelle of Mirbeau kept for you at Morston."

For a long moment, the hawk-bright eyes stared without blinking. Queen Eleanor's features took on a trace of color and seemed, for the space of a heartbeat, to lose the burden of age.

"You should take care, deBauzan, that you do not begin to think as those strange folk in your wild lands must do. Give them a fact and they will turn it into an ancient secret within a single breath."

"As I said, your grace, no one in my family or on my lands would begin to understand what I have brought you. I am the only one who could possibly—annoy you in that way."

"Then cease to annoy me with your incomprehensible talk, or I shall set a second ransom tax upon you and confiscate your lands if you do not pay it." She raised her chin and looked down the arch of her nose. "It has happened, deBauzan, to men more cautious than you will ever be."

"I am cautious, your grace. And discreet."

Queen Eleanor smiled. Raimond's lack of deference and her own triumph in the exchange seemed to have enlivened her. Above her upturned mouth, the eyes were watchful still. "Where is your wife?" she asked.

He willed his voice to remain steady. "I did not bring her."

"You annoy me, Raimond deBauzan. I told you I wished

to see Isabelle's daughter. And you left her behind, on the lands I gave you?''

There would be no profit in lying to the queen. Of course she knew Alyse had traveled with him. Any one of her spies could have told her. Raimond attempted a smile. ''She traveled with me, your grace.''

The queen looked beyond him, to the door. ''Then where is your lady now?''

''In a religious house.''

The predator's gaze snapped back to him. ''Where?''

''Not far from here.''

The ancient smile broadened. ''Oh yes. Prior Eustace's house. I had forgotten—one of his servants came to me last night, to beg my guards to rid them of a violent and blasphemous guest. Of course it was you.'' She paused. ''I have not yet given him my answer.''

There was a small sound from the corner of the hall. With effort, Raimond kept his gaze upon the dowager queen and ignored the possibility that her guards were even now unsheathing their daggers. If it was to be treachery, today, he had no doubt he could kill the first two guards. But others would come. And shedding blood in the presence of Queen Eleanor would almost certainly lead to accusations of treason as well as murder. He would die for such an act, and his lands would be taken from his widow.

Queen Eleanor stretched forth her hand. ''Give me the coffer,'' she said.

Raimond removed the cloth from the age-darkened wood and held the small casket before her. She lifted the lid and reached within.

He had left the Assassin ring on top of the gold coins and the bracelets, nestled upon the coiled silver-mounted pearls. Queen Eleanor reached into the coffer and slipped the small talisman onto her finger. She shut the lid. ''Put it there,'' she said, and gestured to a low table beneath the window.

To do that, he would have to turn his back upon the queen and her two guards. Raimond looked at Queen Eleanor's slender, wrinkled hand and the crude ring which now adorned it. There was no tension in the long, curved lines of her fingers, no sign that she might raise her hand to send her guards' daggers to his throat.

He raised the coffer. "Alyse does not understand what this held, your grace. If her mother knew, she died without telling her daughter. I swear this, your grace, upon my honor and my hope of salvation."

"Marriage has sobered you, Raimond deBauzan. Made you mindful of the state of your soul, has it? How did young Alyse Mirbeau manage that? Through sentiment, or severity?"

Her voice was low and indifferent, but there was a fierce demand in those old, dark eyes. With caution, Raimond answered the question the queen had not uttered. "A man who weds must think of his own fate and those of his wife and unborn children. He becomes more sober, knowing that his family and his lands will prosper only if he speaks and acts with prudence. A man who weds, your grace, must no longer allow himself to be—indiscreet. If I was discreet before, your grace, I must now be doubly so."

The black gaze narrowed. "You seem devoted to Isabelle's daughter. For her, you speak of prudence and discretion; last year, you were not so careful with your words. Hubert Walter said you left Palestine a bitter man with no words of praise for your king."

"I gave him my respect, and my loyalty."

"And might have given him your life, they say, at Acre, when you stopped an assassin's knife. Your deeds have been without blemish, Raimond deBauzan, but your speech has not been prudent. Not until now. You are fearful that your wife will suffer in some way?"

He lowered his voice to a whisper. "She has suffered, your grace. Every year of her life she has suffered for your sake, living as she did to watch over that coffer. And that—talisman—within, had it been discovered and recognized, would have cast such suspicion upon her family that she could have been called a heretic, or condemned as a witch."

She did not flinch, nor was there regret in her proud features. "Better Isabelle Mirbeau's child than one of my own. You snarl, Raimond, to hear those words? Any honest woman would say the same, should she be confined, and her children in danger.''

From the coffer came the faint crackle of rotten wood under strain. Raimond unclenched his fingers.

Queen Eleanor ignored the sound. ''You will understand, should you have sons of your own. I did what was necessary.''

''Was there no other place to keep your talisman?''

The still-graceful brows rose in surprise. ''You presume to question me?'' Again, the faint flush touched her cheeks. ''I was imprisoned, deBauzan, and closely watched. I do not regret my caution.'' The long, white hand rose in a small gesture of impatience. ''There was small chance that Isabelle or her daughter would be accused, living where they did. And much greater risk to me, and to my sons, had Henry discovered such a thing in my possession.''

''Yet you had carried it with you from Palestine when your first husband tore you away from your uncle's fortress at Antioch. Why did you risk keeping such a thing, if you did not intend to use it?''

The queen's color deepened; her eyes flashed in anger. ''The old stories continue. Only three years ago, tales of my Saracen lover were still green, and repeated among Richard's men in Sicily as they were embarking for Palestine. It is a cruel thing, Fortebras, for an old woman to be haunted by such stories. A widowed queen of my years has only her good name to keep the loyalty of her subjects. And I need their loyalty now, while Richard is in distress.''

''You will use that ring to free him?''

She hesitated. ''If you value the life of Alyse Mirbeau, you will speak no more.''

The guards had not moved. They were the room's length away , too far to have heard the dowager's whispered words. Far enough that Raimond would hear their footsteps before the daggers reached him. There would be time for one last demand. ''My wife knows nothing which could harm you. Send her to my father at Bauzan. You owe her that much.''

Queen Eleanor's brows descended upon hooded eyes. ''A man who serves the mother of a king must not offend her—

not with his words, nor with his fears that she will be ungrateful. Now put the coffer on the table, deBauzan.''

He had done all he could, said all he could. Whatever happened now, whether he would leave this room alive, or be carried from it with the guards' daggers in his back, Alyse would have a chance to survive. If the queen's guards found his wife at the inn where she waited in concealment, the dowager might remember these last words. Alyse might live. His wife might live—

He turned his back upon Queen Eleanor and her guards and walked to the low table beneath the embrasure. There was a small, explosive sound behind him. And then the low laughter of an ancient queen.

Alyse had watched her husband ride north to Windsor keep. The intensity of the night's passion had not diminished Raimond's determination to leave her behind. There had been no further words about it, and no apology. He had kissed her farewell and had gone alone, leaving all his men with Alyse and Wat at the priory.

He would not tell her why he had left them all behind.

Long weeks ago at Kernstowe, Alyse and Raimond had planned for this day. There was a risk that Queen Eleanor, in greed or in the forgetfulness which came with age, would imagine that some of the gems were missing, and accuse Alyse of treason and theft. Alyse's absence might cause the queen to hold her in suspicion; Raimond had agreed that Alyse must appear with him in the queen's audience room.

They had delayed their arrival at Windsor until the date when Raimond's brothers had agreed to reach Canterbury, ready to make their move should the queen threaten their kin. A distant cousin was in place at Windsor. All was in readiness, Raimond had said.

Why, then, had he brought her this far, only to change his mind last night and leave her behind?

He had denied that there was a woman—or women—from the dowager queen's court to whom he owed an account of his marriage. It was what a man would say to his wife, before

leaving her behind. And any wife, waiting for her man to
return from the royal court, would know her husband would
be tempted by the women whom he had bedded in his years
unwed.

For the first time, Alyse wondered whether Raimond had
given up a betrothal in order to wed her. He had come back
from the Holy Lands, he had said, to find the queen's messengers waiting for him. Had there been a woman waiting for him
at Bauzan? At Windsor? Was there a woman at Queen Eleanor's
court who had wept to hear the news of Raimond deBauzan's
marriage to another?

Wat appeared beside her. "My lord promised that I would
see the castle today."

Alyse tried to smile. "You saw it yesterday, Wat. The big
tower above the town."

"My lord said I would see all of it."

"Your lord has changed the plan."

"Erec will take me there."

"He will not. We are to remain here until I go to the village.
Lord Raimond wishes us all to stay together."

"Not me. He didn't tell me to stay. And yesterday when we
came here, my lord told Erec and the others that four of them
must stay with you wherever you go. The other four are free
to go visit the brothels."

"Wat! Watch your tongue."

"That's what Erec said to me, Lady Alyse. Erec said that
if I want to see the castle, he will take me now, for later today
he will go with the others to visit the—"

"That will be enough."

"Please, my lady Alyse. I want to see the castle, and tomorrow we will be gone from here. Erec said so. Please?"

"Bring Erec here. If you are telling the truth, Wat, I will
allow you to go with him. But only for a short time. Lord
Raimond wants us to go to the inn by mid morning, to wait
for him there."

Within the hour, Erec had left for Windsor. Wat rode behind
him, clutching the wide belt which encircled Erec's waist and
held his broadsword.

* * *

Raimond returned two hours later, his face darkened in anger. Beside him rode Erec and a silent, wide-eyed Wat.

Alyse saw them from her window over the orchard and ran out to the priory gate. The relief she saw in Raimond's eyes put her imaginings to rest. No errant husband who had gone to court to renew old liaisons with the queen's ladies would look so grateful to see his own wife watching for his return. Or so grim.

"You were not in the village," he growled.

"I did not think you would come for me so soon. Why is Wat crying?"

"Madam, you were to leave for the village this morning. If the queen's men had come here—"

He broke off and turned to Erec. "Do you think you could take my horse to the stables? Or will you think of another errand at Windsor to occupy you instead?"

Erec paled. "My lord, I—"

"Silence," Raimond growled. And he pulled Alyse with him into the priory hall.

"It is not Erec's fault—"

"Later. We will not speak here."

He kicked open the door of the chamber. "So far, despite Erec's stupidity, we are safe," he said, "but we are invited to Windsor keep this day. All of us. You will have your time with Queen Eleanor, Alyse, but you must stay within my sight."

Alyse brushed the sudden tears from her eyes. "Raimond, I had begun to doubt you would take me to the court."

"You waited sixteen years, Alyse. Why were you impatient?" He sighed. "Now that I have seen the queen, I believe you will be safe enough. But when I saw Wat wandering about the queen's hall, and you were not at the inn—" he broke off with an incoherent growl.

"I was just as safe here—"

"No, you were not. The queen was bound to have report of your presence here. In fact, she knew last night. Had she decided to act against us after I saw her, she would have sent her guard to seize you." He kicked the door shut. "That, Alyse, is why I wanted you in the inn by mid morning."

"Raimond, I was going to the village—"

He sighed in exasperation. "It does not matter now. Please, Alyse—promise you will do as I say, whatever I ask you to do, until we are safely away from Windsor this night. The queen is well disposed towards us now, but she may change."

Now that the moment was upon her, Alyse's eagerness to see Queen Eleanor had vanished. The chamber was suddenly cold, and the light streaming through the window had dimmed. Alyse wrapped her arms across her chest. "Was she angry about the jewels? Did she think them lacking?"

Raimond drew his cloak from his back and set it upon Alyse's shoulders. "Don't fear—I believe she found what she expected. She is in good humor." He smiled. "We are all to present ourselves this day, and bring young Wat."

Alyse gasped. "What does the queen know of Wat?"

Raimond's brows rose in speculation. "Discovering how much the queen knows on any subject is impossible." He smiled and shook his head. "She must know, by now, that he's an uncontrollable lad, much given to wandering and snooping in places where he has no right to be. Queen Eleanor's guards damned near killed him when he appeared in her audience room."

"But how did he—"

"Erec lost track of him. Wat, it seems, has been all through Windsor keep, from the kitchens—especially the kitchens— right up to the battlements. He was on his way across the bailey yard when he saw the passageway to the queen's great hall. He trod on a few slippers, and began to stuff himself with sweetmeats from the great table. Erec found the lad and had nearly seized him when the little churl moved on—right into the queen's audience chamber. He was running, young fool, and almost got the point of the guard's sword in his gut before he reached us."

"Oh, thank God he was not harmed."

"Do not be grateful too soon. When Wat discovered whose floor he had muddied, he asked Queen Eleanor whether her shift was embroidered with the riches of the Orient."

"Dear God."

"Dear Queen Eleanor was amused. If she had not been, I would not have returned to you this day. Even now, I might have found new lodgings in the dungeons of the keep. The dowager queen in a temper is not forgiving."

Alyse cursed, using one of Raimond's favorite epithets. In her low, husky accents, the crude words had lost their sting. "I do not see how you can smile," she finished. "Wat will stay here when we go to the queen. He must not have a second chance to outrage her."

"Impossible," Raimond said. "Queen Eleanor asked that we bring him. I believe she recognizes a kindred spirit in your Wat."

She cursed again. Raimond grinned and corrected the order of her words. "If you wish to use guardroom language, you must speak it correctly, my love."

"I will need to learn stronger oaths if Wat continues as he is." She picked up the kirtle she had taken from her sumpter pack and frowned at an uneven lattice of wrinkles which warped the fall of the silk. "I cannot wear this."

"I'll try to find a woman to help you."

"There are no women. You heard the prior. There are no lay servants here—only the monks."

"Erec will bring the clothseller from the village."

Alyse dropped the gown. "Raimond, I cannot go."

"You must. The queen expects you." He picked up the garment and placed it upon the bed. "You are an odd creature, wife. Last night you were angry I would not take you to Queen Eleanor. Today you don't want to go."

"And yesterday, my lord, you were as grim as an executioner. Today, you speak of ladies' maids."

He brushed her hair back from her shoulders. "Trust me, Alyse. And remember what we agreed. Do not leave my side, even in the queen's presence. But if I tell you to leave without me, do not balk. Go quickly. Erec and Alain will follow you. And when you are clear of Windsor keep, do not return here. Follow the road east, and send Erec ahead to Canterbury where my brother Ivo waits."

"But you told me you had seen your cousin here at Windsor. If there is trouble, he would help—"

"Yes, he would. But you cannot approach—you cannot be seen to approach my cousin Montbazon for help. He will be watching, and will choose his own time to aid us, if he can. Queen Eleanor must not even know that we have seen him."

Alyse sighed. "I will remember it all, if I can. Stay with you, leave if you tell me, don't ask for Montbazon, send Erec to Canterbury—Raimond, I do not think I want to see Queen Eleanor's court."

"In troubled times, her court is not a thing to be enjoyed, but an ordeal to be survived. There are other places, Alyse, where you may see the things your mother remembered. We will see them, together. Even at Bauzan—"

"Will we have to run to your father, Raimond? Do you still expect more trouble? Why should the queen be displeased with us, since she has already accepted the jewels?"

He pulled her into his arms. "Surely it will not take a war or Queen Eleanor's temper to persuade you to go with me to my father's lands?"

She smiled back. "Of course not." There was something wrong—something Raimond had not told her. And in his eyes, she saw that he would say no more. Dear God, she prayed. Let us not be fugitives when we cross the water to Normandy.

Raimond set her from him and smoothed her hair from her brow. "If you would keep us from trouble, Alyse, keep young Wat at your side. Do not leave him alone with Queen Eleanor. She will know all our secrets, after one hour with that young knave."

CHAPTER
TWENTY-ONE

There were crowds, milling clusters of noble folk, prosperous merchants, and well-dressed servants, within Windsor's bailey walls. As congested as the muddy track through the village, the courtyard was swollen with fine mounts and well-curried packmules, and high-chinned women mincing past the inevitable puddles upon pattens more finely carved than the old altar front at Morston. The men who had gathered outside the keep were as unlike Raimond as colored finches were to the black hawks upon the moors. Only the men-at-arms and knights bickering over a cartload of spear hafts before the armory doors resembled Raimond in demeanor and sober clothing. Few of them were as tall, even fewer as broad of shoulder, and none of them possessed the far-seeing eyes which set deBauzan apart from other men.

The grey mare followed Shaitan through the gates and passed the large wooden storehouses which contained the royal supplies of food, armory, and harness. Beyond, Raimond and Alyse made their way past serving women and stable boys streaming in errands from the great round keep to the surrounding settlement. Nearer the stone tower, beside the great timber hall built by old King Henry for his queen, Alyse saw men and women dressed in finery which surpassed anything the wool merchant's daughters had worn at Muchelney.

At Raimond's signal, Erec turned his mount and led his comrades and young Wat to the garrison to seek Rollo, the aged sergeant from Eu.

Raimond lifted Alyse down from her saddle and straightened the soft circlet of gold upon his wife's samite-covered brow. She frowned as she smoothed the translucent veil down to her shoulders. "Do Beda's stitches show?"

"No," Raimond lied.

"She will think I was careless with her gift."

"If she seems to notice, I will tell some tale of a sumpter horse tipping its pack into a thicket. Take my hand," he said. "We will go alone from here. If Queen Eleanor asks for the others, we will send for them. She may have forgotten she asked for them all."

They left their horses in the care of the royal hostlers and walked to the queen's hall, east of the great stone keep. There was a long moment, at the end of the door passage, when Alyse stood in mute and motionless wonder at the sight of Queen Eleanor's courtiers moving about the enormous room in loud and many-colored splendor. Raimond's hand at her elbow gave Alyse the confidence to step forward upon legs gone suddenly numb.

Mercifully, no one came forward in the first few moments. Serving maids were dragging forth the frames upon which the trestle boards would be placed for the midday meal. Women in exquisite silks drew their hems away from the path of benches dragged from the high walls to the tables. Alyse was relieved to see that Raimond had told the truth about her court dress. The long creases which had vexed Alyse were no worse than the wrinkles she saw in some of the fine clothing of the ladies in the great hall.

Raimond followed her gaze. "Many of the queen's ladies," he said, "most of the younger ones, have traveled far from their own lands to be fostered with the queen. They live as best they can, and few have chambers where servants may tend to their robes."

"Surely they have servants. They are very grand ladies."

Raimond smiled. "They are grand ladies with rich garments, but they seldom have more than a pallet and a chest in a warm corner for themselves."

Alyse smiled back. "Then they must go willingly with the husbands the queen finds for them."

He shrugged. "That may be it. God knows, they have enough dalliance at court to keep them happy. It must be the crowding and the noise that drive them to wed."

"You know much of these women's habits," Alyse said.

"Only by report," Raimond said. "I courted one, from time to time, but never dared seek them in their chambers."

Which of them had lain beneath Raimond's body, and taken pleasure with him? Alyse brushed a mote of dust from her green silk sleeve. "I had thought you a bold man."

Raimond sighed. "Not that bold. No, I crave a quiet place with no one but my lady to hear my words." With sly skill, he caught her hand and stroked his thumb across her palm. The sensation gave a subtle promise of intimacy to come, sending a hot flush to the hidden places beneath her fine linen chemise. "For that reason, Alyse, I will give that God-blasted tent of ours to the first pilgrim I meet on the road near Kernstowe. It was torture to have you so near, yet have the ears of Wat and the others so close."

He had distracted her, as he must have intended, from the splendor of the queen's ladies and turned her thoughts to the passion they shared. The noise of the courtiers' voices grew distant, and the long chamber only a space in which Alyse and Raimond stood together. The eyes of the curious, and the half-smiles of the women, the amusement with which the serving maids looked upon Alyse's simple finery and lack of jewels—all had ceased to offend. They were no more to Alyse than the chattering of the exotic birds in their silver cages beside the passageway.

"Come," Raimond said. "Look at the hangings. One day I will find you such a cloth, Alyse."

As she passed through the noisy crowd, looking with hungry approval upon the brilliant colors of the tapestries as they lifted and billowed in the chill drafts of autumn, Alyse thought of her parents. Had her mother fostered with the queen when she

was as young as that black-haired maid in the rose-colored
surcoat? Or had she come to the queen's court as a young
married woman? Had her father been trained in the use of
weapons in Poitiers, or had he stayed at Mirbeau to learn his
skills? Had they been at Windsor in the years before she was
born? Had they ever stood together in this long room, looking
upon the same broderie cloth which their daughter now longed
to touch? Had they waited here, as Alyse and Raimond did this
day, for a summons to pass together through the portals of the
queen's private chamber?

When the young guard came to fetch them, Alyse found that
she had lost her reluctance to face Queen Eleanor. For the
dowager queen possessed the answers to the questions which
Alyse only now had thought to ask.

The ancient woman in the deeply carved chair beneath the
window beckoned Alyse and pointed to a low bench at her
side. "Do you remember me?"

Alyse glanced at her husband and found courage in his smile.
She raised her eyes to Eleanor of Aquitaine and shook her
head. "No, your grace."

One grey brow arched in delicate irony. "I did not expect
you to remember. You were a restless child, not one to sit
quietly and heed your elders. You were a great burden to your
mother in our chambers at Salisbury, and her only joy." The
dark eyes focused upon her face. "How did she die?"

"A fever, your grace. The same that took her second husband."

"He was good to her?"

"Yes, your grace. He was kind to us both. I called him
Father."

A small frown appeared between the royal brows. "He was
honored, then, to have Philip of Mirbeau's daughter call him
so." Queen Eleanor inclined her head and fixed Alyse with the
half-lidded stare of a predator at rest. "Did the lady Isabelle
teach you to respect the memory of your father?"

A small seed of rebellion took root within Alyse's heart.
"She did," Alyse answered at last. "She loved my father's

memory all her days, but held William of Morston in the respect he deserved.''

The heavy-lidded eyes opened wide and grew darker still. ''Your father, Philip of Mirbeau, was a brave man, a brilliant warrior and a gentle knight. The day he died, Poitiers was lost. Even in the destruction which followed, there were those who mourned him more than the dismemberment of my court.''

The black gaze turned to Raimond, and back to Alyse. ''Did Isabelle tell you how he died?''

Alyse nodded. ''She told me he fell in a battle outside Poitiers on the night I was born.''

Eleanor closed her eyes. ''Not a battle. A skirmish. On the road outside Poitiers, at the end of my failed rebellion against Henry. Your husband could describe it to you, though he was but a child of ten years when he saw it.''

Alyse's breath stopped. Queen Eleanor's eyes were wide open again, and upon her mouth was a small smile. Alyse's hand dropped from Raimond's slackened grasp.

''That night?'' His voice was hoarse with surprise.

''That night,'' Eleanor answered. ''The night you and your father and his Bauzan knights came upon my party on the road. The night you saw, in the torchlight, that it was a woman whom the few remaining Poitevin knights were defending. The night you may have saved my life by staying your father's hand, and most certainly sent me into years of confinement. Philip of Mirbeau was the captain of that party, the first slain by your father's men.''

In that moment, Alyse saw the virtue in Raimond's distrust of King Richard, his mother, and the warlike Plantagenet brood. The sudden manner of this revelation of Raimond's connection with Philip of Mirbeau's death could be forgiven, for the queen was old, and her mind might move without reason from one memory to the next. What Alyse would never forgive was the cold curiosity with which Queen Eleanor observed Alyse's dismay. And Raimond's grief.

Alyse sought Raimond's hand and took it in her own small grasp. She brought it to her lips and kissed the scars which crossed her husband's palm. ''My mother would thank you, your grace, for sending to me a knight as fine and great as my father"—beside her, she heard Raimond's breath catch suddenly in his throat—"for sending Raimond deBauzan to wed me."

The royal gaze shifted from face to face. The queen sat back against her carved chairback in sudden weariness. "And I would tell the lady Isabelle that I wish her daughter well of the marriage."

With a quiet word, Queen Eleanor summoned her serving maid to bring wine. They drank the dark wine of Poitiers from silver cups held in steady hands, and spoke of the ancient court of Aquitaine. After a time, the talk turned to small matters of little import.

A long, whitened claw descended upon Alyse's hand and raised it to the light. "My chambermaids have fairer hands than yours, lady Alyse. My own, though I am old, are softer. Did your mother not train you to keep them covered when you went abroad?"

"She did . . ."

"Go on."

"But there was work to be done, your grace."

"I see." The narrowed, bright eyes glanced over Alyse's shoulder. "You are impatient, Raimond Fortebras?"

"I am content." His voice belied his words.

Queen Eleanor turned her gaze back to the young woman at her feet. "And you claim you are content, lady Alyse, with the husband I sent to you."

"Yes, your grace."

"He seems to have a high regard for you. You wed a warrior and made him a courtier."

Alyse smiled. "I would not call him that, your grace."

"For your sake, Alyse Mirbeau, your husband has learned the cunning of a justiciar and the discretion of a chancellor. Shall I put him to use his new-formed skill in my service?"

"Oh no, your grace." Alyse stopped her breath. "I mean to say, I do not think he would be useful to you. At court, I mean. Your grace—"

One grey brow arched in amusement. "You are well wed, Alyse. I sent you a husband as plain-spoken and awkward as yourself. The pair of you would make fledgling courtiers at your most eloquent, and would certain fall from the nest should you remain in this company.'' The yellowed smile narrowed, and mirth vanished. ''Yet you have done much in my service, and must expect some small favor.''

''No, we—''

The black eyes looked beyond Alyse. ''I would not have your husband reproach the crown for ingratitude. How, then, am I to reward your loyalty, and your husband's journey on my behalf?''

Alyse followed the queen's gaze to the tall figure of her husband. Raimond's face was impassive, but within his eyes there was a warning.

She turned back to her mother's liege lady. ''We would like to be left in peace, your grace. We want nothing more than peace.''

Queen Eleanor's mouth curved down in disapproval. Alyse caught her breath. ''And to live our lives your loyal servants, of course. And the king's.'' Her voice dwindled into a frightened croak.

There was an ominous silence, then a frail cough of laughter. ''Did your mother not teach you the judicious use of flattery?'' The pale, curved claw moved to caress Alyse's cheek. ''No matter. For all her graces, Isabelle of Mirbeau lacked a courtier's tongue. Never, in my presence, did she mask falsehood beneath pretty words. It is why I loved her, Alyse. And trusted her with my honor and my life.''

In the end, Alyse did not remember the questions she had meant to ask. Her eyes were filled with tears and her mind with Queen Eleanor's words—words of gratitude to the late Isabelle of Mirbeau, words of comfort to Alyse, and later, tales of the past. There were stories which Isabelle had left half-told at Morston, now completed by Queen Eleanor. The dowager queen had given, in one brief evening, the gift of her family's heritage to Alyse Mirbeau.

After a time, Queen Eleanor had sent Raimond to the keep. ''Find your people and tell them they may come to me after they have eaten, deBauzan. I will send for you, when your lady wife and I have finished our talk of her family's history.''

''I am content to stay, your grace.''

''And I insist that you go. I would speak freely, woman to woman, with Isabelle's daughter.''

Alyse gave a look of mingled apology and contentment to her husband. She would be safe enough in this closed chamber with the royal guard at the door, and she wanted Queen Eleanor to speak until all was said. The dowager was old; Alyse knew that this might be her only chance to hear the aged Eleanor speak of Mirbeau's long-dead knights and all that had befallen them in King Henry's time of vengeance.

Raimond looked back from the wide door, uneasy at the prospect of leaving Alyse. There was nothing he could do in the face of Queen Eleanor's orders; to protest now would be to raise Queen Eleanor's suspicions once again, and mar the fragile bond which had begun to form between the two women. Reluctantly, Raimond made his way out the passageway and to the great round keep.

His cousin Montbazon was there, deep in speech with a crimson-garbed woman of exotic, almost Saracen features. His garments were black—a deep, costly black which seemed not a color but the very absence of light. At his side, sheathed in fine leather, was the legendary longsword of the old Viking grandfather of both Raimond and Montbazon, its great size unremarkable beside Montbazon's tall frame. The great hilt with its single red pommel stone outshone the splendid robes of the woman who looked aside and caught Raimond's gaze.

Montbazon followed her glance and saw Raimond. A subtle nod and a slight shrug communicated all that the cousins dared. Montbazon turned his back and drew his companion with him to speak with a hard-jowled man-at-arms.

''Raimond of Bauzan.''

Raimond turned to find Hubert Walter, dressed in dark wool and the heavy, hard-woven cloak of a traveler, followed by three servants carrying heavy panniers.

''Your wife is with the queen?''

"Yes." Raimond glanced back at the passage. "They are speaking of Alyse's family."

Walter's florid face creased in a smile. "Then you are wise to leave them. I am for the road, deBauzan. I will not meet your lady wife until I return."

Upon the bishops upraised hand, Fortebras saw the Saracen stone within its deep silver mounting. And at the bishop's back, their travel cloaks already upon them, had appeared three Templar knights. There was a fourth man, dressed in a Templar surcoat though he had taken no vows.

The impostor, Payen, had come back to his keeper.

With effort, Raimond kept his expression unchanged. "Do you go north, my lord bishop, to collect the last of the ransom tax?"

Hubert Walter's smile remained in place. "No, I will go east. Of course."

Of course. "To Hohenstaufen's court, to give heart to King Richard in his prison?"

"And beyond. I have seen Jerusalem, deBauzan. There would be no better place to pray for the king's swift release."

Raimond fixed his gaze upon the bishop's face, ignoring the ring which he displayed so plainly. Ignoring the presence of Payen, who had earned the respect of King Richard's knights by returning alive from the lair of Rashid ed-Din Sinan, Imam of the Assassins.

"Then God speed you in his cause, your grace," he said.

The bishop's features stiffened into a mask of piety. Only his gaze, flickering from Raimond to the Templar knights who had moved to stand at his side, hinted at the enormity of the danger he must now face. "I will advance the king's cause, God's own, and no other. I pray for God's justice to defend Richard Plantagenet and deliver him from captivity."

Raimond felt a rush of pity for the churchman. He knew what it was to receive from Queen Eleanor's hand a task which would grow more dangerous as its mysteries were revealed. He doubted that Hubert Walter would find a reward at the end of his ordeal.

He met the bishop's gaze. "May you be safe, your grace, among the infidels."

''Pray for me, Raimond deBauzan. And I will pray that the swords of the infidels will slay no more Christians in our time.'' With those words, Hubert Walter took his leave.

The three Templars and the impostor Payen followed, their eyes never straying from the bishop and his servant.

Raimond passed his hand across his brow. Walter had uttered a curious prayer. England's most capable bishop, soon to be enthroned as Archbishop of Canterbury, was traveling to the east, taking with him the most powerful talisman of the Assassin sect, capable of summoning the obedience of that invisible army of silent killers.

What had Queen Eleanor intended in sending the ring back to the lands of the east? Did she wish to bring the lethal skills of the Assassins to the throats of Richard's captors? And why would she send honest, godly Hubert Walter to deliver her demands to the Assassins?

With difficulty, Raimond kept himself from returning to Queen Eleanor's chambers to drag his wife away from the brilliant and ruthless woman who held the lives and deaths of thousands within the grasp of her long white hands.

He drained a cup of fine Burgundy wine and slowly turned back to the corner where he had seen Montbazon and his woman. As Raimond had expected, his cousin was gone.

Back in the queen's hall, there was a singer—a man of Poitiers, a scarred soldier who plucked the strings of his harp with gnarled hands and sung with a voice hoarse with age. Hearing him, Raimond remembered that summer nearly two decades ago when his father had brought him south to serve King Henry. To see, through a child's eyes, the capture of Henry's errant queen. And to witness, all unknowing, the skirmish in which his future wife's father had been killed.

What turns would his life have taken if he had not darted into the fighting to cover Queen Eleanor's torn tunic with his small cloak? He had screamed in his thin young voice that the slender soldier on the white horse was a woman, dressed as a man. He had saved her from the swords of his father's men, but had ended her desperate flight from King Henry's army.

The time passed in a blur of memories. Only when Erec

stirred beside him did Raimond realize how long he had been in a waking dream.

"Where is Wat?" Erec asked.

"God knows. In the dowager's chamber, I imagine, spying upon my wife and the queen. This time, if he finds the queen's wrath too great, I will do nothing to save the little wretch."

Erec shook his head. "If he's spying on anyone, it will be upon that young smith he found this afternoon."

"What smith?"

"His name is Hans or Hound—Hund, it was. Works in the armory here. Wat must be pestering him as we speak."

Raimond rose. "I would speak with the man."

"Will you punish him, Lord Raimond? He may have run away from Morston. Wat said the man left without so much as—my lord?"

Raimond glanced at the queens' chamber door. It was closed, and the guards were in place. "Take me to the man," he growled. He followed Erec the length of the great hall, to the dark timber passage which led to the bailey yard and the hiding place of Morston's missing blacksmith.

Alyse said farewell to Queen Eleanor, knowing it might be many months—or an eternity—before they spoke again. She moved past the chamber guards at the door, and walked beneath the torches flickering against the walls of the great hall. The writhing patterns of fire and shadow cast life upon the tapestries, making the figures of men and beasts seem to move beside the yellow flames.

It had ended now—the burden of the queen's trust, the journey to the ancient woman who had known Isabelle of Mirbeau as a child, and the precious hours during which she had discovered, through Queen Eleanor, more of her parents' early life than she had learned from her modest, self-effacing mother.

If she had not been weeping, if her sight had not been obscured by the stream of tears she could not control, Alyse might have seen the darker shadow of a burly man within the dimness at the end of the passageway, where the light of the last torch met the darkness of the bailey yard.

With sudden, searing pain, Alyse felt her arm nearly wrenched from its socket. She cried out once as she struggled; then the cruel hands moved from her arm to her face to choke her scream and drag her through the door, into the darkness beyond.

The choking continued as a guttural whisper began to speak—a muttered demand, repeated again and again—words which made no sense, which merged into a low growl. The violence of the hands about her throat was sudden and powerful—almost enough to break the bones of her neck. Her last thought, as the darkness came over her, was surprise that she had survived long enough to smell the stale, acrid odor of her attacker's sweat upon his rough woolen sleeves.

She remembered the dagger Raimond had given her. She freed her arm and reached for her boot. She wrenched the blade from its place against her calf and brought it down upon the back of her attacker.

There was a rapid pounding, a distant shout and then release.

Raimond was halfway across the bailey when he heard Alyse scream. One hellish moment later, he found his wife half-crawling in the darkness beyond the torch light, writhing upon the hard-packed earth with her hands at her throat, her fear-glazed eyes upon the blackness beneath the sentry walls. She made a hoarse, guttural attempt to speak.

The queen's guards, rushing from behind, knocked Raimond to the ground and narrowly escaped death when he came up with his sword in his hand.

Queen Eleanor's outraged shout reached their ears in time to force Raimond deBauzan and the three guards to put down their weapons.

The guards gave futile chase to the assailant who had long since taken refuge in the shadows of the walls, or in the tower keep.

Queen Eleanor stood watching the lord Raimond deBauzan, called Fortebras, weeping in relief, holding his wife in his arms. She summoned her guard and sent him in search of the child

Wat, who had gone to the armory with the younger Bauzan knights.

DeBauzan would not be stopped. Not the guards, nor Queen Eleanor herself, nor any of the Bauzan men could dissuade him from taking his wife away from Windsor that night.

His wife had spoken only a few words, and those so obviously painful that he kept her from attempting more. Her dagger was missing, and her clothing had been bloodied, but she had not been cut in the struggle. Raimond set four of his men to searching Windsor keep for a man with torn clothing or other signs of the dagger's work upon his body.

Of the treacherous blacksmith and his discovery within the Windsor armory, Raimond said nothing to his wife. Alyse would defend the smith, and make herself ill fretting for pity of the bastard. As it was, the hoarse pain with which Alyse drew each breath sent keen, killing agony into Raimond's heart. He would leave his wife in safety, this night, while he found the smith and killed the murderous knave.

He had left Alain and Erec to watch the gates of Windsor's walls, to let no man pass without seeing that his clothes were whole and his skin unbloodied. To the queen's guards on duty at the gate, Raimond had given a tirade of curses and a threat that if they hindered the Bauzan men in their search, he would return to nail their hides to the gates.

His two remaining men rode with deBauzan and his lady to the priory. At the place where the track south from Windsor met the narrow road through the orchards, they waited in the light summer rain as their lord placed his wife in the care of the prior and rode back up to Windsor's hill to find his wife's attacker and kill him.

The men he left behind took their place at the priory crossroads. They must, deBauzan had demanded, swear on their immortal souls to allow no one, even the dowager queen's guard, to pass onto the priory road before Raimond himself had returned.

No man in Windsor, not even the queen's closest advisors, could be trusted. That left the house of the prior—the maiden-hearted, woman-fearing prior—the only safe refuge for the lady Alyse for the rest of this night.

DeBauzan would return, he swore, when his wife's injuries had been avenged with the lifeblood of her attacker. He rode back to Windsor keep, his naked sword in his hand, to end forever the threat to his wife.

By dawn, the head of Morston's treacherous blacksmith would decorate the sentry gate. And if the dowager objected, Raimond deBauzan would damn Queen Eleanor to perdition.

The prior, roused from sleep and threatened with violence by his fierce-eyed, blaspheming guest, had taken Raimond deBauzan's lady wife into his care. Only when the hard-eyed knight had placed the lady Alyse in the prior's own chambers and summoned, at swordpoint, the terrified monk who worked in the infirmary, had the prior begun to believe that he would survive the night. And only when the crazed warrior had spurred his devil horse out the gates, had the prior's fear of Raimond deBauzan ceased to turn his guts to water.

The cleric's mind turned to his present dilemma. He had a sorely distraught lady, the wife of a murderous brute, in his own bedchamber. The monster deBauzan had not said when he would return.

Keep her safe, deBauzan had demanded. Do not leave her. Hide her. Place her in a monk's cell, if necessary. Watch over her yourself in every waking moment.

The angry knight had thundered away, and the priory was quiet once again. The lord's wife was silent, after straining to whisper her thanks. Now she had subsided into an exhausted stupor at the abbot's hearth.

It would not do for her to stay in the abbot's celibate bed-chamber.

In the days before he had forbidden women within the house, there had been chambers for male pilgrims and others, at a distance from the first, for married ladies in the company of their husbands. And for young men with gold to spare to bring ladies who were not their wedded wives.

Where should a respectable abbey, if it allowed a woman at all, place a lady of good birth who needed watching in the absence of her husband and her maid?

DeBauzan's wife would be safe enough in the guest quarters, in the room she and her husband had shared the night before.

It was not an easy decision. The crude beast deBauzan had threatened to disembowel the entire population of the house, from the smallest chicken to the prior himself, should his lady come to harm.

With this in mind, the prior decided to send his youngest postulate monk, the simple Brother Edward, to guide the lady Alyse to her empty sleeping chamber and stand watch outside her door.

None of the prior monks and none of the ordained priests would go anywhere near the lady before matins. Her husband was a dangerous man, and might be as jealous tomorrow as he had been protective this night.

If anyone was to feel the wrath of Lord Raimond deBauzan, it would be the young monk Edward, too ill-favored to inspire thoughts of fornication in even the most lustful woman, and too simple to have many lustful ideas of his own.

An hour later, the child-minded Edward had wakened the lady at the prior's hearth and taken her down the dark passageway to the guest chamber. The lady deBauzan had recovered her voice enough to agree to the plan, and had gone willingly enough to the chamber where she had slept with the killer deBauzan the night before. The prior had watched the fool Edward lead deBauzan's wife in the direction of the guest chambers, and had fitted the heavy bar to his own door, sought his own bed, and prayed that the priory's guest chambers would soon be empty.

He did not intend to emerge from his own chamber until the dangerous knight and his lady wife had gone on their way in the morning.

Before he slept, the prior rose once again and barred the shutters against the night.

CHAPTER
TWENTY-TWO

Alyse lay awake, staring at the moonlight streaming through the narrow embrasure of the bedchamber. The wind was rising, and the shadows of small winged creatures hurtled across the pale, shining opening in the darkness of the abbey wall.

There was no fire in the hearth. Raimond would return for her before the night was gone, and it would be better, in the long hours she would wait, not to allow the smoke of a fire to betray her presence in the room.

The skittish young monk who had escorted her to the cold chamber was to keep vigil in the darkness outside her room. "I will bring a bench," he had said, "and sleep near your doorway, just as I did for the widowed lady Berchamon last year, when her son stayed past sunset at the court." He had glanced briefly down the passageway, to the wide, battened doors which had stood open by day upon the stable yard. "She saw Herne coming for her across the orchard, and she would not stay alone."

Alyse had shuddered and pulled her mantle across her shoulders. "Who is Herne?" Her voice had returned, but speech was painful; only a rough whisper emerged from her bruised throat.

"The ghost lord of the forest. He hunts by night."

"What is your name?"

"Me? I'm Edward, my lady."

"Well, Brother Edward. You are a man of God. Do you believe such things?"

"No." He had clutched the crucifix which hung about his neck and raised it to his lips. "Herne cannot harm those who live in the Lord Jesus Christ."

Alyse smiled in the darkness. Brother Edward seemed as fearful of Windsor's predator ghost as she herself had been of Morston's wild hunt.

Since leaving the wide, grey spaces of Cornwall for the hills and dark forests of Windsor, Alyse had not been troubled by thoughts of ghosts; never once, in the days and nights she had been on the road with her husband, had she experienced the sickly, floating feeling that had haunted her, since childhood, whenever she left the comfort of familiar places and traveled beneath the empty sky. With Raimond beside her, there had been no need to fear.

His men called him Fortebras. The strong sword arm for which they had named Raimond deBauzan had made for Alyse a safe haven since the day he had come into her life. There was no place in the wide, cold world where Alyse feared to go, with Raimond at her side.

Alyse settled back upon the bed, but lay wakeful. Herbed honey wine from the prior's infirmary had taken the pain from her throat, and a length of closely-woven linen kept the night breezes from her neck.

She could have told Raimond very little about her attacker, had he allowed her to speak. Her rasping attempts to describe what she had seen in the darkness had, after the first few words, caused such anguish in her husband's face that Alyse had ceased to torment him. Once again, when he had ended his tirade in the prior's chamber and had gathered her into his arms to bid her stay in the safety of this place, she had tried to speak. It was the shock of the hot tears upon her husband's face which had stopped her.

And now her husband was abroad in the night, searching for the one who had crushed the breath from her throat. She had no doubt that Raimond would find him. Alyse drew her mantle closer still, and turned her face to the window.

Raimond deBauzan and his men-at-arms had descended upon Windsor's stableyard to find that the young smith from Cornwall, newly apprenticed to the garrison's armorer, had left in haste. The fire at the forge, still glowing with the day's embers, was banked neatly, but elsewhere there were signs of struggle or hurried flight. Mallets and tongs lay scattered across the earthen floor of the armory, and beside the firewood was a leather sack spilled open to reveal a rough woolen tunic and three pennies.

Erec had roused Rollo from his bed to bring him, loudly complaining and squinting painfully in the light of the torches, into Fortebras' presence.

"He's gone," the aged sergeant had said. "The man's in trouble, I vow. You'll not find him this side of the living." Rollo shrugged. "Had I been here, close at hand, it might have gone better for the him. But when the knight came for him an hour ago, and took him and the lad, there was only the wagoners who saw it and they were afraid—"

"What lad?"

Rollo sighed. "The young boy who was pestering them today at the forges. The lad and the apprentice tried to run, I hear. They were halfway across the stable yard when they were stopped."

"By the queen's guard?"

"No. By the knight. Just one single knight. Big fellow, they said. Black armor and a fine red stone on the hilt of his sword."

"Black-haired." Fortebras' words were not a question.

"Might have been. The wagoners didn't say. Could have been the devil's man, for all he seemed . . ."

Fortebras had wheeled his mount and led his men to the bailey gate, leaving Erec to scramble onto his horse to follow.

A short distance outside the walls, Fortebras pulled Shaitan to a sudden, bone-jarring halt. "Montbazon," he bellowed.

The shutters facing the road were closed. Thin blades of firelight pierced cracks in the wood, and disappeared briefly when blocked by the restless shadows hovering near the windows. Windsor's village was silent, its doors barred shut, the air heavy with fear.

From the darkness beyond the road, Montbazon nudged his mount forward. Behind the black knight, with hands tied to a stout rope held within Montbazon's gloved fist, stumbled a broad, slope-shouldered giant of a man. The Morston smith Hund shook thick, snarled locks from his face and narrowed his eyes against the sudden glare of the torch thrust near to his face

At his side trotted the child Wat, wide-eyed and indignant.

"My lord Raimond," the child began, "this man will not let Hund go free. Tell him Hund is my lady's blacksmith from home. She will make this man let him go."

"Take the child back."

Erec grabbed Wat by the back of the tunic and hauled him up to his saddle. "Take him where?"

DeBauzan never moved his gaze from the smith's staring face. "Back to the queen's hall. Keep him there until I send for you."

"What are you going to do?" The child's shrill voice had risen even higher in distress.

Raimond closed his eyes briefly, then turned to the struggling child. "I am sending him home," he said softly. "I will send him where he belongs."

He waited until the hoofbeats of Erec's mount and the sound of the child's voice had grown faint. Then he swung down from Shaitan's back and walked, dagger in hand, to where Hund the smith strained at his bonds.

"I thank you, cousin," he said to Montbazon. Over his shoulder, he called orders to his men. "Draw back. Leave us and draw back." On either side of the deserted village street, the firelight rimming the shutters ceased to blink; the shadows of the listeners were stilled.

DeBauzan seized the rope from Montbazon's hand. "And you, cousin. Leave us." In silence, he held his dagger to the fleshy throat of Morston's truant blacksmith and waited for the men of Bauzan to move their horses back up the road to Windsor's gates.

There was an alley between the main street and the river road. With sudden force, deBauzan sent the cringing bulk of the blacksmith into the darkness of the lane.

Before the man landed, Raimond was at his throat again. "Shall I cut your bonds before I carve your heart from your body? Or shall I leave you tied like a pig for slaughter—like a murderer for the hanging?"

A piteous sob bubbled from the thick throat.

"Before I kill you," Raimond said, "You will tell me where you left the body of Harald deRançon. If you do not tell me, or if I do not believe your words, your death will be more painful than you can imagine."

Behind him, Montbazon called through the darkness. "He says he did not harm your lady, Fortebras. And the child said he was with this man from the time you and your lady reached Windsor's gates."

"He might have forced the child to say it." Raimond said. He turned back to gaze into the smith's white eyes. "How did you compel that child to lie? Speak now, or I will begin your living dismemberment."

"I—I did nothing to the child. May God strike me dead if I harmed the child." The voice, slubbered with fear, spoke the Frankish tongue in awkward bursts, but the words could be understood. There was an echo of Morston, of Wat's country accent, in the brute.

Raimond steeled his heart against the resemblance. "And my lady?" The dagger rose higher; its point threatened the quivering jaw.

"Never," the man sobbed. "Never would I hurt the lady Alyse. She would tell you. Ask her, my lord. She will tell—"

DeBauzan eased the pressure upon Hund's throat. "And deRançon's body? Where did you leave it? Speak now or by Satan's prick you die."

"Forgive me, lord. I could not stay. I was afraid—"

Raimond struck him with the back of his fist. "I care not why you deserted your lady. Tell your coward's tale to God when you meet him this night. Tell me of deRançon. And why you attacked the lady Alyse."

"I would never, never—"

"Tell me, smith. Or die."

"I have not seen the lady Alyse. Wat saw me at the forge, and told me that my lady had wed and that she was here at Windsor. I never saw her, lord."

"And deRançon's body? I ask you for the last time. Speak now—quickly, or you die."

"He was not dead, my lord."

Raimond dropped the rope and stepped back. So there were two. Two men had followed Alyse to Windsor.

The sobbing began again. The smith Hund crouched at Raimond's feet, unmoving but loud in his fear. With difficulty, Raimond did not strike the lout to silence him. Through this shambling coward, he must find deRançon. "Tell me," he said.

Hund raised a tear-streamed face. "The lady Alyse had struck the lord Harald hard, but she had not killed him. He started— he moved, my lord, as I began to fill the well. He woke when the earth began to fall upon him. I could not—I did not bury him, but brought him away from Morston."

Raimond lowered the dagger. Through the red veil of his anger, he began to hear a hint of frightened truth in the blacksmith's words.

Raimond drew an unsteady breath. "The well was filled with earth in the morning. You did it."

"Yes, my lord."

"Why?"

"He told me to do it."

Raimond seized Hund's neck. "Why did you do it?" he asked softly. "Were you his man?"

Hund dared to shake his head. "For gold, my lord. And for fear of God's wrath. He was a lord, and it was a sin to strike him. I—I put him on his packhorse and I took him away."

"How long did he live?"

"I don't know." It was a desperate cry from a terrified soul.

Raimond released the smith's throat. "Tell me where you left him."

"I bound his wounds and took him east, as he told me to do. He would not permit me to stop. It was when his fever came that I took him to the abbey for the monks to cure him. He gave them a name not his own—"

Fear shot through Raimond's veins. "Which abbey?"

"In the marsh. The one on the high ground in the marsh."

"Muchelney."

"That was the name."

"He died there?"

In the growing moonlight, Raimond saw that the smith had begun to weep. "I was afraid, my lord. When he recovered, I was afraid. I ran—I left him. I found a place in the armory here, lord. And have worked here since. That is all I did, my lord, and may God forgive me for running away."

Raimond did not hear his last words. He dropped the rope which bound Hund the smith and turned his back upon him.

The abbey. Muchelney Abbey. There had been a monk who had brought water and lingered near them, until Raimond had warned him away. A burly monk, with the well-developed shoulders and arms of a fighting man, traveling behind them to Windsor, riding at the end of the file, never raising his eyes, never pushing the brown hood back from his face. Pulling his mule off the road to allow Payen and the Templars to pass, turning his face aside—

A monk could travel the length of the country and be given lodging. A monk could pass through the gates of a royal stronghold to beg for shelter.

Few, if any, ever looked at the face of a monk working in an abbey.

Or in the orchards of the priory.

Brother Edward had said he would not touch the door unless he heard her stir. If he heard her moving about, he would enter the room and see that she was safe. The lady was not, he said, to take offense if this happened. And the lady's husband was not to burn the settlement to the ground, as the prior feared, if he returned to see his wife back in the guest chamber and Brother Edward at the door.

Alyse had agreed to Brother Edward's stammered words and tried to sleep. It had not been not easy. She was not surprised, therefore, when the door opened and Brother Edward's brown-clad figure appeared once again beside her bed.

"Go back," she murmured. "I am well."

Brother Edward laughed. It was a low laugh, and unpleasant. And he smelled—Alyse sat up in alarm. He smelled of stale sweat and an acrid scent she had not forgotten—

In the darkness, there was the sudden gleam of a knife. Her own small dagger, taken from her in that dark struggle at Windsor. This was not Brother Edward. Sweet Jesu, it was not.

"Did you tell her?"

It was the same guttural voice she had strained to hear over her death struggles only hours ago. And it was the same question.

He did not wait for her answer. The dagger was at her ribs and his hand over her mouth, stifling her life's breath. He pricked her side painfully when she refused to go through the door, and dragged her past the blood-spattered body of Brother Edward.

She struggled in the doorway to win her freedom, but the cruel pressure of the knife stopped the attempt. Once past the door, he smothered her face in a foul-smelling cloth and dragged her out into the night. Out into the vast, open space where Raimond would never find her—

"It was the body of the guard at your door. It is your fault he died, Alyse Mirbeau. His death is on your soul, like all the others. But this one I will bury with you."

It was a voice she had not imagined she would hear this side of hell's fires.

There was a tugging at the linen cloth about her throat, as if the man would strangle her. But the cloth came away beneath the dagger's blade, leaving nothing between the steel and the flesh of Alyse's throat. The foul cloth over her face was torn away, and the cold night air was upon her.

Harald deRançon drew the dagger upwards, and pressed it in a line of searing pain beneath her jaw.

She held herself stiffly, each shallow breath an agony as her throat pulsed at the edge of the blade.

"You are afraid," he breathed. "Yet I have only begun to kill you."

Above them, the sky was a turning spiral of stars. Suddenly, the knife lifted. "No—" where the knife had rested, a hand closed upon her neck. "You will not swoon. You were poor game, lady Alyse, the day I took you. Do you imagine I would allow you to escape your death pangs in the same way?"

His fingers spread wide, and moved to her jaw. "There— at last. The honest sweat of fear. I have lived with fear—fear that you would find that I was not rotting in the earth. Fear that you would tell the old queen I had come for her gold. Fear to claim my lands—my own lands—while you lived, ready to cry treason."

He drew a long, rasping breath. "Did you tell her I came for her gold?"

"There was no gold—"

His blow stopped her words. "I shall ask you again. Once more. And if you lie to me, I shall cut out your tongue before I find better uses for this knife." And he dragged her, step by struggling step, out of the abbey, his hand stifling her very breath.

They were behind the stable yard, where the orchard stretched in dark rows to the wild forest beyond. DeRançon's dagger chafed against her neck as he pulled her with him. Was that how she would die, with the blade sawing deeper with every step she was forced to take?

He took his hand from her mouth. "Did you tell him, Alyse? Did you tell your thick-skulled husband?"

The knife pressed harder. Alyse moved her lips in denial, but the words would not come.

One wrenching, violent motion later, deRançon's hand had closed upon her hair and pulled her head back. The knife was higher, pressing against the very spot where deRançon's hands had tried to wring the voice from her throat.

"Your man will die next, some few days before the miracle of my return from a Saracen prison. And then the smith will disappear." DeRançon's laugh was a familiar horror, fetching the deeds of the past to crowd within her mind. "You should have tried to kill him too, Alyse. He was the one who brought me to Morston with his tales of hearthstones come loose before dawn. I will find him next." His voice slowed to a low, droning pulse. "I saw you, today, looking out the window toward your grave."

He wrenched her face toward the forest. She saw the dark patch in the ground just beyond the edge of the orchard. There had been three monks at work, one of them digging beyond the taller trees—

Above them, the moon shone grey in a vast, windy space with no end to it. She was to die here, beneath a sky more open, more barren than the moors which had held such terror for her. She could feel herself drawing away from her body as she had always done when the dread of open places came upon her. This time, she would not try to stay. This time—

She dug her nails into her palms. This time she must resist the oblivion; she must keep her eyes upon the horror before her, and live to warn Raimond—

The world righted, leveled, and no longer trembled beneath her feet.

DeRançon stopped a few feet from the long darkness in the ground. "Do you know, Alyse, what it was like to lie in the earth, my blood upon my face, waiting for the first shovelful of filth to fall upon me? To imagine, at that moment, that I would die in the darkness, with the earth pressing down upon me, filling my eyes. My mouth. You left me there, to be buried alive."

He raised the blade. "If you would have my mercy, if you would be dead before the earth's creatures come to devour you, tell me of the queen. Did you tell her?" His words slowed to a deadly cadence. "Did you tell Queen Eleanor that I would have taken her gold from you?"

She shook her head.

"My sword is there beside your grave. Which shall it be, Alyse? The weight of the sword, or the slice of your own dagger?"

The knife began its slow descent; at the last instant, it shifted to trace a thin line between her breasts.

She turned her head and bit his arm. The hilt of the dagger came down upon her temple. There was a burst of painful light behind her eyes.

The crimson light did not fade. Alyse opened her eyes. There was fire beyond the orchard, upon the priory road. Torch light. Many torches and shouting.

There were horsemen on the road.

Alyse brought her knee up into deRançon's belly and twisted from him. On the road, too far away to hear her hoarsened cry, the riders had turned their mounts to the priory gates. One torch lay sputtering upon the hard-packed earth, dropped in the wake of the swiftly moving horsemen.

DeRançon fell upon her and seized her hair again. He dragged her back to the gaping blackness beneath the trees. "It must be quick, then. Weep for me, Alyse. I might have had your slut's body beneath me one last time—"

A shudder passed through the burly arms of her killer.

Before them, a dark, massive form moved down the orchard, making its way slowly towards the grave. The rising moon reflected upon the glossy black coat of the beast and the pale hair of its rider.

Alyse screamed Raimond's name as deRançon released her to snatch up his sword and to level it at the chest of the great black horse bearing down towards them.

She clawed at deRançon's arm, and weighted it with her body. Behind Alyse, the horse bore down upon them, and swerved aside an instant before his hot breath touched her neck.

There was silence. DeRançon backed away, dragging Alyse with him past the open grave.

"Let her go." Raimond's voice was calm, cold as the blade which shone silver in the moonlight.

DeRançon stepped closer to the dark pit. Before Alyse lay the deep maw of the grave. The earth beneath her feet was soft, and would not hold her if she tried to turn. Had Raimond seen the pit? Or would deRançon lure Raimond to bring his mount too close, to turn away too late? She drew a panicked breath "Raimond don't—"

DeRançon stopped her words with a savage blow. "Come for her," he called into the night. "Come for her, if you want her still. Did she tell you that I had her? I had your wife—"

Great clumps of earth flew against the tree trunks as Shaitan carried his bellowing rider to bring Fortebras' scarred, deadly broadsword to deRançon's head. At the edge of the open grave, horse and rider turned aside to leap the breadth of the pit.

DeRançon pulled Alyse before his chest and pushed her

toward Shaitan's deadly hooves, only to cry out in rage when Alyse turned once again to claw at his face, and to jostle aside the hilt of the sword which was to sweep across Shaitan's saddle.

Shaitan's empty saddle.

The riderless mount ran free in the moonlight.

Alyse sobbed for her husband. There was no answer from the moonlit spaces between the trees. And no sound from the gravepit.

"He's down," deRançon said. "There will be three of you dead this night."

"No," came the voice behind them. "Not three."

DeRançon pulled Alyse back against his chest and shoved the heavy sharpness of his broadsword to her throat. He turned, using Alyse to shield him, to face Raimond Fortebras.

"Her life for mine," said Harald deRançon.

"Let her go and fight for your own life as a man should do."

DeRançon laughed. "Fight you, a man who has not had his sword from his hand since childhood? I have been cloistered these past years because of your slut of a wife. I am not stupid, Raimond deBauzan. I will keep my life and have my lands back."

"Then you must kill me to have them." Slowly, Raimond lowered his sword. "Or give me my lady unharmed."

"I will have your word on it. You and your whore will say nothing to the queen. Nothing, do you understand me?"

"Put your sword down, deRançon, and speak."

Alyse felt the edge of the blade shift slightly. At her shoulder, she could feel the bulk of deRançon's arm harden and begin to tremble. The man who held death to her throat was as tense as a wolf near its prey—ready to strike. "Raimond—" she whispered.

"Be silent," Fortebras said. In the moonlight, his eyes answered her warning.

At the far end of the orchard, too far to reach their lord in time, Raimond's men had come out of the priory, and milled with muffled voices at the crossroads. At the very corner of her vision, Alyse saw a dying crimson light—the guttering torch which Raimond had dropped upon the road.

"And when I return to claim my lands," deRançon said, "you will say nothing to deny me."

Alyse willed herself not to turn her head towards the priory and the men who had left the road to search for their lord. They would never reach him in time, but the sight of them might make deRançon strike earlier.

"I will say nothing," Raimond agreed. "Put down your sword."

"Swear, Fortebras."

"I—"

DeRançon's sword sliced towards Raimond's unprotected eyes.

To where Raimond had been.

DeRançon never felt the pain of Raimond Fortebras' sword rising to sever his hand, not did he feel Fortebras pull the Mirbeau bitch clear of his other arm.

All he felt, in that flash of hard, grunting combat, was the final blow, when Raimond Fortebras drove his sword through the robes of a monk to pierce the heart of an exiled and desperate man.

CHAPTER
TWENTY-THREE

Alyse did not remember how she came to be back in the bed at the priory, cleansed of deRançon's blood and the black earth of the orchard. Raimond was beside her, keeping vigil in the last of the low moonlight. Telling her, when he heard her stir, that she was safe. Showing her, with the comfort of his arms, that she was beloved.

She tried to speak, many times, of deRançon, but Raimond would not allow it. He had barred the door upon the agitated voices echoing down the dark stones of the passageway, and had demanded that they close away the world in that way, until the moon was down.

Still, she did not sleep. Long after Raimond had dismissed his men from the chamber and had with his own hands treated and bound the ravages of deRançon's hands and blade upon Alyse's throat, she lay wakeful.

The marks of the knife were shallow, and would heal quickly. The bruises across her throat had turned ugly, if there were truth in the expression upon Alain's face when he had brought the honey wine he had taken while ransacking the infirmary.

Raimond had lit a fire in the small chamber hearth but refused to bring candles, and had claimed that he could not find the polished steel looking piece in Alyse's saddlepack. Instead, she had a flask of herb-laced mead to heal her throat and a husband who watched her every breath as he amused her by speaking of Normandy and the severe beauty of his father's fortress at Bauzan.

It was impossible to see, in Raymond's face, any fear of the queen's displeasure. Yet he spoke of a journey east, and said nothing of returning to the west country, and to Kernstowe.

Alyse struggled to rise. "Emma—" she whispered.

He settled her back upon the bolster and placed his hand upon her brow. "She is safe. Go to sleep, Alyse."

She shook her head. "The queen—"

"Emma is safe," Raimond repeated. "She and Hugo will be in Normandy, at Bauzan, long before we arrive." He forestalled her next words with a gentle finger upon her lips. "We had an agreement, Hugo and I, that if he did not have a message from me by the end of the late harvest, he would take Emma south to the coast and buy passage to Normandy." He pulled the coverlet up her neck and smoothed it upon the linen dressings. "If we had failed to keep peace with the queen, or if we had gone into hiding, there would have been no need to fear for Hugo and Emma."

Alyse closed her eyes. Raimond had known long known what she also had feared—that they must choose whether to ride for Canterbury, where his brothers waited, and cross to Normandy to commit themselves to his family's protection. If they did so, Kernstowe and England would be lost to them for as long as Queen Eleanor lived. Perhaps longer.

If tomorrow they returned to Windsor to tell the queen of deRançon's death, and to ask for her pardon, Count John would hear of the death of his vassal. He would take quiet but final revenge, if it pleased him to do so; Queen Eleanor his mother had her own reasons to permit her son to silence Raimond deBauzan and his wife, to ensure that her own secrets would be kept forever.

When she opened her eyes again, the moon had set. Raimond had not moved from the bench he had drawn up beside the bed.

Alyse shifted to one side. "Please," she whispered. "Come sleep beside me."

Raimond glanced at the darkness between the shutters. "We have an hour before dawn."

"Then talk to me, before the others come to wake us."

He moved to sit beside her, his back against the stone wall. "Rest your voice," he murmured. "I have much to tell you. Rest, Alyse, and listen."

"About deRançon?" she asked.

"About deRançon," he said. "And worse." He took her hand between his own, and began to stroke her palm. "DeRançon was not the greatest danger we faced at Windsor. Hush—," he said. "I will tell you all. And forgive me, Alyse, for keeping you in ignorance. But had you known what was the real treasure within the coffer we brought the queen, you would have been in greater peril from Eleanor Plantagenet than you faced this night."

"How—"

"The ring. The ugly silver ring with the marks upon its stone. I saw such marks, in Palestine, upon the daggers found with the Assassin dead."

"The Assassins—the Saracen murderers?"

"It is a religion. When sent out by their leader, Assassins will persist in their tasks until death—the death of the victim named by their chief, or the death of the murderers themselves, should they be stopped."

Alyse touched Raimond's tunic where it covered the dagger scar. "Assassins did this?"

He covered her hand. "Yes."

She swallowed painfully. "Why did Eleanor—"

Raimond shook his head. "I know not. A ring such as the one we brought her is a sign of the Assassins' obligation to the one who wears it. She may ask for one thing—a murder, most likely. Or any other task. Queen Eleanor said she wanted the coffer to help free King Richard. Now I understand that it was only the ring she wanted."

Alyse shivered. "How would she—"

"Let us pray," Raimond said, "that we never discover how she will use it."

Alyse pulled herself up to sit beside him. "Does she know that you recognized the mark?"

"She knew I would. I spent two long years in Palestine at King Richard's side."

"Why send someone who would know?"

For the first time in two days, Raimond smiled without bitterness. "Do you complain that she sent a weather-beaten, scarred survivor of the pilgrimages to wed you?"

It hurt to laugh. Alyse put her fingers upon his lips. "Tell me."

He kissed her hand. "She must have fretted over the choice. A man who saw no value in the ring might have been careless with it. But a man who would recognize the thing might use it himself, or take it to Count John, who might have used it against King Richard and his mother, accusing them of an alliance with those devils."

Alyse closed her eyes. "She trusted you. It is a curse, to have her trust."

Raimond's smile remained. "You and my father, Alyse, are of like minds. Yet another reason why he will love you."

She placed hands beside his face. "We must go to your father," she whispered. "There is no other place where you will be safe, if the queen decides she cannot trust you. With deRançon dead—"

"Shh. Not so many words. Rest your throat."

"Raimond—"

"Hush." He pulled her closer, and tilted her head to his shoulder. "I will say it. DeRançon is an unwelcome new piece in this game of the queen's. If she learns he died at my hand, she will be tempted to have me killed for it, though she might know the monster deserved to die."

"She must not know. He was a man in the guise of a monk. Nothing more. He lived as a simple monk—"

"If we do not tell her, and she discovers who he is, she will trust us no more. And then she will be dangerous indeed." His voice lowered. "Hund is at Windsor, working in the armory."

Alyse started. "He's here? He knows deRançon's face. If he had seen the body—if he sees it tomorrow, we are lost."

Once again, Raimond stopped her words with a caress. "Your voice will be lost, my lady, if you continue so." He sank back against the wall. "Hund will not speak of deRançon. He promised me." He sighed. "No more talk of the smith. I left him free to stay at the armory, though I might have sent him back to Kernstowe."

"You were kind, my lord."

Raimond frowned. "It was the only thing to do. He will stay where he wants to be, and I will not be troubled with the sight of his idiot's face."

"Hund is not—"

"—he is an idiot, and lucky he escaped with his life. I will call him what I please, and he should thank me for it."

"I thank you for his life."

"His life is not worth the smallest word you have spoken, nor the pain it caused you to utter it." Raimond cast a swift glance at the shutters. "Enough talk of the damned idiot smith. Soon it will be dawn, and we must have a plan by first light."

"To reach Normandy, and leave your lands behind?"

He ran his hand through his hair and closed his eyes. "You must decide," Raimond said at last. "I thought I had earned those lands and a few years' peace in return for my service to King Richard. But what you did for the queen went beyond a warrior's courage; you must choose what we will do in the time we have left. You have the right."

She raised her hand to touch his face. "You would give up your lands so quickly?"

He caught her fingers and raised her palm to his mouth. "I will have you. I will find other lands for us, and earn them with my sword."

"You wanted peace, Raimond."

He placed her hand back upon the bed and pulled the coverlet over her. "I will have you."

"Later, if you regret—"

His mouth brushed hers in a kiss so gentle she might have imagined it. "Sleep now," he said. "I will keep watch."

She pushed the coverlet down. "Come sleep with me, Raimond."

He touched the cloth which covered the wounds upon her neck. "You must not move."

"Hold me, Raimond. Hold me until dawn."

He had not expected to sleep so deeply, as soundly as if his body had taken the pleasure his soul had found, holding Alyse safe within his arms. It was dawn when Raimond woke to find the hearth still warm, and the sun beginning to touch the shutters.

Upon his shoulder, Alyse slept easily. There had been a bad moment, when he first awoke and did not hear the slight, painful rasp which had accompanied her breathing earlier in the night. But she had stirred at the sound of his frantic whisper, and smiled into the curve of his arm. And when she spoke, her words had held only a trace of her earlier hoarseness.

"We must tell her," Alyse said without preamble.

He kissed her warm cheek. "It is your choice, as I said. There is nothing you must do. And many destinations you may choose." He drew the coverlet back and stepped onto the cold planked floor. "But you shall choose none of them until you break your fast."

Alyse reached for his arm. "There is no real choice, as I think of it. The queen would find us, Raimond, if we left now. If we did not speak to her, and if she heard of the—of the body in the orchard, she would trust us no more. And she would send the routiers once again to your father's castle."

"Yes, she might send Mercadier." Raimond covered her hand with his own. "Given time to prepare, the Bauzan fortress could stand against Mercadier's army. Do not make your choice out of fear for my family. They do not need it." He touched her face and brought her gaze to his eyes. "Are you sure you wish to place your trust in the queen?"

"I am not sure, but it is the better wager. If she takes our part, the queen will forbid Count John to move against you, to take your lands."

Raimond bowed his head and kissed her brow. "As you said, it is a good wager. If we run from her now, she might be a danger to us as long as she lives."

But it was a wager—with much to win and everything to lose.

With a knot of fear in his belly, Raimond opened the door and called for Alain to find food in the hushed refectory.

The young knight brought news of the night's aftermath. The body of deRançon, left to lie where it had fallen, had been discovered at first light. In the orchard, six monks had placed the body upon a board to carry it upon its last journey, through the stable yard gates, to be buried within the priory's consecrated ground.

And the monk Edward, found bleeding from many wounds when Raimond's men had stormed into the passageway, was lying in the infirmary hall, and had not yet opened his eyes.

As strange as the rest, and causing uproar within the confusion in the refectory, was the disappearance of Prior Eustace; he had left his chambers at dawn, and could not be found.

A wide-eyed servant, younger still than the unlucky Brother Edward, brought cold meat and bread and ale to their door and stood staring at the bloodstained flagstones in the passageway. Raimond took the wooden platter from him and closed the door upon his greening face.

Alyse had packed her belongings in the pannier she had dragged from the corner of the chamber. Her court garments, ruined beyond repair, were heaped beside the hearth. From the saddle pack, Alyse drew forth the crimson wool kirtle which had seemed so elegant when she had first found it at Kernstowe. "I will have to wear this as we travel."

Raimond looked up from the loaf he had begun to cut. "It will be fine."

"I will be all of a color, then. Red wool, red scratches upon my face, and wounds upon my throat. Will the guards let me into the queen's presence, looking as I do?"

He touched her cheek with gentle fingers. "They will. If they had used the ears the Almighty gave them, they would have come to you sooner, and killed deRançon when he first attacked you at Windsor. If those knaves look askance at you, I'll put my sword through their black hearts."

There was a cold draft from the passageway. The door stood open upon a straight, slender figure in a richly bordered mantle.

"Black hearts?" Queen Eleanor asked. "You speak of black hearts once again, Raimond Fortebras?"

Slowly, Raimond placed the knife back upon the platter and stepped between Alyse and the stern visage at the door. "Your grace," he said. "Would you speak with me in the courtyard?"

Queen Eleanor advanced to the table and lifted one arched brow towards Raimond's bench. "I would speak with you here, Raimond deBauzan. With both you and the lady Alyse."

Raimond brought the bench.

The dowager queen turned to her escort behind her in the passageway. "Have someone put rushes over that floor—the child must not see the bloodstains when he arrives. Then wait for me with the horses. All of you." She turned back to Raimond. "There was a butchered man lying dead in the stable yard and your cousin Montbazon watching this passageway with a cold eye for my guards. And the prior has begged my protection—told me he must remain at Windsor keep until you are gone from this place, as he fears you will turn your sword upon him."

She gestured to Raimond to close the door. "You may speak to me," she said. "You have a great many things to explain, Raimond deBauzan. To Richard's justiciars, if not to me."

"Tell her."

The queen's gaze turned to Alyse. Upon the mask of aged royalty, a small tremor could be seen. "Your voice, child—"

"—Crushed by the bastard outside your hall." Raimond said.

"—No, Raimond—" Alyse's voice rose to a ragged treble.

"—within earshot of your guards."

"Be silent, deBauzan." The queen's voice softened. "And you, Alyse, must not speak. It pains you?"

"It does," growled deBauzan.

The narrowed gaze moved back to Raimond. "Then speak for your wife, as she has asked. And do not cheat me of the truth, deBauzan. I will have all of it, or never again count you among those I may trust."

"That would be a sorry thing, your grace."

Queen Eleanor placed a single, exquisite hand upon the table. "That, Raimond deBauzan, would be more than a sorry thing.

It would go badly for you. You would be worse than sorry.''
Upon the oaken board, the long fingers curled into an aged
knot. ''Now tell me, deBauzan, the entire truth of what happened here.''

Alyse had chosen to trust the queen. Raimond took his wife's
hand and began to speak. ''The dead man is Harald deRançon,
your grace. The former lord of Kernstowe.''

''So he did not die in Palestine.''

Raimond drew a long breath. ''My charter for the lands in
Cornwall is not binding, as it was written in the belief that
deRançon was dead—''

The queen made a dismissive gesture. ''It is not for you to
decide that a royal charter is not binding. How did deRançon
die?''

''Under my sword.''

''Why?''

''He harmed my lady.''

''Why?''

''She had struck him down, years ago, as he tried to take
the coffer.''

There was a long silence. ''He was John's man, much given
to greed,'' the queen said at last. ''And from a family noted
for its rebellious ways.'' She closed her eyes briefly, then
smiled. ''The man will be buried here, and none will know his
true name. The prior will record the death as a struggle with
thieves.''

Alyse cried out in relief. She lowered her fingers from her
lips. ''Thank you, your grace.''

Queen Eleanor frowned. ''You, Alyse Mirbeau, have the
look of a snared rabbit, with the marks of the noose upon your
throat. DeRançon's doing?''

There was a low growl from Raimond's chest.

''Yes, your grace,'' Alyse whispered.

''And your voice is weak. Too weak, I believe, to repeat to
me the tales your husband has told you to put the fear of Eleanor
Plantagenet into your eyes.''

Alyse rose to her feet. ''Your grace—''

With a careless gesture, Queen Eleanor bade her sit. ''I am
too old to listen to idle stories. But,'' the dowager continued,

"if I should hear that you have repeated those idle stories—or spoken of anything touching the matters with which I have trusted you—you will lose more than your lands."

Alyse raised her gaze to those darkened eyes. "We will not fail you," she said.

There was a slight tremor in the queen's hand as she reached across the table to touch Alyse's cheek. "So you will not, for the sake of Isabelle's memory." She turned to Raimond. "Keep my secrets, deBauzan, and you will keep your life. God grant that it will be so."

She rode with them out of the priory gates to the crossroads. Her mounted guard, following behind them, drew back at her command, and waited out of earshot with Raimond's men and the young boy, Wat.

"I will leave you here," Queen Eleanor said. "When Richard is free, you must come to his court to swear homage for your new lands. Until then, do not come near."

She drew a small roll of red-sealed vellum from her sleeve and held it out to Raimond. "There are lands in Aquitaine which shall be yours. When I am dead you may have need of them, if my sons cannot keep the peace in England, or if the barons make war against Richard in Normandy. You have the means, now, to stay distant from the court, and from those who will test my son's patience. I expect you to use them." She turned her dark gaze full upon Raimond's face. "Now, Raimond deBauzan, do you still believe that to be trusted by the Plantagenet brood is to be cursed?"

Alyse turned to her husband in confusion.

Raimond's features flushed a deep, dull red.

"Your grace, Raimond did not mean—"

"Alyse Mirbeau, you are fortunate that your husband did not seek a place at court. His blunt speech might have been his ruin." Queen Eleanor tilted her head towards the small group of riders surrounding Wat. "Go now, before that odd child repeats any more of your imprudence."

Raimond took a deep breath and opened his mouth. And

glanced at his horrified wife. "I beg pardon, your grace, for my words."

"You will have it, Raimond deBauzan—if you learn to mind your tongue. Value discretion, my children, and you will live in peace."

Queen Eleanor rode north to Windsor, followed by her guard. She did not look back to see which road they chose.

Raimond drew a long, unsteady breath. "She is unpredictable, our Queen Eleanor. Before the pendulum of her favor turns back against us, we must put ourselves beyond her reach."

"Where?" Alyse whispered. "She will know what we do."

The Bauzan men waited, their mounts restive in the sharp autumn wind. From his perch upon the larger packhorse, Wat's distant chatter filled the silence.

"Kernstowe?" Alyse asked.

Raimond shook his head. "Too soon," he said.

"To Bauzan, to your family?"

He smiled. "A good choice, but easily predicted." Raimond raised the vellum scroll still in his hand. "Queen Eleanor might not expect us to go obediently to claim our new lands in Aquitaine. She would expect us, instead, to lose ourselves in the countryside until King Richard is free."

Alyse smiled back. "And she would never expect us to reach Aquitaine before winter."

From the Bauzan party came a sudden silence; Wat's voice had ceased its cheery drone. The child lay on his back, comfortably invisible within the largest packhorse pannier, one thin arm pointing to a break in the translucent clouds.

Far above them all, a black hawk traced slow circles in the sky.

Raimond untied the laces of his saddlebag. "We should keep moving, for the next few months, until King Richard is free. By then, the queen will be content and we may settle in Kernstowe or Aquitaine, as you wish." He placed the queen's gift within the bag, and frowned at the hawk's path.

The chill of the morning was in the air. Raimond drew the cloak from his shoulders and placed it upon Alyse's scarlet mantle. "I will divide our company, and send Wat along with Erec and six of the men." He smiled. "He will be safe enough, and your voice will recover sooner without the lad's constant questions."

"He will be safe enough if Erec and the others stay clear of the brothels." She smiled at her husband. "Speak to them, Raimond, if they are to care for Wat."

"Hmm." He glanced down the road. "Alain and the rest will ride with us to Dover. I will find a quiet place where we may spend the next few days, until your strength is back."

"I can ride, Raimond."

"There is no need. No hurry." He nudged his mount closer and took his lady's hand. "My men will watch the road while we have a fortnight of peace."

Alyse smiled. "And then, if we still can ride—"

"Dover." Raimond moved his hand to her waist. "There will be the sea to cross, and half the length of King Richard's lands in Normandy and Aquitaine—"

"With you beside me, the sea will seem no more than a pool upon the moor."

Raimond laughed. "And a river or two, for good measure."

Alyse raised her face to the sky. There was no spin, no dizzy need to look away from the vastness. The blue space above her was no more than a great silken canopy above her lover's countenance.

Above them, the dark hawk banked from its circle and flew east, into the clouds.

HISTORICAL NOTE

In February of 1194, King Richard of England was questioned in Mainz by the Holy Roman Emperor concerning the death of Conrad of Montferrat. Richard produced a letter from the Old Man of the Mountain, the leader of the Assassins' sect, in which the Old Man claimed full responsibility for Conrad's death. Within a week, Richard was free.

ROMANCE FROM JANELLE TAYLOR

ANYTHING FOR LOVE   (0-8217-4992-7, $5.99)

DESTINY MINE   (0-8217-5185-9, $5.99)

CHASE THE WIND   (0-8217-4740-1, $5.99)

MIDNIGHT SECRETS   (0-8217-5280-4, $5.99)

MOONBEAMS AND MAGIC   (0-8217-0184-4, $5.99)

SWEET SAVAGE HEART   (0-8217-5276-6, $5.99)

ROMANCE FROM FERN MICHAELS

DEAR EMILY   (0-8217-4952-8, $5.99)

WISH LIST   (0-8217-5228-6, $6.99)

AND IN HARDCOVER:

VEGAS RICH   (1-57566-057-1, $25.00)

Available wherever paperbacks are sold, or order direct from the Publisher. Send cover price plus 50¢ per copy for mailing and handling to Kensington Publishing Corp., Consumer Orders, or call (toll free) 888-345-BOOK, to place your order using Mastercard or Visa. Residents of New York and Tennessee must include sales tax. DO NOT SEND CASH.